HEART FIRE
A NOVEL OF REDEMPTION

JOHN M. HUTCHINSON

Praise for John Hutchinson's

Heart Fire: A Novel of Redemption

Author John M. Hutchinson creates a brilliant 1830s/40s tapestry of tales interweaving the lives of two quite dissimilar men and an intelligent, strong-willed woman that begins in England and ends in the Mormon city of Nauvoo, Illinois. Poignant. Personal. I laughed, I cried at the end, and sometimes with nail-biting tension, I couldn't wait to read on. The story includes elements of early Mormon history. Within these pages, the reader finds good and evil. Love and hate. Marriage and adultery. God and religion. Truth and lies. Definitely worth the read.

We both cherished the accurate and very passionate presentation of the early Mormon ethical intrigues intertwined with the lives of those who endured this uniquely American religious deception. Heart Fire tells the authentic story of the foundational years of the Mormon Church through the eyes, actions, and aspirations of those who both fell victim to, or were protected by the treacherous character, control and corruption of Joseph Smith, Jr. This engaging work brings the human tragedy of a trusting heart into direct conflict with the deceitful intent of men hiding behind a totally false presentation of Jesus Christ. If it were not so accurate, this captivating story could be merely dismissed as an invented account of religious repugnance driven by power, sex, and lawlessness. An inspirational work that removes the more clinical portrayals of deceitful men by reviewing the effects they had on their very real human targets.

I have to say that I'm delighted in Heart Fire. I like very much the switch back and forth between characters and location. The first person style is very, very good. It makes the characters come alive and the use of "antique" words makes it even more alive.

Heart Fire
Copyright © 2019 John M. Hutchinson
All Rights Reserved

Publishing Coordinator – Sharon Kizziah-Holmes

Paperback-Press
an imprint of A & S Publishing
A & S Holmes, Inc.

ISBN -13: 978-1-945669-90-3

DEDICATION

For Jean Ann - A Loving Editor

PART ONE

My heart was hot within me, while I was musing the fire burned: then spake I with my tongue, "Lord, make me to know mine end, and the measure of my days, what it is: that I may know how frail I am.

Psalm 39:3-4

Behold, the destroyer I have sent forth to destroy and lay waste mine enemies, and not many years hence they shall not be left to pollute mine heritage, and to blaspheme my name upon the lands which I have consecrated for the gathering together of my saints.

Doctrine and Covenants 105:15
Church of Jesus Christ of Latter Day Saints

PROLOGUE

Kevil

Questions

On a rain-soaked night – the night of May 6th, 1842, to be exact – I crouched below the side window of a house on South Spring Street in Independence, Missouri. There, with rain slashing my face, trickling in rivulets down my spine, I prepared to assassinate the Honorable Lilburn Boggs, sixth governor of the great State of Missouri. When I saw him walk into the room, sit in his favorite brown leather chair – one studded with brass upholstery nails – I asked myself, how had it come to this? How had I – Kevil Pape, Esquire, a once prominent Southern attorney and plantation owner – come to be on the brink of such an ignoble act? Why had I, a felonious prison escapee, allowed myself to be lured into the role of a hired gun? Why had I permitted my services as an agent of vengeance to be purchased for the modest sum of six thousand dollars? Why had I abandoned the comforts of a warm home, to squat in the miseries of a wicked downpour cradling a forty-four caliber pepperbox pistol?

CHAPTER ONE

Kevil

Walls

"Out of the wagon, Pape. Stand up straight, eyes forward, y'hear?" The prison guard, a little rat man with scabs on his face, paced to and fro before me slapping his left palm with a scarred black truncheon. "This ain't no Greene County Jail, y'hear! This ain't no gentleman's club like you been in down there to Springfield. This here is the *Walls*. Yessir, the Missouri State Pen, newest, finest, and strongest prison in all of these here *You*nited States, y'hear?"

"I'm not deaf," I said. For this I received six vicious blows of the truncheon.

"Don't you never mouth me, y'hear! Now git up and march your sorry white arse through them doors."

So began my incarceration in the Walls. A sentence of seven years of hard labor.

Once through the doors, guards hurled me into the *reception cell*, as it was called, a damp, dark, foul little dungeon furnished with a crusty slop bucket. There, I would stew in my own filth. There, the warders would dash any desire for resistance and extrude all hope for escape from the putrid miasmas of the Walls. However, it so happens that I am made of finer fettle than most. Thus, my powers of endurance were quite sufficient to survive whatever abuse the guards would inflict upon me.

Two days later, I was dragged from the reception cell, marched to a small room, and ordered to take a bath in a tub of fetid water. Then, in a comic moment, the guards forced me to don ill-fitting garb consisting of a striped shirt, pantaloons, and a silly pillbox cap. Chains were affixed to my waist and ankles. One half of my head was shaved to mark me in the unlikely event that I should escape. Despite my appearance as a court jester, I bore myself with a dignity proper to my aforementioned station in life. I refused to accept the disgrace intended by my prison attire.

I was prodded on to the warden's office where I endured a long, incoherent tirade of insults. I watched with fascination as large globules of white spittle formed in the corners of Warden Rayford's mouth only to be forcefully expelled on the stream of his invective. From thence, I was paraded past a honeycomb of one-man cells emitting the groans, pleas, and commiserations of the convicted. These wretched cells appeared to be about four feet wide and seven feet deep. The doors were low and I could not determine the interior height. Straw beds rested upon metal floor racks and, though I could not clearly see the remaining appointments, I thought I spotted assorted commodes and washbasins.

I did not display any outward emotion but I must confess to groaning inwardly, wondering how to endure such desolation for the full measure of my sentence. Escape had to be a part of my thinking and since my intellect was of superior quality, I could surely devise a way to steal away from this god-forsaken hellhole.

As we marched along, the lead guard, a brutish man with sloped forehead and single eyebrow, barked the prison rules: "You ain't to talk, in or out of yer cell. Never look up to a visitor even if it be yer own kin. You do, I gonna flay you with the cat-o-nine. Take off yer cap when you is speakin' to yer superiors an' none o' these wretches is to be called *Mister*. You followin' me?"

"Yes sir," I said and was rewarded with a sharp blow from the guard's cudgel on my right shoulder.

"Said take yer cap off when you is speakin' to the authorities! How many times I gots to tell you?"

I said nothing more.

One can imagine my surprise and relief when the guards threw me into my cell. I didn't land in one of the small stone cubicles by which I had just passed, but in a more commodious room nearly twice as large in width and depth. Later, I learned that such a cell would normally have housed four inmates. However, only one other person occupied the space, sitting upon his straw ticking, deep in prayer.

When the cell door slammed with its unsettling clang, he did not move. Having no pressing obligations, I saw little need to invoke my usual impatience and allowed him to finish his supplications. When he returned to the present moment, he saw me sitting opposite him and reached across the three feet dividing us to extend his hand in friendship.

"Good day, sir," he said in a whisper. "Doctor Tobias Mercer at your service."

"*Doctor*?" I asked, also in a whisper and with raised eyebrows.

"Medical College of Ohio, class of 1832."

"Do tell," I said. "Kevil Pape, University of Virginia School of Law, 1833. Note, I pronounce my first name *Keh*vil, not *Kee*vil."

We loosed our hands and studied each other in silence for a moment, I presume mutually delighted by our unexpected pairing. We had been spared the company of unrefined and thuggish cellmates, at least for the time being.

"Why are we in this cell?" I asked sweeping my hand around the stone walls and glancing at the domed ceiling.

"You mean as opposed to the small one-man cells?"

I nodded.

"No clear idea. Perhaps because we are learned and professional men."

"So a slight act of mercy on someone's part?"

"It would seem so."

Suddenly, Doctor Mercer held his hand up and pursed his lips for silence. With measured pace, a guard walked by the iron latticework of our cell door. We held our breath. When the guard had moved out of earshot, my cellmate lowered his hand.

"I notice you are a man of faith," I said.

"I am indeed sir. A member of the Church of Latter Day Saints."

"The what?"

"The Mormon Church. Have you not heard of us?"

"To be honest, I do not occupy my mind with matters of religion."

"Nor did I for most of my life," Doctor Mercer admitted. "That is, until I met and heard Joseph Smith preach on restoration of the priesthood and fulfillment of the Gospel."

"Who is Joseph Smith?"

"You've not heard of Joseph Smith? Why he is a genuine prophet of God sent in these latter days to prepare mankind for the second coming of our Lord."

"I see," I said, regretting my decision to raise the issue.

"I should like to enlighten you with more about our beliefs," Doctor Mercer said. "Would you have a mind to listen?"

I held up my hand. "Perhaps another time. I am rather addled from the indignities of my reception and, if I have a moment of solace, I should like to rest."

"Most certainly," he said. "I do understand. The brutalities of the guards know no bounds."

I settled myself on the filthy straw mattress and closed my eyes. Of course, I had no real need to rest my mind but I desired to veer away from this religious palaver. When I judged a suitable span of time had gone by, thirty minutes or so, I reopened our conversation. "So what offense brought you to this place?"

"Protection of my family and defense of my property."

"Hardly a criminal act."

"Unless you are a Mormon."

"Do tell."

Doctor Mercer raised his eyebrows as if to question whether I truly wanted to hear his story. When I nodded in encouragement, he took a deep breath. "Some years ago, the Prophet Joseph Smith received from on high a revelation that the New Jerusalem, the Promised Land, was to be centered in the western regions of Missouri."

"Missouri? The Promised Land?" I stifled a smile. "Hardly an auspicious locale to my mind."

"So it turned out," he said. "Our people came to Jackson County settling around Independence. However, conflicts with the old settlers forced us to remove to Clay County, where our reception was somewhat more cordial. That benevolence lasted for two years and we were forced again to move, this time to Caldwell County. My family and I located and settled just south of Caldwell County. This was 1837, after I had converted to the true faith."

"Did you open a medical practice?"

"Yes and I also ran a small farm on the road between Caldwell County to the north and Ray County to the south."

I studied him as he spoke. The man presented a thoughtful and solemn mien, no doubt formed by the travails of his life. Curly dark hair, now graying at the temples, and a pair of gold-rimmed spectacles added to his air of sagacity. Despite the man's religious lunacy, I found his story compelling and bade him continue.

"Caldwell County was a Mormon county," he said, "by designation of the State. Ray County, on the other hand, had been populated largely by old settlers. Between the two counties there lay a geographic buffer known as Buncombe's Strip. Our farm and the small community of Buncombe sat squarely in the center of this borderland. No doubt you can begin to see the potential for problems. Mormon settlers encroached upon Gentile homesteads. That's what we call non-believers – Gentiles."

"Indeed."

"In short order, a flood of Mormon immigrants from Canada and England poured into Caldwell County and spilled over into the surrounding counties. This population growth, coupled with the growing political power of the Church, caused tensions to flare once again. I must say I can understand the natural uneasiness of the old settlers who feared a wholesale takeover of their land by the Saints. No doubt our preaching and proclamations about the end of the world inflamed the passions of our Gentile neighbors. Perhaps violence was unavoidable."

He picked at a straw poking through his mattress ticking. When he had it extracted, he rolled it around in his fingers as if to study its makeup.

"Throughout our history," he said, "Mormons have tried to respond to persecution in a peaceful and Christ-like manner. However, the patience of the Saints came to an end at precisely the same moment the rage of those old settlers burst into flame. On Independence Day, two years ago, one of our leaders, Sidney Rigdon, gave a provocative and incendiary speech. I was present on that occasion in the city of Far West and remember it as if it were yesterday. In fact, I have committed a portion of it to memory." He stared at me, took a deep breath, raised the right forefinger, and launched into his memorized discourse.

"We take God and all the holy angels to witness this day, that we warn all men in the name of Jesus Christ, to come on us no more forever, for from this hour, we will bear it no more; our rights shall no more be trampled on with impunity. The man or the set of men who attempts it does it at the expense of their lives. And that mob that comes on us to disturb us; it shall be between us

and them a war of extermination, for we will follow them, till the last drop of their blood is spilled, or else they will have to exterminate us: for we will carry the seat of war to their own houses, and their own families, and one party or the other shall be utterly destroyed. Remember it then all MEN."

Doctor Mercer paused for several long seconds and removed his spectacles, breaking the gaze he had directed upon me. "I think of myself as a man of peace," he said, in a softer voice, "but that speech, those words, became my personal creed. *We will bear it no more; our rights shall no more be trampled on with impunity.* On that hot summer day in Far West, I vowed that I would strive to repel any unjust aggressor who tried to force my family from our home. In October of 1838, a mob unit of old settlers under the leadership of one Captain Bogart entered Buncombe's Strip, harassing the Mormon settlers, disarming them, and forcing them at gunpoint to leave the county. I was in no mood to comply. At the first sign of trouble, I dispatched my wife and two young daughters north to Far West and prepared to defend my property.

"On the morning of October 24th, ten of Bogart's men, including Bogart himself, came onto my farm and called me out. I told these invaders to get off my property or I would let fly. They paid me no heed and moved toward my house. I fired a warning shot through the window. While I was reloading, they stormed the house and breeched my front door. The first man through the door met the butt of my musket, swung with the fullest force I could muster. The blow crushed his face and he crumpled to the floor. Though he survived for a time, he later succumbed to his injuries. I had dealt him a mortal blow. Of course, I was subdued in short order, beaten, and brought to trial."

We paused again to let the guard pass in silence.

"It appears at first glance," I said, "that you have not been hanged by your neck until dead, the standard punishment for such a crime. I must therefore assume you were convicted of a lesser charge."

Doctor Mercer was a humorless man, but he offered a rare smile in response. "Quite right, I reckon two facts persuaded the judge. First, Bogart had gone beyond the scope of his orders and trespassed upon my property. Second, I had a justifiable argument of self-defense. I might even have expected acquittal, given these mitigating circumstances, but we Mormons are not always the beneficiaries of justice. For me it is a four-year sentence on the charge of

8

manslaughter. I have served eighteen months."

He replaced his spectacles. "And you, Mr. Pape," he said. "How did you come upon this misfortune?"

I had no desire to go over the circumstances that led to my incarceration but since Doctor Mercer had been so forthcoming, I thought I ought to reciprocate. I agreed to tell him my story, at least in broad outline. There seemed no reason to offend by stonewalling him. After all, he might well be in a position to help me later. As will soon be seen, in this supposition I was uncannily accurate.

"I am here because I chose to defend my family's honor," I said, pausing to let the full weight of my remark settle upon his mind. "In the spring of 1838, my half-brother Jedediah had intimate relations with a Cherokee squaw during the relocation of her tribe through Missouri to Indian Country. Allegedly, he forced himself on the young woman. No proof exists. Nevertheless, the barbarian Cherokees elected to avenge this alleged transgression by the capture, brutal torture, and murder of Jedediah.

"To my everlasting consternation, those rustic chawbacons in String Town, where this set of events unfolded, elected not to pursue the matter further. They made no effort to bring to justice the savages responsible for my brother's murder. The String Town leaders fatuously reasoned that the punishment fit the crime. Now, I ask you, does flailing, dismembering, and burning a man for a mere dalliance with a squaw constitute a fitting punishment?" Before he could answer, I rolled on, "I engaged in my own pursuit of the culprits. I found them and, in defending the honor of my family, I was attacked, beaten, and incarcerated without trial. For an inhumanely long period of time, I should add. Of course I petitioned for a writ of *habeas corpus* but in the wilds of southwest Missouri, such a petition fell upon deaf ears. I daresay most of those citizens couldn't even pronounce *habeas corpus*, let alone issue a writ thereof."

"So you have been dogged by the hounds of injustice too."

"Well put. When finally I came to trial I defended myself brilliantly but the winds of justice blew away from me. Despite my brilliant self-defense, I was convicted of assault and sentenced to seven years. The judge lay hard upon my sentence."

"I should say so. You said you defended yourself?"

"I did. Ironically, it is the first case I have lost in many years, a realization that causes me no small measure of embarrassment. In these forsaken wilds, there is little hope for appeal. For the past three months, I have languished in Springfield, in the Greene County Jail, awaiting transfer here to Jefferson City."

Doctor Mercer held his hand up once again. Clearly his ears had sharpened over the months for I did not myself hear the guard approaching.

Keys rattled and the cell door creaked open.

"Here's yer grub," the guard said. While a fellow officer trained his gun on us, two chunks of dry corn bread and two cups of water were slid into the cell.

Upon receipt of these meager rations, Doctor Mercer closed his eyes and mouthed a prayer of thanksgiving, which I found curious. How could one muster thanks for moldy bread and water drawn from an uncertain well? We ate in silence. Just as we swallowed our last morsels, the lights were extinguished leaving us in pitch-black silence broken only by the moans, shrieks, and curses of our fellow inmates. The fusty straw mattresses offered little comfort. Our so-called *Indian blankets* were so thin and short that my cellmate and I found no shame in huddling close, drawing upon each other's warmth.

Periodically, we were awakened by one of the guards dragging some hapless soul from his cell and beating him senseless for a minor infraction. I discovered in time that our night guard, a man named Worrell, preferred to beat prisoners with a stout wood paddle riddled with holes like a slice of Swiss cheese. The holes enhanced the speed and force of the blow while giving rise to bloody welts.

The next morning we were awakened before dawn and paraded to our several workstations. I was assigned to the brickyard alongside Doctor Mercer, where I labored as a hod carrier, moving fired bricks from the kiln to the stacks. When we broke for breakfast, I was thoroughly exhausted and despaired of my ability to continue for the remainder of the day. Surprisingly, the stale cornbread and soggy bacon, which I ate with dust-smeared fingers, revived me. I found myself able to return to productive work for the balance of the day. Thus began the drudgery of prison life.

+ + +

To my great relief, one month after my arrival at the Walls, the leg irons were removed. My conduct had been sufficiently compliant to permit this small measure of freedom. Work in the brickyard became much easier when I was allowed to walk around unfettered. To my further relief, I had not yet been removed from my cell during the night hours for one of Mister Worrell's undeserved beatings, nor had Doctor Mercer. He attributed our reprieve to the efficacy of his daily prayers. I simply counted it as good fortune, bearing no divine stamp whatsoever. However, I did not disabuse the good doctor of his nonsensical appeals to the Almighty. As I have already noted, Doctor Mercer could be of value to me. Humoring him was by far the only sensible course of action.

In due time, the act of humoring him reached heroic proportions as I was obliged to listen to his missionary spiels. I was taught more about the Church of Latter Day Saints than ever I desired to learn. For example, Doctor Mercer regaled me with the incredulous story of Joseph Smith who, at age fourteen, was visited simultaneously by God the Father and the Lord Jesus. These apparitions directed Joseph not to join any particular church. I suppose this prohibition indicated divine dissatisfaction with all denominations. Later, at age eighteen, an angel named Moroni came to Joseph and informed him of the existence of certain golden plates containing a history of the ancient Americas and a new testament of salvation. Four years later, the soon-to-be prophet unearthed these golden plates from a hillside in upstate New York. With the aid of a set of *peep stones*, he claimed to have translated the ancient language imprinted on the plates. And *voilà*! The *Book of Mormon* was loosed upon this apostate world.

Of course, all of this beggared my imagination and caused me to wonder how anyone in his right mind could believe such swill. Upon further reflection, however, I concluded that all forms of faith involve delusion. That is, all religious belief is grounded in the unproved. I could not castigate Mormons any more than I could castigate Methodists. They both believed in fantastic irrationalities. Why, I reasoned, is the Virgin Birth, or the Resurrection, or the Damascus Road event any less whimsical than a fortuitous visit from an angel named Moroni?

On more than one occasion, Doctor Mercer nudged me to accept the revelations of his mighty prophet and the absurd doctrines flowing from that man's fertile imagination. Gracefully, I resisted. I had no doubt that my cellmate's quiet persistence in seeking my conversion earned him jewels in the crown of heaven. Or so he must have thought because he never gave up.

+ + +

September 13, 1840, turned out to be a propitious day in the fortunes of Kevil Pape, Esquire, and his humble companion, Doctor Tobias Mercer. On that day, Mister Worrell was relieved of his duties. Mister Nathan Philpott replaced him, a kind man and one given to compassion for prisoners. He did not so strictly enforce the rules. The strictures on speaking among ourselves loosened. When other guards came around, Mister Philpott feigned cruelty but we all knew that it was merely for appearance's sake.

During work breaks, Doctor Mercer engaged Mister Philpott in conversations about the Mormon faith. The latter seemed intrigued by this twaddle. Initially, this irritated me because it showed the naïve gullibility to which our species is heir. As I thought about it further, however, it occurred to me that pulling Mister Philpott directly into Mercer's orbit – and indirectly into my own – could have its benefits.

In the meantime, another boon came my way. Several of us who worked in the brickyard were selected to take part in a prison lease program. Prison officials identified a dozen of the more trustworthy inmates to work as masons and carpenters on municipal construction projects outside the Walls. Doctor Mercer and I were among them. Five guards accompanied our work crew as we passed through the confines of the Walls and into the streets and byways of Jefferson City. Though still under guard, we had the opportunity to breathe fresh air. We savored the day-to-day goings on in a world that had become for us a distant fantasy. To our great fortune, Mister Philpott was placed on the day shift and served as one of the guards during these outings from the Walls. Because speaking restrictions were suspended during the work details, a certain camaraderie developed between the guards and trustees.

Of course, Doctor Mercer wasted no time in trotting out his religious wares and, before long, he had begun to persuade a few convicts and guards that the last days were at hand. Conversion to Mormonism, he said, provided the opportunity for exaltation, regardless of one's station in life. Even a convict could be guaranteed glory in heaven. Doctor Mercer's focus on glory in the next world had great appeal to those suffering nothing but despair in this one. As I watched my companions listen to Doctor Mercer with rapt attention, I could not help but draw to mind the observation of Edward Gibbon. He contended that throughout history, the conquered often become the conquerors. Gibbon noted, for example, that the Romans successfully civilized their conquerors – the Visigoths, Vandals, Lombards, and Huns. In a microcosmic way, this phenomenon appeared to be playing out among the members of our crew in Jefferson City. Doctor Mercer, the conquered, was conquering the religious minds of his own guards. Nothing could have been more providential.

One evening in mid-November, following a grueling day, Doctor Mercer and I shivered beneath our flimsy Indian blankets and tried to muster as much body heat as possible.

"Mister Pape," he whispered, "I have a proposition for you."

I said nothing, waiting for him to continue.

"As you know Mister Philpott looks upon us Saints with favor and grace."

I remained silent.

Doctor Mercer continued. "He has indicated a willingness to help us escape."

My ears pricked. "Do tell," I said.

"It seems we are going to have a change in our labors. They are shutting down the brickyard so we are to be sent into the forest to chop wood. There will be one guard leading our work column, another on each flank, and two in the rear. Mr. Philpott will arrange to be one of the rear guards. You and I are to assume our place in the back of the detail. We are to proceed slowly, thereby causing the two of us, and the two rear guards, to fall behind the others. Then, we are to surprise Mr. Philpott's companion guard, overpower him, snatch away his rifle and strike out into the woods. Mr. Philpott will put up token resistance and let us escape."

"You can't be serious," I said, instantly aware of the many flaws in the plan. "Where, pray tell, would we go?"

"Mister Philpott and his wife will harbor us."

"You trust him?"

"Completely. He has asked me to baptize him upon my escape. I agreed. He looks forward to this with all of his heart."

"So what is the plan?" I asked.

"After work on a prearranged date, while we walk back to the Walls from chopping wood, we will pass through a forested stretch near the Missouri River. You no doubt recall it. It is there where we will make our break, pushing hard through a dense belt of trees to the north and west. Not far from the road, the river bends abruptly to the north. On its west bank, a mile or so upriver, an abandoned farmhouse sits secluded in the trees. Behind the farmhouse, we should find a deep root cellar hidden in the underbrush. We are to locate this root cellar and hide there through the night. In the early hours, just before dawn, Mister Philpott will come for us, hide us in his wagon, and transport us to his house. We are to stay there for several weeks under his hospitality until things die down and we can leave town. Then we will be free to go our separate ways."

At first pass, I understood the ingenuity of this plan. Who, for example, would suspect a prison guard of aiding and abetting an escape? The security and success of this subterfuge, however, could be compromised if others reflected upon Mister Philpott's obvious zeal for his new-found religion. The relationship between guard and prisoner could bring suspicion upon Philpott and prompt inquiries and even searches of his home. When I mentioned these reservations to Doctor Mercer, he responded with quick assurances.

"There is a space beneath the floorboards of the house. I am told that this cellar has a low ceiling but suitable for sleeping quarters. While in the house itself, we are to keep a low profile and not to drift far from the hidden trap door to this undercroft. If a search party arrives we are to jump into the cellar. We will take our meals down below. This is not an ideal habitation but no worse than what we now suffer. I am confident we can endure it for as long as necessary until we can take our leave of Jefferson City."

I told Doctor Mercer that I would ponder this opportunity. I passed a sleepless night during which I ran a series of events through my mind. The escape plan was a high-risk operation. Yet, I had few other options. The Walls proved to be a robust facility guarded by vigilant brutes. I myself had not yet devised a suitable plan for escape so this one proffered by Doctor Mercer was opportune indeed. When at last we were rousted from our beds the following morning I whispered my acceptance.

CHAPTER TWO

Elena

Mission

A few minutes after two o'clock in the afternoon, the Reverend Mister Fielding raised his hand for silence and attention. "The Lord be with you."

"And with thy spirit," came the congregational response. Though a majority of those in attendance were not Anglicans, they knew the prescribed responses from years of exposure to the established Church of England.

"Let us pray." *Mister* Fielding continued with a rote prayer for the beginning of a church meeting. He demanded that no one call him a *priest* of the church, though that was his office. Nor, heaven forbid, was he to ever to be addressed as *Father* Fielding, being a man of militant low church persuasion.

I listened to his prayer, not to the content of his petitions, but to the way he spoke. Mister Fielding, an itinerant minister and not from Lancashire, spoke the Queen's English. I say the *Queen's English* because one month earlier, in June of 1837, King William died and his daughter Victoria ascended to the throne. Though I had never traveled far from my home and had never strayed beyond the boundaries of Lancashire, I did not want to think of myself as a *provincial* girl, one of a simple character and superficial mind. To elevate myself from this status, I had been working for years to shed the Lancashire dialect of my mother and father. So, when I had the opportunity to listen to one who spoke the Queen's English, I did so with an alert ear.

When he finished his prayer, he lifted his head to survey the assembled congregation. More than two hundred souls had squeezed into Vauxhall Chapel, a small box-like building quite unlike most parish churches. The building had lately been used by the Particular Baptists but they made it available to Mister Fielding for his ministrations among the working poor of Preston, our home village. My Da, Thomas Arkwright, who was one of the town's blacksmiths, had been attending Vauxhall Chapel. I occasionally accompanied him but I did not find the tepidity and mechanical prayers of the Anglican services to my liking. However, Da insisted that I come with him on this occasion to hear missionaries who had come from America.

"As I mentioned during the morning service," Mister Fielding began, "my brother Joseph and two of his companions have journeyed from America to tell us about the *restored Gospel*. I am informed that our first speaker will be Brother Heber Kimball and so I welcome him to the pulpit."

Mister Kimball rose and bobbed his head several times in the general direction of the congregation. Timid and tentative-appearing, he took his place behind the pulpit. There he paused and gathered himself, rising to his full six-foot height. In a quick nervous gesture, he smoothed his thinning black hair and peered at us with eyes bright and piercing. Anticipation filled the room. Save for an occasional cough or sniffle, Vauxhall Chapel was as quiet as a cemetery.

"Dear friends," he said in that flat, broad dialect of Americans, "I come and bear testimony to you that not long ago an Angel of the Lord come visited these lower regions of the earth. That angel have committed an everlasting Gospel to all mankind." His grammar and vocabulary betrayed limited education and rustic beginnings. Still, there was an unmistakable power in what he said.

As he spoke, his voice swelled, bearing testimony to what he claimed was a series of divine revelations to a man named Joseph Smith. Mister Kimball exhorted us to prepare for the Second Coming, which he assured us was near at hand. Acceptance of this revelation, baptism by someone in the authentic priesthood, and commitment to a new life in Christ would bring us everlasting salvation. He declared further that all denominations, Protestant and Catholic, were but partial and incomplete expressions of the full Gospel. They had all gone astray upon the death of the last apostle. Therefore, a new order of things became necessary and God had chosen Joseph Smith to receive His instructions for a restored church.

"Every human being," Brother Kimball thundered, "every one – rich, poor, sinful or innocent, male or female – every one can have a personal relation with God. You need not have priests and pastors to find the true god. And He be not a god without body or parts, as the denominations preach. Nay, the god of the denominations is a false god. Not the god of true Christians to whom the Gospel has been restored in these last days. All of you can become pure Christians and I hold this to be true: you will possess miraculous gifts in proportion to your faith. Brothers and sisters you are now strangers to the truth and yet you are candidates for immortality. May the blessings of heaven rest upon all of you."

When Mister Kimball had finished his testimony, an excited murmuring rolled through the chapel. I saw Molly Miller and Thaddeus Atherton overcome with emotion, weeping into their kerchiefs. My dear old impulsive Da was also quite beside himself, enthralled by what he had heard. I harbored reservations.

After Mister Kimball's speech, another American, Orson Hyde, and the Reverend Mister Fielding's brother, Joseph, addressed the assembly. Their remarks added little in the way of new information but upon their completion, shouts of *glory to God*, *praise to the heavens*, and whispers of thanksgiving filled the air. When the excitement had subsided, Mister Fielding seemed caught up in the moment and invited everyone back that evening to hear from the missionaries once more. As the meeting broke up, Da rushed to the front of the chapel in a throng of people seeking personal blessings, healings, and other charities from our visitors. I waited patiently by the door for Da, offering greetings to those I knew, particularly the families of the doffer boys whom I supervised in the mill.

I watched Da coming toward me swaying back and forth on bandy legs, his face lit up like a lantern. I took him by the arm and we left the chapel. Though my father came only to my shoulder, I never got over just how strong he was. His upper body was like a block of granite, hardened by a lifetime of labor in the blacksmith's shop.

"T'wern't that somethin' Lanie? Did ye ever hear o' such a thing? An angel comin' t' a simple man in these latter days. 'Tis like Bible times anew."

"It is something to think about, Da. I'll give you that."

"Aw'm pricked to me heart, Lanie. Aw'm a-comin' back tonight.

Wilt thou be a-comin' with?"

"I don't know, Da. I shall think on it."

"Ah, but Lanie, 'tis seldom we get visitors from America. Our little village o' Preston has received the Lord's magnificent blessin'! Why the Prophet hisself sent these men t' come among us. Canst thou believe such a thin'?"

"So now you too call him *the Prophet*?"

"He must be, lass. He must be. 'Tis is a powerful testimony and a whole new Bible testament t' boot. Angels and prophecies – dead for so long – be now back among us, Lanie. Can the Second Comin' be far behind?"

"I don't know, Da. I'll ponder it some."

"Aw feel lik Aw'm half way to heaven, Lanie. My owd heart is swole with joy at the thought o' becomin' a true follower o' the Lord an' receivin' the gifts o' the Spirit."

Da had a lift in his old bow-legged step on that half-mile walk back to the cottage. Despite my own misgivings, I felt warmed by his delight over the afternoon's events. My Da had spent his entire life, from the age of nine, in the sweltering confines of the blacksmith shop. His labors left him little time for recreation and pleasure. He had a smattering of school, enough to read, write, and cipher a bit. My sweet mum died three years before the arrival of the missionaries and Da had rarely smiled since her passing. Indeed, I couldn't recall the last time I had seen him so full of excitement. The smile on his lips brought one to my own.

I did not accompany Da to the evening meeting with the American missionaries, choosing instead to spend my time at home.

"Lanie, Lanie," Da said on his way out the door, "Ye'll miss the crownin' o' the day. Subject tonight is baptism. Aw wish ye would come alon'."

"You go on, Da. I have some reading to do."

"Ah, Lanie, thee an' thy books. Always readin'. Most readin'ist girl in Preston, Aw do declare."

"Bye, bye, Da," I said and gave him a peck on the forehead.

It is true. I no doubt was the *readingest girl* in all of Preston. I had only a few years of schooling before going to work in the mill but took to the classroom like a moth to flame. I read every book, pamphlet, newspaper, magazine, and tract I could find. Even when I started work in the mill as a little doffer, I found I had some time to read. The hours were long. I began work at five in the morning and carried on until seven at night. The work of the doffer required extreme speed and dexterity. When the bobbins in the throstle room were full, the spinning frames were stopped. We had to remove the bobbins, replace them with empty ones, and set the frames going again. Most of the doffers were boys. Indeed, for a long time, I was the only girl but much faster than the boys.

Between doffings, our time was our own. As long as we were within earshot of the throstle jobber, who would whistle to us when the bobbins were full, we were free to do as we wished. The boys spent most of their time out of doors playing games – rounders, knucklebones, tag, or jackstraws. I curled up with a book except when the boys called for a game of dodge ball. That brought me to my feet. I threw a ball harder than most of the boys – truer too – and despite my skirts, I ducked and dipped better than most.

As I grew older, I assisted the younger boys in their apprenticeship and became a big sister to them. Because of my coaching, most of them became excellent doffers and productivity increased. The overseers observed my leadership and, against all convention, appointed me the first woman throstle jobber in the mills of Preston. I earned much better money than the other women, worked only from seven in the morning to six at night, and had Saturday afternoon free. A woman could find no better work in all of Lancashire. As one might imagine, my fellow workers, especially the women, looked upon me with envy and disaffection. I became isolated from all but the children, which added to my peculiarity.

"Thou art a queer one, lass," Da had often said. "Aw love thee full and all. Thou art as keen as a rippin' saw and a jobber in the weighvin' shop, no less. But Lanie, thou hast no man t' help thee and time's a-movin' on. An owd spinster ye'll be afore ye know it. All thy readin' an' thinkin' is a puttin' thee off th' lads, Lanie. Aw'm worried about thee, lass."

And Mum would chime in, "Now Tom, don't ye ride 'er back. Elena's a lovely girl, a prize for some good man. She'll be a-bidin' 'er time 'til the right one comes along. Go and poor thee another cup o' tea and leave the lass be."

Da loved me. Of that I was certain. I took no offense when he talked of my oddities. His worries were well placed. Since I had no prospects I accepted the fact that I might never be married. I hadn't yet met a man who met my standards; namely intelligence, sensitivity, industry, and height. With reference to the last feature, I should mention that I'm two inches short of six feet. Most of the men in my acquaintance were much shorter than I. Intelligence, sensitivity, and industry could have trumped height, but no one had ever come my way with the right trump cards. Further, while I could imagine kissing a man, I did not favor leaning down to do so.

I didn't accept Mum's description of me as a *lovely girl*. I did not have the fullness and curves of a lovely one. Others felt the same way about my tall, slender appearance because I had been subject to such taunts as *Long Lanie, Upright Arkwright*, and *Elongayna*. Mum herself once said, "A bonny fair lass thou art, Elena, long and willowy, but strong as wych elm." *Willowy* and *wych-elm strong* did not amount to loveliness in my mind. Of course, Mum would often add, "Such a pretty face thou hast with flaxen hair and curls. Thy mouth is like a rosebud, to be sure. Ah, Elena, a man would be proud indeed to have thee as his own."

And so it went. Da and Mum would debate my condition, sing my praises, and offer different predictions about my future. That is, until Mum died of the cancer leaving Da with but one woman in his life. He became increasingly reliant upon me, almost clingy. With this dependence came an abrupt halt to his concerns about my future. If I found a good man, Da would be left alone.

+ + +

Just as I closed my book and prepared to put out the lanterns Da burst into the cottage.

"Lanie! Aw'm t' be baptized on Sunday! Baptized into the one true faith. Aw'm t' be a Saint, a Latter Day Saint. A Mormon! Canst thou imagine such a thin'?"

"But, Da, you've already been baptized. Christened as an infant."

"Aye, but that wasn't a true baptism."

"Grandmum said the Bishop himself christened you. What's not true about that?"

"The Bishop had no true priesthood. Ye see, my Lanie girl, the Lord himself gave t' the Prophet the *true* priesthood. John the Baptiser, Peter, James, and John come down from heaven and ordained the Prophet. So now only men ordained by the Prophet hisself can perform a valid baptism. Dost thou follow?"

"I understand Da but you are accepting too much and throwing away more. You have heard these men on two occasions and now you are ready to cast your lot with them and abandon all your family has given to you."

"The disciples dropped awl to follow Jesus."

"The *Prophet* is not Jesus."

"Ah, but a good deal closer than most."

"I would ask that you give it time, Da. Sunday is very soon."

"Thou shan't stay me on this, sweet Lanie. Aw'm t' be baptised. And that's the Lord's will."

Da could be stubborn. Any future arguments would bounce off of him like arrows off a castle rampart. I said no more.

The missionaries spoke again the following Wednesday but, as Da reported to me, the Reverend Mister Fielding shut the doors of the chapel to them for all future meetings. Dozens of the faithful were on the verge of conversion to Mormonism and Mister Fielding saw his congregation slipping away. Da and the other Saints considered this rebuff as a minor inconvenience and selected the market square for future preaching and meetings of the newly formed flock. Early on Sunday, I returned to my small Methodist congregation while Da hurried to the market square.

"After yer service, ye'll come t' the river, Lanie? T' see thy owd Da baptised?"

"I'll come," I said, though I still bore deep misgivings about it all.

That morning during the Methodist meeting, the Reverend Walter Cumberland, preached a diatribe against all denominations but our own. Beginning with the Catholics and proceeding in order, he skewered the Anglicans, Baptists, Presbyterians, Unitarians, Congregationalists, and Aitkinites. He even made passing mention of the dangers he saw in the Latter Day Saints' teaching to which he had just been exposed. Ironically, the central theme of his sermon was that all of the denominations were partial and incomplete, having succumbed to one heresy or another. He argued that Methodism, especially his primitive form of Methodism, came as close to the truth as one could find on this earth.

As I listened to him, I could not help but recall the testimony of the American missionaries who said essentially the same thing. The Mormon insistence that the apostasies of all of the historic denominations resulted from an inauthentic priesthood, had a measure of logic, I had to admit. Wouldn't it be something if what the missionaries were saying could be true? Had the Lord Himself, through the visitation of John the Baptist, Peter, James, and John the Apostle, restored the true priesthood? I pondered these questions as I left the church that morning, bound for the River Ribble.

By the time I reached the river, over a thousand people had gathered to watch the Mormon baptisms. The Saints baptized outdoors by immersion in a river, a practice seldom witnessed in Preston. Standing on the river bluff, I cast my eyes back toward the skyline of the city. I saw the tall steeple from Saint John's church and the chimneys of thirty-eight textile factories chuffing smoke and soot. The tip of the city obelisk peeked over the row houses. As I gazed upon our town I wondered what the future would bring to a place that in one week had become absorbed by the homespun preaching of the Mormon missionaries. Lancashire as a whole, including Preston, was quite weak in church attendance. To witness this multitude gathered for a religious ceremony was striking indeed, even if it were motivated more by curiosity than devotion.

I turned my eyes back to the river. Those to be baptized had changed into long white gowns and even from my distant vantage point, I could see Da beaming with pride. A man named George Watt, a weaver and recent member of the Reverend Mister Fielding's congregation, broke from the group of soon-to-be Saints and ran pell mell to the river. He outdistanced another man to become the first Saint baptized in England. In his earlier years Da would have joined the race. Now his bandy legs would be no match for younger ones.

The baptisms themselves were brief but the missionaries did not miss the occasion to preach to more than a thousand souls. Fascination gripped the audience and many lingered. When the service had ended, I made my way through the crowd to find Da. He had just finished changing back into his clothes when he saw me approaching.

"Ah, Lanie, my sweet Lanie, thou come after all! Thankee sweet lass. Aw'm filled with light, Lanie, the light o' Christ. To me dyin' day, Awm a servent o' the Most High God. Aw just wish thy mum could have been here on this day. Bless 'er soul."

I could not bring myself to say or do anything that might lessen my Da's joy on that occasion. I put my arms around him and just held him for a time as if to say, *I love you Da, no matter what.*

+ + +

From that point on, our lives were consumed by the Latter Day Saints. Since they had no indoor meeting place, the missionaries accepted invitations to preach in the homes of faithful converts. On three occasions during that summer of 1837, our little cottage was packed with Saints and their sympathizers. When not at meetings, Da prattled on at length with the fervor of a convert. At times, I thought I would go mad with the smothering influence of the Church.

There were few copies of the *Book of Mormon* available to recent converts. Mister Kimball loaned Da a copy because he was among the first to be baptized. Though Da could read, he struggled with the printed word and asked me to read the book aloud to him. Thus, every evening for days on end I read the *Book of Mormon* to my Da. He would sit with his eyes closed, enraptured by this strange tale of the ancient Americans.

One evening, as we were nearing the end of our reading, I turned to face my father. "Da, I have a question for you."

He nodded for me to continue.

"I have noticed something. Do you remember a few nights ago we were reading in the book called *Third Nephi?*" Da remembered with a nod and smile. I opened to *Third Nephi* and read a portion of the eleventh chapter. "*And he that believeth and is baptized shall be saved, but he that believeth not shall be damned. And these signs shall follow them that believe – in my name they shall cast out devils; they shall speak with new tongues; they shall take up serpents; and if they drink any deadly thing it shall not hurt them; they shall lay hands on the sick and they shall recover.* Do you remember that passage Da?"

"Aw believe Aw do. Why dost thou ask?"

'Then let me read you something else. I removed the family Bible from a nearby table and opened it to the Gospel of Mark. Reading from the sixteenth chapter I quoted Jesus, *He that believeth and is baptized shall be saved; but he that believeth not shall be damned...*" "Do you see that the two passages are the same?"

Da nodded.

After a short pause, I continued, "Do you think the Prophet

Joseph Smith copied from the New Testament?"

Da furrowed his brow and after several long seconds, shrugged his shoulders. "Aw cannot answer thee," he said, "but the Prophet would not do wrong." His brow relaxed and he leaned back in his chair, no longer troubled by this coincidence.

I watched him for a few minutes. "Perhaps," I said. "Let's leave it at that."

He smiled.

+ + +

As the summer wore on, Brothers Kimball, Hyde, and Fielding stayed in Preston while others journeyed to Bedfordshire and Cumberland. The church grew at an astonishing rate. Da told me in early August that their number had grown to forty, enough to organize a *branch* or formalized congregation of the church. This took place in the home of my friend Ann Dawson who lived on Pole Street. Many of the new members were former parishioners of Vauxhall Chapel. The Reverend Mister Fielding became an ardent opponent of the Saints, bitterly denouncing them for sundering his little church to pieces. Sadly, he broke ties with his brother Joseph, as did other members of the Fielding family.

By September, the Saints – now one hundred in number – had outgrown Ann Dawson's home and other worship venues. They began to hold their meetings in a musty old building, called the *Cockpit*, which, as its name implies, was once used for cock fighting. When Parliament banned cock fighting, the Cockpit became a lyceum and concert hall. This facility served the growing Church well because it held seven hundred people in amphitheater seating. To my relief, as the church grew and gained structure, Da's enthusiasm settled a bit and our home enjoyed relief from the religious frenzy of those early weeks.

For the next two years, the church continued to grow steadily in Britain with membership exceeding three thousand by New Year's Eve, 1839. Of course, the Saints interpreted this impressive growth both as divine favor and confirmation of Mormonism. Several ordinations had taken place, providing leadership for the many branches that had been established. My Da was one of the first in England to receive what the Mormons call the *Priesthood of Aaron*. An unlettered working-class man, one of limited education and untroubled by complex thought, he was quite beside himself at having been set apart for ordination. This would have been impossible in most other denominations.

Despite its phenomenal growth, as time wore on, the Mormon Church in England suffered many of the problems of other dissenting denominations. Limited finances, splintering, lukewarm devotion, quarreling, troubled leadership, and persecution plagued the Saints. I once overheard Joseph Fielding, now in charge of the Preston church, describe conditions as bleak with *the powers of darkness raging on every side*. Of all the church leaders, Da remained optimistic and unconcerned. That was my Da, a naturally cheerful man who, through his devotion to the Saints, had overcome the depression that settled upon him when Mum died. I continued to attend the Primitive Methodist Church. It was hardly a place of inspiration but, of all the available options, it still seemed to me the best.

One of the Mormon missionaries from America, Doctor Willard Richards, remained in Preston to assist Joseph Fielding in oversight of the local branch. He took my Methodist loyalty as a challenge. I spent many evenings in religious conversation with Doctor Richards, a soft, frail, intellectual man. He had fallen from a scaffold as a child, leaving him weak and unable to perform manual labor. This handicap may have spurred his interest in a wide range of intellectual matters. He found our evenings as stimulating as I, or so I assumed. To my delight, he created any number of excuses for visiting Da. After perfunctory chitchat about the Church, we would settle in for lengthy discussions, mostly on matters of faith. At first, Da struggled to follow what Doctor Richards and I were saying but in time he simply excused himself and left us to our debates.

Doctor Richards had an ulterior motive, of course, wanting more than anything to convert me to the Mormon faith. I remember one particular evening when we were discussing the truth of the *Book of Mormon*. "Here," he said. "Listen to this teaching that I have copied from one of our early newspapers, *The Morning Star*." He retrieved a small piece of paper from his pocket. His handwriting appeared beautiful and uniform in appearance. I wondered at the time how a man with occasional palsy could produce such precise penmanship. "This is what the Prophet wrote, *Search the scriptures — search the revelations which we publish, and ask Heavenly Father, in the name of His Son Jesus Christ, to manifest the truth unto you, if you do it with an eye single to His glory nothing doubting, He will answer you by the power of His Holy Spirit."*

He paused and looked at me with a steady gaze. "Elena, you have searched our scriptures. I know this because your father told me that you read the *Book of Mormon* to him from beginning to end. But you have not asked Heavenly Father to manifest the truth unto you. You have not done so with an eye to His glory. You have harbored doubts. Otherwise, the Holy Ghost would have visited you and confirmed the truth to you."

"But, Elder Richards, I *have* sought God's direction. On many an occasion, at night, when the lanterns have been extinguished, and all that can be heard are the gentle snores of Da, I have asked God to reveal to me the truth. I am not blind. I can see the growth of the Church. I marvel at the fervor of many of your new converts. I have witnessed the transformation in people who were once lost and now lead purposeful lives. I can see it most fully in my sweet Da. He is a new man and, I daresay, a happier and better man. I see in him a new joy and charity. I cannot ignore all of this. I assure you, I have taken it to God in prayer. But I've had no revelations, no confirmations, no assurances. All remains silent to me."

"Then there must be some defect in your attitude."

"But, Elder Richards, do you not see how this goes round and round in a circle like girls dancing the maypole in spring? If the truth is manifest to me, I am in a right attitude. If not, I am in the wrong attitude. If I say my mind and heart are sincere but receive no revelation, then you would say my mind and heart are not sincere. It is an unbreakable circle. How is one to know?"

"Elena, if you do not receive the revelation of truth, you must read the scriptures and pray again."

"And if I do and still nothing comes to me, what then?"

"Read and pray once more."

"I'm sorry but this is a futile process. Perhaps I am not capable of sincerity of thought and cannot cast an eye to God's glory."

"May I suggest, Elena, that you are all wrapped up in your mind. You think too much. You have not yet had that burning deep within your heart that tells you the truth of a thing." He raised a pudgy finger. "*Heart fire.* Until this emotion assails you, until you know heart fire, you cannot know God. Your spirit is…*defective.*"

"Defective?"

"I would say it is true."

His words pierced my soul. At that moment, I was assailed with an overwhelming sense of inferiority, weakness, and incapacity. I said nothing more and struggled to stay calm in Doctor Richards' presence, not wanting him to see how he had hurt me. Certain other feelings magnified my pain. Secretly, I had been wondering if perhaps Doctor Richards might wish to court me. He was shorter than I and giving way to portliness but his attentions had begun to affect me. However, the pain he had just inflicted struck me like a slap in the face. I sat there, weak and superficial, unable to see the truth of his beliefs. In that moment I knew I could not live up to his spiritual expectations.

One week later, near the obelisk in our market square, I saw Jenetta Richards, a casual acquaintance of mine, walking with Doctor Richards. Though they bore the same last name, they were not kinfolk. I could tell from the messages passing between their eyes that theirs was more than a chance meeting. A sense of foolish embarrassment flooded me and I realized that a man of Doctor Richards' stature and learning would have little to do with the likes of Long Lanie. As Doctor Richards and Jenetta rounded the corner out of sight, tears burst from my eyes.

+ + +

In December, 1839, three new missionaries arrived in Preston. Two more came in January and my life changed forever. One of the latter arrivals was Elder Wilford Woodruff who, in his early thirties, had already been appointed to the Quorum of the Twelve, the leadership council of the Saints. I first saw him in the town square, emerging from the Liverpool carriage. Brother Woodruff was a robust man of medium height and weight, dark-haired and ruddy in appearance, a veritable embodiment of this rollicking new religion.

That evening, when Da came home for supper, I asked him about Brother Woodruff.

"Aw'm tellin' thee Lanie, Brother Woodruff is a saintly man. A gracious lover of souls, 'e is. A great man, indeed. Aw canno' wait for thee t' meet 'im."

Da's wish came sooner than he might have expected. Two days after his arrival and a day before departing to conduct missionary work in the Staffordshire Potteries, Brother Woodruff knocked on the door of our cottage. I was alone at the time. Da had gone to minister to a woman suffering from *evil spirits*, as he put it.

I opened the door. Brother Woodruff stood there cradling his black hat.

"Good day, Miss," he said. "I'm looking for Brother Arkwright. Would he be in?"

"Not just now," I said and opened the door further. "Would you wish to come in and wait for him?"

"If it is no imposition."

"None at all. May I serve you a cup of soft cider?"

"That would be delightful," he said and took a seat near the fire.

When I returned he asked me to join him by the fire. We sat in silence for a time. I stole glances at him as he sipped his cider, his eyes focused on the flames.

"Your father is a fine man," he said, breaking the silence.

"Thank you, sir. I surely do think so."

"A true Saint."

"You would know."

"I'm told you have not yet accepted the restored Gospel."

"No sir, I have not," I said, on edge.

"Do you find your current spiritual circumstances satisfactory, fulfilling?"

"Not entirely."

"I can sympathize," he said taking his last sip and handing me the cup.

"More?" I asked.

"No but I thank you." He sniffed and let out a long breath, eyes still focused on the fire. "When I was young, my mind became exercised and at times vexed by religious subjects. I, like you, could not find fulfillment in any of the denominations. The denominations have partial glimpses of the truth. But that is all they have, *partial* glimpses of the truth."

"I know this argument," I said. "It has some logic."

He nodded. "I suppose I was most troubled by the message of so many ministers I encountered. They argued that the miracles of ancient times, the graces and ordinances, were but things of the past,

no longer necessary. Some even argued that the miracles were untrue
– mere stories designed to quicken one's faith. This dry and
uninspired religion I could not accept. I believed – and this belief has
been confirmed – that when the true church of Christ was again
restored upon the earth, these many gifts of yesteryear would be seen
once more. Miracles would abound and the gifts of the Spirit would
flourish. Of course, that church has now been restored. The miracles
and graces have begun anew. More importantly, we have discovered
that we – each of us – can converse with God and receive revelations
from Him."

He took a deep breath and, pausing at full inhalation, he began
slowly, softly, in a deep baritone on perfect key, to sing,

Come, let us anew our journey pursue,
Roll round with the year
And never stand still till the Master appear.
His adorable will let us gladly fulfill
And our talents improve
By the patience of hope and the labor of love.

With each line, his voice rose until it filled the entire cottage.
Suddenly, my heart began to beat rapidly, fluttering like the wings of
a wren. I feared I would be overcome and faint away. To still myself,
I took several deep breaths and glanced at Brother Woodruff who
seemed quite unaware of my condition.

By the patience of hope and the labor of love.

My syncope gave way to a bright clarity of thought and my mind
seemed to expand, capable of more lofty and penetrating insights
than I had ever experienced. In that instant I remembered the words
of Doctor Richards, *until you know heart fire, you cannot know God.*

This must be it! Heart fire!

The last thing I remember is descent into blackness as my mind
coursed out of sight and I fell into the vast expanse of nothingness.

CHAPTER THREE

Kevil

Escape

December 9th, the day appointed for our escape, dawned with a sky bleak, gray, and foreboding. We had barely arrived at the stand of trees to be felled when snow began to fall in large, cottony flakes. As the snow swirled around us and the day grew colder, I cursed our misfortune.

"Snow's a problem," I whispered to Doctor Mercer between synchronized swings of our axes.

"I know. Tracks. Turning very cold too. Could be a rough night."

"If we make it."

"We'll make it."

"I don't share your confidence," I said, swinging my axe with increased force.

"Trust me."

"Not much choice, do I?"

"We'll make it."

That ended our conversation.

At five o'clock, when dusk settled upon us, the lead guard called it quits. As required, we surrendered our axes and formed up in a two-by-two column. We began the four-mile march back to the Walls. As planned, Doctor Mercer and I managed to finagle our way to the rear of the column. We were relieved to see Mister Philpott fall in behind us, side-by-side with a second guard. Doctor Mercer feigned fatigue, and I mentioned a strained muscle in my left leg, which produced a malingered limp. These ploys allowed us to slow our gait and fall behind the other convicts and guards.

"Get a move on!" the second guard barked and hammered my back with the barrel of his rifle. "Colder'n a well-digger's bottom out here, so step to!"

To keep up the deception, Mister Philpott prodded us with his rifle. Each time we received these encouragements, we picked up the pace for a minute or so before falling back into our labored tread.

After a mile of trudging and slipping in the snow, the column before us slid out of sight into the stand of trees where we intended to make our break.

The snowstorm intensified. The prison coats were insufficient and our limbs stiffened. I wondered how fast we could run in this weather.

The stand of trees loomed before us.

Snow swirled in gusts of wind.

Doctor Mercer cleared his throat twice in quick succession – our signal.

I planted my foot, spun on my heel, and drove my fist hard into the face of the second guard. His eyes opened wide in surprise.

Doctor Mercer shoved Mister Philpott to the ground and turned to join my attack on the second guard.

Hard labor in the brickyard had added to my strength, and I had little difficulty wresting the rifle away from the guard before he could fire a warning shot.

"Shoot him Philpott!" the guard screamed

I planted the stock of his rifle squarely in the guard's mid-face.

I put the full weight of my body into several more arching blows on the guard's head until I was certain of his death.

Doctor Mercer and Mister Philpott looked at me with horrified expressions.

I swung again, this time rendering Philpott quite senseless.

Doctor Mercer stayed my arm before I could swing again.

"Enough! You have murdered the man! Philpott is to be spared."

I held up. Doctor Mercer stared at me with an expression of horrified revulsion. I held his gaze for several long seconds. Mercer tore his stare away from me and sprinted into the trees. I raced to follow. We slashed through the underbrush, slipping, sliding, and falling in the wet snow. After five hundred yards of all-out running, we pulled up behind a row of cedar trees, leaned upon our knees, and gulped large volumes of air. We listened but heard no one in pursuit.

"For mercy's sake, Pape, did you have to kill him?" Doctor Mercer said between ragged breaths.

"Happens in prison escape."

"Entirely unnecessary. Now we will be charged with murder. Bounty on our heads too. Killing a guard will stoke their pursuit. Did you ever take that into consideration?" He shook his head. "Unnecessary and stupid."

"The man was in our way. Had to be eliminated."

Doctor Mercer shook his head and stared into the snowy distance. Just then we heard the snapping of twigs behind us. The other guards were in pursuit, tracking us in the snow. We took flight once more, pounding hard until we came to a bluff overlooking the Missouri River.

"Down to the river!" Doctor Mercer shouted.

Falling to our backsides, we slid down the embankment on the accumulated snow. When we reached the river we splashed upstream in the shallows to avoid further footprints in the snow.

A shot rang out.

Then another.

"Aagh!" Mercer slapped the side of his face. Blood spilled between his fingers.

"Just grazed. Keep going!" he shouted.

We crouched low and continued to splash through the water.

More shots hissed past us, popping the water and snow with muffled nips.

We made our way to a stand of cottonwood trees growing near the riverbank and pulled out of the water. We ran along a narrow game trail that coursed near the river. The voices of our pursuers faded, dusk shaded to darkness, and the advantage was ours. In time, we slowed. For the moment, we had eluded those on our trail. Doctor Mercer held his arm out and drew me to a halt.

"We must find that cellar," he said. "According to my directions it should not be far."

"I'm turning to ice," I said. "Can't feel my feet."

"No small problem," was all Doctor Mercer said in return.

To our great relief, the game trail led us to the abandoned farmhouse. Upon arrival we scrabbled around in the brush to the rear of the house. Our fingers were icicles but, after twenty minutes of searching in the snowy underbrush, we located the cellar. We tumbled out of sight into the dank pit below and pulled the door over our heads. Doctor Mercer allowed his eyes to adjust to the darkness and began rummaging around on the shelves.

"Philpott was to leave us a lantern," he said.

"Do tell!" I said. The possibility of light and even a modicum of heat buoyed my spirits.

"Aha!" Doctor Mercer said. "Here it is! Thank God for the invention of these locofocos. There is a whole tin of them right by the lamp."

He struck a locofoco and in no time, we were warming our hands in the small flame of the lantern.

"Take your shoes off," Doctor Mercer said, unbuttoning his shirt.

"Shoes off, why?"

"Put your feet on my stomach. If we are lucky we will stave off frostbite."

I confess I was taken aback by his remedy for my petrified feet but did as he directed. When feeling had returned to my feet, I reciprocated, though not out of compassion.

We then built a small fire with bits of wood and rotten shelving scattered around the cellar. The fire produced copious plumes of smoke that billowed around us. Doctor Mercer periodically opened one of the doors to vent the fumes. With each exposure of the back-lit cellar we worried about discovery but no one appeared to be out on this dreadful night. The search had been suspended until morning when it would no doubt be resumed with a much larger posse. Our safety now depended upon an early retrieval by Mister Philpott who, we hoped, had regained consciousness and remained committed to his heroic plan.

Doctor Mercer leaned against the rough wall of the cellar, sullen and subdued over the murder of the guard. No matter, I thought. Doctor Mercer would have to make peace with it. I resolved to drop the whole affair from my mind.

The sun had not yet risen when we heard a sharp knock on the cellar door. I grabbed the guard's rifle and aimed it at the opening while Doctor Mercer hid behind the wall.

"It's Philpott," came a muffled voice.

We both sighed in relief. Mercer raised the door. I kept the gun at the ready, putting it down only when I saw the familiar guard lower himself into the cellar, his head wrapped in a bloodied bandage.

He glared at me. "To the wagon," he said, never taking his eyes from mine.

We ascended the cellar steps and plodded to a wagon where Mister Philpott directed us to lay on the floorboards. He covered us with a blanket and proceeded to place one row of small cordwood over us. The cumulative weight was considerable, but not enough to cause us harm. In this condition we were transported to the Philpott home. Upon arrival we dropped into the undercroft of the house. Two straw mattresses on a dirt floor and two buckets reminded us of the Walls. Indeed, the mattresses and buckets appeared to be prison issue. This low-slung room would be an acceptable hideaway for several weeks until it would be deemed safe for us to surface and blend into some distant and unsuspecting society. Looming freedom made our discomfort bearable. We uttered no complaints.

Several days lapsed before Mrs. Philpott graced us with her presence. When finally she did, we were subjected to a withering invective about our treatment of her husband, for which we apologized. I felt no remorse whatsoever for what I had deemed as a necessary act. Nevertheless, it was clear that contrition was the prudent course. It had a dual effect. My apology softened Doctor Mercer's standoffishness toward me and mollified Mrs. Philpott. Thereafter, my interactions within the Philpott home were cool but cordial. Our hosts were wary of me, if not frightened. Doctor Mercer enjoyed a much warmer reception.

One evening, after several days in hiding, I surfaced from our basement confines and walked into the parlor of the Philpott home. There I found the guard and his wife reading by the fire. He eyed me charily.

"I have a request," I said. I received no response but continued. "I would like to borrow a small carving knife. Only for a short time."

"For what purpose?" Mister Philpott asked.

"I mean no one any harm. I want to do some whittling to while away the time."

The Philpotts looked at one another.

"I don't trust you," Mister Philpott said. His wife nodded in agreement.

"I do not blame you for your concern, but I assure you my purposes are quite innocent."

Mister Philpott stared at me. He glanced at his wife. She nodded and returned to her book. From a rough-hewn chest of drawers Mister Philpott withdrew a small paring knife in a soft leather sheath. He held it out to me.

"I thank you," I said. "Please be assured that I shall take good care of it."

He returned to his seat with neither nod nor comment.

Later that evening I found myself alone in the cellar. Doctor Mercer had gone upstairs to prepare for Mister Philpott's baptism. I retrieved a handkerchief provided to me soon after arriving at the Philpott home. I had earlier contracted a mild case of the grippe as a result of running in the shallows of the river and shivering through that cold night in the cellar. My nose ran incessantly and Mrs. Philpott, either out of pity or annoyance, provided the handkerchief.

I sat down upon my mattress and placed the handkerchief on my knee. I studied the knife blade and tested its edge with my thumb. It was not razor-sharp but it would suffice. I inserted the knife behind my upper lip, just to the left of the midline, and turned the blade until it faced outward. I took several deep breaths, closed my eyes tightly, and in a swift forward thrust, sliced my lip through from back to front.

Pain shot through my face.

I let out a scream and rocked backward.

Blood gushed from my severed lip and fell in large droplets on the mattress.

I slapped the handkerchief over my wound and took several deep breaths.

Doctor Mercer and Mister Philpott heard my scream and came rushing down the cellar steps.

Doctor Mercer raced to my side. "Good heavens, man, what has happened?"

I threw my voice in my nose and said, "I melieve I have ngut my lip?"

"What are you saying? You cut your lip? Whatever for?"

I shrugged my shoulders. "Ngow I am a harelip."

"A harelip? Have you gone utterly mad!"

"Mart of my nisguise."

"Your disguise?"

I discontinued my nasal voice. "Yes, part of my disguise. Kevil Pape was a man with perfect diction. Sadly, Edwin Freeman, my new persona, is a poor man born with a harelip and a hole in the roof of his mouth. Simple soul can barely be understood. Then too, there is this problem." I hobbled around the room with the same malingering limp that I had used in the minutes before we overpowered our guards.

Both men shook their heads in disbelief.

"Let me see the lip," Doctor Mercer said. Gently, he inspected my self-inflicted wound. "You best pray this does not become infected. It will heal with a scar, likely a tight one. Of course, I presume that was your intention."

I nodded.

"It will soon form a scab. You should come upstairs so I can clean the wound and dress it with turpentine."

I thanked the good doctor and followed him up the stairs.

"Crazier than a privy rat," was all Mister Philpott had to say.

We stayed in the Philpott home for three full weeks. During this waiting period, I practiced my nasal speech and limp to the point that they became second nature to me. My lip healed and a noticeable scar had begun to form. Mister Philpott and his wife provided clothing for us to use and trimmed our hair so the shaved side did not appear so obvious.

The night after Doctor Mercer cracked open the ice and baptized Mister Philpott in a frozen tributary of the Missouri, we took our leave of Jefferson City. Despite the absurdities of their religion, I was thankful for the mutual support given by the Saints to one another. I had already benefited greatly from my connections to Doctor Mercer. Little did I know that I was soon to be further graced by the Church of Latter Day Saints.

Shortly after one o'clock in the morning, on the first day of 1841, Mister Philpott bundled us into his wagon once again. This time we were spared the layer of cordwood. We traveled for twelve miles, first over an iced bridge across the Missouri River, and then along an undeveloped river trail. At Cote Sans Dessein, pronounced *Cote sawn DUsaw* by the locals, we met by a man named Tanner, another Saint, who provided us with two horses. I was astonished by the munificence of these people, especially to me, a Gentile.

"How did you manage to arrange for these horses," I asked as soon as we were out of earshot.

"There are many more of us than you might imagine," Doctor Mercer said. "Through our network of believers and sympathizers word reached the leadership, now headquartered in Nauvoo, Illinois, and they arranged for us to have two horses. On loan until we arrive in Nauvoo."

"But I have no intention of going to Nauvoo. I'm bound for Saint Louis."

"As you wish. You may keep the horse for now. Let us simply agree that you owe the Mormons a horse."

I thanked Doctor Mercer and inhaled the crisp air of freedom. I had growing hope that our escape from the Walls would indeed be successful. While lying low in the Philpott cellar and waiting for my lip to heal, I had begun to make my own plans for the future. I intended to lose myself in the relative anonymity of the only urban setting in Missouri. Saint Louis had grown to twenty thousand residents and, as a burgeoning commercial hub, presented opportunities for employment. I intended to take up temporary residence there, obtain work, and live as modestly as possible. Once I had saved sufficient funds, I would move further east to more civilized environs.

Mister Philpott had informed me that I had a two thousand dollar bounty on my head so I could not afford to practice law in Missouri. Sooner or later, someone would recognize me at the bar, despite my scar. To my great chagrin, neither could I return to my beautiful home and lands in North Carolina. During my trial, I had disclosed to the court whence I had come. Two thousand dollars is a good deal of money. Bounty hunters would no doubt investigate my property in the Carolinas to see if I had been foolish enough to return home. Saint Louis it would be.

Doctor Mercer and I rode hard through the clear night reaching Mexico, Missouri around dawn. Tanner had provided us with venison jerky and a small block of cheese, which we ate on the outskirts of town. Prudence directed us to take a northern by-pass around the town. We occasioned little notice from the townspeople on that early morning and reconnected with the main road, which led on to Pinkney and Marthasville.

In the afternoon of our fourth day of travel, we arrived in Saint

Charles. Here we were to part ways. Doctor Mercer would head north into Illinois and on to Nauvoo, where his family awaited him. He suffered little of the apprehension that occupied my mind. There could be a warrant for his arrest but he knew, if he made it to Nauvoo, he would be spared extradition back to Missouri. The Mormons protected their own. I could certainly vouch for that. I also suspected that when he made his report, Mister Philpott would put the blame for the guard's murder squarely upon me. He would have done so to throw the posse off of the trail of his mentor and spiritual guide. Doctor Mercer, a prison escapee on a charge of manslaughter, was hardly worth the chase in those days. No, they would be after me, not Doctor Mercer.

After bidding farewell to Doctor Mercer in Saint Charles, I purchased a small lump of potter's clay and headed down the road to Saint Louis. The road was rather heavily traveled but after about five miles, the traffic thinned and I stopped to perch upon a stump. From my vantage point, I had a good view of the road in both directions. Satisfied that I was alone on this stretch, I kneaded the lump of clay, spreading it into the general shape of my right sole. I inserted it in my boot and stood, pressing down, further molding the clay. This served not only to remind me of my limp but it acted to create one. I stood and walked around a bit, smiling at my own ingenuity.

I reached Eighteenth Street, the western corporate limit of Saint Louis around two o'clock on the afternoon of January 6th, a Wednesday. The houses were sparse as I coursed eastward from Eighteenth to Ninth Street where urban bustle began to increase. I rode around for a time, casing the city. Stone cottages and narrow, winding streets, marked the older sections, originally settled by the French and Spanish. As I rode away from the city center, I found myself on wider roads. The commercial and residential architecture reminded me of the eastern cities with which I was familiar, Philadelphia, New York, Boston, and Baltimore. Here, in the newer districts, the buildings were constructed flush to the unpaved streets.

The city revolved around the waterfront along Main Street where commission merchants clustered. Despite the January chill, Main Street itself was a beehive of activity on that Wednesday afternoon. I rode the full extent of its length from the Purvis Livery Stable on the south end all the way to Pierre Choteau's Fur Company on the north. The nucleus of all activity appeared to be the Tontine Coffee House, flanked on either side by Andrews and Beakey's sheet metal factory, Anderson's dry goods shop, several grocers and druggists, assorted professional offices, and the hat factory of Beltzhoover and Robb.

Upon completing my reconnaissance, I found a small boarding house on the corner of Sixth and Locust. Mrs. John Perry, the widow landlady, agreed to take me in on the promise that I would pay my rent as soon as I had enough money. Her willingness to board me on credit reflected the optimism of the Saint Louis citizenry in those days. Opportunities for employment abounded with the growth of the city as a center for manufacturing and transportation. Steamboats had put in and launched from Saint Louis for three decades but now there was talk of rail lines to connect the city with the rest of America. As depressed as my spirits were about having to live apart from my rolling lands and beautiful brick mansion, I did see the favorable prospects for Saint Louis.

The following morning I arose to begin my search for work. The limp, scar, and simulated speech impediment, while an excellent disguise, turned out to be a handicap when trying to secure work. Proprietors and foremen thought of me as a half-wit. I had to minimize the limp and the nasal tone in my voice to gain any reception at all. Near day's end, I chanced upon a small shop on Third Street, not far from Mrs. Perry's boarding house. I peered in the window to see a man building a set of shelves. Piles of books lay strewn about the shop. Thinking I might be able to help him for a few coins to buy my supper, I knocked on the door. The man let me in and listened patiently when I explained I was new in the city and anxious for employment.

"Do you have any manner of education?" he asked, a fair question given my appearance.

"Indeed," I said. "I have studied some years at university." For obvious reasons, I did not disclose that I had earned a Bachelor of Laws degree. The shopkeeper, Lewis Crabtree, seemed both surprised and pleased by my answer.

"Very well then," he said. "We do not have many well-educated people in Saint Louis, though this is changing. As you can see, I am preparing to open a bookshop. It will be the first in the city. I need someone to assist who possesses an interest in and a familiarity with a broad range of subjects including classical literature. May I assume you have such qualifications?"

"You may, good sir. I would delight in assisting you with this venture and may I also offer my carpentry services. I have no special skill in this regard but I can surely respond to your capable direction."

Mister Crabtree studied me for a moment. "I had not planned to hire anyone until I had the shop ready for business. However, the construction of shelving and counters is too much for one man. I take it you could begin on the morrow?"

"Certainly but...I wonder if I might have a small advance in my wages to pay for my dinner." Mister Crabtree hesitated, not certain of my intentions. "Here," I said. "Permit me to write my name and address. I am staying at Mrs. Perry's, a mere seven blocks from here."

"No need," he said, his apprehensions fading away. "I know Mrs. Perry. I shall place my trust in you."

He reached into his pocket and withdrew several coins, which he placed in my hand. "This should purchase you a good meal. Until tomorrow."

I returned to the boarding house and informed Mrs. Perry that I had secured employment. In spite of her earlier optimism, she appeared quite relieved. That evening at supper, I met the two other boarders. Theodore Jones, a metal worker, occupied the other room on the third floor. The Widow Wilson lived in the only occupied room on the second floor. As I ate my stew, I studied Widow Wilson. I learned she had lost her husband in a carriage accident several years before and had been forced to hire out for domestic work. The bloom was clearly off the flower, no doubt as a result of her sad circumstances. Yet I could detect a fine figure beneath her billowy uniform and resolved in due time to press my intentions upon her. She could prove to be a delightful diversion, taking my mind away from the depressed circumstances in which I found myself.

Two days following my employment, we completed the shelving and arranged the merchandise, thus allowing the grand opening of *Lewis Crabtree – Bookseller and Literary Promoter*. I had been hired to manage the bookshop while Mister Crabtree busied himself with the deployment of traveling salesmen who would spread out through the region to sell books, magazines, and subscriptions. This work deadened my mind and I deemed it far below my intellectual station. Nevertheless, I appreciated the opportunity to manage the shop with little or no interference from Mister Crabtree.

We did a lively business in the first few days of operation, no doubt due to pent-up demand for reading material. After the initial rush had subsided, traffic remained steady, and the hours passed quickly for me. Commerce with the public was not at all to my liking. I had to force myself on many occasions to bite my tongue and subdue my acerbic comments. So successful was the business of bookselling that over the course of the first few months, Mister Crabtree presented me with two wage increases. These increases were enough to permit me to set aside funds for my anticipated relocation to the east. In addition, I was able to begin the restoration of my once splendid wardrobe.

By the end of summer, 1841, I rebuilt my once excellent collection of stylish clothes. I had become a steady customer of Bill Grady who still referred to himself as a *barber-surgeon*. Bill kept my hair in perfect trim and I daresay I've never had a closer and more comfortable shave than those I received at his hand. To my great delight, I had become a figure in the city center and seemed daily to gain the respect of the townspeople. *That Ned Freeman* – Edwin had been reduced to Ned – *is a right respectable man*, they would say. *A man with a sweet and sober disposition, so kindly favoring his customers. And such an intelligent and insightful young man.* Occasionally, I would hear something akin to *poor man, born with that harelip and all…does very well despite his impediment.* Comments of this nature made me smile in the assurance that my disguise was successful and, despite the natural prejudices to which the defective are heir, my intellect shone through.

During the fall of that year, in late September, I greeted the Widow Wilson at the door of Mrs. Perry's boarding house. I asked if she might wish to accompany me to Tontine's Coffee House the following Saturday for biscuits and a cup of tea in the fashion of the English.

"Why Mister Freeman, I am indeed flattered by your invitation," she said, "but I do not yet know you well. Do you think it proper?"

"I assure you Mrs. Wilson – "

"*Cassie*, please."

"Thank you, Cassie. As I was saying, my intentions are entirely honorable."

"I should not have thought differently."

"Consider a further advantage…" I said, "By these means you will get to know me better and I you."

"I should like to think about it. May I give you my answer tomorrow, Mister Freeman?"

"Most certainly, madam. I shall await your response on the tiptoe of expectation."

She nodded and slid gracefully past me, turning back with a smile.

"Propitious," I whispered to myself. "Quite propitious."

From that point on, Cassie and I became close companions, seen often about town, thrilling the gossipmongers and fueling their speculations about our future. Though my memory is somewhat dim on this point, I believe about two months after our initial foray to Tontine's Coffee House, I arose in the wee hours of the morning and descended from the third to the second floor. I rapped gently upon her door just the once. She must have been awaiting my knock. She opened the door, pulled me inside, and embraced me with an unexpected hunger. What a delightful night we had behind her closed doors. All I shall say on this matter is that my earlier speculations regarding her comely figure were quite accurate.

Thus, I settled into what I assumed would be the routine of my life for the foreseeable future – clerking at Lewis Crabtree's bookshop by day and bedding the Widow Wilson by night. That is, until one day in early April, 1842 when I turned from shelving books to see Doctor Tobias Mercer standing at the counter. At his side was a short, slender man of dour countenance who sported a long black beard, plaited in two stiff braids.

"Doctor Mercer! What a most pleasant surprise," I said, trying to disguise my astonishment. "What brings you to Saint Louis?"

He extended his hand in greeting. "You were not easy to find. In my inquiries, I finally had to refer to *the red-haired man with a scar on his lip.*"

"Do tell," I said. "Have you come to reclaim your horse?"

"Not at all. We are here on other business. Permit me to introduce Mister Porter Rockwell."

Mister Rockwell and I nodded to one another but did not extend our hands in greeting.

Doctor Mercer looked around and seeing no customers, asked if we might have some privacy to talk. His solemn demeanor led me to believe his mission was serious.

"But of course," I said. "Let me put out the *Closed* sign. We can discuss matters in the back room."

When we had seated ourselves around a small oaken table, I repeated my question, "How may I help you?"

Doctor Mercer studied me for several long seconds. "We want you to assassinate Lilburn Boggs."

I flushed in surprise. "What did you say?"

"We want you to assassinate Lilburn Boggs."

"The former governor?" I asked, surprise rising in my face.

"That's the man," he said.

CHAPTER FOUR

Elena

Conversion

I awakened to the sound of embers softly crackling in a dying fire. I stared at the coals trying to gather my thoughts. After a time, I realized I was lying on the braided rug that lay in front of our fireplace hearth. Someone had placed a quilt over me and a pillow under my head. I touched my head and arm. I wiggled my toes. My shoes rested by the fire with my bonnet laid neatly on top of them. To my relief, no one had removed my housedress. I had no great wish to move and savored the unexpected comfort I found lying on the floor in front of the fire. I snuggled into the quilt and turned my mind back to the events of the last evening.

"Good mornin' lass. Are ye come back?"

"Da?"

"Aye," he said and his rocking chair began to creak behind me.

"What happened?"

"Couldn' rightly say. When I come home last ev'nin,' Aw found Brother Woodruff standin' o'er thee. Brother Woodruff said ye swoont upon the floor. Jes' out o' the blue, ye keelt o'er. Thy face was all flushed an' ye were breathin' like a field mouse – fast 'n' shallow."

I sighed. "I don't know what came over me. I was listening to Elder Woodruff sing and that's the last I remember."

"Brother Woodruff says the Holy Ghost come upon thee, lass. Caught up in the power o' the Spirit, 'e says. Th'art soon to join the Church, Lanie lass. Aw feel it in me bones."

"I don't know about that, Da," I said but I could not deny the possibility of a divine sign, a visitation of the Holy Ghost. I had to admit to myself that whatever happened to me the previous night – the tempest in my body and the expansion of my mind – were strange and unfamiliar experiences. What did they mean?

Upon my request, Da agreed to inform my supervisor that I had taken ill and could not work that day. I spent the morning wrestling with myself over the significance of my collapse and, though my mind stirred up many natural explanations, my heart said otherwise. At last I decided I had to talk with someone – a woman – about my experience. After a light dinner I walked to Pole Street and sought out Ann Dawson in whose home the first branch of the Mormon Church had been established. Mormons and non-Mormons alike held Ann in high regard for her wisdom and insight. Though she was an ardent Saint, I felt she could honestly evaluate what had happened to me.

When I arrived, Ann welcomed me with open arms and served me a cup of tea in a white china cup. It had a blue scalloped rim that made sipping difficult. After small talk – inquiries about the mill and Da – she put her cup back upon its saucer. "Dear Elena, I daresay you didn't come calling just to be neighborly. What is on your mind?"

She listened attentively as I explained what had happened to me. When I finished, I stared at Ann who had a knowing smile. "The Holy Ghost?" I asked.

Ann nodded her head. "There is no doubt in my mind. To be sure, you were warmed by the fire, impressed by Elder Woodruff's attentions, and overcome by the quality of his wonderful voice. But such circumstances would not have caused you to swoon and fall into a deep sleep. God has visited you, my dear Elena. In the presence of one of His apostles, He has given you an unbidden revelation of the truth of the Mormon faith."

"How can you be so certain?"

"Elena, think upon it. You are a woman of faith. Yet there is no expression of the faith that fills your heart. The Church of England is arid and full of dry bones. The Methodists renewed things for a time but they have fallen back into the same spiritual desert. These churches cannot stir your soul, they cannot fire you with enthusiasm, and they certainly cannot cast you into a fainting sleep! They lack what the Saints have been given. We both know what happened. So, my dear Elena, do not fight it any longer. You have been called into the one true faith. Join your Da, join me, join all of us, and gain an eternal life of everlasting joy, felicity, and above all, *love*. Love is the Prophet's key message. An eternity of love. Is that not your heart's deepest desire?"

I nodded. Ann Dawson was right. I could reach no other conclusion. I had been smitten by the Holy Ghost.

On the following Sunday, Elder Woodruff announced my name and plunged me into the icy waters of the River Ribble. When I came gasping back to the surface, I looked up at my Da whose copious tears mingled with darts of sleet shooting from the heavens above.

+ + +

Three months later, in early April, five high-ranking leaders of the Church arrived from Nauvoo. The Saints in our city were beside themselves in the presence of Brigham Young, Orson Pratt, George Smith, and Reuben Hedlock. All three hundred of us flocked to the Cockpit the first Sunday after the arrival of these men. We marveled at their preaching and thought ourselves uncommonly blessed to receive the Sacrament from their hands.

Throughout the following week, the apostles conducted a series of gospel events. I could not be present at all of them. However, I did attend the Thursday evening meeting when a bold idea was unfurled for the first time. We had arrived at the Cockpit after supper and took our seats in anticipation of further preaching by our visitors. After several minutes, Elder Brigham Young stood and held up his hand. Silence descended upon the room.

I studied Elder Young as he rotated to engage the entire congregation. I judged him neither handsome nor homely. His sandy hair curled around his collar, from which a black cravat extended. A slight smile had formed on his lips and I sensed a man of strength and conviction, still trim, vigorous, and ruddy-complexioned. When he spoke, his voice was higher in pitch than I had anticipated but he projected his words with strength and assurance.

"Beloved Brethren," he began, "a full decade ago, the Prophet Joseph Smith put forth a decree from our Father in heaven. All the elect in the true church are to be gathered into one place on the face of the earth. There, the Church is to prepare for the time of tribulation when desolation shall be loosed upon the wicked. That one place is in America, in the State of Illinois, where the Saints have found asylum and a gracious welcome after the persecutions in Ohio and Missouri."

Da leaned forward in his chair, lips parted, breathing deeply as if enraptured.

Brother Brigham thrust his right forefinger into the air, "Nauvoo is the place! On the banks of the mighty Mississippi River, Heavenly Father has given to us a sanctuary – a place called *beautiful* in the Hebrew language. The cornerstone has been laid in Zion. The time is now ripe for the gathering. All who have received the blessings of the gospel and obey the commandments of heaven are admonished to ready themselves for the general gathering of the faithful in *Nauvoo*. Prepare ye! Prepare ye! As fast as your circumstances allow, remove yourselves to the Kingdom. There you will find the land cheap and fertile. Factories are under construction and the temple of God will soon rise to the sky. In that temple the saving ordinances and blessings will be bestowed upon you. Let the rich be the first to go and share their wealth in the building up of the kingdom so that it may be readied for the arrival of the poor."

When Brother Brigham finished his discourse on the gathering of the elect, the congregation exploded into a frenzy of excited chatter. Whispers of this doctrine had been heard here and there prior to that Thursday evening in the Cockpit. However, this was a thunderous call. We received it as a commandment from the Lord himself. As soon as Brother Brigham stepped down from the platform, Da rushed to the center of the Cockpit and engaged the apostle in a spirited discussion. I could not hear what they were saying but I could tell from Da's gestures to the west and the smile on Brigham's face, that my father had already accepted the call to Nauvoo.

I must admit that my own stomach fluttered at the thought, an excited flutter at that. Da and I, with no kinfolk and good incomes, were ideal candidates for relocation. There was little to tether us to Lancashire and ever since I was a young girl with a fertile imagination, I had dreamed of traveling to distant lands. I never held any hope that it would actually happen. Could such a thing now come true? I put my hand to my bosom, breathless at the thought.

When we arrived back at our cottage, Da grabbed my hands and we circled around in a jig of joy.

"We're comin' home to Zion, Lanie, me girl! Aw'm flushed wi' excitment! Could such a thin' come to pass wi' thy owd Da an' his beloved daughter?"

Around and around we went until we collapsed on the floor laughing like school children. That night, after calm had once again descended upon us, we began to make our plans to gather to Nauvoo. Though there had been suggestions of a loan fund to help Saints relocate, none had yet been established. Da and I agreed to save enough before relocating to avoid going into debt. We realized that it would take more than a year to save the necessary amount to pay for the Atlantic crossing and subsequent journey to Illinois. However, prudence dictated that we postpone our departure until we were certain we had enough money to set up our home in America. Our elders urged this caution on all Saints preparing to gather to Zion.

The relocation began in June of 1840 and continued month after month. Droves of Saints journeyed to Liverpool for embarkation across the Atlantic Ocean. Da and I tried to see off as many families from Preston as possible, wishing them godspeed and a safe crossing. Members of the Quorum of the Twelve, who remained in Britain, blessed the first voyages and gave our emigrants every good encouragement. However, most of the Saints departing for America were terrified of the ocean voyage. They had heard many a tale of shipwreck in the treacherous waters and roiling skies of the North Atlantic. We all tried to assure them that God would protect His elect but this assurance was a thin blanket on cold dread.

We were told that the voyage to America took anywhere from five to eight weeks depending upon the port of arrival. By the early fall of 1840, letters arrived from those who had completed their journey. The Saints remaining in Preston would gather of an evening to hear the reading of letters from loved ones who had gone before. We listened to frightening tales of storms, seasickness and a host of other maladies, broken masts, vile food, and accidents of one sort or another. Yet, so far, every ship carrying Mormon emigrants from Liverpool made it safely to port.

What I found more exciting were the early portrayals of Nauvoo, which I hoped would one day be my home. *The Prophet Joseph Smith himself greeted us!* said Fanny Chadderton in a letter to her parents, still residing in Preston. *He is a tall man with piercing blue eyes. I shook his very hand and felt as if I had touched the hand of God. He walked us from the dock into the city and shewed us the industry of our fellow Saints in building up the Kingdom. Nauvoo is a beehive of activity. There are many new houses, streets have been laid out, factories are being built, and the Prophet also shewed us where the great Temple would be built come spring. What a wondrous place it is and to think that, day-by-day I walk in the precincts of the Prophet!*

Descriptions such as this would swell my anticipation to the breaking point. Nauvoo was constantly in my thoughts. When I lay my head on the pillow each night I would paint a picture of the place in my mind as a prelude to my dreams. I had never held hope of anything beyond long hours in the *weighvin' shop*. Now, the thought of journeying to the other side of the world was nothing short of a wonder. Perhaps in America I might find the man who would meet my standards and provide the life of security I so wanted. Throughout the long winter of 1840 and 1841, my yearning knew no bounds. The *Kingdom of God* was no longer just a biblical phrase; it had become my new reality.

Our delay in departing for America gave us several advantages over those early emigrants. Liverpool pickpockets had left many an unsophisticated convert from Lancashire without a farthing. Those who managed to avoid the pickpockets were often swindled by dockside merchants. By the time Da and I were ready to embark on the sea voyage, the Church had established an agent in Liverpool. He provided protection for the emigrants and guided them through their preparations for the voyage. Also, a new law in England required ship captains to provide sufficient food for the passengers, which relieved us of the need to procure our own victuals for the Atlantic crossing.

Da burst into the cottage on New Year's Day, 1842, and brushed the snowflakes from his woolen coat.

"Aw've got it, Lanie girl. Right here in me hand."

I walked over to where he stood and watched his soot-creased forefinger as it coursed over lines of print on a wrinkled sheet of paper.

"See, girl, we're to be in Liverpool by the twelfth. 'At's when the *Tremont* sails. We're to report to the agent, Sam Richards, on the 'leventh."

The reality of what we were reading hit me like a sharp slap to the cheek.

"My heavens!" I said. "This doesn't give us much time."

"Let's get to packin' girl," Da said and started rushing around the room grabbing things at random from the mantel, shelves, and tables.

"Da!" I shouted. "Calm yourself. We must do this in an orderly fashion."

He stopped and took a deep breath. His smile melted me.

"Aw'm jes' so excited, Lanie, but Aw'll give it all o'er t' thee. Thou art in charge. Tell me what Aw'm t' do."

From that point on, I saw to the packing. As excited as I was about the voyage to America, I grieved as I set aside those items we could not take. The kettle in which Mum cooked her lovely rabbit stew, the rocking chair that had squeaked ten thousand times, and the brass mantle clock that had filled Da with such pride. All set to the side.

Da looked wistfully at the discarded items. "Couldn' we take th' clock, Lanie girl?" "I will try, Da," I said, "but I can't close the lids on the two trunks as it is."

He nodded and shuffled off to market to buy us some potatoes for our supper. I dug in one of the trunks and removed three of my precious books to provide room for the clock. I hid the books under some cast-off bedding so Da would not discover my exchange. The clock would be a surprise for him when we unpacked the trunks in Nauvoo. This thought washed away my sadness at leaving the books. Nauvoo!

+ + +

The morning of January Tenth dawned crisp and clear. The air crackled in the lemony sunlight and smoke from the mills stood still in the frigid sky like columns of soiled cotton. Da teetered back and forth on his bowed legs, clapped his mittens together for warmth, and expelled little puffs of excited chatter. We stood on that platform, eyes peeled for the stagecoach.

"There she be, Lanie girl! Th' coach for Liverpool. Soon, we'll be on our way!"

The stagecoach pulled to a sharp stop, and the drivers jumped down and began to load our trunks. Da and I settled in the coach side-by-side and gave each other a hug. To my surprise, I felt no great sadness at leaving the place of my birth. Whatever pangs of nostalgia

I might once have suffered had long since slipped away. Thoughts of a far better place in the company of the Saints gave rise to an unquenchable excitement. From his behavior, I knew that Da felt the same way, though I wondered if he had any regrets about leaving Mum buried in the cemetery behind the litchgate of Saint John's Church. If he did, he never said so.

Just then the door to the coach opened. In stepped an odd little man. His long protruding nose led his stooped frame into the coach and so diminutive was he that once inside he could almost stand upright. I daresay he did not top the five-foot mark. I marveled at his hair, which was gray, not the gray of senescence, but a drab mousy gray. His closely cropped beard was of the same color. The protruding face, gray hair, bright eyes, and tiny circle of a mouth, not larger than a farthing, set me to humming in my mind. *Hickory dickory dock, the mouse ran up the clock.* I giggled to myself but then felt a pang of shame at my uncharitable thoughts.

"Top of the morning to you fellow Saints," he said with a bob of his head. "Permit me to introduce myself to you, Elder Arkwright, Miss Arkwright. I am Arthur Walmsley."

"Aw'm delighted to meet thee," Da said, extending his rough hand to meet Mr. Walmsly's pale, soft palm. "How is it that thou knowest our names?"

"Elder Arkwright, you are well known throughout Lancashire for your great service to the Church as are you, m'lady, for your intelligence and great learning."

"But good sir," I said blushing, "I have no great learning. Only six years of schooling."

"Yes, and look at what you have done with that schooling. You are known as a well-read young woman, no doubt more conversant with our English literature than I, despite my years at university."

I flowered inwardly. "I do thank you Mister Walmsley for your kind words but I must say you exaggerate."

"Not at all, I'm sure."

"Thine is th' advantage," Da broke in. "Thou seems't to know much about us but we have no knowledge of thee. How cames't thee to know us?"

"My late step-mum, Agatha Cooper, God rest her soul, told me all about you in the many letters she wrote to me before she died."

"Oh," I said. "So you are Sister Cooper's step-son. Our

condolences on your recent loss. Had I but known you were her step-son I would have sought you out at the funeral to offer my sympathies."

"Thank you, Miss Arkwright but, alas, I was not there for her burial. I had been studying at Vienna. For a host of reasons, I could not make it back. I've just lately arrived here in Britain. I came to settle some of Mum's affairs and prepare to gather to Zion."

"How then dids't ye come to th' true faith?" Da asked.

Just then the coach lurched forward slamming poor Arthur against the seat. His eyes widened and a slow grin spread across his face. Once the carriage had settled into a steady pace, he leaned forward. "Interesting story, if I may say so. It all began with a chance meeting. Elder Orson Hyde stopped in Vienna on his mission trip to the Holy Land. I met him in a small café one evening and we talked well into the wee hours. Did you know he was of Hebrew descent?"

"Nooo," Da said, extending the vowel in disbelief.

"Indeed. That is what he told me. And the Prophet Joseph Smith knew this, though Elder Hyde had never disclosed it to him."

"How?" Da asked.

"Heavenly Father has given to the Prophet certain *keys* to compel the gathering of the Saints from distant lands. One of those keys was – and is – Orson Hyde. When the Prophet confirmed Elder Hyde, he prophesied that the latter would go to Jerusalem, to the *land of his fathers*. The Prophet said he would do a great work in the land of our Savior. And so it came to pass."

"Amazing! Truly amazing," Da said.

We rode in silence for a time savoring the wisdom of our Prophet. Mister Walmsley had forgotten his stream of thought. He stared through the window of the stage at the passing countryside, unaware that he had not finished the story of his conversion. I stole glances at him, transfixed both by his appearance and his marvelous command of the Queen's English. He spoke in that unmistakable Oxford accent I so envied. As I studied him, I beheld a gentle man, frail, with a rounded chest that reminded me of the breast of a small woodpigeon that fluttered around our cabbage patch. When not in conversation, he occupied himself by reading a scholarly tome, the title of which I could not discern. Periodically, his small pink tongue would dart through his rounded mouth.

Risking disruption of his thoughts I reopened the conversation,

"Mister Walmsley?"

"Please call me Arthur."

"Thank you and you may call me Elena."

"Aw'm Tom," Da chimed in.

"Sir, it will be difficult for me to call you Tom, so great is your reputation among the Saints. If it is all the same, I should prefer to call you Elder Arkwright."

"'Tis a great honor to hear thee say so but Aw'm just a simple smithy caught by the scruff of 'is neck to do the work o' the Lord."

"And a wondrous work it is too," Arthur said. His smile stretched that little round mouth into an oblong shape.

"Mister Walmsley," I said again, "We did not hear how your time with Elder Hyde ended. How did you come to join the Church?"

"Yes, yes, dear me. I do apologize. My mind often wanders off course. It is most interesting what happened that evening in the Viennese café, at least I find it most interesting."

"And I'm certain we shall as well," I said.

Arthur closed his book and clasped his hands. "For a time we discussed Elder Hyde's Jewish ancestry, which he admitted was a matter of family lore rather than a confirmed genealogy. I shared with him my research interests. You see, I had just completed my reading of a most interesting book, *A View of the Hebrews* by one Ethan Smith. I told Elder Hyde that I bore a great curiosity about the fate of the Ten Lost Tribes of Israel. Ethan Smith, an American clergyman, argues in his book that the aboriginal tribes of America are the descendants of the Ten Lost Tribes. As I explained this theory, Elder Hyde broke out in a wide grin that threatened to erupt into laughter. I must say I found his demeanor somewhat unsettling. 'Good sir,' I said, 'what amuses you?' At that point, he reached into his budget and pulled out a copy of the *Book of Mormon*, which he handed it to me."

Arthur cleared his throat and pressed on with his story. "He explained to me that Ethan Smith's theory is not a theory at all but the plain truth of the matter. He pointed out in the *Book of Mormon* certain passages that confirmed the journey of the Ten Lost Tribes to the Americas. 'Mister Walmsley,' said he to me, 'it is no coincidence that we have met in this far corner of the world in the back room of this small establishment. Heavenly Father has commissioned me to go to the Holy Land and, on the way, He foreordained that we should meet. Please take this book and read it to your eternal edification and salvation.' With that he excused himself to his room but agreed to meet me on the next day for light repast. I stayed up the entire night and by noon, I had completed the entire *Book of Mormon*."

Da's jaw dropped. "The entire book?"

"Yes, sir. It was a feverish read, to be sure, but therein lay the spiritual confirmation of what had been lodged in my mind by the reading of Ethan Smith's book. I should add that since that night, I have read several other books by Gentiles that confirm the veracity of the *Book of Mormon*. It is a marvel and wonder to my mind."

"Were there other Saints in Vienna?" I asked.

"None. When I met with Elder Hyde the next day I knelt before him and committed myself to the Church of Latter Day Saints. He reached down and drew me up to embrace me. We hired a carriage and drove out of the city until we found a suitable embankment along the Wien River. We walked into the river up to our waists and Elder Hyde baptized me. At that moment I became the only resident Saint in all of Austria."

"Meanwhile your step-mother had come to the same point?" I asked.

"Yes, to add to the curiousness of our circumstances, two letters – one hers and one mine – passed in the sending. In our letters we each disclosed to the other that we had become Saints. It was for us a great and mutual joy. Of course, not long after, Heavenly Father called my mother home. The rest you know."

"What will you do in Zion,?" I asked.

"Interesting you should ask," Arthur said, "for it is on this very subject I wish to engage your attention."

"Oh? Pray continue," I said, tilting my head to the side, as I'm told I often do when curiosity comes upon me.

Mister Walmsley poked his little pink tongue through rounded lips as he prepared to disclose his intentions. "Elder Hyde recommended me to the leadership in Nauvoo as a teacher and school master. The city charter of Nauvoo grants authority to establish a university, which is charged with the education of people at every level. There are three levels of instruction in the University of Nauvoo. Common schools have been formed in each of the wards for the younger children. A seminary for secondary education is now run by a Mister

Cole and his sister, Adelia. Higher studies in the liberal arts are provided at the university level. The need for education is great.

"The gathering to Zion has gained steam and families with children are streaming into Nauvoo. Most of the schooling of these children has been left to the families. The University Chancellor, John Cook Bennett, having heard from Elder Orson Hyde asked me if I would gather to Zion myself and form a second seminary. I agreed, but only on the condition that I may use my own ideas in the education of children. You see, I fear that our schools – both here and in America – are places of drudgery with mindless repetitions, unceasing recitations, pointless memorizations. These days teachers deposit information into young brains and demand senseless parroting without engaging the students in the *process* of learning." He paused, took a deep breath, and placed his hand on his little bird breast. "Oh, how I do go on," he said. "However, Doctor Bennett agreed. Within the confines of the prescribed curriculum and with use of the appointed textbooks, he will allow me freedom in how I conduct the classes."

I waited for him to continue.

"Elena, as I said earlier, you are known for your broad knowledge of many subjects and for your ability to teach. In the latter matter, your skill in helping the doffer boys become the best in Lancashire is well-attested. Would you join me as a teacher in my new school?"

Silence ensued as I tried to process what I had just heard. Slowly, a wave of joy washed over me and I could barely stammer out my affirmation. "Oh, Arthur, what a splendid opportunity. Of course, I accept."

"Ho ho!" Da said and clapped his hands in delight.

For the rest of the journey, Arthur and I bubbled with enthusiasm as we discussed seminary organization, pedagogical techniques, and mutual responsibilities. Da slept in blissful contentment.

When our coach crested on the hill above Liverpool, a great vista spread before our eyes. The masts of a hundred ships lay before us like a forest of slender trees garlanded with pennants. For several minutes, I drank it all in then closed my eyes, filled with an ecstasy and joy I could never have imagined.

CHAPTER FIVE

Kevil

Destroyer

I sat in dumbfounded silence listening to the syncopated ticking of a Seth Thomas wall clock. Doctor Mercer and Mister Rockwell waited for me to come to grips with the astonishing offer they had just made.

"Gentlemen," I said feigning indignity, "I find myself quite shocked at your request. The answer is *no*. I will not do as you ask." I paused for effect. "Why would I? Why would you even consider me for perpetration of this outrageous crime? I must say I take umbrage at your suggestion."

Doctor Mercer nodded. "Money," he said. "We are well aware that you wish to return to the east. You need funds for this purpose. We are prepared to pay you four thousand dollars."

"A handsome sum," I noted.

"Indeed."

"But why, if I may ask, do you so desire the death of Governor Boggs?"

"He is an avowed enemy of the Saints," Doctor Mercer said. "Moreover, the Prophet Joseph Smith predicted his violent end in accordance with a revelation from God; to wit, a *Destroyer* will be sent forth to destroy the enemies of the Lord. Sometimes it falls upon the Saints to assist the Lord in fulfillment of his revelations."

Mister Rockwell sat up in his chair. "And to boot he's a miserable son-of-a..." Doctor Mercer held up his hand cutting off his companion's invective.

"Did Joseph Smith put you up to this?" I asked.

"Not at all," Doctor Mercer said. "He merely prophesied the man's death."

I smiled to myself. It's easy to be a prophet when your followers assure fulfillment of your *prophesies*. "So why don't you assassinate him yourselves?"

"Deniability," Doctor Mercer said. "The Mormons will certainly come under suspicion of the authorities. It is no secret that every Saint desires punishment for Boggs."

"So I take it if I were to carry out this deed and be caught, you will disavow me?"

"Exactly."

"How convenient."

"We have a further offer."

"Go on."

"You need not accept this option. However, if you succeed in eliminating Governor Boggs and retreat to Nauvoo, the Saints will shelter you. The Prophet will offer sanctuary. Only a few discreet individuals, four or five, will know of your involvement. The Nauvoo city charter offers protections and securities not seen in other cities."

"Such as?"

"Our city council has passed an ordinance that permits the municipal court to investigate charges against its citizens. If the charge against a Mormon is judged to have been issued for purposes of malice or persecution, the court can dismiss it. If you make it to Nauvoo and are later charged in Missouri, you will not be extradited. It would not be difficult to see persecution in such a case. After all, Boggs drove the Saints out of Missouri on pain of extermination. His assassination is a matter of *spiritual justice*."

"Interesting perspective."

"As a lawyer, I thought you might find it so."

"Well, gentlemen, fascinating though all of this may be, I must decline your offer. I have no wish to commit this crime and further compromise my circumstances. Nor do I have any intention of becoming a citizen of Nauvoo. I do not doubt the sincerity of your beliefs but the Mormon Church is not for me."

"Four thousand dollars is four thousand dollars," Mister Rockwell said.

Such profundity deserved no reply.

"May we ask you to sleep upon it before giving us a final answer?

We shall stay in the city until mid-day tomorrow. We will return to see if you have had a change of heart."

"Well, I suppose I could grant you that courtesy," I said. "After all, four thousand dollars is four thousand dollars."

Mister Rockwell smiled.

+ + +

I did not become fully aware of the reversal in my mind until the midnight hour. Cassie Wilson lay beside me basking in the oozy afterglow of lovemaking. In contrast, I found myself in a peevish and mean-spirited mindset, which caused me to snap at Cassie when she turned to me and asked, "Ned, do you love me. Please tell me you love me."

"Given the last hour, shouldn't my feelings be obvious?"

"I know, it was wonderful, but can't you just say it? Say you love me?"

"Actions speak louder than words."

Her exasperation seeped out in a quiet sigh.

"It is late," I said. "I must work tomorrow. You should go."

She turned her head toward me. Even in the darkness I could sense her silent pleading. My emotions remained unstirred. I had important considerations to ponder. I did not wish to suffer a mewling woman. She stood and gathered her robe. Without a word she slipped away. Relief washed over me. Our lovemaking had become tedious, unfulfilling.

As my bed cooled from her presence, it dawned upon me that it was not just Cassie. All of my current circumstances had become dreary and mind-numbing. I needed a rush of excitement to crack this shell of weariness, something sparky, nervy, and risky. Such as the assassination of a governor? Could this be just the right antidote? For the first time in many weeks, I fell asleep excited about the morrow and the return of my Nauvoo conspirators.

A brisk morning business had tapered off by the time Doctor Mercer and Mister Rockwell eased through the front door of Crabtree's. Doctor Mercer tipped his hat. Mister Rockwell stood stiff as a statue, unblinking. I completed a sale to the only customer lingering in the shop. When he left, I put out the *Closed* sign. Once again, I ushered both men to the back room. Seth Thomas ticked away.

Before Doctor Mercer could ask the question, I said, "I have given your offer further thought."

"Yes?"

"I shall do it."

Doctor Mercer smiled.

"But," I said, "the price has gone up."

"To?"

"Six thousand dollars."

Doctor Mercer and Mister Rockwell looked at each other, then back at me. Doctor Mercer pursed his lips.

"Very well, then. Six thousand it is."

"And should I come to Nauvoo for sanctuary, I will suffer no pressure to join the Church."

"Guaranteed," Doctor Mercer said. "There are Gentiles in Nauvoo."

"That settled, I presume you have further information. For starters, I have no idea where Governor Boggs is now located."

"Independence. He has a home in Independence where he is running for the United States Senate."

"So how do you propose I carry out this...*assignment?*"

"Port Rockwell here is living temporarily in Independence. His in-laws, the Beebes, reside there and the Rockwells have relocated so his wife Luana could be with her family until the birth of their fourth child." Doctor Mercer smiled at Mister Rockwell. "This blessed event occurred not ten days ago. Little Sarah has joined the Rockwell family."

Rockwell showed no emotion at the mention of his new daughter. "Gotta get back to Nauvoo afore long," he said. "Gotta finish this mission in the next six weeks."

"What is your role, Mister Rockwell?" I asked.

"Headin' back to Independence first. When you come there, you find me. I'm known under the name of Brown, Josiah Brown. Move around only in the dark. I will set you up with grub and a dry bed."

"And how do you propose I accomplish all of this? Do you have a time or place in mind?"

"Up to you. You will have to reconnoiter when you arrive in Independence," Doctor Mercer said.

"And how am I to be paid?"

"One thousand now," the doctor said. "That is what we have with us. Two thousand more when you show up in Independence and the balance upon successful completion of the mission. You will have to make your way to Nauvoo for the final installment. You'll be free to stay in Nauvoo or go."

"Seems fair," I said.

Without further comment, Doctor Mercer withdrew a scarred leather wallet from his coat pocket and counted out ten one hundred dollar bills issued by the Girard Bank of Philadelphia, to my mind a venerable and stable institution. He handed them to me. His hand remained in an extended position, palm up, inviting me to shake on the deal, thereby committing each of us to the *mission* of assassinating Governor Lilburn Boggs.

+ + +

I retrieved the *Closed* sign and from the window spotted two young women walking along Third Street. When they saw me remove the sign, they paused. One woman pointed to the store and a few minutes later they brushed through the door. I studied their appearance. The Mississippi River had become a highway for Mormon immigrants on their way upriver to Nauvoo. It took no great powers of deduction to conclude that these ladies – one short, curvaceous, and quite beautiful; the other tall, lissome, and plain in appearance – were Saints. Most Mormon immigrants were, for the most part, a course and uneducated lot. They arrived in America dazed and blinking as if they had just been jerked from the Lancashire coalfields, scrubbed, and dropped in a canvas chair on a holiday beach. Whatever their circumstances, these unlettered English immigrants were not inclined to frequent literary houses. To see two of their lot – women no less – in my bookshop was an unexpected occurrence.

"Ladies," I managed finally to say, as I offered a brief bow.

They smiled but said nothing in response. It became apparent that the taller of the two had a genuine interest in literature. The pretty one paid scant attention to my stock and focused on the repair of a bent spoke on her parasol.

"Can I help you find something?" I asked.

"No thank you," the taller one said, "we are occupying our time before the steamer arrives."

Browsers irritated me. They were prone to banal and time-consuming chatter, upon which I seldom remarked. By way of avoidance, I said nothing to the young women and busied myself re-shelving several books that had been examined by an earlier customer. Out of the corner of my eye, I watched both women, my eyes lingering on the shorter one. Delicious. However, preoccupied as I was with her tumbling black curls, I could not help but notice when the taller woman picked up a new edition of Ralph Waldo Emerson's *Essays*. She began to leaf through the book, stopping every few pages to read a passage.

"Are you familiar with Emerson?" I asked.

She shook her head. "I'm afraid not. I've not had access to many American writers. Though I must say this looks interesting."

To my surprise, she did not speak with the unsophisticated dialect I had heard among so many of the immigrants. Hers was a cultured tongue and her intellectual curiosity piqued my interest. She paged further through the volume until a particular passage caught her eye. Her eyes swept over the lines.

"What passage are you examining?" I asked.

"It is from the essay entitled, *Self-Reliance*. Have you read it?"

"Indeed," I said and walked to where she stood. "Show me."

"This…" she said and pointed to a long paragraph.

"Read it aloud," I said. "Emerson begs to be read aloud."

"Very well." She swallowed and offered me a brief smile. "*An institution is the lengthened shadow of one man; as, Monachism, of the Hermit Antony; the Reformation, of Luther; Quakerism, of Fox; Methodism, of Wesley; Abolition, of Clarkson. Scipio, Milton called 'the height of Rome'; and all history resolves itself very easily into the biography of a few stout and earnest persons.*"

She looked up. Our eyes locked for a moment.

"What strikes you in this passage?" I asked.

"We should be on our way," the shorter woman said.

"In a moment," the taller woman said. "As you may know, sir, we are Latter Day Saints on our way to Nauvoo."

I nodded.

"This passage seems to apply to us."

"How so?" I asked.

"The Prophet Joseph Smith is such a *stout and earnest person*, as it says here, one whose institution – our Church – is the lengthening of his shadow."

"I should think it too early to tell."

She raised her eyebrows. "Perhaps. But I note the Saints are thriving in Nauvoo, even after persecution and exile from Ohio and Missouri."

"Your Church is not yet fifteen years old. Hardly a sufficient span of time upon which to claim a long shadow for its founder."

"But good sir, our Church is centuries old, dating back to the Patriarchs. The restoration of the Gospel is recent, to be sure, but the foundations are of ancient origin."

"So you think Joseph Smith is a man destined for greatness in the centuries to come, in the path of Antony, Luther, and Wesley?"

"I do."

"You should read on," I said. "May I see the volume?"

She handed me the book.

I flipped ahead several pages. "May I now read to you?"

"Of course."

I cleared my throat and eased back on my nasal speech. "*As men's prayers are a disease of the will, so are their creeds a disease of the intellect.*" I paused to skip a sentence or two before continuing. "*But chiefly is this apparent in creeds and churches, which are also the classifications of some powerful mind acting on the elemental thought of duty, and man's relation to the Highest. Such is Calvinism, Quakerism, Swedenborgism. The pupil takes the same delight in subordinating everything to the new terminology, as a girl who has just learned botany in seeing a new earth and new seasons thereby. It will happen for a time, that the pupil will find his intellectual power has grown by the study of his master's mind. But in all unbalanced minds, the classification is idolized, passes for the end, and not for a speedily exhaustible means, so that the walls of the system blend to their eye in the remote horizon with the walls of the universe; the luminaries of heaven seem to them hung on the arch their master built.*"

I put my finger between the appointed pages and handed the book back to her. In receiving it, she preserved my place with her own finger. For the briefest of instants, our forefingers touched, and I felt an unexpected spark, like the glint of a striking flint. She drew in a quick breath.

"I…I fear I do not understand," she said, blushing.

I drew myself up a notch as if to enlarge my explanation. "Emerson is saying that to study or worship under a revered master is ultimately limiting and if one does not rise above the tenets and admonitions of this *stout and earnest person*, to cast one's self entirely on the resources of his – or *her* – own mind, horizons narrow, freedom becomes restricted, and the intellect is stunted."

Her blush deepened. "I fear I am out of my depth."

"Not at all. Emerson can be arduous to read. Would you want to purchase the book to study it in more detail?"

"Oh," she said, replacing the book on its display stand. "I cannot afford such a thing. I am sorry to have wasted your time. We must go."

"Take it," I said.

She turned back to face me.

"I…I couldn't."

"Please," I said. "I am entitled to a free book each month. I have not yet selected for April. I would be honored if you would accept this book as my gift."

She paused to weigh the offer in her mind. Satisfied that my gift was unrestricted, she picked up the book and curtsied in gratitude. Then she swept out the door, her beautiful companion in tow.

I smiled, amazed at my uncharacteristic charity and felicitous mood.

+ + +

The following day I took an extended lunch, which gave me the opportunity to walk along the riverfront. There I hoped to spot the two ladies who had wandered into Crabtree's. I cannot say what I thought such a meeting might accomplish. I suppose, at a minimum, I hoped to re-engage the taller one in conversation and perhaps entice the pretty one into a different sort of congress. After wandering the riverfront and seeing no evidence of the immigrants, I inquired of a dockworker if he knew where I might find the Mormons. He told me they had departed earlier in the day aboard the *Maid of Iowa*, a side-wheeler bound for Nauvoo. "Ah well," I said to myself, "Perhaps it is for the best. Further entanglements with the weaker sex could cause me problems and I wanted nothing to compromise the beginnings of my *mission*."

I should add that my churlish behavior with Cassie had its intended effect. After one more evening of her tearful entreaties, which fell upon my deaf ears, Cassie disappeared from my life. So, as I returned from the docks to Crabtree's that afternoon, I sighed in the comforting thought that I was unencumbered by any relationship whatsoever.

Three weeks later, in the small hours of April 24th, 1842, I left Saint Louis. I told no one. I paid my rent to the end of the month, which gave Mrs. Perry a bit extra. To slip away unnoticed from Crabtree's, I forfeited my last week's wages. I filled my panniers with as much of my fine clothing as possible and rode into the night, fortunate to have a full moon to light the way.

Seven days later, I arrived on the outskirts of Independence and slipped into a secluded grove of trees until nightfall came upon me. An ominous mass of black clouds rolled through the sky at dusk. The clouds were accompanied by a dramatic drop in temperature, forcing me to retrieve my fleece-lined coat. Within moments, sheets of rain poured from the sky. Excellent.

I kept my vigil for an hour before beginning my search for the Beebe residence where I hoped to find Porter Rockwell. When I located the house, now assailed by torrents of rain, I dismounted and walked my horse to the back porch. Mister Rockwell sat alone in the darkness, cradling a pistol in his lap.

"Where you been?" he asked.

"Settling my affairs. I've been on the road a week."

"Expected you earlier. Gittin' more 'n' a might dithery waitin' for you."

"You gave me no deadlines."

"Told you I needed to git back to Nauvoo. Been nigh unto a month ago since we talked."

"Your urgency was unclear. I make no apology."

Mister Rockwell glared at me in silence. I held my tongue though my aggravation at his surly demeanor festered just below the surface. It would not have taken much scraping to release it.

Sensing my irritability, he softened. "Come up here and set a spell."

I accepted his invitation.

"Ever see one of these?" he said, as he hefted the pistol and passed it to me.

"Looks like a pepperbox to me, though bigger than most I've seen."

"Yup, it's a pepperbox. German. Barrels revolve when you cock it. Smooth bore but accurate at close range. Can fire a forty-four caliber ball. Recommend you use it but you is goin' to have to git a close shot."

I nodded and continued to examine the gun.

"Ever shot one of them afore?" Mister Rockwell asked.

"Not this large."

"Got a kick to it. Might recommend you fire it a few times afore you set out on the mission."

"Not necessary. I'm not a stranger to firearms."

"Suit yourself."

We sat in silence for a few minutes until Mister Rockwell rose from his chair and bade me follow him. We walked half a mile in the pouring rain to a barn on the edge of town.

"This is where you'll hole up," he said. "Someone will bring you food. Blankets on that old tick mattress in the corner there. Stay out of sight during the day. Boggs lives on Spring Street not far from the town square. He spends his days roamin' the district campaigning for the Senate. Comes home at night. I recommend you track him a few days afore you strike. Figure his whereabouts. Plan your escape. Gotta be in close range with that pistol. Remember, you is on your own."

"Where can I find you if I need you?"

"Better be a mighty good reason to look me up. I been workin' horses for Cyrus Ward out east of town. You passed it on the way in. However, I don't hanker to see you unless you got a serious problem. Don't want you around the Ward place or here at the Beebe's. Git my drift?"

"Where's my two thousand dollars?"

"Got it right here."

Mister Rockwell retrieved the cash from his coat pocket.

"Any chance for some food tonight?"

"Nope. Tomorrow morning."

"Your hospitality knows no bounds."

He did not reply. He turned on his heel and left me dripping in the cold, dark confines of the abandoned barn.

For the next three evenings, I covered my face with lampblack and staked myself in a stand of trees several hundred feet to the rear of the Boggs home. From this vantage point I could watch Boggs's return after his days of campaigning. On the third occasion, I stole up to a window on the side of the house. Just inside was a well-appointed study with a large, brass-studded leather chair to which the former governor repaired after dinner to read his newspaper. His head and shoulders were visible above the back of the chair. I could fire through the window and drop him with little difficulty. The range was close, as recommended by Mister Rockwell.

Satisfied my three-day reconnaissance was sufficient, I resolved to take action on the fourth night – Friday, May 6th. The rain had not eased and seemed to intensify on the appointed night as I crept from the stand of trees behind the Boggs home and positioned myself to the side of the study window. My nerves sparked. I sneaked a quick glance around the side edge of the window. The governor sat in his leather chair, a newspaper spread before his eyes.

I checked my pistol, counted to ten, took a deep clearing breath, wheeled, and fired all four barrels into the back of Lilburn Boggs's head.

Shards of window glass blasted into the room. The governor shot forward, snapped back, and slumped forward again. I saw a glass splinter embedded in the back of his leather chair.

CHAPTER SIX

Elena

Voyage

Despite an icy chill blowing off the Mersey Estuary, the Liverpudlian docks were a beehive of activity. Artisans stood in the doors of their shops hawking their wares. Dockworkers loaded, carried, and stacked all manner of goods in patterns and places I did not comprehend. Seamen rolled out of the pubs and prostitutes offered opportunities that brought a blush to my face. I had never seen so much energy in one place. I stopped from time to time to stare in awe at the clippers, barkentines, brigs, and full-rigged ships, some moored hundreds of yards from the dock and accessible only by tender. The ships loomed large in port – behemoths before our eyes – soon to be crumbs on the roiling Atlantic Ocean. The thought kinked my stomach.

And the smells – such a wondrous mixture of scents! Fish, brine, gull droppings, hemp, pine tar, unknown spices, and that indefinable odor of the sea gave the air a fresh pungency that I hoped would follow us across the ocean. I wanted this aroma to greet me each day as I walked out upon the deck in early morning.

After searching for the better part of an hour, Arthur, Da, and I found the small office leased by Mormon Agent Sam Richards. Upon our arrival, Agent Richards drew us into his office, shutting its door to the din and clamor.

"Elder Arkwright, Miss Arkwright, Mister Walmsley," he said. "Welcome to Liverpool, a modern-day Corinth if ever there was. A den of iniquity and sin but still the best departure point in Britain for the gathering of the Saints. Please, please, do have a chair and warm yourself."

We accepted his invitation and rested our aching feet.

"You are out on the *Tremont* in two days' time. You can board tomorrow so you will need lodging ashore for one night. You will sleep on board tomorrow night. Until then, we have secure rooms available up the hill. I will take you there after a simple supper. Elder Arkwright and Mister Walmsley, I have you placed in a room for six men. Miss Arkwright, I'm hoping you won't mind sharing a room with another Saint, a woman of your age."

"Not at all," I said.

Agent Richards oriented us to the details of our departure and advised us to get a bowl of hot porridge at a nearby public house, safe for Christian travelers. Our evening repast extended beyond the meal to include excited conversation with other saints about our upcoming adventure. Arthur left after finishing his meal, claiming infirmity and the need for a good night's sleep. As he minced out of the public house, I feared for his health during the strains of a long Atlantic voyage. His frailty aroused in me a strong protective instinct. Of course, I also had my old Da to care for, as I was soon reminded.

"Aw'm plumb tuckered, Lanie girl. Aw'm bound fer me bed."

"It has been a long and exciting day, Da. I'm weary too."

"Cans't ye b'lieve it Lanie? In but two days we'll be bound fer Nauvoo aboard a great sailin' ship. Tuckered as Aw'm, don't know if Aw can fall asleep."

I curled my hand under Da's arm. "You'll sleep like a babe, Da. And if you don't, what's the worry? You have weeks to catch up on your sleep. The rolling of the sea will be like grandmum's cradle."

"Oh, Aw hope so, Lanie. Aw do hope so."

A portly innkeeper and his wife met us at the entrance of the rooming house and welcomed us with great hospitality. They were not Saints, but they appreciated the opportunity to rent their rooms to our church members. We caused them little or no trouble, a rare circumstance in that boisterous dockside. Satisfied that Da had settled comfortably in his room, I repaired to my own. A solitary bed stood in the center of the room. I had never shared a bed with anyone. However, I reckoned for one night I would survive.

I sat on the bed and took several deep breaths to calm myself from the exertions of the day. In the silence of the darkening room, I reflected on the frantic pace that had brought us to this point. My reflection gave way to anticipation of a whole new life – an ocean and a continent away. Now, on the eve of our departure, I had completed all preparations. I permitted myself to relax and revel in the wondrous adventure that awaited us within but a single turn of the hour hand on the customhouse clock. Excitement stirred the pit of my stomach and I had to pinch myself to be assured this was not a dream.

A gentle knock sounded on the door.

"Yes," I said.

"May I enter?" came a woman's voice

When I cracked open the door, I beheld a striking young woman with dark tresses tumbling from beneath her bonnet.

"Hello. Are you the other roomer?" I asked.

"Yes."

"Then, of course, do come in," I said, as if permission were mine to give.

She gave me a shallow curtsey. "I'm Theodora Littlejohn but please call me Dorrie."

"I'm very pleased to meet you Dorrie. My name is Elena Arkwright but my family and close friends call me Lanie."

"Elena. What a comely name. Are you traveling alone?"

"No, my father is with me. Mum died several years ago. And you?"

"I travel alone."

"It is not good to be alone on such a journey. You may join our company. We are also traveling with Mister Arthur Walmsley, a teacher."

"I am most grateful," Dorrie said.

We settled on the bed side-by-side and any fears I might have harbored regarding my bedmate dissipated. In the first moments of our meeting, I knew that Dorrie and I would become fast friends. At this thought, my happiness soared. I loved my Da and respected Arthur but the thought of having a friend my own age – a woman – with whom to travel and explore the New World was an extraordinary boon. We talked long into the night, sharing our stories of conversion and our plans upon arrival in Nauvoo. I discovered that Dorrie hailed from Manchester and learned the craft of dressmaking at her late mother's knee. She planned to ply this trade once in America. At last, fatigue weighed upon us and we fell asleep.

"Lanie! Lanie! Get up girl! Get up! Time t' rise an' shine!"

"What's that?" Dorrie asked, blinking herself awake as the first rays of daylight seeped into our room.

"That's just my Da. He's quite beside himself with excitement."

Dorrie smiled and rose to a sitting position. We sent Da off in search of a place to eat and scurried around getting ourselves ready to board the *Tremont*. After warm biscuits and hot tea sold by a street vendor, we set off in search of our ship. I looked for Arthur but he was nowhere in sight. No one in our company had seen him since the previous night. Da concluded that he must have arisen and left the boarding house before dawn. A growing uneasiness tempered my excitement as we searched the dock for our ship.

When we finally saw *T-R-E-M-O-N-T* rising in white letters from the black hull of our ship, we clapped our hands and set off to search for our trunks. To our relief, after several minutes of hunting, we found them at the stern of the ship, ready to be loaded. One of the dockworkers told us we were free to board and that some of our group had already gathered on the forecastle deck. Da and I struggled to carry our trunks up the gangplank. One of the deck hands, a handsome young man with sandy hair and a welcoming grin, raced to take my end of the trunk. Once aboard, we were met by Brother Carson Greene, a Mormon bishop from America who would be in charge of our group of emigrants. He checked our names on his manifest, directed us to our quarters in steerage, and asked us to join the others on the *fawks'l* deck, as he pronounced it.

"Has a Mister Arthur Walmsley yet boarded?" I asked.

He ran his forefinger down several pages of crinkly, salt-laced pages.

"Ah, there's his name. No, miss. I do not show that he has boarded."

More worry.

Da and I were permitted one trunk in steerage or the tween deck where we would sleep and eat. The other was to be stowed until disembarkation in New Orleans. We had not been aware of this limitation and set about to do some quick re-packing. To my relief, the rearrangement of our belongings did not expose Da's precious clock. The ladder descending to the tween deck was perpendicular and I worried about Da's ability to negotiate these steps. Several times on our descent I looked up to see if he could manage the ladder.

"Don't worry 'bout me, Lanie girl. Aw can get down. Aw'll be fine."

The moment we set foot on the tween deck I sensed the first midges of dread. A low, dark room greeted us with rudely constructed bunks arranged two-by-two on both sides. A table ran full length down the middle of the deck. Support beams rose from the center of the long table and extended to the ceiling. Sawdust had been strewn on the deck, I presumed to ease cleaning. Two lanterns were positioned near the hatch and I feared that these would be our only light in the dark hours of the voyage.

Single women were directed to the far end of the tween deck; single men, to the other. A canvas sheet cordoned off the women's quarters to provide a measure of privacy. The married couples and families were housed amidships on a lower deck comprised of small sleeping compartments with wider berths. At once, we heard young men half-seriously proposing marriage aboard ship so as to claim the more commodious quarters.

The fresh pungent odor of the dock dissipated in the tween deck, overpowered by the stink of decay and human waste. From a lower bunk, a toothless old woman grabbed my arm with a claw-like hand. "Take a top bunk, dearie. 'At way no-one will spew on ye." I nodded, held my breath, and moved toward the canvas curtain. When I pulled it aside, I saw Dorrie sitting on a lower bunk.

"There you are!" she said. "I lost track of you during the rush of boarding. Come I've saved you a bunk next to mine."

"A top bunk?"

"It seems the old lady caught your arm too. Yes, a top bunk. This one right above me."

After we stowed our few belongings on the upper bunks, Dorrie and I went up to the forecastle deck as instructed. After a wait of nearly an hour, Brother Carson Greene strode to the center of the deck below us and called for our attention. I swept my eyes over the crowd. A wave of relief surged through me when I saw Arthur sitting on the steps to the forecastle deck with his head leaning against the banister. I excused myself and hurried to his side.

"Are you faring poorly Arthur?"

"Aye," he said. "I periodically suffer from an unnamed spell. My limbs shake, my head aches, and I cannot clear my vision."

"And you are suffering now?"

"Yes, but it will pass."

"Does this happen often?"

"Alas, it does. This one is severe." He groaned "I nearly reversed my decision to gather. I arose early to find fresh air. I managed to climb the street above our boarding house where I found fresher air. It revived me and I mustered the strength to board." He looked at me with his deeply set gray eyes, now bloodshot from fatigue. 'You are most kind to inquire."

"Is there anything I can do, Arthur?"

"No, Elena. I must simply wait until the shaking and pain subside."

Risking a breach in propriety, I put my hand on his shoulder. "Let me know if I can help."

He smiled his little oval smile and mouthed the words, "thank you."

"Dear friends in Christ Jesus…, may I have your attention please!" Elder Carson shouted from below us on the main deck. "May I have your full attention…"

We listened as Elder Carson Greene introduced two high priests who would assist in leadership. We were advised there would be morning and evening devotionals each day and two services on Sunday. Most of Elder Greene's instruction focused on the need for extreme cleanliness. We were to be responsible for washing our own dishes, keeping our bodies scrubbed, and our clothing laundered. Elder Greene concluded his orientation by warning the single women of our group not to fraternize with the sailors.

When he finished, Elder Greene bade us bow our heads in prayer. Upon the utterance of our collective *amen*, someone in our company began to play one of my favorite hymns upon the violin. We sang it often in the Methodist Church, *Come Thou Fount of Every Blessing.* Many of the Saints knew the words and we joined in such a moving rendition of this great hymn that it shattered the chill of winter. To my wonder and delight, next to me I heard Arthur's angelic tenor soaring far above the ranges of other men in descants that pierced my soul. I could not help it. My throat tightened in joy and, no longer able to sing, I swayed in time with the music.

+ + +

"Lanie! We're moving!"

I opened my eyes, felt Dorrie's hand on my shoulder, and listened to the creaking of beams and decking. Yes, we were moving! While we slept, our ship now loosed from its moorings and under weigh, sailed out into the great Atlantic Ocean. Swarms of butterflies fluttered in my stomach. I turned to Dorrie. We clasped each other in a long hug.

"Keep us safe, good Lord," I said.

"Amen," Dorrie responded.

A bell sounded three times and a man's voice hollered, "Devotions, twenty minutes."

We jumped from our beds, donned our dresses, bonnets, and winter cloaks before racing to the women's lavatory in the forecastle. We waited in line, bouncing on our toes in the chilly air. The stench below decks intensified in the lavatory, forcing me to take deep breaths through my mouth. I pinched my nose, breathing through my cupped hand. To my surprise, the closets were clean but the piping could not be rid of the mucky residue that accumulated over years at sea. Our first contributions to those maritime sewers revived the smoldering stench like a bellows blast on simmering coals. Water for the washbasins had a brackish odor, but I was thankful to have the opportunity to scrub, even with stinky water and abrasive soap.

After a devotional period of hymns and prayers, we ate a quick breakfast of hot coffee and biscuits smothered in unrecognizable gravy. When finished, we scraped the residue of our food overboard and cleaned our tin plates in gravy-clouded water bobbing with biscuit crumbs. Arthur had not joined us for breakfast so I immediately began to search for him. One kindly Saint told me that *the wee man* continued unwell and wished to stay in bed for the day. With worry in my heart, I returned to the top deck. There I joined other passengers watching the ship sail away from our homeland and all that had sustained our forebears for unnumbered centuries. We were now on what the sailors called the *uphill passage* from Europe to America, a term derived from the headwinds encountered in traveling west across the Atlantic.

The first days at sea were deceptively calm. Fair winds filled our sails and moved us gently through the low gray waves. Few of the Saints became seasick and many of the fears that had once gripped our faithful began to ease. Dorrie and I continued to develop our friendship, often talking well into the early morning hours and occasioning frequent hushing from our berth mates. To my great relief, Arthur rallied and soon joined us for meals and devotions. He still slept several hours during the day but never complained about his frailty. In occasional moments of selfishness, I wondered what might happen to my exciting future in the Nauvoo schools should anything happen to Arthur during this long voyage. I forced myself to confess these self-centered thoughts to God, asking His forgiveness, and offering genuine prayers of intercession for Arthur's recovery and sustained good health.

In contrast, day-by-day, Da grew more robust and energetic as if the sea air had blown the soot out of him. He stood on the deck for long hours, hands clasped behind his back, breathing deeply, and engaging one and all in high-spirited conversation. A perpetual smile graced his lips, and it warmed my heart to see my Da in such fine fettle.

+ + +

A week into the journey, I had taken to my bed early with monthly vapors and fell asleep. Some hours later I awakened and, as was often my custom, I turned to rub Dorrie's shoulder, a common gesture of affection and security for both of us. To my surprise she wasn't in her bed. I raised myself on one elbow and looked around but saw nothing behind the shroud of canvas that separated us from the dim lantern light beyond. Suspecting that she had gone to the forecastle deck, I settled back under my blanket and fell again into a light sleep. Perhaps an hour or so later, I reached again for Dorrie and, despite my somnambulant state, I realized she was still not in her bed. "Dorrie," I whispered but there was no reply. Now fully awake, I waited several minutes wondering what I should do. "Dorrie," I whispered again, louder this time. Still no answer. Several minutes passed, and I decided to go in search of her. As I crawled over her bed to the crude ladder, I saw her slip around the canvas curtain and tiptoe toward our paired bunks.

"Dorrie, where have you been?" I asked in a wave of relief. "I was about to go in search of you."

She crawled up into her bed. "Shh," she whispered. "I have

something to tell you."

"What?"

"Promise you won't tell anyone?"

"I promise."

"I've been with a sailor." She covered her mouth to mute her giggle.

"What? Dorrie that's forbidden!"

"Shh. Keep your voice down."

"Who is it?"

"His name is Piet Van Rijn. He's Dutch. He has a funny accent. Very charming."

"I know who he is. He helped us haul our trunks on board. But Dorrie, if you are caught out, you could be excommunicated." She giggled again and I became annoyed with her insouciance. "What have you been doing?"

"Nothing that you might imagine. We've only talked."

"But Dorrie, fraternization with the sailors – which certainly includes this…this talking – is forbidden. You heard Elder Greene say as much on the first day."

"I can't see the harm Lanie. He's such a nice young man. We talked about our native lands, life at sea, and America. All well within the bounds of respectability."

"Is that all you talked about?"

"Well…mostly."

"Dorrie, talking in the dark of night in a secret place – even if it is innocent conversation – will not be condoned."

Dorrie let out a long sigh. "No. I suppose you're right but please, dear Lanie, don't tell anyone."

"I won't. Tell me, will you see him again?"

"Yes."

"You are frightening me."

"I know. Good night sweet Lanie. You are a wonderful friend."

"Good night Dorrie," I said sighing. "Please be careful."

I could not sleep, thinking about what Dorrie had said. I understood the limits of propriety and the reasons why our leaders sought to prevent socialization with the sailors. On the other side of the coin, though, I could not condemn Dorrie, a pretty young woman, for having a conversation with a handsome sailor. I prayed for her protection.

+ + +

Our good fortunes came to an abrupt end on the 22nd day of January, ten days into the uphill passage. A powerful storm erupted just after daybreak with gale-force winds, pounding sleet, and waves that could have swamped the Pennine peaks of Lancashire. The *Tremont* pitched and rolled. With each sweeping arc of the *Tremont*, we feared we would capsize and meet Heavenly Father in the salty depths of the North Atlantic. Passengers were confined to the tween deck, which became a living hell of flying boxes, cookware, bottles, tins, chamber pots, unsecured clothing, and vomit. People clasped their bedposts for dear life. More than one could not hold on, suffering severe contusions and broken bones as they flew out of their beds. Waves crashing over the decks poured into the hatches and mixed with the effluvia below to form a sloshing sewer under our feet. The stench was unbearable. The few of us who remained healthy tied strips of cloth over our noses and mouths in order not to contribute further to the nasty slop that splattered our leggings and shoes. No fires were lit, no food could be cooked, and we survived on water and dry biscuits.

There must have been something in the Arkwright constitution that kept Da and me from becoming seasick. We tended to those who were bedridden, serving food and water to passengers who could eat. We emptied brimming chamber pots, offered words of consolation and encouragement, prayed with the terrified, and attempted to restore a measure of order to the rolling confusion. We relayed orders from the captain, reported conditions to our puking bishops, and tried to keep the lamps lit to minimize the horror of bucking and tossing in utter darkness.

On the third day of this unremitting tempest, Da pulled aside the canvas and grasped my arm.

"Lanie! Lanie! Ye must come! Arthur Walmsley is sick t' death!"

Arm-in-arm we staggered back to the men's quarters where Arthur lay under a thin blanket, ghostly pale in the dim light.

"Aw found some rope t' tie 'im to 'is bed, Lanie. Poor soul cannot 'ang on. Aw don't know what t' do."

I sat at the head of the bed, loosened one of the ropes, and placed Arthur's head in my lap. His forehead burned.

"He's got a fever, Da. This isn't seasickness. Can you find a cloth and soak it in cold water? See if you can fetch the ship's surgeon."

Da scurried off and returned with a cold compress, which I applied to Arthur's head.

"Aw looked for the doctor. Couldn't find 'im. Left word for 'im to come by."

"There's nothing more we can do now but pray, Da. Please use your office as a priest and anoint him for healing. I'll stay with him for a while and wait for the surgeon."

Da rushed around until he located a jar of lamp oil with which he anointed Arthur in a fumbling prayer of unction. For the next six hours, I sang to Arthur, cradling his head, praying for him. I cooled his fever with cloths soaked in cold water. The doctor came by midway through my vigil. He checked Arthur's pulse, felt his forehead, and based upon these two observations, diagnosed his condition as *relapsing fever*. He prescribed brandy. I tried to give Arthur small sips of the liquor but he was so debilitated, he could not swallow. The liquid spilled out of his mouth and dribbled off his chin. Judging the brandy to be ineffective and, absent any other remedies, I resolved to hold him in my arms and petition Heavenly Father to receive His sweet soul into the arms of mercy.

After three days in my lap, Arthur showed signs of recovery. His fever broke and his body temperature plummeted. We piled blankets on him and fed him bits of biscuit, which he tolerated well. As instructed by the ship's surgeon, we rubbed his feet and limbs vigorously with spirits. He said little during these ministrations save for brief, whispered thanksgivings.

The storm eased after eight days. The winds abated, rains receded, and glimmers of sunlight could be seen in the far western sky. To our relief no one died in the storm. As the Saints recovered, they mucked out the steerage with the industry for which they would later be known. Hymns of thanksgiving, and invocations of relief rose from the decks of the *Tremont*. In a matter of hours, things were once again ship shape and our faith in the Almighty soared. And what a joy it was to have that first sip of hot tea and spoonful of warm stew. It nearly brought tears to my eyes.

+ + +

The instant Elder Carson Greene and the other two bishops could stand and retain food, they wasted no time in summoning Dorrie Littlejohn to a private meeting.

"I've been found out," she whispered to me from her bed late one night. "I've got to go see them first thing in the morning. Oh Lanie, I'm scared. Will they excommunicate me?"

"I don't know."

"That would be devastating. But I don't feel like I've done anything so very wrong."

"Did you...?"

"No. No. Not that. Piet kissed me though. Once. I'll admit that. That's all. He never touched me improperly. He's been a fine gentleman."

"So you love him?"

"I think so."

"And does he love you?"

"He has declared as much."

"Oh Dorrie! You have such a terrible choice. Your heart is being pulled in two directions."

"Only one direction now, it seems."

I put my arm around her and drew her to me. I could do little to remedy her troubling circumstance save for the succor of my arms. She cried herself to sleep in my embrace and did not stir when I lowered her to bed and pulled the quilt over her shoulders.

The following morning, Dorrie slipped into her finest clothes and prepared for her ominous meeting. I whispered a brief prayer, wished her luck, and told her I would wait for her topside. She nodded and crawled up the ladder, fighting valiantly to withhold her tears. Thirty minutes later I basked in the warm weather that had swept the storm away. The seas had a gentle roll, and I became entranced by the white-crested waves curling against the hull. So rapt was I that I did not sense Dorrie's presence for several minutes. I finally felt her standing by my side and I snapped out of my reverie. She bore a smile.

"My dear Dorrie! I did not hear you come."

"You were captivated by the sea. I did not wish to disturb you."

"So, tell me, what happened?"

"I am still a member of the Church."

"I'm so thankful! Tell me."

"The bishops were very kind. I couldn't believe their forbearance. I expected them to be harsh and unforgiving. In quiet and measured tones, they told me that I had been observed with Piet on the night before the storm hit. They did not chastise nor condemn me. They repeated their reasons for prohibiting fraternization but also gave me a chance to explain myself."

"What did you say?"

"I told them that our meetings were quite innocent and that nothing of an immoral nature had taken place."

"Did you tell them of the kiss?"

She covered her mouth to hide a quick smile. "No, I confess I left that part out."

I smiled back. "It will be our secret," I said. "But tell me, Dorrie, can you continue to see Piet?"

"Only in the presence of another Saint, a man, and only if Piet agrees to hear and receive the restored Gospel. Then I may entertain his suit."

"Do you think he will agree?"

"I hope so. He says he is a Calvinist and a stubborn Dutchman to boot. He tells me he doesn't cotton on to new ideas."

"We shall pray for his conversion."

"Yes, we shall. Prayer may be the only weapon at this point."

"But a stout weapon it is."

+ + +

A week later we reached the halfway point in our voyage. We emerged from the frigid dangers of the North Atlantic and sailed into calm seas and warm days. Heavy coats were laid aside, and we spent long hours in the fresh sea air as the ship plunged toward America and our new life in Zion.

Piet Van Rijn accepted the invitation to learn of the Mormon faith. Our three bishops instructed him during his off hours and, from Dorrie's perspective, he seemed to be *fathoming out* the material. (Dorrie had begun to pick up some nautical terms.) In the full flush of beginning love, she accompanied Piet to these catechetical sessions. I could sense her drifting away from me, which produced in me a wistful left-behind feeling. I tried to concentrate my thoughts on Dorrie's happiness but could not help the twinges of envy that came upon me as I saw the two young lovers walking together in the cool of the evening.

It was Arthur Walmsley who rescued me from my doldrums. Back in fair health, he proposed setting up a short-term school aboard ship. The parents, of course, were quite enthusiastic at the prospect of relief from their children for a few hours each day. The children themselves jumped with excitement. Though many had no great academic appetite, school held the promise of relieving their boredom. With about a month to go in the voyage, we obtained permission to use the steerage dining table to begin our instruction.

Teaching proved to be a challenge without slates or textbooks. However, Arthur conceived of a set of oral examinations to determine levels of education. The fifteen pupils ranged in age from six to seventeen. Seven of them could neither read nor cipher. The seventeen-year old girl, Roseanna Butler, had been to school for several years and Arthur tapped her to assist in teaching the younger children. Arthur asked me to choose a set of moral stories from the *Bible* and *Book of Mormon* to give the children further grounding in the faith. I found I had to adapt the stories to at least two levels of complexity for the older and younger children. I took great pleasure in the work and each day after our school recessed, I spent several hours preparing my instruction for the following session. The ship's captain gave Arthur a large unused ledger, in which he wrote out mathematical problems, scientific diagrams, and other visual aids to assist in his teaching. After supper each day, Arthur and I met to review the lessons for the next day.

+ + +

On February twenty-eighth, one week before our scheduled arrival in the port of New Orleans, we thrilled to two momentous events. First, we sailed through the Gulf of Florida and into the Gulf of Mexico. This passage elevated our spirits. To be sure, the first sighting of land several days earlier had caused uproarious *huzzahs* and *thank-Gods,* but our entry into the Gulf signaled a great victory. The dreaded Atlantic, with all of its terrors, had been conquered.

The second delightful event occurred during the supper hour one evening. Piet dropped into the steerage and banged on the table with a tin cup. Dorrie joined him at his side and, when all eyes were upon them, Piet burst into a full smile and told us that Dorrie had agreed to become his wife. He also revealed that he was to be baptized upon disembarkation. The marriage would take place when we reached Nauvoo. I was happy for Dorrie though her betrothal loomed as one more reminder of my spun-out spinsterhood.

Later that night, after Dorrie crawled into her bunk, I had the chance to speak with her alone.

"Dorrie, I am so happy for you."

"Thank you, Lanie. He is a wonderful man. He is leaving the ship's service to come with us to Nauvoo. I can hardly believe my good fortune."

"What will a sailor do in Nauvoo?"

Dorrie giggled. "Lanie, the ever-practical one. Well, my dear, as it turns out, Piet is a carpenter's mate and carpenters are in great demand in Nauvoo. So we know he will have employment. Perhaps he will work on the Temple. Would that not be a splendid tribute to Heavenly Father!"

"Providence has smiled upon you, Dorrie. Now, to sleep and sweet dreams."

"You are a great friend, Lanie. Thank you."

I clutched the blanket under my chin. A friend, a *spinster* friend. *Spinster* - a spinner of yarn. How apropos, I thought. Elena Arkwright, a throstle jobber, a spinner of yarn, a *spinster*. O how I hated that word!

+ + +

Our days at sea drew to a close. The children grew restless and yearned for freedom from school so they could stand in the glorious sunshine and watch the undulant dolphins escorting us to America. I confess I too wished to be above decks to bask in a sunlight unknown to Lancashire, where the rays were always tentative, tepid, and patchy. Arthur and I decided to draw our teaching to a close.

We begged our ship's cook to bake a cake for the children as a reward for their attention at *Sea School*, as we called it. The cooks did well with their dwindling ingredients and turned out a delicious spice cake. The children and their parents savored this special treat to the envy of the other Saints. Arthur cut out fifteen unused pages from the borrowed ledger and, in his ornate penmanship, wrote a special message to each of the children. He rolled each of these pages and tied them with a leather string. These certificates of achievement from Sea School turned out to be treasures beyond our expectation. Even Roseanna, our mature, seventeen-year old assistant, ran to her father to show him her *diploma*, as she called it. Arthur had given special attention to Roseanna's certificate. At the top of the document, he drew an eagle with a globe in its talons. He added extra flourishes to the lettering and curlicues around the margins. The certificate read:

Maritimis Seminario
Salutem in Domino
To friends and patrons of scholarship: Be it hereby known,
Roseanna Butler
having furnished satisfactory evidence of competent
knowledge in several subjects and having supplied notable
service in the instruction of younger scholars, is presented
this certificate of laudable achievement and excellence on
the Sixth day of March, in the Year of our Lord, 1842.

Elena Arkwright   *Arthur Walmsley, M.A.*
Teacher   *Master*

The following day opened with a cloudless sky and flocks of shorebirds soaring around the masts of the *Tremont*. Dorrie, Arthur, Da, and I strolled the deck bursting with the excitement of pending arrival. The Gulf had begun to show variegation in color from the deep navy blue of the stern waters to emerald green in the distance ahead. We stood at the deck rails for hours staring at the swaying masts above and the foamy trails below. Now and then a Portuguese man-of-war floated through the ripples swirling around our hull.

As the afternoon waned into evening, we could see a thin black line on the horizon bisecting sky blue and emerald green. However, as the black line thickened, the water shaded from green to yellow. Not thirty minutes after I noticed the color change, we felt a scraping shudder as the *Tremont* plowed through semi-liquid alluvia. Suddenly, the ship came to a full stop, broached in the foul-smelling Mississippi silt. The startled passengers panicked at having run aground so close to port. However, the ship's crew assured all that this was a normal event. In the early morning, the captain would dispatch a shore-bound ketch to secure the services of a steam tug that would tow us to port.

That evening we held devotions celebrating a safe journey across the perilous seas. We concluded our service by filling the skies with the refrains of that joyful hymn, *Sing Praises to God*. Surely our chorus rolled over the waters that night borne on the winds of the Holy Ghost.

We awakened to furled sails and crewmembers scurrying about in preparation for docking once the tug hauled us to port. High in the rigging we watched Piet and two other crewmen repairing one of the yardarms on the mizzenmast that had been damaged in the North Atlantic storm. We smiled at their daring as they swung from rope to rope like monkeys in the trees of a tropical rainforest. I had just looked down to swat a flying insect from my hand when I heard Dorrie join a sudden chorus of gasps and cries. I looked up just in time to see Piet falling, his white shirt and britches a plummeting cloud against the bright blue sky. Dorrie collapsed into my arms just as Piet struck the taffrail with a loud crack of his spine and catapulted into the murky waters below.

CHAPTER SEVEN

Kevil

Nauvoo

The last shot kicked with sufficient force to jerk the rain-slippery pistol from my grip and it fell into the mucky underbrush at my feet. I left it in the mire and sprinted into the night. After a short circular dance with one foot in the stirrup, I mounted my horse. Spurring to a full gallop, I raced out of Independence along a small road bound for the northeast and what I hoped would be a clean escape.

I rode hard for an hour along the road to Fort Osage, an outpost on the Missouri River. When the lights of the fort came into sight, I went off road, through the cleared fields to the east until I picked up the east-west road to Lexington. The road neared the river, and I stopped to let my horse drink. Cascades of rain rinsed the lather from her coat. Her breathing slowed. I patted her neck, "We'll go slower now." The mare's head jerked up and down as if to suggest she understood and appreciated my assurances. I strained my ears but heard nothing. I turned to face the east and, through drops of water coursing off the brim of my hat, I contemplated the long, wet slog to Nauvoo.

+ + +

Seven days later, as evening shadowed a cloudless sky, I stood on the west bank of the Mississippi River in the small Iowa hamlet called Montrose. On the opposite bank stood my destination, Nauvoo. I secured the services of a ferryman to take me across the river but he said with the water running so high and nightfall upon us, we would wait until the early morning. I took this delay as an occasion to study the sunset-burnished skyline of America's Land of Zion.

Nauvoo had been laid out on a semi-circle of land that appeared to be plowed into the river by the blade of a high bluff to the east. Atop the bluff, pinkish-orange in the setting sun, rose the first story of the celebrated Mormon Temple. On several occasions, Doctor Mercer had spoken of this edifice, which the Prophet intended to be the *finest in the Middle-West*. I scanned the horizon from the southern-most building visible on my right to the downward slope of the bluff as it slipped into the river upstream to my left. I judged this scan to be on the order of four to five miles. Nauvoo appeared expansive – perhaps as large as Saint Louis – with clusters of fine buildings and homes. I was amazed that the Mormons could have built such a thriving community in a mere three years. It gave proof to the uncommon vigor of the Saints so often described by Doctor Mercer.

I stood there until the sun winked out and the river turned to ink. I took deep sighs commensurate with my growing confidence that I had escaped whoever might have been on my trail, if anyone had been there at all. Nowhere along my journey from Independence had I heard a whisper of Governor Bogg's assassination. I took this to be a good sign, knowing that the more distance I put between the scene of the mission and me, the safer I would be. However, I hearkened back to Doctor Mercer's warning that the Mormons would be accused of vengeance. Thus, crossing the river into the heart of the LDS empire could spell future danger for me if Missouri lawmen pressed their inevitable suspicions. I had to take Doctor Mercer at his word that the Saints promised to protect me in Nauvoo for as long as I wished to stay. However, I would not linger long. Once I received my final payment, I planned to retreat further to the east and the obscurity of urban life.

After a restful sleep in the small log house of the ferryman and a tolerable breakfast of johnnycakes, molasses, and sugary coffee, we boarded the ferry to cross the menacing Mississippi. My fellow passengers consisted of an ignorant backwoods Iowan, his wife, and three dimwitted children. This pitiful family spent the better part of an hour loading an ox, cow, two calves, a table, several chairs, and four steamer trunks loaded with God-knows-what. I found myself annoyed at the delay and incensed by their unending prattle about the *one true church.* The ferryman, an obvious Gentile, shared my irritation, as evidenced by his unsympathetic commands to "hurry it up there; ain't got the whole day, fer cryin' in the beer."

Despite the treachery of the river and the stomping uneasiness of several of the animals, including my horse, we made the crossing without incident. The ferryman left the backwoods family to unload their belongings and offered to show me parts of Nauvoo as he made his way up mud-clotted Parley Street toward the center of town.

"Case you might be a-wonderin', 'ese Mormons shun strong spirits. Beer an' wine is available in several 'stablishments. Howsomever, whiskey an' the like is hard to come by. Ole Amos Naismith, a hard-core Gentile, operates a grocery up on White Street. He'll pour you a shot or two in the back room. 'At's where I'm headin' now. Care to join?"

"No, sir, I am in search of a one Doctor Tobias Mercer."

"Come on, then. He's got an office up on White Street as well. I'll fetch you there."

We turned north and walked the four blocks to White Street. Naismith's stood opposite a small two-story building with gilt lettering in the lower window that read,

Tobias Mercer, M.D.
Physician and Surgeon

I thanked the ferryman for his services, hitched my trailing horse, and stepped from the street up to the wood porch of Doctor Mercer's office. When I entered his office, I beheld him sitting with his feet upon his desk reading a medical journal. He did not rise upon seeing me but offered a slight nod.

"Have you completed your mission?" he asked.

"I have."

"Good."

"I want my final installment."

"We must see the Prophet."

"When?"

"Now. In his office."

"Where is the office?"

"It is on the top floor of his store."

"How far?"

"Six blocks to the south."

"I just came from down there." As intended, my annoyance showed.

Doctor Mercer stood up and laid his journal on his desk. "My apologies for the inconvenience. Walk with me."

When we arrived at Joseph Smith's two-story Red Brick Store, Doctor Mercer led me through the mercantile floor with its long counter running the full span of the room. We passed through a doorway in the rear to a small storeroom with ascending stairs. At the top of the stairs we passed by a large assembly room.

"What is this room?" I asked Doctor Mercer.

"It serves for general meetings," he said, without further explanation.

I didn't press the point but walked a few more paces to a closed office door. A sign had been tacked on the door that read *Office of Jos. Smith, Jun., President of the Church of Latter Day Saints*. Doctor Mercer knocked on the door.

"A moment," came the voice from within the office.

Several seconds later, the door opened to reveal a tall man, six feet or more. He smiled at seeing Doctor Mercer, revealing a chipped front tooth.

"My good Doctor Mercer. How good to see a man who heals cramp colic and consumption." He glanced up at me. "And who do I have the pleasure of meeting today?"

"It is best that we make our introductions behind closed doors," Doctor Mercer said.

"By all means." The Prophet stepped aside, widened the door and, with a sweeping gesture of his hand, drew us into his office. With the door shut, Doctor Mercer introduced me as the *avenging angel of whom we have spoken*. Smith's eyes widened. With solemn mien, he bowed in my direction.

"I am at your service," he said. "You have fulfilled the prophecies and avenged the Saints. We are in your debt."

"Indeed you are," I said. "I want my fee. Three thousand dollars."

Joseph Smith looked at me through deep-set eyes, dark blue in the dim light. His long eyelashes lowered several times. He ran his hand through his flaxen hair and stared at the floor. I became irritated by his gestures of delay.

"Mister Freeman," he said at last, "We have a problem."

I waited in silence.

"We have no money in Zion, no money at all except for useless bank paper. We have invested everything in land, the Temple, and the Nauvoo House."

I did not believe him. "How then do you conduct business in your store?"

"We sell on long credit, in order not to distress the poor."

I gathered myself and prepared for verbal battle. "*Mister* Smith," I said. "I have no patience with this plea from poverty. I contracted to execute Governor Boggs for the sum of six thousand dollars, only three of which have been paid so far. I expect payment in full with specie or paper backed by stable institutions."

The Prophet nodded. "I understand your concern but I pray the opportunity to present a counter-offer."

"Counter-offer?"

"Yes. Please, be seated."

He coursed around his desk with a slight limp and sat lightly in his chair, elbows upon the desktop.

I stood my position.

"Please," Smith said softly, "a moment in the chair won't hurt."

"I would ask that you make it brief," I said, lowering myself into the chair.

"Here is what I propose," he said. "While most of our collective wealth is committed to building projects, we possess considerable expanses of real property. I should like to offer you eighty acres to the east of town, high on the bluff. The parcel I have in mind is mostly prairie but the northeast section is timbered."

I shot out of my chair and hammered both fists on the desk. I leaned to within an inch of the Prophet's face. "You can't be serious! Offering me useless prairie land as payment of an agreed-upon fee! Find the cash or I will broadcast your knavery throughout this…this kingdom of yours."

He raised his hand. "Hear me out," he said. "There is more."

I did not move.

"It has been my intention that the farmers who have gathered to Nauvoo would have their tillable acres outside of town but homes within the city. In this way, they can partake of the events and activities of the Saints. They won't be isolated on outlying farms. To this end, I have built several fine houses on speculation. I have one on the north end of town in the old section, once called Commerce. It is a handsome house and sturdy. It is vacant and can be yours along with the acreage."

"In case you hadn't fathomed my intentions, Mister Smith, I have no desire to own land in this marshy hell-hole. I need money to return to the east and to re-establish myself within the bounds of civilization."

He raised his hand again.

"I understand. However, Nauvoo is not just a center for the faithful Latter Day Saints, it is destined for greatness as a commercial and industrial center. Contrary to the opinion of many, this prairie land all around us is rich and can produce yields never seen in the east. So the properties I offer are worth considerably more than the balance of your fee and will appreciate in value over time."

I cocked my head and studied the man for a moment. He had stilled me with a reasonable argument. Yes, I could take the land and sell it at some point in the future. With swarms of Saints pouring in from afar, land values would go up. I harbored doubts regarding the usefulness of the prairie as agricultural land. If it were so rich, I wondered, why aren't there more trees on it? Nevertheless, Nauvoo seemed destined for growth and Joseph's offer might be in my best interests. I fingered my shirt button for several seconds. "I want time to consider the offer," I said.

"You'll have it," he said. "I should add that the house is furnished. I'll make it available to you for as long as you wish while you reflect upon this opportunity. The Saints owe you our gratitude for services rendered. I have no wish to offend you. I believe this is a fair proposal and urge your favorable consideration."

I nodded. The man had charm. I began to see how he had duped so many people into believing he was the latter day prophet and mouthpiece of God. Of course, I was not for a moment taken in by the allure of this manipulator and charlatan. Without further comment, I took my leave of the Red Brick Store. With directions from Doctor Mercer, I made my way on horseback up the bluff in the direction of what might become my new properties. Husbandry of this untilled prairie did not interest me. This land hardly matched my beautiful plantation in the Carolinas. However, becoming a country squire once again, albeit in this rude environment and for but a short time, did have its appeal.

When I arrived at the appointed tract of land, I walked through knee-high grasses and tall wildflowers, the names of which were unknown to me. The only familiar plant was what appeared to be a type of phlox with clusters of pink flowers nestled here and there among the grasses. I gave the matter little further heed, having no interest in natural history. After traipsing around the field for a few minutes, I made my way to the stand of timber on the northeast corner of the property. I noted that it would make a suitable location for a farmhouse, were I inclined to build one. Though a handsome piece of land, I still had reservations about its potential. Smith had said it would be good for growing crops but I didn't entirely trust the man. He had reasons to lie in order to conclude his deal. However, if he were honest in this matter, I could possess a fine parcel of land, no doubt worth considerable money in the years to come. That is, if Nauvoo continued to prosper.

I spent an hour striding through the prairie grasses before setting a course back to town in search of the clapboard house that would serve as my temporary abode. In the neighborhoods of Nauvoo, I became somewhat confused by the layout of streets. The new city, under Smith's leadership, had been arranged in an orderly east-west and north-south configuration. The blocks were large with only four lots per block. By contrast, Commerce, the older settlement, had streets running roughly parallel and perpendicular to the river in a northwest-to-southeast and northeast-to-southwest direction. Thus, the streets of old Commerce were diagonal to those of Nauvoo. However, after several inquiries, I managed to arrive at the white clapboard house.

I must say my initial impressions of the place were favorable. Large oak trees flanked the house and a small willow bowed gracefully in the breeze as I paused to examine the premises. Grass had been planted in the front of the house and kept trim. The house was hell for stout, had been recently whitewashed, and the shutters boasted a fresh coat of glossy black paint. I wondered if these attentions had been given to the house in anticipation of my arrival. A split-rail fence, in good repair, enclosed the lot and I noted behind the house a small shed, which could serve as a stable for my horse. (The Saints had made no effort to reclaim the horse they had lent me.) A two-hole privy stood several paces behind the house.

Though far below my standards and inferior to my estate in the

Carolinas, I admitted to being pleased by the property. The house boasted two front doors, the reason for which escaped me. The left hand door was unlocked, permitting entrance to a parlor, painted lemon yellow with a dark oak wainscot. The floors were of oak, tightly laid. A simple table with two chairs stood in the center of the room. To the right, behind the other front door, was a *relaxin' room*, as we might have called it in the South, robin's egg blue above the wainscot. A brick fireplace graced the far wall, promising warmth to whoever rested in the lone rocking chair to read by the light of a lard lamp. Behind the parlor and relaxin' room stood a kitchen with a modern cooking stove that raised my eyebrows. I had not anticipated such a modern appliance in this rude environment. Upstairs I found two spacious bedrooms, one of which was furnished with a lattice-rope bed. All-in-all, though sparse, the furnishings were certainly better than I had imagined.

Having reviewed the house, I returned to the relaxin' room and sat in the rocking chair, swaying back and forth and pondering my situation. Though little had been said regarding the outcome of my mission, it did appear that the Saints would protect me. The land and house were worth more than the cash balance owed me. While toiling at Crabtree's, I had nurtured a nebulous ambition to go further east, perhaps to New England, and blend into a city far from the dangers of Missouri. However, beyond this vague notion, I had given the matter little thought. So I asked myself, as I rocked to and fro, where would I go? How secure would I be? Was I able to improve upon the current possibilities? It did not take long for me to reach a conclusion. My best prospect was to take up temporary residency in Nauvoo among the Mormons. I nodded to myself and stood to return to the Red Brick Store where I would accept the Prophet's offer.

+ + +

The sun had begun its descent in the western sky when I made my way south on Granger Street toward the Red Brick Store. As I drew near, I noticed a large crowd gathering just to the east of the store. People were congregating from every direction just outside a log cabin. I soon learned this was the Prophet's homestead. I dismounted and asked one of the passers-by what had occasioned the assembly.

"An Englishman, name of Caswall, has brought an ancient book for the Prophet to examine, maybe translate," the man said. "If anyone can translate it, our Prophet can."

My curiosity piqued, I joined the throng gathering around the front door of the cabin. Saints packed inside, anxious to witness the Prophet's pronouncements concerning this ancient document. I managed to push through the crowd to a point just outside the door.

"What manner of book is this?" the Prophet asked.

"I believe it to be a Greek Psalter," came the reply.

A brief silence ensued.

"There may be some Greek but I believe most of the writings to be Egyptian," the Prophet said. "I surmise it to be a dictionary of Egyptian hieroglyphics."

The Saints issued a murmur of affirmation. Their Prophet had confirmed what they all believed, that he was an oracle of God capable of unparalleled discernment and mastery of ancient languages.

"My good man," said the other, presumably this Caswall, "it is nothing of the sort. I know for a fact that it is an ancient Greek Psalter, perhaps six hundred years old. My own studies in Greek confirm that the characters are indeed of that language. There is nothing of *Egyptian* origin on these parchments. Here, allow me to illustrate."

I heard the rustle of brittle pages. The crowd waited in breathless excitement.

"I have turned to the famous Psalm Twenty-Three. It is actually Psalm Twenty-Two in the Septuagint, the Greek translation of the Old Testament. See here the first two words, *kyrios* and *poimainei*." Caswall uttered these words slowly, with exaggerated pronunciation. "The Greek words for *lord* and *shepherd*, don't you see? If you do not believe me, I urge you to take the matter before any respectable scholar of the classic languages for confirmation of what I have said."

There was no response from Joseph Smith.

I elbowed several aside so I could get a glimpse through the open window. I saw Caswall standing before the Prophet with arms folded across his chest, a smug smile upon his face. I found his demeanor arrogant and irritating. He had traveled to Nauvoo for the sole purpose of duping the Prophet. While I had no great affection for Joseph Smith, I felt a growing impulse to intervene.

Before I could do so, the Prophet offered to purchase the document so he could study it further. Mr. Caswall refused. He placed his document in a heavy envelope and buckled its leather belt.

"Having seen my document," Caswall said, "may I ask in return that you explicate the characters on the ancient documents and celebrated antiquities your storekeeper showed me yesterday."

The Prophet immediately agreed to this request and led the multitude to his store. I made certain I was among those in his immediate presence. Fifteen of us joined the Prophet in his office. He produced several glass frames containing what appeared to be sheets of papyrus. Caswall studied them for several minutes in silence. The Prophet offered no commentary whatsoever on the documents. As the visitor was thus occupied, the Prophet slipped from the room and disappeared.

Unaware of this defection, Caswall pointed to one of the characters. "What is the meaning of this?" he asked and looked up to hear the Prophet's explanation. "Mister Smith? Are you here? Where have you gone?"

We waited with anticipation and rising embarrassment until it became clear that Joseph would not be returning to his office. Caswall pushed through the crowd and descended the stairs of the Red Brick Store. I followed directly behind him. When we came to the street, we could see the Prophet's wagon in the distance as he whipped his horses away from the Red Brick Store. Caswall bore a triumphant smile.

"Did our Prophet's explanation satisfy thee?" one of the Saints asked.

"Not at all," Caswall said. "The man is a fraud."

At this the crowd began to murmur. Shouts in defense of the Prophet rose above the swelling din and in less than a minute the mood of the Saints grew ugly, menacing. Several wiser heads wasted no time in ushering Caswall out of the throng and on to the ferry landing.

A short, porcine man with two bulbous chins raised his hand in an effort to draw the attention of those milling around.

"My brothers and sisters," he said. "Please, may I have your attention. Please." The murmuring abated. "What we must remember is that sometimes Mister Smith speaks as a prophet and sometimes as a mere man. If he gave a wrong opinion respecting Mister Caswall's document, he spoke as a mere man." The short man's explanation brought nods of understanding and the temper of those gathered began to soften. Within a few minutes, the crowd disbanded.

"Who is that fat little man?" I asked one of the Saints.

"He is Doctor Richards, Doctor Willard Richards, the Prophet's private secretary."

I pushed through the crowd to the doctor's side.

"Your point was well stated," I said, "though just as well refuted."

"Who are you?" Doctor Richards asked.

"Ned Freeman," I said.

Richards's eyebrows raised in recognition. He knew who I was, and that put me instantly on edge. I worried that my name and erstwhile mission were more widely known than I had been led to believe.

Richards extended his hand, "It is a pleasure to meet you," he said in a whisper, "And thank you for your service to the Church. I noted the look on your face. Be of good comfort. Only a handful of us know you are the man who avenged the Saints."

"Where has Mister Smith gone?" I asked, relieved by Richards's assurances.

"No doubt to the Grove west of the Temple. There is a favorite tree, a venerable oak, under which the Prophet often sits to meditate and, in this case, recover from what has been an occasion of embarrassment."

"Will you take me to him?"

"I shall but I do urge you to be gentle. The world is not worthy of this man, but he is a man, after all."

"I assure you my intentions are to bring him solace and satisfaction."

"Very well, then, follow me."

We walked with my horse in tow for the ten blocks between the Red Brick Store and Temple Grove. Along the way, Doctor Richards told me of his conversion, missionary work in England, and other dull tidbits regarding his service to the Church. When we arrived at the Grove, we found Joseph seated under a giant oak on the north side of an open grassy trace. His elbows rested on his knees and his head drooped. He fiddled with a twig. As we approached he jumped to his feet, smiling as if nothing had happened. "Ah, Willard and Mister Freeman, good to see you. No doubt you witnessed the black-hearted efforts to trick me. Think nothing further of it. He is entitled to his opinion, but I found him to be iron-hearted. Though I must at all times be charitable, I cannot engage in debate with obdurate souls. We must pray that his mind will open and his heart be warmed."

"I believe I offered the Saints an explanation that will be of good value henceforth," Doctor Richards said. "I reminded those gathered that you were both a man and a prophet. At times you speak as a man; at times, as a prophet. You can err in the former role but not in the latter."

"I thank you Doctor Richards, I cannot agree with you more. I have never presented myself as infallible. A prophet is only a prophet when acting as such."

"An unsatisfactory argument," I said.

The two men looked at me, taken back by my bold statement.

I met their icy stares. "Permit me to continue," I said. "At first blush, the good doctor's argument appears invincible. However, consider these points. If you make a mistake in anything, dear Prophet, one can simply opine that you are speaking as a man. If you pronounce something that is widely accepted as true and inspired, well then, you are speaking as a prophet. Yet the problem of your credibility still looms large. How often can a prophet, as man, err before his prophecies become suspect? And what if one of your prophecies, proclaimed in your role as God's prophet, turns out later to be in error? How then shall you recover? Moreover, I submit your followers do not make the distinction between Joseph Smith the Prophet and Joseph Smith the Man. For them, you are always the Prophet and, if you will pardon the crudity, they linger on every word that drips from your lips."

Neither man said anything in response.

I raised a forefinger. "There are ways out of these predicaments, of course."

"What do you suggest instead?" Doctor Richards asked.

"To begin, as the power of the Church continues to grow, there will be many cozeners and skinners who will journey to Nauvoo with schemes to trap you. I urge you never to make an immediate pronouncement, no matter what pressures you might feel from your faithful. Always, always take the matter under consideration and gather to yourself those who can confirm whatever impressions you might have of the matter at hand. In other words, prophesy from a position of knowledge."

"Then it is not prophecy," the Prophet said.

"I disagree. Who is to say that prophecy must be impromptu? Must the Holy Ghost only work in the moment, or mightn't He work over a span of time and through the support of faithful followers?"

Joseph Smith studied me with his piercing blue eyes. Suddenly, he threw his head back in a hearty guffaw, put his arm around my shoulder, and led me across the Grove with Doctor Richards in tow.

"You have given me sound advice," Smith said. "I know from Doctor Mercer's description of you that you are an attorney. It is obvious. You could be of great value to me as an advisor. Please join me this evening for one of Emma's fine meals. By the way, have you made a decision on the offer I tendered earlier?"

"Indeed I have. I accept."

CHAPTER EIGHT

Elena

Zion

He's alive! He's alive! Lower a boat!"
I leaned over Dorrie, prostrate on the deck of the Tremont. "Dorrie! Dorrie!" I screamed. "They say Piet's alive. Wake up! A sailor dived in after him. He's shouting he's alive! Wake up!" I slapped her face several times to no avail.

"Here, try this." I looked up to see the ship's apothecary remove a small cylinder from his budget and hand it to me. "It is spirit of hartshorn," he said. "Place the wand under her nose. I must help with the rescue." With that, he raced to the side of the ship where all on deck had gathered to watch the recovery of Piet Van Rijn.

I pulled the cap off the small cylinder and tentatively put it to my own nose. Instantly, I jerked it away and gasped. My eyes watered and I could sense a strange fluttering in my heart. When I caught my breath, I inspected the looped wand affixed to the cap of the vial. I dipped it into the solution and when a bubble had formed in the loop, I held the wand under Dorrie's nose. In a few seconds her cheeks flushed and her eyelids fluttered.

"Dorrie, can you hear me? They say Piet's alive!"

It took her several more seconds to comprehend my meaning and raise herself to a sitting position, still cradled in my arms for support. I repeated my explanation, "One of the sailors jumped in right after Piet fell. They are lowering a boat so they can bring him on deck."

My words lifted Dorrie straight to her feet, and despite her fainting episode, she raced to the side of the deck and pushed her way through the throng. Knowing she was Piet's betrothed, the passengers and crew drew aside to give her passage. I followed in her wake until both of us could look over the side of the deck rail. The rescuing sailor held the unconscious Piet and waited for the lifeboat.

When they had him back on deck, the ship's surgeon called for a litter. "Bear him to the aft cockpit!" he shouted.

The mates wasted no time in laying Piet on a stretcher and carrying him to the rear of the ship. Dorrie followed the litter, grasping my hand and pulling me along with her. Once in the cockpit, the surgeon requested space and began to examine Piet, who lay pale and unconscious on a feather-tick mattress. The surgeon opened Piet's eyes, moved his limbs, and performed other assessments that I did not understand. Ten agonizing minutes later, the surgeon stood and turned to the captain, who waited among us.

"I fear his back is broken," the surgeon said. "His breathing is deep and regular. I reckon he will awaken in the next few hours. I will know more then. Let us leave him under the scrutiny of these mates. They will notify us when he awakens."

"I will stay with him," Dorrie said.

The surgeon glanced at the captain who nodded his approval.

"Very well, then," the surgeon said. "The rest of you must go."

On the upper deck, I spotted Da standing with Arthur Walmsley. I ran into my Da's outstretched arms.

"Oh, Da," I whimpered, "they say his back is broken."

"Do they know for certain, girl?" I could feel the gentle pats of his big hand between my shoulder blades.

"That's what the surgeon said. Piet's not yet awake. The surgeon will know more when he comes to."

"How is Miss Littlejohn?" Arthur asked.

"In great tribulation," I said. "She is with him now. The rest of us were asked to leave."

"Aw'll ask the bishop to gather us for prayer," Da said when I finally eased out of his arms.

"Very good," Arthur said. "I shall begin to direct the Saints to the forecastle deck."

Just then, the decks lurched and I had to grab both Da and Arthur to keep from falling. In our concern for Piet, we had been unaware that the steam tug from New Orleans had arrived. A cable had been attached to our bow, and we were being towed through the silt toward the Mississippi River and on to New Orleans.

With the ship moving smoothly again, we gathered to pray for Piet's recovery. Bishop Greene led us in a long prayer of intercession followed by that wonderful hymn from my Methodist days, *Love Divine, All Loves Excelling.* When we came to the phrase, *Breathe, O breathe thy loving Spirit into every troubled breast*, the words choked in my throat. Da placed his hand on the small of my back.

"I shall repair to Piet's bedside for anointing and prayers of healing," Bishop Greene announced as our gathering dispersed. Da gave me a brief squeeze on the shoulder and followed the other men down to the cockpit. Along with most of the other passengers, I took a spot at the ship's rail. There we watched our entry into the Southwest Pass toward the main body of the great Mississippi River, the Father of Waters. Despite my worries over Piet, I could not help but feel excitement welling in my breast as we passed so close to land for the first time in many weeks (though to be honest it was more water than land). The tug churned on, slowing as we proceeded through the passage marked by wooden buoys in steel frames. They looked much like barrels and I later learned they were called cask buoys. Pilots periodically reset them to mark a safe course in the shifting terrain below the surface of the water. After about an hour in the Southwest Passage, Da returned to my side at the deck rail.

"How is he?" I asked.

"Still asleep, Lanie girl. Aw'm quite worried about 'im. But we give 'im the anointin' oils an all."

"And how is Dorrie faring?"

"Tha' girl is a brick, Lanie, stayin' right with 'im, moppin' 'is fore'ead, an' pattin' 'is 'and. 'E's a fortunate lad to 'ave 'er, Aw'd say."

"Most fortunate indeed."

The day wore on as we made slow but steady progress through the dangerous channel. By evening, we had drawn near to the main riverbed of the Mississippi and the water deepened. Just as we were passing through the mouth of the Southwest Pass, one of the surgeon's mates approached to tell me that Dorrie was calling for me. I raced down to the cockpit, anxious to see my friend and to lend what comfort I could.

When she saw me enter, Dorrie leapt to her feet and raced into my arms. "Oh Lanie, Lanie. There is no depth to my woe!" And with that she unstoppered her grief and wept for many long minutes. When her tears receded, she accepted my handkerchief. I kept my right arm around her shoulder, cradling her as she dabbed her eyes and sniffled herself into composure.

"Any change?" I asked.

She shook her head. "His eyes fluttered once, but he did not come fully awake. I do not think he knew I was by his side."

"Has the surgeon offered more information?"

Again she shook her head.

"Would you like me to stay with him while you go topside for some fresh air. We are entering the Mississippi River."

"No, I want to be here when he wakes up."

Tears brimmed in her eyes once more. "Lanie, what am I to do?"

I had no answer.

At twilight, the *Tremont* came to a full stop in the middle of the river. We heard the anchor chain clanking through the hull. I followed the other passengers to the starboard rail to see the tug casting off and steaming upstream without us. We had no explanation for this unexpected stop. The murmurs and grumblings of the Saints were assuaged some time later when word passed through the crowd that we were to wait overnight until two other ships arrived. A larger tug would tow all three ships into port. The delay disappointed me but I accepted our circumstances and returned to the tween deck and what I hoped would be our final night aboard ship. I was ready to set my feet on solid ground once again. On the shores of America, no less!

I spent a night of shallow and unsatisfying sleep. Several times I checked to see if Dorrie were in her bed but she had not returned. I prayed for Piet's recovery, hoping for a miracle. Didn't the Saints claim that miracles had returned to the earth? When I arose for the day and completed my morning toilet I returned to the port rail to watch our journey up the Mississippi. Da and Arthur Walmsley joined me. The two other sailing ships had come alongside and a steam tug began dragging us upriver. I marveled at this small tug towing three ocean-going ships without apparent strain.

Several miles later, we encountered the strangest assortment of dwellings I had ever seen. One of the crew informed us that we were passing by a town called Pilotsville. He told us further that the ramshackle houses were perched on stilts to elevate them above the soggy soil below and to prevent swamping during heavy storms. Platforms connected these wooden hovels. Pilotsville, we learned, was home to river pilots and their families. In its earliest decades, it was a dangerous place with all manner of debauchery and crime. Several murders occurred each night and no self-respecting citizen would dare enter its precincts. Now, however, it was a much more savory place as evidenced by the many women and children visible on the stoops and planks connecting the elevated huts. In the distance I beheld the steeple of a church.

Later, as I was cleaning my dinner dishes, Bishop Greene came near to me and whispered, "May I see you for a moment, Miss Arkwright?"

"Of course," I said.

He drew me away from the others and said, "I have spoken to the Captain about Mister Van Rijn's condition and now need to speak with Miss Littlejohn. She has requested you to be present."

"Certainly," I said. "May I assume Piet has awakened?"

"He has but I've not seen him."

I followed Bishop Greene to his quarters.

"Let's all be seated," the Bishop said.

I wasted no time sitting beside Dorrie.

"As I've mentioned," Bishop Greene said, "I have spoken to the Captain who has received a report from the surgeon."

We held our breath.

"Miss Littlejohn, Mister Van Rijn has awakened, and you have talked with him? Is this correct?"

Dorrie nodded.

"What has the surgeon told you of his condition?" Bishop Greene asked.

"Nothing," she said.

Bishop Greene took a deep breath, girding himself for what he must next disclose.

"The surgeon has informed the Captain that Mister Van Rijn has a broken back. It is broken low down on the spine. He will recover and live but he will suffer paralysis of the lower body, the legs…and all." Dorrie gasped. I pulled her more tightly to me. "He can no longer serve as an able-bodied seaman and will be released from his duties. The Captain is bound by orders to return him to Liverpool where he was hired. However, I have told him that Mister Van Rijn wishes to join our Church. The Captain has agreed to release Mister Van Rijn to us if he elects not to return to Liverpool."

"Does Piet know this?" I asked.

"At this very moment, the Captain is informing him of his options."

"Well, then, he will come with us!" Dorrie said. "We are to be married. Returning to England is not an option."

Bishop Greene looked at Dorrie, his face twisted in apprehension.

"Miss Littlejohn, you must understand..." Bishop Greene paused, "How can I..." He looked helplessly at me.

"Bishop Greene," I said, "perhaps it would be best if I told her in private."

He nodded and in great relief, excused himself from his own quarters.

"Tell me what?" Dorrie asked.

I took her hands in mine. "What Bishop Greene is trying to say," I said, "is that should you and Piet marry, the union may not be consummated."

Dorrie drew away from me. "What are you saying?"

"That Piet's paralysis appears *complete* from the waist down."

Her eyes widened in sudden comprehension. "Oh," she said and looked down at the rumpled handkerchief in her hands. Short seconds later, she looked up and fixed me with a gaze of complete resolve. "It matters not. A broken back won't stop me from loving him."

"You realize you may be a wife who cannot bear children?"

She nodded. "That will be our cross to bear."

"It wouldn't surprise me, Piet being the man he is, that he will try to break the engagement."

"Whatever for? I love him whether he can walk or not."

"He may try to spare you, to open the opportunities for what he will see as a more fulfilling life for you."

"I won't allow it," she said. "That is final."

Her voice was barely audible, but I admired her courage. I could not myself imagine living in such an incomplete marriage nor did I grasp what she was feeling because I had never loved nor been loved by another man. My occasional affections, such as the one for Doctor Richards, surely did not constitute the fully blossomed love that Dorrie had for Piet Van Rijn. She took a deep breath, leaned over and kissed me on the cheek.

"As I have so often repeated, you are a wonderful friend, Lanie.

Now I must go to Piet."

+ + +

Bishop Greene gathered the Saints around the forecastle deck in the last hours before docking. There he gave us instructions on what to expect when arriving ashore. An agent would be waiting to help us find suitable quarters. Some of the faithful had no funds for further travel up the Mississippi. They would be staying in New Orleans to find work, relying upon the charity of local people. Thanks to prudence in delaying our departure from England, Da and I had enough money to continue our journey. We were informed that the *Goddess of Liberty* would leave New Orleans in early afternoon of the following day. This seemed propitious to us. While we were excited to see the great port city of New Orleans, we were also anxious to complete our voyage and begin our new life in Nauvoo.

As Bishop Greene concluded his briefing, I searched the crowd for Dorrie. She was nowhere among us. I assumed she would still be with Piet in the cockpit. I excused myself from Da, Arthur, and the others to go in search of her. To my relief, Dorrie's spirits had lifted when she ushered me into the room. Piet sat propped with pillows, quite awake and sipping a cup of tea. I noticed his arm was in a sling.

"Piet," I said, "It jubilates me to see you awake and taking some nourishment. I know what happened to your back. What happened to your arm?"

"Not my arm," he said. "I haff a busted collar bone, vitch de surcheon discovered in his examination. He says it vill heal on its own but I haff to vear dis sling."

"Are you suffering?"

"De collar bone pains me like de devil. Since I've been avake I haff dis low burning in my legs. I can't feel a pinprick but I can feel dis deep burn. Don't kvite seem fair dat I can't move my legs but I still got dat burnin' down derr."

I nodded and glanced up at Dorrie who bore an unexpected and incongruous smile.

I cocked my head.

"All is well," she said. "Piet and I had a glorious argument last night. He tried to break off our engagement. Out of sheer nobility and chivalry, as you predicted. He was, of course, thinking only of me." At this point, she ran her fingers through his hair to which he looked up at her, reciprocating with a smile. I noted that none of the Mormon chaperones were present. They must have assumed Piet was no longer a threat to Dorrie's chastity. I withered within knowing they were correct, that she was *safe*.

Dorrie continued. "I would have none of his gallantry and thus the battle lines were drawn. We fought like two harts in the field and I am happy to say I was the victor." She thrust her fist in the air. "Piet and I will be married soon upon our arrival at Nauvoo."

"Oh, Dorrie! I am so happy for you. Hail to the victor!"

At this we all laughed.

I imparted the information given to us by Bishop Greene. Piet told us that he would stay on board one more night after the rest of us had disembarked. He would be issued his severance pay, discharged, and given over to the custody of the Saints. As we talked, a sharp knock sounded on the entry to the cockpit. Bishop Greene entered, tipping his hat to Dorrie and me.

"Miss Arkwright, Miss Littlejohn, Mister Van Rijn, I bid you good afternoon. Perhaps Miss Arkwright has explained that the *Goddess of Liberty* will embark tomorrow afternoon. I presume all of you will be aboard?"

We affirmed that we would.

Elder Greene knelt down and placed his hand on Piet's shoulder. "Mister Van Rijn, I have come to give you some comfortable words. Great misfortune has been visited upon you and for this I am most sorrowful. However, the Saints care for their own and, though you have yet to be baptized, we view you as one of us. Therefore, you should rest in the assurance that we will provide for you..." He looked up at Dorrie. "...and for Miss Littlejohn should she become your wife."

"She *vill* become my vife," Piet said, without hesitation.

Bishop Greene smiled, "I am pleased to hear this. I have appointed four men to look after you once you are released into our hands. I shall bring them by later so you can make their acquaintance if you have not already come to know them. They are young, strong, and eager to help. Of course, I have no doubt Miss Littlejohn will be of considerable assistance as well."

Before taking his leave, Bishop Greene offered a short prayer of thanksgiving for the sparing of Piet's life, for courage, and for God's protection on the journey to Zion. I too departed, much comforted by the scene just concluded. I could now enjoy, at least in part, the final minutes of our voyage as we rounded a large bend in the river and beheld New Orleans. Ship masts, church steeples, and tall buildings, splintered the horizon. The great city was at hand.

+ + +

It is an indescribably strange sensation, after weeks of rolling, lurching, quaking, and swaying, to set foot on the solid planking of a pier. As with most of my fellow passengers, we all stood still for a few moments, dizzy in our immobility. After a few tentative steps, with shouts of joy, we gathered around a rough-hewn man known by the name of *Agent Ez* (his name was Ezra Dawes). He arranged us in suitable groups and directed us to safe housing in the nearby neighborhoods. Five other women, Dorrie, and I were directed to the large home of a mariner's widow some six blocks from the pier. As evening drew nigh, we decided to make our way to this house while we still had light to guide the way. Da and Arthur Walmsley, joined by several other men, moved to a boarding house often used by seamen. We bade farewell to one another and dispersed into the city.

Our little group walked up a wide street called Jackson Avenue. Small narrow houses flanked either side of the street. We learned that many Negroes in New Orleans were free people and they had built these strange homes. We waved at the Negros sitting on the porches of the narrow houses. Most waved back, but some looked upon us with wary eyes. This was a new experience for most of us who had seldom seen a person with black skin. To our surprise, we had seen no evidence of slavery. Black people swarmed the pier, but we saw not one in a set of leg chains nor did we hear the crack of a single whip. We wondered if the horror stories we had been told were true.

As we continued along Jackson Street, the small, narrow houses gave way to much more elegant homes. At Magazine Street we turned left and beheld a white two-story house topped with a turret. A widow's walk encircled the turret, sadly fitting since this was the Widow Lozeau's home. Dressed in black, with a black bonnet and black gloves, the Widow welcomed us to her house with a wan smile and quiet grace. Sadness permeated the dwelling and we could only suppose that the widowing of Mrs. Lozeau had ushered in this melancholic air. Dorrie and I were to be housed with two other unmarried women on the second floor in a room crowded with two soft beds arranged side-by-side. We surmised that the Widow Lozeau had been forced to take in boarders upon the death of her husband, which led to rooms overcrowded with beds. However, the overcrowding did not bother us in the least. Sleeping on a soft bed in a well-appointed home was an unimaginable luxury.

Darkness had descended upon New Orleans and out of concern for our safety, we all decided to stay in the Widow Lozeau's home until morning. She provided for us some freshly baked bread with currant preserves, an old French recipe she called *Lorraine Jelly*. To this she added glasses of rose water with sprigs of fresh mint. This simple repast was of such elegance that we imagined ourselves in the very cradle of paradise. We inhaled the scents of the food, eating and drinking slowly to savor the flavors. Mrs. Faircloth, one of the matrons of the voyage and herself a widow, dismissed us to our rooms with a prayer of thanksgiving. She added intercessions for safety in travel and healing for Piet Van Rijn.

The morning descended upon us pregnant with moisture in black and pendulous clouds. In the distance, thunder rolled like a giant's ball in a celestial game of skittles. Our conversations were subdued and uneasy as we all hoped the ominous weather would not delay our departure on the *Goddess of Liberty*. After a light breakfast of oatmeal and dark sugar bathed in cold cream, we made our way back down Jackson Street to the teeming pier of New Orleans. I had arranged to meet Da and Arthur at the gangplank of the Tremont. Dorrie accompanied me because she planned to wait for Piet to leave the ship.

"A pleasant good morrow to thee," Da said when he saw us approaching. "Aw hope thee fared well up in the 'igh class distric'."

"It was lovely. And you, Da, sleep soundly?"

"Aw did. Aw did. What would thee say, Lanie girl, to a stroll 'round the place to see w'at we can see?"

"That would be nice," I said, hoping the rain would hold off for a time.

Dorrie excused herself leaving the three of us to investigate this new land that had now become our country. We were about a quarter of a mile through the riverfront district admiring the boisterous industry of these Americans and the many languages that assailed our ears. To be sure, we detected scores of English words but they were embedded in dialects that rendered their meaning virtually unintelligible.

"W'at did 'e say?" Da would ask. Often Arthur could translate the phrase, but not always.

Presently, we came to an open-air building, under roof, walled in the back. Along the back wall, on benches raised two feet above the wood-plank floor, stood thirteen Negros, seven men and six women. The men shifted, uncomfortable in their ill-fitting suits. The women, clad in long dresses of bright color and calico bandannas, stared at the floor. A white man in top hat and coat tails strode back and forth in front of the benches admonishing the Negros and occasionally striking one or another with a whip to enforce the posture and demeanor he demanded. As he thus paced to and fro, he would stop, extol the virtues – strength, intelligence, virility, servility, skill, whatever – to the several gentlemen bent on a bargain in human flesh.

We had chanced upon slavery at last.

"Have a look at this one, George by name, strong as an ox he is," the dealer barked. "George is yours for a mere seven hundred dollars. Or what about Eliza here? A fine cook and domestic. And look here," he jerked her head down to his level and pried her mouth open. "Gots all her teeth, every one. What'll you give for Eliza?"

We stared in horrid fascination as one buyer walked up to Eliza and jerked her dress up to within inches of her waist. He squeezed her calf, then her thigh. "Sturdy legs," he said.

I don't know what outraged me more, the impropriety of his fondling her leg or the inhumanity with which he inspected her.

"Need a cook," the buyer said. "Give you three-fifty."

"My good man, I could not sell such a fine specimen for a mere three-fifty. Five hundred will fetch her."

"Four hundred."

"Four-fifty."

The buyer flinched and turned to walk away.

"Four-twenty-five and she's yours," the dealer shouted.

"Very well," said the man.

At that moment, Eliza let out a high-pitched keen that split the humid sky. She jumped from the bench and ran to one of the men and clutched him around the legs.

"Buy us bof' massa, buy us bof. He my husban'. He Anton. He smart an' strong. See…"

Eliza jerked his sleeve up to reveal rippling muscles.

The dealer erupted in anger, jerked Eliza away from Anton and whipped her back to her position. Her caterwauling continued unabated. I looked up at Anton and beheld an expression of such helpless agony that I could no longer contain myself. The injustice and degeneration cracked something deep within me. I broke from the crowd and threw myself at the dealer, grabbing him around the arms and imploring him to stop beating Eliza. In my fury I kept screaming, "You can't separate them! They are man and wife! Stop whipping her! Stop this lunacy!"

Da and Arthur jumped forward to restrain me but before they could pull me off the dealer, he had twisted to face me.

"What manner of madness is this?" he hollered. "Get this witch off of me!" He freed his hand, grabbed the collar of my dress, and threw me to the ground. My head crashed against the edge of the raised bench knocking me nearly unconscious. Anton leaned forward in an effort to assist me but caught himself, gave me a look of sorrow, and drew himself up again, unwilling to risk intervention. When my head cleared I saw Da clutch the dealer by the throat and, in one fierce movement of his arm, throw the man to the ground as if he had no more substance than a scarecrow. Da fell upon the man and tightened the vice on his throat.

"Ye foul cur!" Da said through snarled lips. "Ye touch me girl again an' Aw'll choke the livin' breath right outta thee."

The dealer's lips faded to blue and his eyes widened in terror. I joined Arthur and several others who had come to rescue the dealer. If I had not known it before, at that moment, I came to appreciate anew Da's uncommon strength. Removing him from the dealer was like lifting a tombstone. Da would not loosen his grip and it took six of us to pull him away from his quarry. I began to panic for fear Da might actually kill the man.

"Elder Arkwright!" Arthur shouted in a voice that rose above the clamor. "Please, sir, remember your station! You are an ordained priest in the Church…a priest of the Order of Aaron."

That did it. Those words sunk in and slowly Da loosened his grip. The dealer choked and gasped, sucking in large volumes of air. Arthur and I helped Da to his feet. Several of the townspeople lifted the dealer and carried him to a chair near the merchandise benches. Recovering his senses, the dealer pointed to Da.

"Grab him! Grab that crazy plug-ugly son of a whore!"

Arthur took Da aside and spoke to him in words of counsel I could not hear. Da nodded. After several minutes, he drew himself up and walked over to where the dealer sat.

"Aw've come to ask thy forgiveness," he said. "Aw lost me grip there. Jesus taught forgive an t' seek forgiveness. Aw've failed to do that and 'ave come to extend me 'and in apology. Aw do 'ope ye'll find it in thy heart t' forgive me."

Da stretched out his hand. The dealer looked at it as if it were filled with goose dung.

"Git this crazy old coot away from me!" he screamed.

Da left his hand in an extended position, waiting. The dealer became silent but did not accept the apology. Slowly, Da turned to rejoin Arthur and me. With our hearts still pounding, we slipped away from the silent crowd.

"Aw'm truly sorrowful about w'at 'appened back there," Da said, shaking his head. "Aw don' rightly know w'at go' into me."

I shook my head in sympathy. "Nor do I Da. I've never lost the hold on my temper in such a way before. I did not know I was capable of such, such...but when that dealer…"

"Do not fret yourself," Arthur said. "Righteous anger is not un-Christian."

"It feels like the Devil has gotten into me."

"I shouldn't think so," Arthur said.

We walked on in silence.

"What do you suppose will happen to Anton and Eliza?" I asked.

"Nothing good, I fear," said Arthur. "Even if both of them are purchased by that beast of a man. He is cruel and mean-tempered."

"Perhaps the sale fell apart," I said.

"We can only 'ope. We can only 'ope," said Da.

Upon our return to the pier, we began our search for the *Goddess of Liberty*. The irony struck me. In this land of freedom, where liberty is celebrated even in the naming of a steamboat, we had just witnessed a crushing disregard for human sovereignty and dignity. This dreadful crimp in the fabric of American life was made yet worse in the guise of respectable commerce. I walked on in the isolation of my own mind, mulling the implications of one human being buying, selling, owning, and subjugating another. Just then, the clouds opened and rain poured down upon us as if God were shedding His very own tears of sorrow.

+ + +

In due time, the weather cleared and the *Goddess of Liberty* awaited us in majestic repose. Her two red smokestacks rose high above the hurricane deck. The railings, paddlebox, pilothouse, and walls, all painted a glossy white, gave the vessel a fresh, pristine appearance. Two men on the boiler deck played a strange instrument called a *banjar* and sang *Yankee Doodle*. Negros, whether slave or free I couldn't tell, rolled barrels onto the main deck. Others toted cotton bales aboard. Fruit and vegetable vendors hawked their produce.

"Lanie! Look. Aw b'lieve 'at man is sellin' pineapples. Aw 'aven't 'ad a slice o' pineapple in Aw don' know 'ow long! Aw'd favor getting' one and each o' us 'avin' a slice or two. Wha' say ye, Lanie girl, an' thee also Arthur?"

"Sure, Da. That would be lovely."

"A right smart idea," Arthur said.

We purchased a pineapple, which Da sliced open with his penny knife. The fruit was juicy and delicious. I savored each bite and, when finished, I threw manners to the wind and licked the syrup from my fingers.

"Did you know," Arthur asked between flicks of his little tongue between his fingers, "that the pineapple is a symbol of hospitality?" Not waiting for our answer, he carried on. "According to legend, the early American sea captains put a pineapple on a pike or fence post outside their homes to let all know they had returned safely home. Since then, it has become a symbol of hospitality."

"And a good omen, I hope," I added.

As the morning wore on, more of our company arrived. Out of the original one hundred and forty-three Saints, plus two babies born on the Atlantic, only ninety would board the *Goddess of Liberty*. Most of us would spend our time on the main deck sleeping amid the cotton bales without benefit of mattress or blanket. The *Goddess* was overcrowded and, despite the Captain's assurances that we would sail hard for Saint Louis, we had to prepare ourselves for a miserable few days. Several of us did arrange a small cubicle of bales with some available blankets for Piet Van Rijn. Dorrie would stay by his side. The bishops no longer made an effort to separate the men and women. Perhaps they assumed that fraternization was an ocean phenomenon never practiced on the rivers of America.

Aside from rather brutish conditions – a lack of sleep and disgusting food – our trip up the lower Mississippi passed without incident. Da, Arthur, and several of the other men took great interest in the practice of sounding the river to determine safe channels through which to navigate the boat. Since the river ran high in the spring, sounding occurred once or twice a day. The process required us to tie up to shore. A yawl would then be dispatched with a pilot and several oarsmen. An officer on deck would identify what appeared to be good water and direct the pilot in the yawl to the location with a series of gestures and whistles. The pilot would probe for the bottom with a long staff. When a safe channel was detected, a buoy was deployed. The oarsmen then raised their oars as a signal to proceed and we were again on our way heading to the buoy and beyond.

The steamboat leapfrogged its way up the lower Mississippi, stopping at river towns great and small. I remember many of them: Donaldsonville, Saint Francisville, Natchez, Sparta, Villemont, Helena, Memphis, Fulton, New Madrid, Kaskaskia, and, of course, Saint Louis. Many of these towns looked stately and inviting from the river but our leaders warned us that they were often dangerous places to be. At night, thieves, rowdies, and all manner of n'er-do-wells lurked in the dark places ready to take advantage of naïve and unguarded passengers. For this reason, we stayed on board most evenings or ventured forth in large groups to find edible food or other necessaries. We were also told to expect persecution, for the Latter Day Saints were not popular among the Gentiles in America. However, to our relief, we did not suffer any such indignities on the lower Mississippi.

We approached Saint Louis in high excitement because it marked the end of our journey on the *Goddess*. Our itinerary called for us to stay two days in this bustling city before boarding the Saints' own steamboat, the *Maid of Iowa*, for the last leg of our journey. The city was much larger than I had anticipated. Steamboats, barges, and tenders clogged the waterfront. Several factories spewed black columns of smoke, warehouses yawned with open doors, and the steeples of many churches pricked the sky. Upon arrival, we were met by a group of Saints who stood ready to take in boarders. Our first concern was Piet, and we made certain he and the four appointed caretakers had suitable lodging in one of the homes. About twenty of us remained unassigned and had to settle for beds arranged in a warehouse. Da, Arthur, Dorrie, and I were among this last group and, though disappointed by our circumstances, we knew that we could survive almost anything for two nights.

The mattresses in the warehouse were filthy, and we despaired of sleeping in them so we stayed up late into the night. Dorrie spent the first evening with Piet returning to the warehouse about ten o'clock, escorted by two of his caretakers. We had purchased some fresh beef in the bustling Soulard Market and roasted it with potatoes right in the warehouse. We had enough left over from this satisfactory supper to offer Dorrie a warm meal upon her return.

"I'm very worried about Piet," Dorrie said as she finished her last bite of potato.

"What troubles you?" I asked.

"I think the reality of his circumstance has come to full roost in his mind. For the first days after the accident, he seemed happy to be alive. Now, he foresees his future as one of invalidity and dependency. In his own mind, he is a useless husk and has said as much in his lowest moments. I've tried to give him every encouragement and urged him to pray with me."

"And does he pray with you?"

"He bows his head, closes his eyes, and listens to my petitions but I fear his heart is not in it. Each day he seems to grow weaker and his spirits more depressed. I don't know what more I can do."

"You've done all you can be expected to do," I said, "and you need some relief yourself. You've attended him now nearly every waking hour since he fell. While I laud your love and commitment, you must think of yourself as well."

Dorrie nodded, but I was certain she did not accept what I said.

"I have an idea," I said. "They tell us Saint Louis is a safe city, and it appears so. Mightn't we consider a leisurely walk in the morning to stretch our legs and clear our heads?"

"Oh, I don't think I shall. Piet will be expecting me."

"Piet will survive a couple of hours without you, my dear. It would be good for you to have a constitutional. What do you say?"

"We'll see," she said.

The next morning, after we withdrew ourselves from the vermin-infested beds, I managed to persuade Dorrie to take a walk with me. Arthur volunteered to notify Piet that Dorrie would be along later in the morning. We coursed up and down Water Street, stopping to admire the merchandise displayed in the many shop windows. We entered a confectionery to take in the smells of sweetmeats and candied nuts. I bought Dorrie a Turkish delight hoping it would buoy her spirits. Perhaps it did for a short time but soon her bearing sagged again. We continued to walk, straying as far west as Third Street. There Dorrie became restless and urged our return to the riverfront so she could resume her vigil at Piet's side. I agreed and as we were proceeding to the end of the block, I noticed a sign for *Lewis Crabtree – Bookseller and Literary Promoter.*

"Oh Dorrie! A bookshop. Could we stop for just a moment? Then we'll be on our way, I promise."

Reluctantly, Dorrie agreed. My soaring spirits were dashed however, when I saw a *Closed* sign in the window. Just as we were passing by, two men emerged from the bookshop. One was quite handsome with gold-rimmed spectacles and graying temples. The other, sporting a long black beard with two braids, walked with an ill-tempered scowl. The first man nodded to us. For a moment and for reasons I cannot explain, I suspected he and his companion were Saints but they were gone before I could query them on the matter.

The door to the shop opened again, and the clerk removed the *Closed* sign. He nodded to us upon entry but said nothing. Dorrie had little interest in literature and turned her attention to the repair of a bent spoke on her parasol. I perused the many books in stock until at last my eyes fell upon a display copy of a newly published book by Ralph Waldo Emerson. I had no familiarity with his writings but Arthur had told me that America had produced some fine literary lights such as Washington Irving, William Cullen Bryant, James Fenimore Cooper, and Emerson, of course. Thus, I was intrigued and began to peruse the pages of the display copy when I chanced upon an essay entitled, *Self Reliance.*

As I skimmed the paragraphs of the essay, the clerk, a tall red-haired man with a harelip and slight limp approached me and asked me what I was reading. I pointed to a paragraph about great men and shared with him my belief that the description fit our Prophet. He found my assessment weak and inconsistent with Emerson's main argument, which flummoxed me. I am certain embarrassment shone upon my face. I prepared to make a hasty exit when the man offered me the book at no charge. I could not believe his generosity and protested, but not too vigorously for I wanted to have a copy to study in greater depth. I accepted the gift with gratitude and bade the clerk farewell.

When we had rounded the corner of Third Street on our way back to the waterfront, Dorrie said, "You and that strange clerk certainly got on well."

"He was most generous. And obviously quite intelligent despite his disfigurement."

"Perhaps he took a fancy to you."

"Don't be light-minded."

"Didn't you see the way he looked at you?"

"He was merely interested in argument."

"I think not. His eyes were all over you."

"But Dorrie, did you see his eyes? I mean really see them?"

"They were blue."

"But that's not all. They were…how shall I put it? Vacant, absent."

"Now *you* are being light-minded."

"Perhaps but his stare thoroughly discomfited me."

+ + +

If we had not suffered persecution on the lower Mississippi, we surely did on the leg from Saint Louis to Nauvoo. In several of the towns along the river, mobs shouted insults and profane slurs from the riverbanks – *Joe's Rats, Gospel Perverters, Barbarians.* In one town, Gilead, Illinois, several young men tossed lighted torches on our decks and pitched large rocks through the windows of the *Maid.* As our men raced to extinguish the torches, the Captain of the *Maid,* a fiery Welshman named Dan Jones, trained his musket on the ringleader. "Ye best back off or I'll shoot ye filthy dogs one-by-one, so help me God, I will!" His warning had its intended effect. The troublemakers slinked away.

Five days after our departure from Saint Louis, the *Maid* coursed through a westward bend in the river and there before us lay our destination – the city of Zion – Nauvoo! The steamboat erupted in shouts of joy. We carried Piet up to the boiler deck to join the other Saints clamoring for the first glimpse of their new home.

"Look Lanie girl! A crowd o' th' faithful is awaitin' our 'rival. Canst thou believe such a thin'? Aw'm beside meself, Lanie. Nauvoo at last!"

Da bounced up and down on his toes and I could not suppress a smile. We were all shouting *huzzah* and *hallelujah*. Even Piet seemed to sit more upright in his chair. The Saints ashore waved as the *Maid* drew near to the southern landing. We could see handsome brick and clapboard houses, stores, shops, and public halls arranged along broad, tree-lined streets. The first story of our long-awaited Temple had already been completed and its limestone walls glimmered in the afternoon sunlight. We marveled at the energy and productiveness of the citizens who had, in just a few years, created a city far superior to most of the towns we had passed along our river journey. And then we heard it. Those gathered ashore were singing a hymn to welcome us, my favorite Mormon hymn, *The Spirit of God Like a Fire is Burning*. Tears burst from my eyes and as I looked around, I could see that I was by no means alone. Even my strong old Da was wiping his eyes with his club-like hands.

Once ashore, we were rushed by our fellow Saints who hugged us, shook our hands, and clapped us on the back. They gave us such a gracious welcome that I felt we had stepped onto the very porch of heaven. Many of those who greeted us were old friends. I was most pleased when Doctor Willard Richards, my old discussant and his wife Jennetta, made a special effort to seek us out in the crowd. I felt no envy for Jennetta and as I gazed upon the swollen torso of Doctor Richards, I wondered what might have once attracted me to him. I felt a measure of peace to think of them now as friends.

"I look forward to some more evenings of conversation and debate with you," he said, and I assured him I would be delighted with such an opportunity.

Brother Wilford Woodruff paid us special attention and nodded to me in recognition, though I don't think he realized how important he had been in my conversion to Mormonism. As we were thus surrounded by our brothers and sisters in the faith, I looked up to see a tall man with sandy blond hair moving through the crowd. I knew at once that he was none other than our Prophet, Joseph Smith. He walked toward us. Honeybees buzzed in my stomach. He greeted Da and Arthur with hearty handshakes and a shoulder clap that nearly toppled Arthur. He turned to me. He took my hands and fixed his blue-green eyes on me. I stopped breathing.

"In the name of Jesus Christ, I welcome you, Sister Arkwright."

He knew my name! I thought I would faint. His strong hands held me until the spell passed and with a squeeze of my hands, he moved on. I remembered the words from Fanny Chadderton's letter, *I felt as if I had touched the very hand of God.*

PART TWO

For every one of the house of Israel, or of the stranger that sojourneth in Israel, which separateth himself from me, and setteth up his idols in his heart, and putteth the stumblingblock of his iniquity before his face and cometh to a prophet to enquire of him concerning me; I the Lord will answer him by myself.

Ezekiel 14:7

And again, as pertaining to the law of the priesthood — if any man espouse a virgin, and desire to espouse another, and the first give her consent, and if he espouse the second, and they are virgins, and have vowed to no other man, then is he justified; he cannot commit adultery for they are given unto him; for he cannot commit adultery with that that belongeth unto him and to no one else. And if he have ten virgins given unto him by this law, he cannot commit adultery, for they belong to him, and they are given unto him; therefore he is justified.

Doctrine and Covenants 132:61-62
Church of Jesus Christ of Latter Day Saints

CHAPTER NINE

Kevil

Counselor

After a restful first night in my new house, I awoke to see droves of people on horseback, in carriage, and on foot speed toward the center of Nauvoo. Remembering it was Sunday, I donned my breeches, blouse, peacock blue cravat, waistcoat, leather shoes, and calfskin gloves. I rode to the Grove west of the Temple, where I assumed I would join a religious service. Attending a religious service of the Latter Day Saints held no appeal whatsoever. However, on this occasion, curiosity trumped disdain. I scanned the congregation and, to my great surprise, I spotted Porter Rockwell standing next to the Prophet. He shifted uneasily on his feet and stroked the right braid of his long black beard. Rockwell must have arrived from Independence the previous evening after the Caswall affair had come to its embarrassing conclusion.

Within minutes of my arrival, a choir began singing a series of hymns. Given the rude environment and lack of instrumental accompaniment, I found the performance more than passable. When the notes of the last hymn faded into the cool morning air, a stern old man with white hair intoned a long and tedious prayer.

"We come to thee in thanksgiving, O Heavenly Father, for the restoration in these last days, for the great signs and wonders you have bestowed upon us…"

At this point, I stopped listening. When the prayer finally ended ten minutes later, I asked a man standing near me to identify this long-winded intercessor.

"That is our Stake President, William Marks," he said, annoyed by my interruption.

I paid the man no further heed because Joseph Smith had walked to the center of the makeshift platform. He made no mention of religion or spirituality, but launched into an unabashed appeal for money to continue work on his inn, the so-called Nauvoo House. "I remind you that one year, three months, and twenty-six days ago, I received a revelation to build a house unto the Lord, a house for the boarding of strangers, a house where strangers from afar may come to dwell therein. We have not sufficient funds for the completion of this house. I command that ye should not be backward in contributing to the building up of this house, so that we may shelter the kings and nobles of the world."

He droned on for several more minutes and I was about to take my leave when he switched his topic and caught my attention.

"Brethren and sisters, I have important news to bear to you. I have lately received word that the vengeance of the Lord has been visited upon Governor Lilburn Boggs, our avowed enemy. He has been assassinated."

A collective gasp flushed the air followed by shouts of joy and acclamation. Final confirmation. My mission had succeeded. I smiled and slipped away from the jubilant crowd.

I returned home and fifteen minutes later heard a knock on the door. There on my porch with a bottle of whiskey stood Orrin Porter Rockwell.

"Figgered we could get into a bit o' celebration," he said.

I ushered him into the relaxin' room.

"I thought you Saints were to avoid strong spirits."

"Bah! I reckon they's rules, and they's suggestions. I b'lieve the Prophet was makin' a suggestion on the matter of spirits. I'll not give up whiskey unless our great Prophet directly commands me to and mayhap not even then. Let's sit an' have a dram or two."

Rockwell's demeanor amused me. The sullen and bad-tempered man who visited me at Lewis Crabtree's had disappeared. Before me, nearly dancing in delight, stood a jovial and high-spirited imp. I retrieved two glasses from the cupboard and allowed Rockwell to pour a few fingers in each. As we sipped the whiskey, he told me of his travels since last we met.

"Reckon I should tell you," he said, pausing to take another sip and giggle. "Hee. Hee. Ole Boggs wa'n't quite daid when I left

Indypendence"

I raised my eyebrows and took a further sip. "The Prophet just said he was dead."

"Oh, I'll wager he is by now. I lingered a spell and picked up some snatches o' the story from thems what gathered 'round his house right after you done shot him. Ole Boggs's brother's a doctor an' he come right away along with a couple more o' his doctor friends. They hauled Boggs out on the porch. Guess he was jabberin' away jest like normal even though you filled him with balls from that big pepperbox. Hee. Hee. Last word afore I lit outta there was that ole Boggs wasn't farin' well and likely would die. So I figger he's daid by now. That's what I tole the Prophet but you know him, though the earth ain't worthy o' him, he'll stretch the truth on occasion. So that's why he tole everbody Boggs was daid."

Rockwell gave himself another generous pour.

"I do hope you are correct Mister Rockwell, lest my payment be in jeopardy."

"I wouldn't worry none about that. The Prophet will honor the contract. Four balls in the back o' the haid orter do it. Hee. Hee. If it don't, cain't sees how you'd be to blame. You done as much as anyone could under them circumstances."

"And what of you?" I asked. "Is your complicity in this matter known? After all you are a prominent Saint and one known to have been in the Independence area."

"Oh I reckon they's gonna pin it on me. Or try to. Not a splinter of evidence though. Them pukes can accuse me but they gotta prove it." He stroked his right braid. "I may be forced to hide out for a time if'n things heat up. I got my reward though. The Prophet give me a fine carriage an' some horses. You kin see 'em out the window there. He asked me to set up a carriage taxi. Wife Luana and the girl are still in Indypendence. Figger I'll hole up in Amos Davis's inn fer a spell. Good spot to run a taxi."

I gave the carriage a quick glance. "I'd advise leaving now," I said. "The Missourians will be after you."

"To hell with them. Cain't touch me. The Prophet tole me afore I left Nauvoo fer Indypendence to *cut not thy hair, and no bullet or blade can harm thee.* I ain't never cuttin' my hair. Reckon that'll keep a shield 'round me if them pukes come after my hide."

"You put a great deal of trust in your Prophet's prophecies."

He drew himself upright in his chair. "Sir, I put my entire trust in his prophecies."

This pronouncement ended the conversation. After another round sipped in silence, Rockwell staggered to his feet and hauled himself and his nearly empty bottle of whiskey out to the carriage. He clucked his horses into a trot and made his way back to the Davis Hotel.

+ + +

Three days later I sat in the lobby of the nearly completed Robert Foster Hotel and Inn to the east of the Temple. Though construction was still in progress on the upper stories, Foster had recently opened the ground floor to serve food and drink. I picked at the crumbs of an excellent slice of fried scrapple. Through the window I watched masons laying limestone blocks on the second floor of the Temple.

Just then, a scrawny young man burst into the room. "General Bennett just resigned as Mayor of Nauvoo!" he said, panting for breath. Startled by this announcement, the patrons pressed the young man for details. He could offer no further information and beat a hasty retreat.

Sensing something momentous in the young man's proclamation, I motioned to the proprietor, Robert Foster, to come near to my table. "My good man," I said, "as you know I am new to these parts so you will forgive my ignorance but who is General Bennett?"

"As you heard, he was lately the Mayor of Nauvoo." Mr. Foster spoke with a slight British accent, now faded from his years in the United States. He drew himself up and placed his hand on his chest in a gesture of importance. "General Bennett is also a Major General in the Nauvoo Legion, of which I am a Brigadier General. He also claims title to Chancellor of the University of the City of Nauvoo, where I serve as a regent."

Ignoring his air of self-importance I asked, "What, pray tell, is the Nauvoo Legion?"

"Why, good sir, it is the largest and best equipped militia in the entire state of Illinois! Though General Bennett is a knave and scoundrel of the first order, he must be given credit for organizing and leading this fine legion."

"Knave and scoundrel? A harsh judgment."

Foster glanced around and leaned closer to my ear. "He is a libertine of the most notorious kind."

"*Libertine*, you say?"

"I dare say. Bennett is famously unprincipled. He ingratiated himself with Joseph soon upon his arrival some eighteen months ago. He has risen to high position in the Church and city, with Joseph's help, of course. Privately, he leads a dissolute life."

"Dissolute?"

"He is a seducer of women. As a physician specializing in the maladies of women, he gains access to their chambers. His indiscretions are all committed under the guise of what he calls *spiritual wifery*."

"Spiritual wifery?"

"It is not marriage in any sense of the word. It is his way of spreading a thin veil of respectability over adultery."

I could not help but smile. "An interesting turn of phrase," I said. "So, tell me, how is it that a libertine and a debaucher can hold such high offices with impunity?"

"I have no answer for this," Foster said.

"No matter. I pose it only in a rhetorical sense. Why do you suppose he stepped down?"

"Perhaps he was pressured."

"By whom?"

"I might suggest the Prophet himself. Bennett's notoriety has become a source of embarrassment. Under the guise of spiritual wifery, he has gone so far as to establish, along with some of his cronies, a house of ill-repute."

"Do tell."

"Yonder near the oak grove. A large sign advertises its purpose right on the building itself, quite visible from the Grove where the Saints often gather for the Sabbath. A disgrace to the city. Joseph has loudly condemned it."

For reasons I cannot to this day explain, at that moment I sensed the nibbling of an opportunity. This intuition had not formed clearly in my mind, but I thought it propitious that Bennett had been unseated within hours of my arrival in Nauvoo.

"Where might I find this *General* Bennett?" I asked.

Foster glanced around again and leaned even closer to my ear. "He has a home in Nauvoo but I'll wager he is not there. In fact, if he did receive private condemnation from the Prophet, he may disappear for a time to lick his wounds. That has been his pattern. If you cannot find him during the day, I would wait until dark and visit his brothel. I happen to know, on good authority, that he spends his evenings there, though I must say he is discreet. As a newly announced candidate for the Illinois House of Representatives, he cannot be seen openly entering a place of ill-repute. I suggest you steal around to the back of the house and see if you spot a large bay horse. That would be General Bennett's. The back door carries the advantage of shelter from a dense tree stand. You will not be easily given to exposure."

"Thank you for your kindnesses," I said. "And may I add that this was a most excellent breakfast. The scrapple is undoubtedly the best I have ever tasted."

Foster bowed in appreciation and withdrew. Throughout the course of the day I searched in vain for General Bennett. As Foster predicted, Bennett had hidden himself away. Several hours after nightfall, having spotted the large bay horse tied behind the house of ill-repute, I stood before the rear door and rapped three times. A sag-eyed woman opened the door and, as if on cue, cracked her painted face with a smile. "Why hello handsome man," she said. "Do come in. The delicacies of the night await you."

"I beg your pardon, madam, but I am not here for commerce. I come seeking General Bennett and I am told I might find him here."

"Is he expecting you?"

"No but he may recognize my name. Permit me to introduce myself. I am Edwin – Ned – Freeman, lately arrived in Nauvoo. He may know me by name."

"Please," she said with the gesture of a hostess bidding a guest to enter. "I shall let him know you are here."

As soon as I entered the house, four ladies sashayed in front of me offering me their enticements. I demurred though there was one curvaceous and saucy redhead who caught my fancy. I noted her name – *Amanda* – for future reference. She fluffed her red curls, winked, and pointed a painted nail at my own red hair.

"We have things in common, sir. Let me know if you would like to explore these things in…more depth."

I smiled but said nothing more.

Several minutes after the parade of *nymphs du prairie* had passed, a handsome diminutive man emerged from the back of the house. He wore a full dress uniform replete with gold epaulettes and a ceremonial sword. With his broad shoulders, narrow hips and waist, and black hair graying at the temples, he struck quite a figure. He seemed quite unashamed to receive me in this notorious house.

"Mr. Freeman," he said offering me the hand of friendship, "I wondered if I would have the pleasure of meeting you one day. Here we are together under this common roof."

"It is a pleasure to meet you, General. I wonder if we might find a place to talk privately."

"There is no more discreet a place than a brothel. Here secrets remain secrets." He smiled in a conspiratorial way and directed me to follow him to a side room.

"I take it you did not come for love, Mr. Freeman, so what brings you here?"

"Curiosity. As you may know, I intend to make Nauvoo my home for a time and thought it prudent to seek counsel from the Mayor. Yet, over breakfast at Mr. Foster's inn I discovered that you have just removed yourself from that office. Even if true, I wish to make your acquaintance, and I do hope your removal from leadership was of your own volition."

Bennett smiled and rubbed his beardless chin as if he had a goatee in need of grooming. After several long seconds, he dropped his hand into his lap. "Yes, it was voluntary. However, I would be less than truthful if I did not disclose that a number of people in the city have spread scurrilous rumors about me. This pack of lies besmirches my good character. These rumors have reached the Prophet and I fear he believes them. Still, I do not want to bring any shame to the City or to the Church, so after discussions with the Prophet, I chose to step down. He is Vice Mayor and will assume the leadership of Nauvoo...as if he didn't hold it already."

"Yours is a noble gesture, to my mind."

Bennett shrugged. "I fear the matter would have come to a head and I might have been forced to resign in less than favorable circumstances. What was it Falstaff said, *the better part of valor is discretion; in which the better part,* etcetera, etcetera?"

"I do take your meaning. What then of your position in the Church, the Legion, the University?"

He shrugged again. "These matters were left open for the

moment. At the least, I will leave the First Presidency and my position as Assistant President of the Church. This is of no matter to me. However, my command of the Legion and leadership of the University are precious to me."

"I find your lack of concern over loss of the Church position, your *ductu ecclesia*, shall we say, *curious*."

General Bennett raised his hand and pinched his nostrils, holding his breath for several seconds. Expelling the air, he leaned forward. "Mister Freeman, I judge us to be kindred souls. If I may, I should like to disclose some personal information trusting in your confidence."

"As an attorney-at-law, I am bound to confidentiality. Please proceed."

He took a deep, clearing breath. "The truth of the matter is simply this: I am an insincere Saint. I have never believed in the Mormons or their doctrines. I became familiar with them years ago in Ohio. I believed then, and still do, that there has long been a scheme afoot to create a temporal and spiritual empire in these western parts. The Prophet plans to conquer Illinois, Indiana, Ohio, Iowa, and Missouri. In these states, democratic governments will be destroyed, and an empire established with Joseph Smith as lord and king."

"That's a preposterous notion. You can't be serious."

"I'm convinced of it. This very belief compelled me to infiltrate the Church, gain the information I could, and expose Joe as an impostor and fraud. I intend to divulge his iniquities to the whole world. Open opposition from outside the Church would have been futile. By getting behind the curtain, I could see for myself the manipulations of the Great Puppeteer."

I raised my eyebrows at the man's audacity.

"I shall tell you one thing more, Mister Freeman, a mite of information that you would do well to consider. If you are a Gentile, you will have no power, no platform, no position of influence in Zion. None whatsoever. You will labor in obscurity. Perhaps that is your wish. However, if you desire to stay in this city and rise to a place of notable standing, you must join the Church. Here is the favorable news for you: I am living proof that you can become a full-fledged member having neither sincerity nor devotion. I'll wager that you find the Mormon faith – as do I – a heap of nonsense. What then is the harm in feigning sincerity to false doctrine? If one *pretends* to believe that which is false, assuming a good and noble purpose, does one betray his principles? I think not."

"Cogent point," I said, admiring the man's intellect.

At that moment the rudiments of a plan began to form in my mind. I had already demonstrated my usefulness to the Prophet over the Caswall matter. He had taken most favorable notice of me. Now, one of his trusted lieutenants had either stepped down or fallen from grace. The circumstances did not matter. The Prophet now suffered a vacancy. One I might fill. To be sure, I would have to remain behind the scenes, a shadow guide, so to speak. Too much public visibility could bring unwanted attention from the Missouri authorities who, to my knowledge, still had no idea of my involvement in the assassination of Governor Boggs.

So energized had I become over this imminent opportunity that upon leaving General Bennett I decided to reward myself with a visit to young Amanda's crib. I must confess that the delights of the little red dove were extraordinary.

On the following morning, I made my way through a thundering downpour to the Prophet's home. I found him relaxing in an oaken rocker reading what appeared to be a volume of Scripture. When his wife Emma ushered me into his presence, he rose with a smile and set his book on the side table. "Mister Freeman, how good to see you. I trust you are finding your house and lands satisfactory. What brings you through this gully washer to me?"

"I've come on a personal matter," I said after assuring him that I was most pleased with my accommodations and the settlement we had reached.

He pointed to a stuffed chair. "Please be seated and tell me of your personal matter."

"Brother Smith," I said, "I have for some time considered the doctrines and beliefs of the Mormons."

He raised his eyebrows. "Oh, and how have you come to this knowledge?"

I recounted the many evenings I spent with Doctor Mercer in the Walls and how I came to a deep understanding of the *Book of Mormon* and the Prophet's revelations.

"I am most gratified to hear this," he said. "So may I assume you've read the *Book of Mormon*?"

"Cover-to-cover, twice," I said, lying with a brief smile. "A compelling testament, *the* divine revelation for our present day."

His own smile widened to a grin. "Rarely do I encounter such awareness. Surely I must thank Doctor Mercer for his good and holy work on our behalf. Then do you seek to join the Church?"

"Indeed I do."

He slapped his knee with his hand. "I shall baptize you myself! Come, let us kneel in prayer, thanking Heavenly Father for his hand in drawing you hither."

With that he dropped to his knees like a stone, and in one swift, unbroken motion, grasped my forearm and pulled me down to his side. There we paused in silence for a moment before he launched into a tedious and rambling prayer. I paid him little heed until his voice became strangled at mention of the *whoredoms* and *abominations* of General Bennett. I found it both odd and encouraging that he would mention the Bennett affair in my presence and in prayer, of all things.

When we had regained our seats, he called to Emma for a flagon of ale that we might toast my pending enrollment as a Latter Day Saint. After small talk in which the Prophet recounted the many difficulties they had encountered upon their arrival in Illinois, he shifted to a more serious topic.

"Mister Freeman," he said. "I feel as if I can trust you with certain information and I have been most enamored of your capacity to offer wise counsel. Do you know of the Bennett matter?"

I told him I had heard some snippets of gossip and rumor but did not tell him of my meeting with General Bennett.

"The man has become a serious problem," Joseph said. "He has been my trusted confidante for many months. Some time ago, I received a revelation in which the Lord instructed me to use John C. Bennett as my trusted counselor, to stand by me in times of affliction. Yet, of late he has been the very source of my affliction by his seducing of women, acts which he also attaches to me. He claims that I endorse and ratify his depravity, that I myself am similarly engaged. It is outrageous!"

"Such rumors I have heard."

"Yesterday, the matter came to a head. After a most unpleasant argument in which our voices were raised, he acceded to my wishes that he resign as Mayor of Nauvoo. I assured him that the City Council would accept his resignation with accolades and thanksgivings for his service. Thus, his dignity will be preserved. The Council meets this afternoon but I fear Bennett's presence because he simply cannot be trusted. Who knows what the man might do when he has the floor. He may try to impugn my character. He has threatened to do so. What would you advise, Mister Freeman?"

I leaned forward in my chair, locking my eyes on his. "Simple. Have the man prepare a statement to be read into the record in which he avows publicly that you have had nothing to do with his depraved behavior. He should state further that you have always condemned these immoral acts in the strongest language possible. This will place him on the horns of a dilemma. On the one horn, failure to offer such a statement could lead to his own public condemnation, a risk he cannot take. On the other, he cannot issue such a statement and in the same breath attack you. In so doing he would jeopardize his own supposed reputation as a man of honor and truth."

"An excellent plan. Excellent indeed. I shall have Willard seek him out in advance of the meeting and gain assurances that this statement will be forthcoming. I am in your debt Mister Freeman."

"Think nothing of it. I would go one step further. Have your man Willard prepare the statement for him."

"I shall. I shall."

I edged forward on my chair and prepared to leave. "Very well, then, I am ready to assist you in this way any time you so desire."

The Prophet raised his hand. "There is one more matter."

I slid back on the chair.

"There is one Hiram Kimball. Perhaps you have met him. He has a home near where you now live."

"I know of him, though I have not met him."

"He is not yet a member of the Church, though his very beautiful wife has long been among us. Mister Kimball is a City Councilman, and it has come to my attention that he has insinuated evil against me. He claims I tried to draw his wife into an illicit affair with me. Of course, such is a lie. I do not know how this might be handled. Your counsel?"

"May I ask you a question or two?"

"Of course."

"I know that from time to time, divine revelations come to you."

"Yes."

"What is the typical response of your followers to such revelations?"

"They treat them as if they were divine messages...as indeed they are."

"To be obeyed without question?"

"That is correct."

"Is it not possible that you can receive – with prayer and petition to God, of course – a revelation concerning Hiram Kimball's lies?"

The Prophet studied me for a moment, I suppose gauging my confidence in his revelations. "That is not without possibility," he said at last.

"A revelation from God condemning these slanders and warning Kimball to cease on pain of condemnation would, it seems, put the matter to rest."

"Intriguing. But there is this problem: As I mentioned Kimball is not yet a member of the Church so he may not feel the full weight of the condemnation."

"Ah, but his wife will and I rather imagine she can provide a curb to his tongue."

The Prophet broke into a smile. "I see your point Mister Freeman. Good. We shall see what the Lord has in store for us. You might wish to attend the Council meeting this afternoon to see the impact of your good guidance."

"I shall consider it," I said.

Again he slapped his knee. "A most satisfactory time. I am overjoyed to have made your acquaintance. This should prove to be a mutually beneficial relationship."

We both stood.

"Before I leave, I have one further question," I said.

"Please."

"Do you sell jarred preserves in your Red Brick Store?"

"Yes we do. There is a fine variety."

"Some apple preserves, perhaps."

"Yes, locally grown and preserved by none other than my devoted wife."

"Ah. How splendid! This most definitely assures their quality. I have a hankering for some."

"Please go to the store and tell the young clerk that the preserves are to be given without charge, a gift from me."

"Please accept my gratitude but I shall not prey on your generosity. I can pay and shall do so. Should you need me, I am at your service."

I trudged through the rain down Water Street to Smith's store reflecting upon my good fortune. I could not have imagined becoming so involved, so incorporated, so quickly in the doings of the Prophet and his Church. It staggered my mind and bode well, I thought, for my future in this frontier town.

Once in the Red Brick Store, I wasted no time in locating several jars of apple preserves and took them to the clerk seated at the counter.

"Cash or credit?" he asked.

"Cash, of course."

"Ferry goot sir. Cash iss alvays velcome."

"You are Dutch?"

"Ja. From Hulst. Piet Van Rijn, I am."

I expressed my pleasure at meeting him, paid for my jellies, and walked to the door. I paused to raise my collar in anticipation of the unremitting rain. When I opened the door, I beheld a tall, flaxen-haired woman. I recognized her immediately, as she did me. After an awkward pause, we exchanged brief greetings.

"How did you fare with Mister Emerson's essays," I asked.

She smiled. "I should say, well. Very well indeed. I thank you again for your generosity, sir."

"My pleasure."

I stepped aside. "Please. Do come in. The weather is dreadful."

She slipped past me, and as I turned to look back, she gave me a slight curtsey to match her smile.

CHAPTER TEN

Elena

Grove

G ood day, Piet," I said, thankful to be inside the Red Brick Store and out of the rain.

"Goot tay to you, Elena. Do you know dat man?"

"Yes, in a manner of speaking. When we were in St. Louis waiting for the *Maid of Iowa*, Dorrie and I went for a stroll. You may remember. Along the way we stopped in a bookstore where that man clerked. He gave me a book of essays by an American author named Ralph Waldo Emerson."

"Vat do you suppose hass brought him to Naufoo?"

"I have no idea."

Just then, the door to the Red Brick Store opened and Dorrie blew in with rain cascading off of her parasol.

"Oh, Dorrie, how nice to see you," I said. "It seems like months since we last talked though I know it's been but a week."

"Why it's good to see you too, Lanie. Hello darling Piet."

Dorrie leaned across the counter and kissed Piet.

"Dorrie," I said, shaking off my twinge of envy, "I was just telling Piet that I encountered a gentleman from St. Louis that you might remember. He was the clerk in the bookstore, the one who gave me the book."

"The tall man with red hair. Yes, I remember him. You saw him here in Nauvoo?"

"Yes, just a moment ago. Here in the store."

"What is he doing in Nauvoo?"

"I asked de ferry same question," Piet said.

I shrugged my shoulders.

"Did he say anything?" Dorrie asked.

"He asked how I had fared with the book of essays. That's all."

"It seems strange that he would be here in Nauvoo."

"Indeed it does."

Dorrie giggled. "Perhaps he is looking for you."

I rolled my eyes.

Piet and Dorrie exchanged glances.

I dismissed the whole notion by putting my hand on Dorrie's shoulder to change the course of the conversation. "So how are you Dorrie? Mightn't we sit for a spell and catch up?"

"That would be lovely."

We made our way to a pair of chairs next to a warm stove, a godsend on this cold wet day in late May.

"Lanie, I can't tell you how wonderful it is for Piet to have this job, thanks to Brother Joseph. It has kept food in the larder." She turned to Piet. "Hasn't it been wonderful, Piet?"

He said nothing but smiled and waved in affirmation.

"And you, Lanie, how have you been – in that tent and all."

"Agh! The tent. Seven weeks now Da and I have been living in that infernal tent. I hope he will have the log cabin finished in a few days, finished enough so we can move in. It has taken forever but you know my old Da. He is a perfectionist and insists the cabin be airtight and sound of construction."

"And the seminary? When do you and Arthur start?"

"Good news. We will be opening next week, on Monday. It will be a short term, just six weeks. This will allow the children to join in summer farm work, harvesting and laying by. We will resume again in September. As you know, Arthur has rented Elder Campbell's house while he is on a mission to the eastern states. It is perfect. His house is south and east of the Temple. The ground floor is large enough to permit several tables and benches for the students. Arthur has moved upstairs."

"Did Mrs. Campbell go with him on his mission? That seems strange."

"No, she has returned to Ohio to care for her aging parents. Her mother had a fit of apoplexy and has numb palsy. She can no longer manage the home or care for her husband. Mrs. Campbell is an only child, so the duty fell to her."

"I am so sorry to hear of her mother. And what of our own illnesses? Nauvoo is awash in sickness – bilious fever and malaria, colic, the measles, ague. So many are sick. So many are dying."

"Yes, it breaks my heart. Every day a coffin is borne through town. I sorrow the most when I see a small box with the grieving parents walking behind. Nauvoo is truly our Zion and I am happy here but I did not know we would suffer so much. It is a terrible thing to say, but the Lord protected us throughout our voyage but it feels as if He has let His guard down."

Dorrie shook her black curls and took my hands in hers. "Let's talk of happier things, Lanie. So much has happened since we arrived not yet two months ago. Just think. Piet has been baptized, we were given a cabin, Piet received the blessing of this job, and we have been married. I thought all had been lost when Piet fell but the Lord and His servant, the Prophet Joseph Smith, have provided. It is more than we could have hoped."

"Yes, yes, and I have much for which to give thanks as well. We have not really suffered in the tent except on the very cold nights. We have a nice rock fireplace in the new cabin. I cannot wait to warm myself by that fireplace. It won't be long. Da will then go to work on the Temple once he has the cabin finished. That is his dream. And Arthur tells me we have at least thirty students who will start their seminary studies next week. Whatever hardships we have had to endure, it has been worth it. To be taught at the feet of God's prophet for these last days is a wonder."

"And who knows," Dorrie said with a playful smile, "mayhap you now have someone to talk to about those essays."

"Yes, I should like that. I miss having such discussions. I had hoped I might become so engaged with Doctor Richards again, but I fear he is too busy and his work too important to be interrupted. As for this St. Louis clerk, I don't even know if he is here to stay. He may just be passing through. Perhaps he is selling books or subscriptions."

"Perhaps. He is rather handsome, don't you think?"

"No, I don't find him so."

Dorrie widened her impish smile.

I rolled my eyes again but said no more. In the back of my mind, I pondered the tall, intelligent, red-haired man with the scar on his lip. As I thought of him, I wondered what had happened to his limp.

During our short exchange at the entrance to the store, he appeared to move gracefully on his two feet.

After another fifteen minutes of chitchat, I purchased a bolt of calico to sew curtains for the new cabin. Normally, Da handled all of our commercial transactions. Because of the need to barter, the purchasing of goods fell to the men of Nauvoo. A woman would be at a disadvantage in such negotiations, or so the men thought. However, because Da and I were still able to pay cash out of our reserves, he had no qualms about sending me. Cash prices were always less than trade terms and did not prompt as much dickering. Since Piet was the storekeeper, we knew he would protect our interests and, in this case, Da wouldn't have known calico from burlap.

The next few days flew by as Da and I prepared our cabin for occupancy. I finished the curtains and Da added the last interior appointments – pegs for hanging, the final chinking with small wedges of wood, a generous fireplace mantle, lantern hooks, and necessary pieces of furniture. The final touch came on the day we assumed occupancy. Da polished the brass clock and set it on the mantle. He stepped back and put his hands on his hips. "Ah, Lanie girl, ain't she a grand old clock?" That night, in my own room, I snuggled under the covers of my tightly drawn bed. As sleep stole me away, I felt as if heaven and earth had kissed one another.

When I arrived at the Campbell's house early on Monday morning, Arthur was up and dressed in white breeches and a gray waistcoat that matched his whiskers and hair. The chairs and tables had been arranged in order, the distance between each precisely measured. Arthur stood as straight as his curved spine would allow and slapped his hand with a pointer fashioned from a branch of the black walnut tree growing beside the house.

"Ah, good morning, Elena. Are you ready for this grand adventure?"

"Indeed. What am I to do?"

"Today, we observe. We attempt to estimate the pupils' knowledge. They will come from different American states, our own fair land of England, Ireland, and who knows where else. It will be much like our maritime school. Some will have had considerable time in classes, others not. We have older lads that will no doubt try to challenge us – me in particular – and undermine our authority. Some of the girls, I suspect, will be simpering and silly. They are of that age, after all. Thus, today we will take stock of the lot of students and do our best to craft their studies according to their several abilities."

I took a deep breath. "I confess I am apprehensive."

"As am I, Elena. As am I. Our good fortune is that the Prophet has sought to emphasize education. Did you know that he received a revelation to this end back in the early days of the Church? I say this is fortunate because it means we can count on our elders to assist in the chastisement of errant children. We shall do what we can to resolve problems of discipline here but if we fail, we need only to report the matter to others. I daresay proper steps will be taken to, how shall I say it, *reform* the rapscallions, quite out of our hands."

The students arrived in due course. We were disappointed at the attendance because we counted only eighteen of the thirty or so who had indicated they would come. Undaunted, Arthur launched into a long litany of questions, ranging across subjects. He pointed randomly to students in search of answers, not proceeding to the next question until he was satisfied with a complete and accurate response to the previous one.

"Learn from the questions. Learn from the answers," he intoned. Before long, he had queried each student several times. Some of the boys offered flippant answers, which occasioned giggles and guffaws. Arthur deftly parried these outbursts, often turning them into additional teaching opportunities. I remember one particular exchange with a boisterous boy of fifteen, named Milo Crookston. Milo had reached the height of six feet and towered over his diminutive teacher.

"Mister Crookston," Arthur began, "would you be so kind as to tell us who sailed the Atlantic in Fourteen Ninety-two from Spain to the Americas?"

"Frankenstein," Milo said to a chorus of laughter.

"Interesting response, Mister Crookston, and one that betrays your uncommon knowledge of English literature in the early period of this century. I am anxious for you to share your insights on the writings of Mary Shelley to the rest of the students. Some may not know of Frankenstein. Who was he, Mister Crookston?"

"A monster."

"A monster? Permit me to turn to the rest of the students who found great amusement in your answer. Class, do you agree

Frankenstein was a monster?"

No one stirred in the silence of the room except Arthur whose shoes clicked on the wooden floor as he paced to and fro.

"Well, well, Mr. Crookston it appears that no one rises to contradict your assumption that in Fourteen Ninety-two, the monster Frankenstein sailed from Spain to the new world."

Another round of giggles ensued, more muted this time. Arthur pirouetted on one heel and jabbed his pointer into the air to recapture silence.

"I would make one adjustment in your response Mr. Crookston. Do you wish to hazard a guess as to what that adjustment might be?"

Milo Crookston stared slack-jawed at Arthur parading before his table.

"Perhaps a clue would be helpful. Can you offer the general gist of the Frankenstein novel, also known by the title, *The Modern Prometheus*? Mr. Crookston, the floor is yours."

Milo looked around the room and shrugged his shoulders.

"Oh come now, Mr. Crookston, surely you know the basic story."

Milo cleared his throat and offered a few tentative words, "I...I b'lieve it's about a man who creates a monster and brings him to life."

Arthur thrust his pointer forward like a fencer stepping from *en garde* to *flèche*. "Splendid! An answer on point. You are quite right, Mr. Crookston. This is a story of a scientist who creates a monster of old body parts. And the monster comes to life! The only adjustment I would make to your insightful response is this: Frankenstein refers not to the monster but to the scientist himself, Victor Frankenstein. The monster is never named in Mary Shelley's book."

Arthur spun to face the class, pointed to one studious young girl and said, "Miss Robinson, it is Miss Robinson, isn't it?" Her eyes darted around as she nodded in affirmation. "Miss Robinson," Arthur continued, "I should like you to join Mr. Crookston among the learned of our society by telling me who sailed from Spain in Fourteen Ninety-two."

Nancy Robinson offered the correct response and Arthur continued through the morning firing questions from his little round mouth like the balls of a repeating Puckle gun. He had no further disruptions by Milo Crookston and the rest of the class remained silent except to answer the questions posed to them. As predicted, the boys and girls varied in their skills and knowledge, which created a challenge for us in developing suitable groups and lessons. Despite these issues, by the end of the first week, we had the seminary well organized under Arthur's capable leadership.

The end of that first week of seminary also saw Da hard at work on the Temple. Blacksmiths were in demand for crafting tools, fasteners, chains, and other assorted hardware, not to mention the constant need to keep the horses shod and wagon wheels in good repair. Forges had been set up in the Temple precincts and from dawn until dusk one could hear the clang of hammer on anvil.

Not long after Da finished our cabin, and we had moved out of the tent, several Church leaders determined it was a good time to secure tithes from our cash reserves. We refused, harboring our hard-earned funds. Da elected instead to *tithe for the Temple* by giving a substantial portion of his time as a skilled craftsman. I argued that my service as a teacher should be considered an acceptable contribution. Since my payment came in form of goods, not bank notes or specie, I had little of use to offer the Church. Apparently, our arguments were sufficient because for a time we suffered no further pressure to provide a cash tithe.

The following Sunday, the last Sunday in May, 1842, Da and I walked to the Grove to attend the Sabbath meeting. As we drew near, we could hear the singing of hymns. Arthur had lent his splendid tenor voice to the choir. I spotted him in the second row singing with his eyes closed in rapturous contentment. Soon upon our arrival, Dorrie rolled Piet to our side in the Bath chair Da and several of the cartwrights had fashioned for him.

"Is it not a glorious day, this last day in May!" Dorrie said, breathless from her exertions.

"Most glorious," I said.

Da nodded with a smile. After the exchange of a few pleasantries, I stole a moment to scan the congregation in search of the red-haired bookseller from St. Louis. After several seconds, I saw him across the way and immediately realized that he was staring in my direction. Our eyes seemed to lock though, from the distance, I couldn't tell if he had focused his attention on me or upon the beautiful Dorrie, who stood beside me. I felt that tiny prick of envy again and averted my eyes.

The service began with a long litany of announcements and

exhortations by the Prophet's brother, Hyrum Smith. These were of no particular concern to me and I listened with scant attention. Nor were Hyrum's remarks of great interest to those around us because muted conversations continued without interruption. At last, Elder Sidney Rigdon stood and delivered an angry tirade about the persecutions of the Mormons. He recounted the sufferings in Ohio and Missouri, which he noted were now beginning in Illinois as well. To be sure, we knew of mob actions by residents in the outlying settlements but thus far Nauvoo had experienced few civil disturbances or skirmishes with the Gentiles. Elder Rigdon sounded grave warnings but followed with assurances that the Nauvoo Legion would protect and defend the community. After fifteen minutes, Rigdon's countenance flagged, and he collapsed in a chair.

"'Is 'ealth suffered since 'e was jailed in Missouri," Da whispered. "'E wants for a full recovery."

We nodded in sympathy.

The Prophet then rose to preach. "You have heard it said," he began, "the mobs that plagued us in Ohio and Missouri have anon reared their ugly heads to fight us anew here on the banks of the Mississippi. Take heart and consider well the words of the prophet Ezekiel in his lamentations over old Pharaoh, the king-devil of the mobocrats, miracle rejecters, Saint killers, and hypocritical priests. To them he saith, *I will water with thy blood, the land wherein thou swimmest, even to the mountains, and the rivers shall be full of thee.* If the mobs and the kings of the mobs repent not, they shall go down to the pit there to be ruled by old Pharaoh. I remind you of what I wrote to the Saints when I was imprisoned for Jesus Christ's sake in the infernal jail of Liberty, Missouri under the influence of the exterminating Governor Boggs. On that occasion, I wrote, *God forbid! Hell may pour forth its rage like the burning lava of Mount Vesuvius or of Etna or of the most terrible of the burning mountains and yet shall Mormonism stand. Water, fire, truth, and God are all the same truth is as Mormonism. God is the author of it he is our shield it is by him we received our birth, it was by his voice that we were called to a dispensation of his gospel in the beginning of the fullness of times, it was by him we received the Book of Mormon, and it was by him that we remain unto this day and by him we shall remain if it shall be for our glory and in his almighty name we are determined to endure tribulation as good soldiers unto the end.*"

It was a magnificent discourse and a great encouragement to us. In my mind it made ever more firm the assurance that Joseph Smith was a genuine prophet of God in these latter days. For who could speak of such portentous things, save for a true prophet? At the close of Joseph's sermon, Hyrum rose again and offered a prayer for the prosperity, protection, and perseverance of the Saints.

As we prepared to leave the Grove, Da helped Dorrie spin Piet around on the wheels of his chair. I glanced over my shoulder to see the tall bookseller coming toward us with long strides. Unaware of his approach, Dorrie, Piet, and Da went on but I lingered to see what prompted the man to approach.

"Pardon me, miss," he said. "Might I detain you for a moment?"

I nodded and waited.

"My manners deserted me when we met some days ago at the Prophet's store," he said. "In coming upon you that day, I seem to have lost my presence of mind. Not surprising given your grace and beauty, but I do offer my apologies. Permit me to say it was and is good to see you again, a woman of such lofty interests and learning. I understand you teach young people. No doubt, theirs is the great advantage."

With that he gave a short bow at the waist. At that moment, my nerve floundered and I'm certain my blush was in full bloom. "Why thank you sir," I managed to say. "I shan't think any apologies are necessary. I was a touch unsettled myself."

"You are too kind, Miss…?"

"Arkwright, Elena Arkwright."

"And I am Edwin Freeman, but most people call me Ned."

"I am pleased to make your acquaintance," I said, offering my hand. He bowed again, raised my hand, and kissed it. As he rose, he looked into my eyes. "I wonder if we might meet again sometime, perhaps for a longer session to discuss matters of mutual intellectual interest."

My blush flared again and, despite my reservations about the man's rather forward invitation, I thrilled at the possibility. "Why, yes," I said, in too much of a rush. "I would enjoy that."

"Where might we meet?" Ned asked. "It is such a splendid day, a venue in the great out of doors seems in order. How about here in the Grove?"

"A lovely suggestion."

"May I suggest later today? Say, three o'clock?"

"I shall be here," I said.

"And I await our time together with great anticipation and hopes that time will fly."

With that he gave another bow and walked across the Grove, now vacant save for those few who lingered in the presence of the Prophet. When I rejoined the others, Dorrie met my gaze with a smile spreading from ear to ear.

"My, my," she said. "Is something afoot?"

I blushed...again! "We are simply meeting for conversation."

"Is that what you call it?"

"Dorrie, don't be puerile!"

Dorrie squelched her smile and in mock seriousness said, "Oh, of course, Miss Arkwright. I wouldn't want to be *puerile*."

"Honestly!"

+ + +

I arrived first at the Grove, searched for potential sites to meet, and selected a shaded spot on the north side near the intersection of Durphy and Knight Streets. I spread a remnant of the calico curtain material on the mossy soil and opened a basket containing wheat bread, a jar of soft cider, and currant preserves. I had no sooner completed these preparations when Ned Freemen joined me on the calico spread.

"How nice of you to bring refreshments," he said.

"'Tis nothing," I said. "Just some bread and jam. Would you care for some soft apple cider?"

"Most assuredly."

I poured him a small glass. "So, Ned, what shall we discuss?"

"I should consider it a great honor to know more about you Elena. You are from the British Isles. This I know from your accent. How did you come to be here? Tell me the story of Elena Arkwright."

I had not intended to devote time to my own personal history but with questions and promptings, Ned managed to learn a great deal of my life and times. At certain junctures, I attempted to turn the tables to discover more about my companion. He offered cryptic answers and deftly re-directed the conversation back to me. At one point, after recounting the events of that momentous evening in Preston, I managed to insert a question of my own. "And you, Ned, have you ever found your heart warmed by the presence of the Holy Ghost, as happened to me on that night?"

He lowered his gaze to the calico spread and took his time answering. When he raised his head to look at me, he had an eerie smile on his face and I was instantly disquieted by that vacant look in his eyes. Those icy, sky-blue eyes that betrayed a want of...*something.* I knew not what.

"In a manner of speaking," he said, cracking my thoughts. "I have not swooned by a hot fire as in your feminine experience but I have sensed, shall we say, the *potentialities* offered by the Mormon faith. Have I mentioned that I am to be baptized in the Mississippi River on the morrow?"

"Ned, how wonderful for you!"

"The Prophet himself will perform the ordinance."

"I should like to be present."

"It would be an honor."

For the briefest of moments, I wondered if the baptism of Ned Freeman could bring life to his eyes. Perhaps what he lacked could only be supplied by the workings of the Spirit. I did not know.

Two hours in the Grove passed in the blink of an eye. I glanced to my right and saw the sun trailing off in the western sky.

"I must soon take my leave," I said. "My father will be home before long, ravenous, and ready for his supper."

"It has been for me a most gratifying afternoon," Ned said. "Would you consider further conversation at a convenient time in what I hope will be the very near future?"

"That would give me great pleasure," I said. "I am occupied much of the day in the seminary but perhaps in a week's time we can meet. If weather permits, this shady spot would be suitable, methinks."

"I shall fervently anticipate the reunion," he said.

Upon our parting, I walked the ten blocks to our home on Sidney Street. As I proceeded, my uneasiness over Ned Freeman's vacancy shaded to commiseration. What had happened to suck the life from his eyes? His outward gentility masked an ill-omened disturbance of the spirit. In that long walk home, I felt compassion rising within me. I wondered what I could do to quicken his humanity. I must hastily add that my sentiments were not those of a woman falling in love. No, I suppose, if anything, I felt myself called to be his spiritual friend and a nursemaid to his soul.

For the next four Sundays Heavenly Father provided sunshine, which permitted us to meet in the Grove at the appointed hour of three o'clock. To my great disappointment, he showed little interest in discussing historic literature and the writings of contemporary authors. Each time I introduced such a theme, he provided a few half-hearted comments. He preferred to talk about the goings-on in Nauvoo. He had a particular obsession over the events surrounding General John Cook Bennett. I did not know General Bennett save by reputation. I had listened to him speak on two occasions and found him to be a bit of a popinjay. (Each time these mean-spirited thoughts about the man arose in my mind, I became ashamed of my un-Christian attitude, often whispering a brief prayer of confession and repentance.) Ugly rumors had circulated regarding General Bennett's unchaste conduct with certain women in the community. However, having no first-hand knowledge of such indiscretions, I passed them off as unsubstantiated rumors.

Ned, on the other hand, condemned him roundly. "General Bennett – if he is still a general – is a pathetic little man, vile and unscrupulous." Immediately, Ned recognized that his remarks unsettled me and lowered his eyes. "Forgive my uncharitable comments about the General."

"Thank you." I said.

He did not, however, drop the subject. "You may have heard that a week ago yesterday, the Prophet denounced General Bennett and exposed his treacheries to the public. No doubt you were then attending to your duties at the seminary but, I wonder, did you see the Prophet's condemnation in yesterday's issue of the *Wasp*?"

"I did not. Political matters are not of concern to me."

"Here it is," Ned said, withdrawing from his budget a copy of the paper. He pointed to two particular paragraphs. "Read these sentences I have underlined with a pencil. These are the words of the Prophet himself regarding Bennett."

I did as he instructed and found myself mired in the reading of quite salacious and unpleasant material:

He had not been long in Nauvoo before he began to keep company with a young lady, one of our citizens; and she being ignorant of his having a wife living, gave way to addresses, and became confident, from his behavior towards her, that he intended to marry her; and this he gave her to understand he would do. I, seeing the folly of such an acquaintance, persuaded him to desist; and, on account of his continuing his course, finally threatened to expose him if he did not desist...But, like one of the most abominable and depraved beings which could possibly exist, he only broke off his publicly wicked actions to sink deeper into iniquity and hypocrisy. When he saw that I would not submit to any such conduct, he went to some of the females in the city, who knew nothing of him but as an honorable man, and began to teach them that promiscuous intercourse between the sexes was a doctrine believed in by the Latter Day Saints, and that there was no harm in it; but this failing, he had recourse to a more influential and desperately wicked course; and that was to persuade them that myself and others of the authorities of the Church not only sanctioned but practiced the same wicked acts...

I was blushing when I handed the newspaper back to Ned. I looked down at the calico spread and fiddled with the strings of my bonnet, not knowing what to say. The discussion of such matters in mixed company was most inappropriate but Ned continued, once again insensitive to my discomfort.

"I told the Prophet to publish that condemnation in the *Wasp*," he said with pride.

"Oh? You did?" I said, my voice barely above a whisper.

"Yes. Quite. After Joseph's public censure of Bennett last week, the latter repaired to Springfield. The Prophet became most agitated, wondering what could be Bennett's intent in making the journey. You see, Elena, there may be a modicum of truth in what Bennett alleges."

"Why I'm sure that is quite untrue! I cannot believe such a thing. Just now, in the words I read, Joseph condemned General Bennett's behavior in the strongest possible language."

"True. I advised him to do just that. Lighting a back-fire is often the best way to fight a fire."

I gave my head a little shake. "Ned, I fear this entire matter borders on the sacrilegious and I would beg to talk of other matters less distressing to me. I am confident the Prophet has always acted with the noblest of intentions and with purity of heart. If he has committed any indiscretions I'd warrant they are insignificant and only evidence of the fact he is human. He is happily married to Emma and has a fine family of children. I cannot imagine he has been involved in anything illicit. General Bennett is sadly deluded in this regard. Might we then redirect our thoughts to more pleasant and loftier things?"

"If you say so," Ned said as he focused his icy, empty gaze on me. A thousand millipedes crawled over the skin of my back.

We parted with plans to meet the following Sunday, weather permitting. If the afternoon sun were to become insufferable, Ned suggested we meet on the shaded front porch of his house. This invitation gave me pause but, since he had never acted toward me in an inappropriate way, I agreed. He promised to have fresh lemonade and melon slices. It sounded delightful despite my reservations about propriety. I had little doubt that Ned would want to reopen the Bennett case, the intimate details of which he appeared to be privy. He seemed to have gotten the ear of the Prophet in a short span of time. I found it perplexing that the Prophet allowed a recent convert to become such a close confidante. Ned had a towering intellect and a trained legal mind, to be sure, but so much trust, so soon?

Nauvoo was a beehive of activity the next Sunday, July Third. The community had planned a great Fourth of July celebration on the morrow with speeches, fireworks, and picnics. The Legion would be mustered to lead a parade featuring Pitt's Brass Band, which had been formed by another English convert named William Hill Pitt. While I rejoiced in the celebration of my new country's independence, I had nervous twinges at the thought of the dance to be held that evening. To my surprise, the Mormons were a dancing bunch! We Primitive Methodists in England shunned dancing. I had never been to a dance nor had I any idea how to be a dance partner. Of course, it was unlikely that anyone would ask me to dance...but what if someone did?

After the Sabbath services in the sweltering Grove, I borrowed a carriage owned by Dorrie and Piet to carry me to the north side of Nauvoo where Ned Freeman lived. When I alighted, I looked around the porch and yard. Ned was nowhere in sight. I walked up the steps and knocked on the door. There was no answer. I knocked again, harder this time. Again, no answer. After several more attempts, I became uneasy. I lifted the door latch. The door was unlocked. I pushed it open and peered inside, careful not to cross the threshold. "Ned? Ned, are you within?" Silence answered me. Several long seconds later, I screwed up my courage and entered his home, calling his name again. Nothing. I glanced around the parlor and living room noting the stark paucity of furniture and the lack of any personal possessions. I thought to myself that the vacancy of the home mirrored the vacancy of its owner. As I scanned the interior, I heard a faint groan from upstairs.

"Ned? Ned is that you? Are you upstairs? Are you all right?"

Nothing.

Then, another groan.

I took a deep breath and cast aside my propriety. Up the stairs I went and along the hallway to the far room. There I beheld Ned Freeman, stripped to his waist, writhing on his fetid bed in a torrential sweat. I ran to his bedside and knelt. When I placed my hand on his forehead I could tell he had a morbidly high fever. A quick inspection of the room revealed that he had been sick for days. Dried vomit, urine, and diarrhea smeared the floor. The stench threw me back into the tween deck on the *Tremont* as it pitched and yawed in the grip of that North Atlantic storm. The poor man was too sick to make it to his privy.

I ran downstairs and hailed a lad trotting by on his horse. "Boy!" I shouted, "Do you know Doctor Mercer's office?"

"Yes, m'am," he said.

"Please fetch him. Mister Freeman is deathly ill."

The boy wasted no time in spurring his mount to a full gallop, careened around the corner, and sped out of sight. I found a bucket and pumped cool water from the well to make cold compresses, and raced back upstairs. The application of cool, moist cloths brought a measure of relief to Ned and his writhing subsided. He opened his eyes briefly but drifted off again in the throes of his distemper. Less than thirty minutes later, the boy and Doctor Mercer burst into the room. I stepped aside to give the doctor full access to his patient. Without a word, he peeled back Ned's eyelids and noted the yellow tinge. He pushed on his stomach and took his pulse. Ned began to shiver.

"Cooold. So cooold," he said in a long plaintive moan.

Doctor Mercer nodded and stood to face the boy and me. He put his hands on his hips, took a deep breath, and said one word, *malaria.*

CHAPTER ELEVEN

Kevil

Calling

What a colossal farce! I donned a long flowing white gown and waded in my boots out into the shallows of the Mississippi River arm-in-arm with the radiant Prophet. George Miller, a bishop, and five soon-to-be-dunked dupes joined us. As we stood in the swirling chest-high waters, Smith blathered on for several long minutes concerning the ordinance of baptism. Then, in order, he and Bishop Miller lowered us into the murky water. I have no idea what the other dupes were thinking as the waters of eternal salvation closed over them. I held my breath, not in the hopes of heavenly bliss, but of earthly fortune.

A scattering of witnesses stood on the riverbank to greet us as we returned to dry land with our white robes clinging to every contour of our bodies. I could not help but notice one young woman whose attributes were revealed by her saturated gown.

Elena Arkwright broke my satyric fancy. "Mister Freeman," she said with a joyful smile, "My congratulations to you on your entry into the true church of God where you will enjoy assurance of salvation."

I nodded with feigned delight, adding a simple *thank you*.

"I'm very happy to be here," she said. "Mister Walmsley granted me a brief leave to attend the baptism. I cannot linger. I must return to the seminary but I assure you I look forward to our time together on Sunday next. Lemonade and melon. What a toothsome delight!"

"I shall be waiting for you on the porch, lemonade and melon slices at the ready," I said.

She gave a brief curtsey, and with a wave of her hand, turned to leave. The Prophet led us back to the Red Brick Store where we changed into our dry clothes. As I walked from the large upper room, where the men were dressing, he drew me into his office and shut the door. Three others were present. Brigham Young stared out the window with his back to us. Bishop George Miller leaned against the far wall picking his teeth with a splinter. Willard Richards had settled his enormous buttocks on a chair and fanned himself with the last issue of the *Wasp*. Anxiety brooded over the silent air of the office. Joseph paced back and forth, his limp ever more pronounced. In a matter of minutes he had slipped from the radiant joy of baptizing new followers to the high anxiety of an unnamed doom.

"We have a problem, Mister Freeman," he said. "Two problems actually."

The stalwart Brigham Young turned slowly from the window, his face a pasty white. Willard's *Wasp* shifted to a flutter. George Miller stopped picking his teeth.

"Tell him, Brother Brigham," Joseph said without slowing his pace.

"Governor Boggs survived," Brigham said.

I raised my eyebrows. "I don't see how. I emptied four barrels into the back of his head at point blank range." I fixed my gaze on Joseph. "You yourself declared he was dead."

The Prophet turned his palms up and shrugged his shoulders.

I waited.

"And Boggs has accused the Prophet of masterminding the attack," Willard said. "He's pinned it directly on Port Rockwell as Joseph's agent."

"They'll be after me," Joseph said, his voice strained and low.

"I fail to see how this is my fault," I said and girded my mind for battle. Any effort to recall my fees or properties would meet my stiff resistance.

"We cast no blame upon you," Joseph said. "This is an unfortunate quirk of Providence."

"What's the second problem?" I asked.

Grunting and wheezing, Willard hoisted himself to his feet. After three more swishes of the paper, he proceeded to outline the problem. "John Cook Bennett has threatened to conspire with some Missourians to bring a mob upon us. He has also threatened to bring down the Prophet by publishing a book of scurrilous lies."

"What is the nature of these lies?" I asked.

Joseph stopped pacing and turned in my direction. "He accuses me of seducing women, of harboring several wives, and teaching the benefits thereof. Not true! Not true!"

I looked around the room. All eyes save for mine were fixed upon the floorboards.

I nodded, confirmed in the Prophet's lie. "What do you wish of me?"

"Your good counsel," Joseph said.

Silence descended upon the room.

Auspicious, I thought to myself. On the very day of my baptism, I stood in the inner sanctum of the Church to deliver advice to its leading authorities. My plans were unfolding much more rapidly than I could have imagined. I knew in an instant what must be done but drew out the silence – for effect, of course. "Here is what I propose. First, in the matter of the Missouri mob, I recommend appeal to the highest authority."

"Meaning?" Brigham said.

"Since the mob is forming in Missouri, I suggest you pen a letter addressed to the Governor of Missouri in which you expose Bennett's treachery and request the State's assistance in case mob action arises from that state. Time is of the essence. I am prepared to dictate such a letter to your scribe here and I suggest that it be delivered forthwith."

Joseph nodded. "Done and done. Brother George will deliver the letter to Jefferson City. What about Bennett's book?"

"Are the charges accurate that you levied against Bennett in last Sunday's *Wasp*?"

"Indeed they are," Bishop Miller said. "At the Prophet's request, last year I traveled to Ohio where I discovered Bennett had a wife and three children. Since he has been in Nauvoo, he has proved to be a rascal and a seducer of women. We have on good authority and his own confession that he has had illicit relations with Catherine Warren, Matilda Nymens, and Matilda's sister, Margaret. I wager this list is incomplete. In brief, there is considerable evidence to condemn him."

"Then I would counsel you to reprint this material in the *Times and Seasons*. This paper is more given to religious matters than the *Wasp*.

Since Bennett once numbered among the First Presidency, it's necessary to discredit him in the religious organ of the Church." I looked at Joseph. "Think of it, sir. It is among the devout – those avid readers of the *Times and Seasons* – that such charges against you will have their greatest impact. Therefore, the *Times and Seasons* is the hill from which you must launch your attack."

Joseph nodded again. "Is there aught else?"

"I suppose it goes without saying," I said. "There is a final and irrevocable means of silencing such a critic. You must weigh the consequences – either way."

The four men stared at me, uttering nary a word in response.

"If that is all," I said. "I should like to begin dictation of the letter to Missouri Governor Reynolds."

Joseph sighed. "Of course. You may use my office. Willard will take your dictation. Brigham, George, please walk for a time with me."

+ + +

When the letter had been completed to my satisfaction, George Miller hurried off to secure the Prophet's signature before his hard ride to Jefferson City. I made my way back to my house where I prepared a bowl of apple slices and settled in on my porch to read some of the area newspapers.

As I savored my small repast, I looked over the edge of my paper, to see General Bennett, now back in Nauvoo, hitching his horse to my fence. He had exchanged his military uniform for gray breeches, a white blouse with green cravat and a black waistcoat. He cradled his top hat in one arm and a leather folio in the other.

As Southern manners dictated, I stood to receive him. "General Bennett, welcome to my home. Please, won't you join me in an apple slice or two."

"Thank you, Mister Freeman. I appreciate your hospitality."

"Not at all. To what do I owe the pleasure of this visit?"

"Word has reached me that you were baptized into the Church earlier today."

"True," I said with a wink. "Some days ago, I received wise counsel that such a submission would help to establish my civic position here in Nauvoo."

Bennett smiled at my flattery before sobering to his purpose.

"I thought you should know what is afoot," he said.

I reached for an apple slice. "Do tell."

"I will be leaving Nauvoo. There is no future for me here. It is my intent, once out of the city to bring Joseph Smith to his knees, if not to his permanent demise."

"How?"

"I will tell you but I must be assured of your confidence. I would humbly request that you place what I am about to tell you under the seal of attorney-client privilege once again."

"On my word," I said.

"I thank you. During my trip to Springfield several days ago, I met with the editor of the *Sangamo Journal*. I contracted to write a series of articles exposing the evils of Mormonism and its Prophet. I will continue to collect affidavits from disaffected Mormons who are inclined to speak the truth. These will form the basis of a book I plan to write on the true history of the Church. Prior to penning this book, however, I will be on the lecture circuit in the east where I will inform the country of the depth of Mormon perfidy."

"A bold and dangerous game," I said. "You must realize that the Prophet and his cronies will not take this lying down. They will fight back. They will attempt to expose further your own alleged infidelities and improprieties. Your very life may be in danger."

"I am aware of this. In private conversation, Holy Joe threatened to make catfish bait out of me and cast me into the hands of the murdering Danites if I said anything untoward about him or the Church."

"Who, pray tell, are the Danites?"

"They are a shadow society, a group of Joe's avengers and enforcers, a violent bunch, sworn to secrecy upon pain of death."

"I see. So how do you hope to protect yourself, if indeed this group of Danites is sent to avenge your exposure of the Prophet and his Church?"

"I have friends. We are well-armed."

And delusional, I thought to myself. The resources of the Mormons appeared to me quite substantial, far beyond those of General Bennett.

"We can protect ourselves," Bennett continued.

"If you say so. I don't share your confidence but I shall leave you to your own securities. Permit me to turn to another point. The old adage is that the pen is mightier than the sword. How do you plan to address the public charges against you?"

"To this I will counter with a long litany of character references. My many services and accomplishments have not gone without notice."

For several minutes I listened to the man prattle on concerning the things he had done and the written accolades he could collect. Through it all, I listened for his denial of the charges of adultery and illicit intercourse with certain women in Nauvoo. Hearing none led me to the inescapable conclusion that, in the matter of John Cook Bennett, Smith had spoken the truth. Bennett could inflict damage on the Prophet's reputation, but I judged the Mormon Church to be sufficiently robust to withstand whatever attack the little rooster could launch.

Wishing to hear no more of this self-aggrandizement, I held up my hand. "General Bennett, I do not doubt the extent of your accomplishments and your ability to gather supportive testimonies. Tell me what you intend to write in these letters to the *Sangamo Journal*."

"The first is written," he said. He opened his leather portfolio and extracted several handwritten pages, which he handed to me.

"Do you wish me to read this?" I asked.

"If you would be so kind."

"There are a number of pages here. It will take me some time. Do you wish to wait?"

"I suffer some urgency in the matter but I do not wish to inconvenience you. Might I return in early evening and receive your thoughts on what I have written?"

"That would be satisfactory. I shall see you around seven this evening."

General Bennett bowed and took his leave. Munching on another slice of apple, I began to read his letter to the editor, delighted to be providing advice to both sides in this contest of reputations. The letter contained a number of points. Bennett accused Joseph Smith of issuing death threats, violating constitutional rights, failing to submit to justice, seducing women, land fraud, debasing the Masonic rituals, and a host of other treacheries. When I finished reading the letter I chuckled. When the Prophet reads this, his wheels will fly off. What a delightsome game I was playing!

Upon General Bennett's return that evening, we sat at the dining room table and I offered my guest a glass of brandy.

"A powerful letter," I said. "I offer but one suggestion."

"Please. You have my full attention."

"In his attack upon you, Joe Smith will, in all likelihood, offer up the names of those women with whom you have allegedly consorted. You have not done the same in your letter. Do you know the names of the women the Prophet has attempted to seduce?"

"Indeed."

"And they will support the content of your charge if they are publicly named?"

"I would so believe."

"Disclose their names."

"That is bold."

"That is your defense, sir."

He pondered. "Very well, on advice of counsel, I shall do it."

"And remember, General Bennett, this confidentiality agreement cuts both ways. Not a jot, tittle, or whisper of my involvement. Is that understood?"

"Absolutely."

I stood to signal our meeting had ended and with one final quaff of his brandy, General Bennett left my home. I never saw him again.

+ + +

As soon as Bennett rounded out of sight, I saddled my horse and rode hard to the Prophet's homestead. When I knocked on the door, young Joseph welcomed me into the keeping room. There the Prophet bade me be seated and excused his son. "What brings you to me at this late hour?"

"General Bennett is on the warpath."

Smith sucked in a quick breath. "Yes, please continue."

I then disclosed Bennett's intentions and informed the Prophet that I had been privy to one of the letters intended for the *Sangamo Journal*.

"What's in the letter?" he asked.

"A great many charges. One of the most serious concerns your alleged seduction of women here in Nauvoo. He is prepared to name names."

"These allegations are not new. They never come to anything."

"Bennett claims the named women will back his charge. He also intends to travel to the east where he will give a number of lectures exposing your alleged transgressions."

The Prophet sighed. "What do you advise?"

"First, I would reiterate my advice to light a backfire in the *Times and Seasons.* Second, I suggest you deputize faithful men and dispatch them to points east where they can either debate or countermand the charges Bennett will make in his lectures."

"Yes, yes," Joseph said. "All of this I can and will do. Is there aught else?"

I debated in my mind whether to bring up a final recommendation, but decided to suppress my reservations and offer a third course of action.

"I understand the Church harbors a company of enforcers called Danites."

"Completely false. The Church does not condone such societies."

"I see," I said, knowing full well that the Prophet had no choice but to deny the existence of such a group. "Allow me then to offer a *hypothetical* course of action. Bennett is careless but dangerous, nonetheless. He can inflict serious damage. I fear the only means by which you can defeat this man is to silence his pen – forever." I counted to ten letting my words settle. "In this hypothetical plan, should such a group as the Danites exist, their influence could be most valuable. I'm certain they would be quite, shall we say, *persuasive.* Of course, you must stand apart from any such action." The Prophet opened his mouth. I held up my hand to stay any further objection he might offer. "I understand. Our conversation at this moment is purely *hypothetical.*"

"I take your meaning, Brother Ned. As always, I appreciate your counsel. Great has been your service to me, to the Church, and to the Almighty. I shall ponder what I must do."

The Prophet's reaction was more subdued than I had expected. However, he listened with full attention when I pressed upon him the benefits of a Danite attack upon his apostate general.

+ + +

I cannot identify the precise moment when it hit, but it was in the first hot, sticky morning hours of June 29th. Intense chills shook me awake. Every muscle in my body ached and my head felt like a hammered anvil. I rose to pull a blanket over my chilled body and, without warning, felt the gorge in my throat. I spewed vomit on the floor.

Over the course of the next several days, I wavered in and out of consciousness. At some point, either in a state of thin sensibility or delirium, I could not say which, I saw Elena by my bed. Somewhere in the recesses of my mind I also registered Doctor Mercer's presence, but these were but fleeting images, absorbed by cold darkness. My life teetered on the brink for many hours. I was later informed that the Prophet himself came to lay hands upon me and anoint me with the oils of healing. I have no memory of this.

It was not until early on July 5th, one week after the onset of my malady, that I felt the fever break and sap returning to my devitalized body. Famished, I rose from my bed and wobbled downstairs in search of something to eat. To my relief, I saw on the table a loaf of bread, a jar of current preserves, and a clean white napkin in a serviette ring. These were the same refreshments Elena served during our first meeting in the Grove. I slumped in a chair and ate these delights, ravenous as a wolf at a long winter's end. I returned to bed, so weak I had barely the strength to ascend the stairs. Later that day, Elena came up the stairs calling my name.

"I'm awake," I managed to say, my voice raspy and muted from non-use.

Elena's step quickened when she heard me.

"Ned! It is good to hear your voice. Are you back among the living?"

"It would seem so. I presume you are the angel who supplied the bread and preserves."

"Yes, I have come by each evening to check on you, keep your bedding clean, and your room in good order. Doctor Mercer has been by several times as well. At his insistence, we opened the window to clear the miasma from the room."

"Thank you," I managed to say. "What was my ailment?"

"Malaria."

"Malaria!"

"Yes. You were near death. Doctor Mercer has anguished over his inability to treat you. He has no supply of Jesuit's bark. He says it's the only effective treatment for malaria. You have weathered the illness without medication. He will be mightily relieved to see you recovering."

I mustered a few more sentences of small talk before drifting off to sleep once more. For two weeks I slept, rising only to relieve myself and take a few bites of nourishment from the food left by concerned acquaintances. Given my newly established importance to the community, I rightly expected to be nurtured to health by my fellow Saints. After all, I was keeping a lid on the Prophet's rumbling cauldron of iniquity, which had nearly boiled over with the publication of Bennett's letters. These so-called *kindnesses* to me by my fellow saints were merely my due.

The sickness terminated my Sunday meetings with Elena. This was just as well. I had grown weary of them. She seemed interested in literary discussions only and had no appetite for the politics of Nauvoo. Perhaps she also found the discontinuance of our conversations acceptable because she never mentioned them during her nursing calls, which tapered off with my recovery.

Given this cooling of our relationship, you can imagine my surprise at what the Prophet Joseph Smith proposed when he visited me one day in early August. I sat on my porch browsing several recent newspapers when the Prophet pulled up to my front gate.

"Brother Ned, come ride with me."

I joined him on the seat of his carriage and we drove in silence north and west to a secluded stand of trees along the river. The Prophet often wandered into such places when he planned to disclose something important to his followers. Thus, our arrival at this forested wayside was portentous.

"Walk with me Ned."

We slipped into the canopied stand of trees and secreted ourselves from the sights and sounds of Nauvoo. Joseph perched on a fallen log. He patted a vacant spot on the log. "Please, sit with me."

I sat, amused by his artless preparations for our conversation. We sat in silence for the better part of a minute.

"I rather imagine you are curious about what I wish to say," he said.

"Indeed I am."

"You are familiar, are you not, with our belief in a Celestial

Kingdom?"

"It has been explained to me."

"Then you realize that the Celestial Kingdom is the highest of the Kingdoms of Heaven, higher than the Terrestrial and Telestial Kingdoms?"

I nodded.

"Entry into the Celestial Kingdom is the object and goal of all Saints. It must, therefore, be your object and goal as well." Joseph stood and walked to and fro before me. The limp in his gait and the sibilance in his consonants added peculiarity to the moment. "Brother Ned, I am more than delighted with your service to me and to the Almighty. I am desirous of your eternal salvation in the Celestial Kingdom. It is a magnificent place, beyond description, where we will be in the very presence of God the Father and Jesus Christ. In this Celestial Kingdom, we become exalted, god-like, and we shall enjoy eternal *increase*. By increase we mean eternal procreation, the building up of our own dynasty through the addition of spiritual offspring."

I refrained from rolling my eyes. I could not imagine anything more repugnant than siring an infinite number of troublesome little whelps for all eternity. I could not conceive of anything more disagreeable than the endless management of an infinite family. I said nothing.

"There are, however, earthly requirements for exaltation and entry into the Celestial Kingdom," Joseph continued. "First, one must hear and receive the testimony of Jesus Christ and believe on his name. Second, one must be baptized and receive the Holy Spirit by the laying on of hands. Third, one must enter into the covenant of marriage and be sealed for eternity." Here he stopped and stood before me. "Brother Ned, you have fulfilled the first two of these requirements. But you have not yet completed the third. What say you?"

His attitude annoyed me. I stood to face the Prophet eye-to-eye. "Sir," I said, a purposeful edge in my voice. "I choose the single state. It is my preference for the moment and I do not wish to be married. Should this exempt me from the Celestial Kingdom, well, so be it. Besides, I've not yet found anyone with whom I would want to spend the rest of time, let alone all of eternity."

"Brother Ned, let me be direct. I find you to be of immeasurable value to the Church of Latter Day Saints. The Almighty has bestowed upon you the gift of wisdom and good counsel. I want your earthly sojourn to be as joyful and satisfying as possible. Your position in the Church will be elevated in due time. However, it is difficult to advance someone to a position of authority and leadership who does not qualify for the Celestial Kingdom. Do you take my meaning?"

"I do not seek a position of leadership."

"Come now, Brother Ned. You are a man who sees possibilities. You offered your counsel to me unbidden. Why would you do that if you were not interested in my good fortune and that of the Church?"

"Desire for your good fortune doesn't necessarily translate to ambition."

"Yes, but your desire for our good fortune has caught the attention of the Church's authority. I am dispatched to inform you that you are *called* to a higher service but only upon the occasion of your matrimony. I should add that to refuse a calling is to refuse Jesus Christ himself. So it is for your soul, as well as for the good of the Church, that I urge upon you a speedy marriage."

"Since you are *calling* me, sir, at least conditionally, I presume you also have in mind whom I am to marry."

"Brother Ned, you have been seen in the company of Sister Elena Arkwright on many occasions. She succored you when you were sick. Do you not have a stirring in your heart for her?"

"No. Not in the least. She and I met for intellectual conversation and that has ended. Her tending to me when I was sick was of her own volition. I did not summon her."

"But still…"

"Brother Joseph, while I appreciate her ministrations, I do not wish to marry her."

"Do you not find her attractive?"

"Not at all."

"Is there anyone else?"

I measured my thoughts for a moment.

"There is one," I said.

"Who?"

"The wife of the cripple."

"Dorrie Van Rijn?"

"The very same."

"She is a most beautiful woman, to be sure."

"But married."

"Yes. Yes, she is married."

I watched Joseph turn and walk a few steps toward the edge of the clearing. He put his hands on his hips and stared up at the canopy of leaves, stationary in the windless sky. After a long period of thought, he turned to face me once again.

"There are possibilities," he said.

I raised my eyebrows.

He took a deep breath. "May I vouchsafe a secret to you?"

"Of course," I said.

"The Lord revealed to me that if a man espouses a virgin and desires to espouse another, if the first gives her consent, he may take the second. There is no adultery."

"Go on," I said, intrigued by his reasoning.

"I presume Sister Elena is a virgin."

"I would suppose so."

"And given Brother Piet Van Rijn's condition, I would assume that Sister Dorrie's virginity is also intact. Do you follow where I am heading?"

"I do."

"Then I shall leave the matter to your thoughtful consideration and prayer." He reached over and grasped my arms, pulling me off the log. "Come, I must return to the store and prepare for the City Council meeting this evening. Let me know your decision."

CHAPTER TWELVE

Elena

Portents

A great unease settled upon Nauvoo in late July, 1842. Word reached our city that John Cook Bennett had charged our Prophet and Orrin Porter Rockwell with the attempted assassination of the former Governor of Missouri. I was sure this was a false accusation, and I recalled Ned's opinion that Mister Bennett was a scoundrel of the highest order. Three weeks had passed since last I saw him and I could only conclude that I had upset or failed him. I felt discarded. Despite those times our conversation steered into uneasy matters, I missed our meetings in the Grove.

Mister Bennett threatened to bring mob action from Missouri across the border into Nauvoo. Our Prophet called a meeting of the City Council to approve a petition to Governor Carlin of Illinois requesting protection from the State. After approval of the petition, many citizens of Nauvoo gathered in the Grove to pass a resolution to Governor Carlin condemning Mister Bennett and supporting the high moral character of our Prophet. Eight hundred men signed it. That same day over one thousand women – I include myself in this number – signed a companion resolution and urged its rapid transmittal to the Governor.

Given this atmosphere, it is understandable that both my Da and Piet became apoplectic when Dorrie and I declared we were going on a ladies' outing. We planned to take a wagon along the river road toward Quincy, find a suitable place by the river, and have a picnic. We had not been out of Nauvoo since our arrival. It was time to *air out our minds,* we said. Not since our days aboard ship, had we enjoyed one another's extended company for more than a few fleeting minutes. We yearned to renew our friendship – just the two of us. We assured Da and Piet that the Missouri mobs were not after two young ladies who posed no threat to anyone. Finally, the protestations of both men sputtered out when we promised to be home before nightfall.

We appointed Wednesday, August 3rd, as the day of our outing. In a grudging mood, Da helped us hitch Fancy, Dorrie's black mare, to the Van Rijn's wagon. We loaded a basket filled with good treats to eat, took Piet to the Red Brick Store, and started off on the road to Quincy. The day dawned sunny and hot, but to our relief much of the swampy humidity had blown away on winds from the west. Our ride was most pleasant. Both of us chattered away as Fancy clopped along.

Our conversation ranged over many things – reminiscences of our sea voyage out of Liverpool, the fortunes and misfortunes of that watery journey, and the rapid population growth of Nauvoo. We reflected on the difficulties and joys of living on the American frontier. I shared with Dorrie our plans for the next session of the Seminary. In turn, Dorrie offered the encouraging news that Piet had begun to get partial feeling back in his lower extremities.

"Have I mentioned that I joined the Female Relief Society?" Dorrie asked as we reined to a brief stop for sips of water from the glass canteen we had packed.

"No, you hadn't mentioned it," I said.

"Yes, about three weeks ago."

"Is it to your liking?"

"I'm not sure. Hundreds have joined since it started back in the spring. There are nearly eight hundred members now."

"But you have reservations?"

"I wouldn't say I have reservations, exactly. Perhaps I'm too new in the group to fathom everything. I joined because the Relief Society provides assistance to those in need and I wanted to be a part of that cause."

Dorrie corked the canteen and settled it back in the basket.

I waited for her to continue.

"Let's go on," she said.

The sun had risen high overhead. I unfurled my parasol to shade us as we continued down the road now coursing within a few yards of the Mississippi River.

"There is little doubt," Dorrie said, "that the work of the Society is righteous and good. When we drift off course, as I suppose any group of women might, our President, Emma Smith, returns our minds to the primary purpose for the Society. Spiritual blessings are bestowed upon those in need. Offerings are taken up to assist those in want. What worries me, Lanie, is the frequent effort to expose and admonish those who are presumed to have a less virtuous character. Names are brought up, allegations levied, and actions proposed for the investigation and correction of the errant one. Often the charges are based upon rumor and insinuation. Not upon fact. I find myself quite unsettled by such proceedings."

"Have you spoken to Emma about it?"

"Yes, several of us approached her after the last meeting."

"What did she say?"

"She said the Prophet intended for the women to become the stewards of female purity and virtue in Nauvoo. The Prophet believes no one else in all of Zion is better placed to bring sinful sisters to repentance and a return to moral living than the women of the Relief Society. Joseph views the Society as akin to the Priesthood and it is the priest's role, he reminds us, to bring sinners to judgment."

"So, Emma dismissed your concerns?"

"Yes, she was very firm with us."

"Will you leave the Society?"

"I can't. I joined in part because the Prophet mentioned to Piet one day that my absence from the Society was noted. I'll not bring any shame or misfortune upon Piet. We owe so much to the Prophet and the Church. My resignation from the Society could cause problems for my dear Piet."

"I understand," I said.

A brassy crow called our attention to the surrounding chorus. Squirrels scolded from high in the trees above, cicadas joined with high-pitched thrums, and redbirds commented on the beauty of our day – *purty-purty-purty*.

"Might you join the Society?" Dorrie asked, "I would welcome your company."

"Oh, Dorrie, I'm not much for such groups. I don't doubt the good purposes for which the Society was established but I have my work at the school and Da to care for. It is quite enough for now.

And, I must say, I have no wish to sit in judgment of other women."

"I see," Dorrie said.

My answer disappointed her. "Please, Dorrie, don't think ill of me. I just don't see myself in this service. My work, I think, is better placed elsewhere."

"Of course, Lanie. I understand."

Save for the sounds of the riverside forest, we rode in silence for another mile or so until we came to Sonora Landing. We saw a small cluster of log and clapboard homes, a Post Office, church, and what appeared to be a school in the near distance. We stopped to let Fancy drink from a trough of murky water. Just then, a middle-aged man rode up on a fine chestnut horse. He pinched the brim of his hat as a gesture of greeting. A wide smile spread across his weathered face. "Top of the day to you, ladies," he said.

"And to you, sir," I said in return. "Whom do we have the pleasure of meeting?"

"Ah, English," he said. "I recognize your accent. Mightn't you be Mormon sisters from Nauvoo?"

"We are. And you are?"

"Begging your pardon ma'am, I am Gabriel Graham. Most folks in these parts call me Gabe. I am on my way to conduct a Methodist class. It meets in that church building. May I ask what brings such fair ladies out on this fine summer day?"

"We are simply out for a ride and a picnic, sir. We needn't detain you further."

"It is my pleasure to rest a spell with you. It might interest to you to know we have several Mormons, or perhaps I should say former Mormons, who join us each Wednesday for the Methodist class."

"Oh?" I said.

"Yes, it seems these Saints have become disaffected by the Mormon religion and seek to find a faith more in accord with the Gospel."

His comment provoked a flash of indignation in me. "Sir, the Mormons are the most closely aligned of all churches with the authentic Gospel. Our doctrines far surpass those of the denominations. Heavenly Father has restored the true priesthood and revived the ancient ordinances through the Prophet Joseph Smith."

Gabe's smile did not waver. "I'm certain you believe that with all of your heart, Miss...?"

"Arkwright. My name is Elena Arkwright. This is Mrs. Piet Van Rijn."

Gabe Graham gave a nod of his head to Dorrie.

I pressed my argument. "I daresay, Mister Graham, that I know whereof I speak because, you see, I was once a Methodist and a devout one at that. The Methodists do not possess the true priesthood, the one granted directly by God Himself to Joseph Smith."

Still smiling, Gabe gave a short chuckle, "And I presume you now find that the Mormons fulfill all of your spiritual needs."

"Indeed. There is a joy and sense of fulfillment in these last days."

His smile faded, "Well, may I offer you the utmost respect but I do not share your belief that these are the last days. Perhaps they are, perhaps not. Nor do I wish to leave you with the impression that our Methodist church is a place of cold devotion. Ours is a great and – to use your British word – *rumbustious* delight in the Lord. I daresay no Mormon service can rival ours in the joyful outpouring of the Spirit."

"That is a contest I would like to join, Mister Graham, but not today."

"Then let me offer this invitation. You are welcome to visit our little group. We would be delighted to have you. Every Sunday morning at ten o'clock; every Wednesday, at noon. We do not have an Elder except upon occasion when a circuit rider wanders this way. I have taken upon myself to prepare a message for our gathering each Sunday and we have some glorious singers among our little group. If your admirable faith in all things Mormon begins to falter, we are here for you."

He pinched the brim of his hat again and clucked his horse into movement.

"One moment," I said.

Gabe halted his horse. "Yes?"

"How is it you know the British word *rumbustious* and how is it you speak so eloquently? One is not used to such sophistication in these frontier parts."

"I am a schoolteacher." He pointed to the building I had earlier identified as a school. "Yonder is where I attempt to scale the walls of ignorance. I studied myself for a time at Illinois College before my funds ran dry. So, now I teach. For thirty years and a few more."

"Well, sir, we have that much in common. I teach in one of the seminaries at Nauvoo."

"Aha! I am doubly pleased to make your acquaintance. Now I must be off. Miss Arkwright, Mrs. Van Rijn, enjoy your outing. I shall ask our faithful congregation to pray for your safe return to Nauvoo."

With that, he spurred his horse toward the church where others were beginning to gather. Dorrie snapped our own reins, and we resumed our journey.

"I found that man arrogant," I said.

"Yes I suppose he was, but I think he meant no affront."

"I'm not so sure. He certainly pressed the case for his Methodists."

"And you pressed the case for the Saints. I must say I do envy you, Lanie."

"How is that?"

"You are so intelligent and quite able to engage others, especially those who are learned like Mister Graham. You have no fear of challenging or defending as the situation demands. I can't do that."

"Sometimes I fear I say too much."

"I shouldn't think so. Mister Graham is no doubt a fine man, but he is quite misguided. You pointed that out to him with such grace."

"I didn't feel graceful. His remarks offended me and I felt I had to defend our faith. So many have given so much to the spread of the restored Gospel. So many have endured so much on its account that it is the least I can do. This was but a small and, I suppose, a polite exchange, but it pales in the face of the persecution so many Saints have suffered."

"Yes, but your abilities are admirable, even in polite exchanges. I wish I had such skills."

"We all contribute in our own way, Dorrie. Perhaps your special offering will be to serve our faithful through the Relief Society."

"Perhaps. We shall see."

We fell into silence again, absorbed in our own thoughts. I ruminated over what Mister Graham had said about disaffected Saints and their turning to the Sonora Methodist congregation as a religious haven. If I thought long enough, I suppose I would realize there must be disaffected Saints, but I had never met one. I couldn't imagine giving up the gifts of Mormonism to return to my old Methodist ways, even if they were more joyful and hospitable in this frontier land. However, despite my allegiance to the Saints, I had to admit a smidge of curiosity about these local Methodists.

Two miles south of Sonora Landing, a grassy slope spread out to our right, extending from the road to the river. The slope gave rise to several tall oak and sweet gum trees that spread the ground with wide patches of shade. We selected this lovely place for our picnic. Fancy delighted in the grassy feast beneath her hooves. Once settled upon our quilt, we said brief prayers and dived into the pieces of batter-fried chicken Dorrie had prepared.

Dorrie blotted her lips with a white linen napkin. "Lanie, may I ask you a sensitive question?"

"Of course."

"What do you make of these charges of spiritual wifery among the Saints, of multiple marriages, I mean?"

"I don't believe a word of them. I signed the petition."

"As did I but the rumors don't end."

"But isn't that the nature of a rumor – the repeated telling of something unproved?"

"I suppose but when one hears it over and over, from different people, there might be some truth to it."

"So you're saying, 'Where there's smoke, there's fire?'"

"Yes, Lanie, that's what I'm saying."

"Where have you heard these rumors?"

"There are whispers in the Relief Society. At first, I thought it was the gossip that arises when a group of women get together. Then Piet said something about it."

"Oh?"

"Yes, he overheard Brother Joseph and Brother Brigham talking about it one day in the Red Brick Store. When they realized Piet had overheard their conversation, they quickly left the place. Poor Piet found this a very troubling conversation."

"Perhaps they too had heard the rumors and were devising a way to counter them."

"That's not what Piet said."

My eyes met Dorrie's. Hers were welling.

"Tell me," I said, my voice soft, blending with the lapping of the river waves.

She blotted her eyes with her napkin, leaving an unfelt crumb of chicken batter on her cheek. I reached over and brushed it away.

"Piet says Brother Joseph poked Brother Brigham playfully in the ribs and said, 'I have ten wives. In heaven, I will have ten times the glory of the man who has but one wife, and five times the glory of you, Brother Brigham. You have but two!'"

"Oh, Dorrie, surely he was just jesting."

"I hope so, but Piet came home sorely disturbed by what he heard."

I shook my head. "We shouldn't borrow trouble. Let's leave it as a rumor, nothing more. It is better to let it go, not repeating it, as the gossips do."

"I know that is what we should do, Lanie. But what if it is true?"

"Let us think for a moment, Dorrie. How could it be true? How does one man serve and provide for ten women and keep it a secret from the vast throng of Saints in this place? How would the Prophet keep nine other wives a secret from Emma?"

"I don't know."

"Tell me, Dorrie, if Piet had nine other wives don't you think you would discover it? Wouldn't you wonder where he could be when consorting with the other wives? Wouldn't you sense it? Our fair sex has strong intuition after all."

"I suppose you are right."

"Well, there it is then. Such a notion of nine wives kept in secret from the first wife is preposterous."

"Perhaps Emma knows about other wives."

"How could any woman countenance her husband of many years taking on additional wives? Nine of them? It defies logic and stands against the moral order. It is a violation of one's marriage vows. An abomination before God, for heaven's sake!"

"You must be right, Lanie."

"Think further. If Joseph were serious in his conversation with Brigham in the Red Brick Store, surely he would only claim to have one or perhaps two more wives. I suppose one could hide one or two such dalliances. But he said ten wives! Impossible. He was jesting."

"Then why did Joseph and Brigham run from the store when they realized Piet had heard what they were saying?"

"Perhaps they were embarrassed. Such juvenile conversation is unbecoming two Church leaders. Yet, we must remember they are only human and human *men* at that."

Dorrie smiled. "Yes, I understand. Men can be boyish at times.

Even Prophets and Apostles."

I smiled in return. "Even Prophets and Apostles."

We left the subject of Joseph's multiple wives convinced our assumptions of absurdity were true.

On the return trip, we stopped again in Sonora's Landing. On a whim, I said to Dorrie, "Can we visit the little church? Their meeting has ended."

"Why? What is your sudden interest in this church?"

"Just curious. That's all. It can't hurt."

Dorrie shrugged and drove over to the front of the little clapboard building. I jumped from the carriage and climbed the three stairs to the door. I tried the latch and found it unlocked. When I stepped into the entryway, I saw six rows of rustic pews on each side of the aisle. A pulpit and lectern flanked the Lord's Table, a typical arrangement and familiar to me. To my surprise, I felt a stitch of nostalgia. We had no church in Nauvoo. To be sure, the magnificent Temple would be a most sacred building, the grandest in the west. Yet we had no dedicated, hallowed space such as that upon which I gazed. For a moment, I sensed a yearning, small and perhaps of no consequence, but unmistakable just the same. Why, I wondered, had such feelings come to me unbidden?

When I arrived at home in the late afternoon, I found Da pacing to and fro in front of our fireplace. His hands were clasped behind his neck and he flapped them in synchrony with his paces as if he were a giant moth flexing its wings in preparation for flight. This was Da's typical behavior when agitated, upset, and without a set-upon course of action.

"Da, what is the matter? Did something happen at the Temple today?"

"Oh, Lanie girl, Aw don' know wha' t' do but Aw've got t' tell ye."

"Tell me what?"

"Aw've 'ad a visit from the Prophet Joseph Smith."

My brow furrowed. "And?"

"Oh, Lanie, Aw don' know 'ow t' say it."

"Da, come and sit down. Quit flapping your arms. You look like a rooster in chicken hawk time."

Da did as he was told.

I sat in the chair opposite him and waited.

"Aw reckon it's bes' if Aw just come out wi' it."

"I reckon."

"The Prophet 'as a proposal for ye."

"A proposal?"

"Not a proposal exac'ly – more a proposal 'bout a proposal."

"Da, you make no sense."

Da stamped his foot, I suppose in hopes this could somehow loosen his tongue.

"'E, the Prophet tha' is, says tha' man Ned Freeman wishes to marry thee. There, now Aw've said it."

"Marry? Me? Da, what are you saying?"

"'E, the Prophet tha' is, says Ned seeks thine 'and in marriage, 'e says."

"That is nonsense, Da. I haven't seen Ned in three weeks. When we talked, there were no intimacies. I can't imagine his wanting to marry me."

"'E does. So says our Prophet. It would seem 'e, Ned tha' is, come up an' tol' the Prophet. Asked 'im to urge thine approval. So the Prophet come to me, Aw presume to keep i' all in good order."

"Well it's not in good order. If Ned wants to marry me he should ask me himself."

"Aw b'lieve 'e will Lanie, in goo' time."

"If he does, he will be sorely disappointed. I have no interest in marrying Ned Freeman. I appreciate his mind and he has been a perfect gentleman but I do not love him."

"Ye could grow t' love 'im, couldn' ye?"

"Nothing doing. I will marry for love, not potential love."

Da sighed and slumped in his chair. "Aw'se afraid ye'd say tha'. 'Ow can ye turn down the Prophet?"

"Simple. I shall say *no*."

"But 'e's the Prophet."

"The Prophet, yes; the lord of my life, no."

"Lanie, girl, ye don' 'ave tha' many years left to fin' the righ' man."

"Are you saying I'm getting long in the tooth?"

"No, Lanie, well…yes Aw s'pose Aw am."

I put my hand on his forearm. "Dear Da, I thank you for your worries about me but I would prefer the single state to a loveless marriage."

The next two days passed in agony for my Da. Repeatedly, he raised the Prophet's proposal. In the morning, during his dinner break, and no fewer than two times each evening, he would launch into the subject, each time taking a different tack. He squared his shoulders, sniffed sharply through his nose, and began, "Now Lanie girl…" His pleas and supplications came to no avail. I declined every time, repeating the essence of my belief that love must ground marriage and would surely ground mine.

Finally, on the morning of the third day, a Saturday, I put my foot down – literally. I stomped my foot on the floorboards sending a reverberant *whomp* throughout the cabin. "Da! This is the end of it! I'll hear no more of it. I am not marrying Ned Freeman. That is final. There is nothing you can do or say to change my mind."

He looked at me with widened eyes for I seldom spoke to him in such a fashion. "Awright Lanie girl. Aw'll honor thy wishes. Aw only wan' w'at's best for thee."

"Thank you Da, but you waste your breath."

"Aw'm doin' the Prophet's bidding too, ye know."

"He is a prophet, Da. He is not the Lord Himself. While we owe him our allegiance and obedience, there must be limits to his influence on our private lives. In matters of love – or the absence of love – we must follow our own hearts."

"Aw s'pose ye are right, Lanie girl."

That ended it, or so I thought.

The next day, Sunday will be forever etched in my mind. It was August 7th and the twin miseries of heat and humidity pressed upon us once again. We endured a Sabbath service in the Grove, clumped up in the few spots of shade, fanning ourselves with whatever we could find, including our sweaty palms. Joseph preached a long tirade on the need for steadfastness in the Lord as the "clouds of doom formed on the western horizon." He mustered the Nauvoo Legion and bade us prepare for the certain battle to come.

Besides the alarm I felt at Joseph's dire warning, I became worried because I could not spot Arthur Walmsley in the choir. He had always been such a faithful member, and he loved to sing. His absence did not bode well. I left the meeting early and made my way to Elder Campbell's house. At my knock, a feeble voice answered from within. "Enter, the latch is unfettered."

Arthur sat at a table in his nightshirt, hair splayed and beard ruffled. His ashen face quickened my step to his side.

"Arthur, are you ill?"

"Yes, the fainting sickness, though a mild bout this time. I shall recover."

"How may I help?"

"If you could bring me a cup of tea, I would be most grateful. There is heated water on the stove and some English tea in the tin on the shelf. If I stand, I become quite dizzy. Your assistance would be a boon."

"Of course," I said and set about steeping his tea. "We missed you at the Grove."

"It was good of you to come."

"Arthur," I said looking into his eyes. "You seem flagged and dispirited. Is it merely the illness?"

He signed. "I fear it is not."

I waited.

"Lanie, you have been my companion and compatriot in the education of children. We have become close. I wonder if I might share with you a burden upon my heart."

"Arthur, you know you can confide in me."

He sighed and looked to the ceiling, gathering his thoughts. "How do I start? I suppose things began to gel for me on Thursday last. I had a visit from William Law, the Prophet's Second Counselor, with whom we are both acquainted."

"Yes, I just saw his wife Jane this past week. She inquired of me whether their oldest, Richard, might be admitted to the Seminary. He is only eight but has quite outstripped his classmates and is ready for a higher level of learning. We should discuss this but now is not the time. Please, continue."

Arthur blinked several times and took a deep breath, gathering strength to continue. When he found his voice, it sounded low, breathy, and barely audible. "Brother William and I share similar thoughts, thoughts that might be deemed as apostasy. I hasten to add neither of us is an apostate nor do we seek an open break with the Saints."

"Arthur, what are you saying?" I asked, my voice rising in alarm. "William Law has been a staunch defender of the faith and of the Prophet. Just days ago he denounced John Cook Bennett and vouched in a public way for Joseph."

"I am aware of this but privately he – I should say both he and I – find ourselves apprehensive over certain things that are afoot."

"Such as?"

"We believe there is an ominous merger of church and state here in Nauvoo. Now that Bennett is gone, Joseph is both the President of the Church and the Mayor of Nauvoo. For all intents and purposes, he commands the Legion as well. He has for some time sought to influence and maneuver politicians to his personal benefit. Brother William is particularly troubled by Joseph's increasing control over the financial dealings of the Saints. For several years now, Brother William has chafed under the Prophet's requirement that property in Nauvoo be purchased only from the Church. As you know both William and his brother Wilson Law have substantial real estate interests and seek to profit from the sale of property. Yet, their commercial ventures have been stifled by Joseph. These concerns burden me and have for several weeks now."

Arthur paused, pursed his tiny mouth, and blew a stream of air across the rim of his cup. I waited. "One thing that so thrilled me about coming to America," he said, "was the constitutional separation of church and state. We English have labored for centuries under the tyranny of an established religion. Our coming to America brought relief from such oppression and the opportunity to worship in freedom. While I love the doctrines of Mormonism, I shudder to see the Church established as the dominant political power in our community – a theocracy if you will. The omens are ill, to my mind."

"But Arthur, we have been here just four months. The city is very young, not yet three years old. We should give things time."

"I could accept that but I do not see power dispersing. It is gravitating to the center, to the First Presidency, to the Prophet himself, the King of Zion. I do not wish to live again under kingly rule."

"I understand your fears Arthur, but you mustn't let them ruin your health. You have too much to offer."

Silence descended upon the room, which I broke a minute later. "Do you wish more of tea?"

"No, thank you, Lanie." He shifted in his chair, trying to become more comfortable. "There is one more thing I must tell you."

"Yes?"

"It has to do with Governor Boggs," he said. "Brother William believes that Joseph personally sent Port Rockwell to fulfill his prophecy, to kill the Governor in revenge for the extermination order in Missouri."

"You cannot be serious Arthur. That is a most treacherous accusation."

"Yes, I know. That is why you mustn't breathe a word of it. Brother William told me that Joseph said, 'I sent Rockwell to kill old Boggs and usher him into hell. They...' Here Arthur paused and looked up from his cup. '*They* missed him,' Joseph said. I found it strange that he used the term *they*. Was there more than one assassin?"

I cupped my hand over my mouth. "It can't be true," I said, my voice low and muffled by the palm of my hand.

"Mister Law, *Brother Law*, is a man of impeccable reputation, Lanie, a man not given to false witness. His credibility cannot be ignored. Murder for revenge, murder for hire, cannot be countenanced among God's people. It is contrary to the Gospel. It is contrary to our own doctrines. I checked." Arthur reached for a tattered copy of the *Doctrines and Covenants* resting before him on the table. He riffled through several pages. "Here it is. Section Forty-two, *And now, behold, I speak unto the church. Thou shalt not kill and he that kills shall not have forgiveness in this world, nor in the world to come.*" He closed the book.

"Do you know what Brother William said to me when we parted?"

I shook my head.

"He said our Prophet has fallen."

Neither of us could do aught but stare at our teacups in the silence of the room.

Our unhappy conversation drew to a close, and I assisted Arthur to his bedroom. I assured him I would return each day to check his health, bring him food to eat, take care of his chamber pot, and tidy up his rooms. He protested, to no avail.

I returned to our cabin, my mind churned by rising doubts. No matter how hard I tried to screen these thoughts from my mind, I could not do so. When I arrived home, I walked into the immediate audience of my Da and the Prophet himself. I wilted. It took no great power of discernment to know what was afoot.

"Lanie, girl! Come in," Da said, as if he were giving me permission to enter my own house.

Joseph stood and flashed me his winning smile. The top of his breeches rolled. He was getting flabby. "Miss Arkwright," he said, gesturing to one of our own chairs, "please, won't you join us for a time."

I nodded and eased into the chair, bracing myself for what was to come. Joseph attempted small talk but my clipped answers and nods pushed him to the purpose of his visit. "Miss Arkwright, Sister Elena, I wish to speak on a delicate matter. You have heard of celestial marriage?"

My stomach dropped. "Yes."

"And what is your understanding of it?"

I nodded and shrugged at the same time. "A man may be married on earth for time and for all eternity."

Joseph smiled again. "Good. You understand it rightly."

I waited.

He slapped his hands on his knees. "So, Mr. Ned Freeman desires your hand in marriage that he might join the Patriarchal Priesthood and assure his increase in heaven. Of course, for you, to be bound for time and all eternity here in Zion assures your entry into the third and highest, the celestial heaven."

A deep sigh overtook me. "Dear President Joseph," I said, still trying to muster at least a modicum of deference. "I do appreciate your coming in person and I do thank Ned for honoring me in such a way. However, I cannot marry Ned Freeman."

"And why, pray tell?"

I glanced at Da whose expression of anguish melted my heart.

"Because," I said, "I do not love him."

"Oh but Sister Elena, many marriages begin without there being a spark of love. Yet, as the years roll on, love abounds. It is the will of Heavenly Father that you should marry Brother Ned and join him as both an earthly and heavenly spouse."

"Brother Joseph, I do not doubt your sincerity in revealing what you believe to be the will of God in this matter. On the other hand, no such revelation has come to me."

Joseph stood and walked to where I sat. He looked down at me with hands on his hips.

"Then Sister Elena I admonish you to deepen your life of prayer, more dutifully read the Scriptures, and listen to the promptings of the Spirit. Then you will know that God wishes this of you."

I glared at him for several long seconds before running to my room and slamming the door in outrage.

CHAPTER THIRTEEN

Kevil

Counsel

Word reached me that the Prophet's approach to Elena Arkwright on the matter of our nuptials had not gone well. To be spurned by that homely wench infuriated me but I would not abandon the quest. Elena provided passage to two important destinations – unconditional admittance to the inner sanctum of the Church and delicious intimacies with Dorrie Van Rijn. Joseph and I vowed to wear down Elena Arkwright. Her initial rejection, while galling, would not hold. Of this we were quite sure. She would accede. Eventually.

Confident of this, I purchased another bed, bureau, and a night table to furnish the second bedroom in my house. I had no intention of sharing my bed with Elena Arkwright. She would sleep in her own room and submit to my infrequent conjugal demands when I so willed it. Having completed the purchases, I rode up the hill toward Doctor Foster's hotel for dinner, my mind teeming with fantasies of Dorrie Van Rijn. Heretofore I had not made her an object of my daydreams because I had assumed her to be out of reach. Now, girded with the Prophet's new, albeit secret, doctrine of plural marriage and assured of his influence, I had every reason to believe my contrivances would come to pass.

As I approached the crest of the hill, my musings were interrupted by hoof beats behind me, coming fast and hard. Turning in my saddle, I saw Doctor Mercer low in the saddle, spurring his horse. I could not imagine what had pushed him to breakneck speed on this sultry August morning.

When he drew near, he reined his horse to a stop.

"Doctor Mercer," I said, "What hastens you so?"

"You must come, Kevil."

"*Ned*, remember."

"Of course, but come with me. You are needed at the Municipal Court."

"Whatever for?"

"Several officers arrested Joseph and Port for the attempted murder of Governor Boggs."

Blood drained from my face. "Have they charged me?"

"No, just the Prophet and Rockwell. We need your legal counsel. It is urgent. Come now!"

In a cloud of wariness, I raced with Doctor Mercer to the Red Brick Store where the Municipal Court gathered. I would have to be careful. Joseph would not betray me. Of this I was certain, but I did not trust Rockwell. Might he give me up under duress?

The justices met us upon arrival. Orson Spencer, a slender, dark-haired, and handsome man had been selected as Chief Justice *Pro Tem*. One of the finest intellects in Nauvoo, he was well-educated and penetrating in thought. He did not suffer fools well, something I greatly admired in a man. However, I remained baffled that someone of such towering intelligence as Spencer could be so slavishly devoted to the absurdities of Mormonism. It staggered the imagination.

Spencer rose from his chair when we entered the large room on the second floor of the store. "Mister Freeman," Spencer said, "Thank you for coming. We need the benefits of your legal mind."

"Tell me what happened," I said.

"Less than an hour ago, an Adams County officer by the name of King and several of his deputies produced a warrant from Governor Carlin for the arrest of Porter Rockwell. He is accused of shooting Governor Boggs with intent to kill. Carlin charged Joseph as an accessory."

"Where are Joseph and Porter now?"

"Sheriff Sherwood has them in custody."

"Gentlemen," I said raising a hand to focus the Court's attention. "We must move with some dispatch. There are three important steps to be taken. First, this town has in its charter the most favorable law in the land on the matter of *habeas corpus*. Therefore, the prisoners must petition for a writ of *habeas corpus*. Once received, this Court shall convene and issue said writ. If I surmise correctly, this will *knock the officers for a loop*, as the pugilists would say. When presenting this writ to the officers, do not demand the arrest warrant in their possession and refuse to take it if they try to give it to you. We *do not*, may I repeat, *do not* want to be in possession of their arrest warrant. No doubt, the officers will be flummoxed by a municipal writ of *habeas corpus* and wonder if it bears on a state-issued warrant. I suspect they will leave the prisoners in custody of the sheriff and run off for advice. The Court can then order release of the prisoners on two premises. One, the writ will be in full force and effect; and two, the arrest warrant will not be in the sheriff's possession. Do you follow?"

The members of the Court nodded in unison.

I continued. "Second, Rockwell needs to leave Nauvoo without delay and stay away until things calm down. The further away he goes the better. Joseph cannot leave for distant parts because his presence and leadership are needed here. Therefore, plans must be made for faithful Church members to hide him when necessary. He can carry on his business while in hiding." (I did not mention I needed Joseph in the vicinity for my own purposes.)

"Not a problem," Orson Spencer said.

"Finally," I said, "the terms in the municipal charter for *habeas corpus* must be strengthened by an additional ordinance which the City Council has the authority to pass. If you will excuse me, I will prepare this ordinance for consideration by the Council, which I urge you to convene forthwith. I shall be writing for a time. When I have finished, I will beg the indulgence of Doctor Mercer here to bear this proposed ordinance to the City Council. It will contain language that strengthens the *habeas corpus* provision of the city charter. This language will be of extreme value when the officers return, as they no doubt will, to re-arrest the prisoners."

The Court members stared at me.

"Go!" I said, with a shooing motion of my hand.

Because of my exceptional skills with legal language, I penned a three-section ordinance in less than thirty minutes. When finished, I summoned Doctor Mercer who had been biding his time with Piet Van Rijn. I gave him the proposed ordinance and showed him the critical language in the second section. This section gave the Municipal Court power to dismiss any warrant against a citizen of Nauvoo generated through *private pique, malicious intent, or religious persecution, falsehood, or misrepresentation.*

"As you can see," I said, "this section is very broad and the *religious persecution* language will become highly protective for the Mormons in days to come. I urge you to present this to Hyrum Smith, the Vice Mayor, post haste."

I lingered in the Red Brick Store for a time to assure the hangers-on that matters were under control and that the Prophet would soon be freed. At my request, those in the store spread through the town urging calm. When the store emptied, I seized the opportunity to start a conversation with Piet Van Rijn. I had rarely spoken to the man and then only in pleasantries. Inasmuch as his wife would soon become my delightsome prize, I reasoned that a fuller friendship with Piet might be worthwhile. *Perhaps I can get to her through him*, I thought. My assumption could not have been more accurate.

"Vell," he said in his silly Dutch accent, "you are stook oop dere in dat house by yerself. Vy don't you come to de house for sooper tomorrow? Torrie vill make a pot of rabbit stew. Vy don't you choin me and de vife?"

Delighted by the prospect, I accepted his invitation and, after suffering through further chatter on *vile harassment of our beloved Prophet*, bade him an indulgent farewell. I retraced my steps to Doctor Foster's hotel where I ordered a belated dinner of peppered pork steak with applesauce and fried new potatoes. When I had completed this most satisfactory repast, I returned home with a renewed sense of security. My complicity in the Boggs affair had not been discovered by the authorities in either Missouri or Illinois. I leaned back in my rocking chair and fell asleep with images of Dorrie Van Rijn in my head.

+ + +

The following day, I made several inquiries around town and discovered, to my relief, that Porter Rockwell had torn out of Nauvoo headed for points east. Joseph attended to his matters with a carefree attitude. His nonchalance worried me. The officers would return. Of this, I had no doubt. Joseph's brother Hyrum assured me that plans had been made to hide the Prophet for as long as necessary, but I remained uneasy.

That evening, I selected a gray suit (the cut of which presented me quite well), a burgundy waistcoat and cravat, my best calfskin shoes, and a new gray top hat. I over-dressed intentionally...to go a-courting. I snipped a bouquet of garden flowers in the window box on the west side of the keeping room. Elena Arkwright had planted these flowers during my illness. I enjoyed keeping them watered and pruned, not out of dutiful thanksgiving to Elena, of course, but for my own pleasure. Flowers in hand, I made my way to the Van Rijn cabin.

To my shock, Piet greeted me at the door in a full upright position, standing on his own two feet, albeit suspended on two wooden crutches. With a quick glance, I noticed he had steel braces strapped to his legs with leather belts.

"Piet," I said, finding my voice. "How splendid it is to see you standing."

"Yah, Elter Arkwright hass been vorking on dese tings, dese braces. Dis is de secont pair. I haff enough feeling in my leks now to tell dey is uncomfortable. Ve are soon to try a new pair. Dey vill be better I tink. But, hey, vat happent to my manners? Come in. De vife is fixing sooper now."

"Thank you, Piet," I said. "May I present these flowers to her?"

"Yah. She is stirring de stew by de fireplace."

Once inside, I saw Dorrie bending over the fire stirring the stew. She wore no bonnet and her black hair cascaded downward in a delightful tangle of curls. When she stood and turned in my direction, I could see that her face was flushed from the heat of the fire. She wore a blue dress with a tight waist that accentuated her lovely curves. I presented the flowers and savored the smile she offered, full of white teeth in perfect array. I could only whisper my delight in seeing her.

"Brother Ned," she said, "It is so good of you to come. Please be seated at the table. The stew is ready."

Piet poled himself over to the table, swinging his legs and landing them with a loud clunk. He unstrapped the braces and pivoted on his bench to face the table.

"I must say you fare right well," I said. "Getting around on those steel contraptions."

"Yah, I just wear dem around de house. Dese things veigh a ton."

As Dorrie ladled the stew into bowls, she turned to the two of us. "And you should see my Piet's arms and shoulders. He has gotten so strong. Show your big arms to Brother Ned, Piet."

Piet lowered his head, embarrassed, "Ah Torrie, don't make me do dat. Brooder Net don't vant to see my arms."

"Oh go on. Piet, show him."

Piet shrugged his shoulders and offered a weak smile. He rolled his shirtsleeves and presented two upper arms humped with strength.

"Well, I shan't engage you in an arm wrestle," I said.

"Yah but you look purty strong yerself Brooder Net."

"Some time ago, I was a hod carrier, and that did toughen me for a time but I have been engaged in less strenuous pursuits of late."

Dorrie placed a basket of rolls and a crock of preserves on the table. "Piet, dear, vould you ask the blessing?"

"Dat would be my pleasure." He took a deep breath. We lowered our heads. "Dear Heffenly Fader, ve give thanks for de restoring of de Gospel. Ve ask for good fortune in dis vonderful place, dis new Zion. Ve ask for your blessing on de good food you haff provided for us in dis meal. Ve ask these t'ings in de name of Jesus. Amen."

Dorrie and I added our own *amens.*

Piet lifted his cup of beer. "Let's have a toast. Dis beer is not so goot as Grolsch, de lager from my country. Ve can toast anyway. Ve say in my country, *proust.* So, Brooder Net, *proust!*"

"Proust!" I clinked his cup with my own and took a swig of Nauvoo beer. I found it palatable but agreed with Piet, there were better brews by far than this local swill.

The food, while superb, did not compensate for the insufferably tedious conversation. I could not keep my eyes off of Dorrie. Once, while lifting her spoon, she caught me staring at her. Of course, I averted my gaze, but she slipped from the table leaving Piet and me to quaff a few more cups of beer.

Dorrie cleared dishes from the table and Piet yawned. He declared that a long day at the store, hauling his heavy legs, and four cups of beer had made him drowsy. He strapped his braces on flaccid legs, stood, grabbed his crutches, and swung himself to a rocking chair by the fading fire. Before I could join him in further conversation, he fell fast asleep.

I seized this opportunity to follow Dorrie out to the back of the house where she was washing the dishes in a lean-to shed.

"May I be of assistance?" I asked. "Piet has fallen asleep."

She smiled. "Poor man. The mere task of living tires him so. But you needn't help. I can manage. You are our guest after all."

"But I insist."

I could see the hesitation in her eyes. I would have to practice custody of my own in order not to upset her further, to regain her confidence in my *noble* intentions.

"Very well, then. You may wash these few remaining dishes and I will towel them off. Perhaps you wouldn't mind helping me to carry them back into the cupboard."

"It would be my pleasure."

When we had finished the chore, I followed Dorrie back into the cabin, my arms loaded with dishes. Unable to help myself, I aped her backside as she strode before me.

Piet stirred as we re-entered the cabin.

"Goodness me," he said, "I must apolochise. I have fallen asleep. You helped Torrie vith de dish vashing. I tank you."

"No apologies are necessary, Brother Piet. It was my pleasure."

And indeed it was.

We reseated ourselves for evening conversation and I suffered through their stories of the harrowing voyage from Liverpool. Obviously, this was a defining event in their lives because they regaled me with story after story, not failing to omit the tiniest of details. Dorrie, though not ashamed of her husband's condition, seemed compelled to tell of his prowess as a sailor in the days before his accident. Several times, she reached over and squeezed his considerable arm. I could tell they were much in love, which consternated me. However, to my relief, by the time I took my leave, Dorrie had relaxed again in my presence. I had finally managed to hold my wandering eyes in check.

During my leisurely jaunt back to north Nauvoo, I smiled to myself. All-in-all, it had been an auspicious evening. They invited me to supper again and thus the friendship between Kevil Pape; nay, Ned Freeman; and Dorrie Van Rijn deepened.

+ + +

As I predicted, Officer King and his men returned with orders from Governor Carlin to arrest the Prophet and Porter Rockwell *at all hazards*. Hyrum and others met the lawmen in the middle of Water Street between the Prophet's homestead and the Red Brick Store.

When presented with the warrant for re-arrest, Hyrum brushed it aside, "Rockwell's gone. Can't say where."

"Why didn't you hold them?" King said, in obvious distemper.

"No warrant. No charge. *Habeas corpus*."

King sputtered, "That's a pile of horse chips and you know it!"

Hyrum shrugged. "Joseph may be around," he said. "If you can find him I reckon you can arrest him."

I couldn't contain my smile. My counsel had come to good avail.

Joseph had gone into hiding in what the Mormons called *Zarahemla* (Iowa to the Gentiles). The officers combed Nauvoo in search of Joseph. Unable to find the Prophet, Officer King became apoplectic with rage and threatened to lay the city to ashes. He found Emma Smith in her garden and poured out his invective upon her with vile threats to shoot her husband on sight. Several of us rushed to her aid. In a moment of grand chivalry, I stepped between Officer King and Emma. "Sir," I said, "your complaint is not with this good woman. I ask you kindly to stand down and leave these premises."

"She's harboring the son-of-a-...."

I put my hand on King's chest. "No need to be profane in the presence of a lady. You have finished your business. I suggest you leave town."

King stared for several long seconds, then sagged. He and his men mounted and rode out of town to join John Cook Bennett who, with his vigilante mob, had surrounded Nauvoo in a virtual blockade. Several times in the days to come, these aggressors invaded Nauvoo in search of Joseph but were never successful in finding him.

+ + +

The night after he disappeared, Joseph convened a council on an island in the Mississippi River between Nauvoo and Montrose. He invited me to attend. Just after dark, William Law picked me up at my house. In the wagon, I joined Newell K. Whitney, and Bishop George Miller, who had assisted in my baptism. Miller had just returned from Jefferson City, Missouri with news to be revealed when we reached the island. We made our way to the Red Brick Store and joined the others, a half dozen or so of the most trusted aides to the Prophet. To my surprise, Emma came along, having been summoned by her husband.

Hyrum drew us into a circle. "There's a small cabin on Dundey Island owned by a man named Walker. He's a Gentile but sympathetic to the Saints. He will hail us ashore. Joseph and Erastus Derby will come across from Zarahemla to meet us. All clear?" Hearing no questions, he continued, "Let us then ask Heavenly Father for safe passage to the Island, protection for our Prophet, and relief from the persecution at hand." We bowed our heads as Hyrum voiced a long and wearisome prayer.

Two men formed a chair with their arms and carried Emma out to the skiff. It took us thirty minutes to reach the southern shore of Dundey Island. When he heard the lapping of our oars, Walker waived his lantern and called out, "Heave her to shore here." The place he selected brought us out of the current allowing us to maintain our position without drifting. We waited in silence, save for a few comments regarding the ongoing dangers posed by King's men and Bennett's mob. I quite enjoyed such cloak and sword action pursued in the dark of night. I felt energized and honored at having been included in this clandestine meeting.

Fifteen minutes after our arrival, a second skiff rounded the bend of the island shoreline. When Joseph came to on our starboard side, he reached across the gap between the skiffs and took Emma's hands. He lifted them and kissed each tenderly.

"Dear Emma, the wife of my youth," he said. Then, looking up, he hailed us, "Brothers, I greet you in the name of the Lord Jesus Christ."

I rolled my eyes.

Joseph also found it necessary to pray for our clandestine meeting, our safety, and our protection in the days to come.

"Let me hear your news," he said upon finishing the long-winded prayer.

"Nauvoo is surrounded," William Law said. "Bennett's men and King's regular officers patrol the roads leading into and out of the city. Several times, they have gone searching for you. It has not yet occurred to them to patrol the river, but I reckon they will before long. We have to hide you away. Sooner the better."

"Word has reached me," Erastus Derby said, "that a warrant has been issued in Iowa for the Prophet's arrest. Authorities from Lee County are soon to descend upon Montrose to capture him."

"All the more reason to remove the Prophet immediately," Law said. "Brother Edward Sayers and his wife, who live upriver, will shelter the Prophet. I recommend that we see to his removal upriver tonight."

Bishop Miller then disclosed the news from Missouri. "I made some inquiries in Jefferson City. Seems that Missouri Governor Reynolds had nothing to do with the demand that Governor Carlin arrest Joseph and Port. Old Boggs made that request before a justice of the peace and it was upon this flimsy appeal that Carlin issued the warrant for arrest."

"Won't hold up under legal test," I said. "However, we needn't tempt fate here. This will all die down within a fortnight. Then Joseph can return home. Even if arrested, there is no proof that the Prophet was involved in the attempted assassination. Of course, Rockwell is in a more precarious position."

After several more comments on the general state of things and Joseph's pronouncement that Governor Carlin was a *misguided simpleton,* we concluded our business. Arrangements were made for a man named Albert Rockwood to ride upstream to a point called Wiggan's Farm, which was not far from the Sayers' place. Rockwood would light two fires on the shore to signal the point of landing. With that, we pushed off and returned to Nauvoo undetected.

As I disembarked from the skiff and prepared to climb into William Law's wagon, Emma drew me aside. "Brother Ned, a moment please. I have a letter for you…from Joseph." She slipped the letter into my hands and I deftly inserted it into the inside pocket of my coat.

"What is this?" I asked.

"I don't know. You were on the far end of the skiff so Joseph could not give it to you directly. When we prepared to depart, he slipped it to me while we embraced. He said, 'See to it that Ned gets this.'"

"I'm sure I am in your debt," I said and bowed.

She said nothing more and gathered her skirts to leave.

Twenty minutes later, I sat in my rocking chair by lantern light and opened the letter to read the following lines.

August 10

My dear Brother Ned,

I take the liberty to tender my deepest thanks for your swift action upon my arrest. I am aware that you orchestrated my release from prison, the actions of the Municipal Court, and the work of the City Council. The ordinance you penned is nothing short of brilliant. We are all in your debt.

These good actions and your noble service compel me to press hard on the matter we discussed in the tree stand to the north of town some days past. As you are well aware, I shall be indisposed for a time until this Carlin business dies down. Upon my return, I shall have further conversation with Elder Arkwright and his daughter. She is strong-willed but I have no doubt we shall prevail. I also want to speak with you regarding admission to the Quorum of the Anointed. However, I ask you to keep this matter in confidence until I can properly introduce you to said Quorum.

Until we speak again, I remain in your debt.
Joseph Smith, Jun.
Mayor of Nauvoo

P.S. It might be well to burn this letter.

I re-read the letter several times before removing the globe from my lamp, igniting the paper, and tossing it onto the cold fireplace grate.

CHAPTER FOURTEEN

Elena

Desolation

The Prophet's arrest and the city blockade paralyzed Nauvoo. Traffic in town thinned to the point of necessity. People stayed behind closed and locked doors. Meetings were canceled, schools were closed, and socializations snuffed. Work on the Temple stopped because so many of the craftsmen stayed home to protect their families. At unpredictable times, our persecutors rolled into town and conducted fearsome searches for the Prophet. They broke into homes, upended furniture, tore open cupboards and closets, and made terrifying threats. To their soaring frustration, these officers and vigilantes had no luck in finding their quarry. I had no intimate knowledge of behind-the-scenes efforts, but learned our leaders and Emma were trying to quash the warrant for Joseph's arrest and lift the siege.

I must confess that I had become so disaffected by the Prophet's unseemly effort to arrange a marriage between Ned Freeman and me that a part of me hoped he would be arrested again. When these thoughts surfaced in my mind, I let them linger for a time and then, ashamed of my hardened heart, sought God's forgiveness. What I could not repent of, however, was my umbrage at the proposition itself. During the days of the siege, when Da and I remained cooped in the cabin, my bitterness festered. Periodically, I seethed, snarling inwardly at the thought that one man would attempt to direct my marital future in such a ham-fisted way. During the snippets of time in which my anger abated, I realized that my reaction was excessive and disproportionate. I tried to fathom why, but could not. I daresay my continued spinsterhood factored into this immoderate set of emotions but I was too distressed to understand why.

All of this emotion became manifest in the banging of pots, slamming of doors, and stomping of feet. Save for these excessive noises, I brought a blanket of silence down on our shut-in circumstances. Poor Da tiptoed around, wincing at the bangs and slams, his brow gnarled like bark on a sweet gum tree. As the days of our confinement wore on, my exchanges with Da became less terse. I knew deep in his heart Da wanted the best for me, but his slavish devotion to the Prophet had corrupted his motives. At the core of it, I could not divine the Prophet's incentive for meddling in my life and thus my resentment remained full to the brim.

For twelve days we endured the dreadful blockade of Nauvoo. Finally, on August 20th, word reached us that during the night, our persecutors had abandoned their cordon of the city. Joseph emerged from hiding and, for the moment, resumed his normal activities. We felt the full bloom of relief and once again took deep breaths. Out of food at the cabin, I bustled off to the Red Brick Store to buy necessities. Other Saints, in the same state of want, packed the place. An atmosphere of joy and thanksgiving pervaded the store. Piet, consumed by his duties, could only wave and smile at me.

As soon as the opportunity presented itself, I hurried to the Van Rijn cabin and fell into one of the rare upholstered chairs to be found in Nauvoo.

Dorrie rushed to kneel by my side. She grasped my hand and held it between her own. "Lanie, you look dreadful! Tell me what has happened."

I took a deep breath and prepared to unburden myself. "Dorrie, troubling matters are afoot. I shall not mince words. I am under great duress to marry Ned Freeman."

Dorrie's expression shifted from worry to bewilderment.

Apprehending her puzzlement, I continued. "Yes. Apparently, Ned Freeman asked Brother Joseph to secure my consent to marry. First Joseph approached Da. Of course, Da will do whatever the Prophet asks."

She nodded. "Of course he will. He reveres Joseph."

"Then, just before the siege, the Prophet himself stood in our keeping room side-by-side with Da and, without batting an eyelash, entreated me to marry Ned."

"What did you say to him?"

"I refused."

Dorrie's eyes widened.

"At hearing my refusal, Joseph jumped to his feet and stood before me. He put his hands on his hips and looked at me as if I were a wayward child. Towering over me, he told me to strengthen my prayers. He lorded over me in a most maddening way. I lost my composure and stormed into my room. I slammed the door on the Prophet. Dorrie, I will not marry Ned Freeman and the Prophet cannot force me to do so."

"Oh, Lanie. I am so sorry for your circumstance. But, pray tell, where is Ned in all of this? Has he spoken to you?"

"That is just it. I haven't seen Ned in weeks. We parted ways – of his volition. I cannot imagine he now wants to marry me and I don't understand why he has not approached me himself. Da says this is the proper way to ask for a woman's hand in marriage. True, I suppose, but why didn't Ned himself seek my father's permission? Why should Joseph be in the middle of it all?"

"Lanie, that is obvious. Ned has rightly predicted you will decline. He seeks greater leverage and feels the Prophet provides such."

"I don't see why Ned assumes I would decline. I've given him far more than he has ever given me."

"Somehow he must sense it."

"He's a coward."

"Or cunning."

"There is the truth of it."

"But Lanie, if the Prophet sees this as the proper future for you, you must listen. He is God's prophet in these latter days."

"Dorrie, not you too!"

She squeezed my hand. "Look at me, Lanie."

I raised my eyes.

"My dear, dear Lanie. I do not mean to press you. I cannot imagine marrying a man I do not love. I have been blessed by love. I pray that for you too." She lowered her eyes and her voice. "One must be careful in turning down the Prophet. A soul could be at stake."

"I cannot imagine a loving God wishes to force me into a loveless marriage. I will not accede to the Prophet's wishes. What hurts me more is how this affects Da. He so wants me to be cared for and loved. After Mum died, he clung to me fearing that no one would succor him in his dotage. Here, in Zion, I have sensed in him new feelings of peace and security. He knows that the Church will not abandon him. He is ready again to see his spinster daughter courted. Truly, I must say it is more painful for me to deny my Da's wishes than those of the Prophet."

"And you are certain there is no chance for you to change your mind?"

"None that I can imagine."

"Well, then…that is how it will be. I shall be by your side. And may I say, the Prophet's urging aside, that I am relieved by your decision."

"Thankful?"

"Yes. Some days ago, before the blockade, Mister Freeman was at my home for supper."

I waited.

"I had thought perhaps Ned would be the right man for you, but his actions during our supper put me quite off that idea."

"What did he do?"

"He unsettled me."

"Unsettled you? How so?"

"I caught him on more than one occasion looking upon me with what I take to be a lustful eye."

"Lustful?"

"Yes. I don't believe it to be my imagination. I would catch him staring at my…my womanly features. He then quickly averted his eyes. It was unnerving, very unnerving."

"This surprises me. Despite my own reservations, I've never known him to be other than a gentleman."

"To be sure. Outwardly, he was every bit the perfect gentleman. He offered to help me with the dishwashing. I must say I found that a most unusual offer for any man to make, especially one under our roof as a guest."

"He can be charming. That I'll allow."

Just then three sharp knocks sounded on the oaken door.

We glanced at one another, then the door.

Three more knocks in rapid succession.

Dorrie stole to the window to peer out from behind the curtain. She relaxed and her shoulders dropped. A man named Markus

Oliver, one of the Temple blacksmiths, stood on the porch. Markus looked around Dorrie and fixed his eyes upon me.

"Ah, Miss Arkwright, you are here. You must come."

I stood up. "Why, Markus? What is the matter?"

"It's your father. He collapsed at his forge. Come quickly."

Markus mounted his horse, grabbed my arm and swung me up behind his saddle, and spurred to a full gallop. When we arrived at the Temple, a small crowd had gathered around my old Da who lay on his back, his ruddy face pale and twisted in pain. I rushed to him.

"Da!" I screamed. "Someone fetch Doctor Mercer."

"On his way, miss," a bystander said.

I knelt by Da and put my hand on his forehead.

"Ah, Lanie, girl. Ye've come."

"Of course, Da. Don't try to talk. Doctor Mercer is coming."

Da clutched his left arm. "Me arm aches like old Billy Hades, Lanie."

Just then his face contorted in another paroxysm of pain.

"Oh Da," I said. "Stay with me. Please Da. Help is on its way."

"Lanie," he said, barely able to muster a whisper. "Lean down thine ear."

I put my ear next to his mouth.

"Aw'm finished. Aw know it, swee' girl. Da has come t' the end o' the road. Aw love thee more than life itself. Promise me somethin', Lanie."

"Of course Da. What?"

"Me dyin' wish is for ye t' be married. Aw'll not be around t' care for ye an' Aw want ye t' be safe and looked after. Please, won't you marry tha' Ned Freeman. It would give thine owd Da a final peace of mind."

I stared at him for several long seconds, my breath caught in my throat. *No, Da. Not this. Anything but this.*

"Please, Lanie girl."

Suddenly, his breath caught. His eyes widened. His mouth formed a single silent word, "Please."

I squeezed my eyes and managed a brief nod. "Yes, Da. I will consent."

A smile of radiant peace crossed his face. He closed his eyes and surrendered his life to Almighty God.

I sat there, numb, clutching Da's hand, the hand that had steadied me for so many years, the anchor of my life. "I love you Da," I whispered.

Dorrie rushed up, having just arrived, and knelt by my side. Slowly, she pried my hand from Da's and turned me toward her, bringing my head into the triangle of her neck. It was then that I poured out my grief on the shoulder of my friend. Through my tears, I saw Doctor Mercer listen to Da's chest through a brass tube. After placing the tube on several points, he shook his head and thinned his lips. "His heart."

+ + +

The next day, Elder Thomas Arkwright was buried in the cemetery to the east of the city. The Prophet preached an appallingly insensitive funeral discourse on the necessity for solidarity among the Saints. He scarcely mentioned my wonderful Da's name, let alone offer praise for the sacrifices and services he so unselfishly gave for the furtherance of the Kingdom. I found myself disgusted by the whole affair. Just as the service was ended I caught Arthur's eye. His sympathy radiated across the fifteen yards separating us. He shook his head. He too found the funeral to be a tactless display of political oratory. Everyone loved Da, and they had hoped for something better - tender words about his goodness and the surety of his eternal rest.

When the Prophet finished his last words and the Stake President William Marks offered a perfunctory benediction, all passed by to offer condolences. All, that is, save for my soon-to-be betrothed Ned Freeman. At least he bothered to attend the funeral but left before its conclusion. Seeing him walk away without so much as a word of sympathy added to the accumulated pain I felt that day. I did not want to marry the man and I knew the Prophet would soon renew his case for my submission.

It didn't take long. Brother Joseph waited until just short of twenty-four hours before reprising his expectation that I marry Ned Freeman. So numb was I by my loss that I simply nodded, hoping he would leave me to grieve alone.

Good people stopped by in the days to come, reiterating their sorrow at my loss and giving me food for which I had no appetite. Each day Dorrie came by and sat with me, often in a silent vigil. I appreciated her presence because the warm and joyful cabin my old Da had so lovingly built now stood as a tomb of quiet heartache. Word must have gone out that I consented to marry Ned Freeman because after several days, people added awkward congratulations to their sympathies. All of this added to my dread. Any hope I might have had in avoiding this arranged union faded with each expression of good wishes. Still, I had not seen hide nor hair of Ned Freeman. Not a good sign.

When I did see him, ten days had passed since Da's funeral. There in the Grove, under a canopy of evening blue, amid a shower of golden oak leaves fluttering in the autumn breezes, Ned Freeman awaited me. On the arm of Arthur Walmsley, I *approached the altar*, so to speak. Of course, there was no altar. In its place stood a beaming Prophet ready to perform our wedding ceremony. Doctor Mercer stood to Ned's left as his witness and Dorrie awaited me as my own. Several hundred Saints had gathered to see our nuptials on this perfect Autumn evening. However, my unresolved grief and dread squeezed from me every ounce of happiness I should have felt. I was oblivious to the beauty of that mid-September day.

Mercifully, the wedding ceremony was over in but a few minutes. A picnic ensued and, once again, I received the handshakes and hugs of my brothers and sisters in Christ. Their expressions of sorrow had given way to smiles and well wishes. Ned did not stay by my side during the picnic but stood aloof, under a tree, munching on a piece of fried chicken. He nodded and offered obligatory thanks to those who congratulated him. This was a scene far from my wedding dreams as a girl in the *weighvin' shop* of Preston so many years ago.

It must have been after five o'clock when the crowd began to disperse. The sun had dipped low to the western horizon and a lovely sunset spread over the rim of Zarahemla. Ned pointed me to our wagon. He did not take my arm nor did he offer to help me into the seat beside him. I drove to my new home next to my husband...my *husband*, an oddly joyless thought. Not a word passed between us, a strange circumstance given the many conversations we once had on the grassy slope of the Grove.

When we arrived at our house, Ned busied himself unhitching the horse, feeding, and grooming him. He took a long time to currycomb a horse that had had merely pulled a small wagon to and from the Grove.

I busied myself with unpacking. Ned had not emptied any of the bureau drawers to accommodate my few undergarments nor was there any room in the armoire for my dresses. I hoped he wouldn't mind if I rearranged things to secure enough space for my few clothes. It was not an easy chore, inasmuch as Ned was a natty dresser and had a number of fine suits.

When I finished these preparations, I sponged myself with a bar of manufactured soap that Dorrie had given me as a wedding gift. I slipped into my nightgown and settled into the bed to await my husband's arrival. I was as nervous as a bride should be on her wedding night but my uneasiness was compounded by Ned's strange and distant silence. He acted as if he, too, had been compelled to enter this marriage against his wishes. Whatever the case, I vowed to be a good wife, dutiful and responsive to my husband. Though I did not love him, perhaps my Da and the Prophet were right. In time, love can develop and grow, sometimes out of nothing. I could only hope.

The candle on our bedside had nearly guttered out when at last I heard Ned's footsteps in the hallway outside the bedroom.

The door creaked open.

He stared at me in the dim light. "What do you think you are doing?" he asked in a low, menacing voice.

"Why…why…I am waiting for you, dear one."

He sprang across the room, grabbed my arm, tore me from the bed, and hammered my face with a tight fist. He threw me into the hallway. "Do not come into this room again unless I summon you!"

He slammed the door and left me sitting there in stunned and crumpled silence, my hand on a battered eye.

I have no idea how long I sat there horrified and frightened by the inexplicable assault I had just suffered. When I managed to pull myself to my feet, I tottered to the second bedroom. I closed the door and secured the tiny hasp, though I knew it would be too flimsy if Ned decided to break into my room. In the darkness I managed to pour a basin of cold water. I soaked a cloth and held it to my swelling eye. I winced at the touch of the cloth and guessed that Ned's punch had torn the skin of my cheek. I took the cloth over to the window and in the dim moonlight confirmed that I had been bleeding. I placed the cloth back on my cheek and sat on the bed.

I cannot describe the agony of misgiving and grief I suffered through the course of that sleepless night. I could not imagine what had gotten into this man whom I had only known as a gentleman. His distance from me in the weeks leading up to our wedding, while unsettling, could not possibly have presaged such a violent outburst. Though I had uneasy forebodings, I surely had no sign that my husband would assault me on my wedding night nor, I fear, had anyone else. It made no sense to me. Had he been drinking while I prepared for bed? Had I done something to provoke such outrage? Had he taken ill? Had something momentarily driven him mad? I could not contrive an explanation nor, strangely, could I weep.

The next morning, as dawn stole through the bedroom window, I heard stirrings in the next room. Then, bureau drawers slammed and armoire doors banged shut, followed by a soft *whump* that I presumed to be the sound of clothes hurled against a hallway wall. I lay still as death until Ned left the house. When I heard his horse trotting away from the yard, I rose to inspect my injuries in the silvered glass. My left eye was a purpled slit. A tight scab had formed over the cut on my cheekbone.

What was I to do? A maelstrom of futile thoughts whirled in my mind. I could not run to anyone for help. Who could believe a man would batter his wife senseless on his wedding night? An educated man. A pillar of the Church. What normal, red-blooded man spurns a willing young wife? Willing to yield her virginity. I was, to put it squarely, left in the lurch. Shame and guilt slithered through this mental lockup.

+ + +

Ned returned in the early evening and met my timorous stare with a look of his own, softer and less threatening.

"I have prepared a light supper," I ventured to say.

"What is it?"

"I found some things in the cellar. I made a salad out of potatoes."

He shrugged and nodded.

"Come," I said and led him into the kitchen. I had set a small table with cloth napkins, silver forks, and china plates I found in the cupboards. When he seated himself, I dished him a hearty portion of the potato salad.

Ned took a fork full and savored it.

"It's good," he said.

I let out my breath. Oddly, I found myself thrilled by his approval.

I took a few bites myself but had no appetite. When Ned neared the end of his supper, I screwed up my courage and broke the silence.

"Ned, have I done something to offend you?"

He stopped chewing and looked at me with those vacant eyes. "No."

"Then what happened last night?"

"You are not to be in my room unless I grant you my permission."

"So I have gathered. Mightn't you have mentioned this to me?"

"Perhaps, but now you know."

"Yes I do. Why don't you talk to me? We used to have such full conversations. Now you barely say anything to me."

"That was then. This is now."

I could not argue with such unassailable logic. "Ned, I want to be a good wife to you. I will honor your wishes about where I am to sleep. I will prepare meals for you, I will keep your house, I will do your bidding…but I will not tolerate any further physical abuse."

His hand snapped forward and clamped my cheeks, squeezing them between my teeth.

"If anyone asks," he hissed, "You fell against the newell post on the stairway."

He let go, stood, and walked into the front room of the house. I heard him unfurl his paper. Our brief conversation had come to a close. I cleared the dishes and went up to *my* bedroom. There I tried to read soothing passages of Scripture but found no solace.

The next day unfolded in much the same fashion. Ned left in the first hours of the morning. Where he went remained a mystery to me. In the early evening, he returned home and ate the warm molasses beans I had cooked on the stove. I had never used a factory stove before and considered myself fortunate not to have burned the beans.

On the third night after our wedding, Ned summoned me to his room and there, in a loveless, mechanical, and painful coupling, we consummated our marriage. Immediately, upon finishing, he sent me to my room feeling used, soiled, and bereft of the proper joy I should have known upon the granting of my virginity.

And so our married life began. To my relief, I suffered no further physical abuse. Yet I remained ever vigilant. I did not know when he might come unhinged again. As they say, I *walked on eggs*, whenever in his presence. When my eye healed, I went out in public once more to purchase food and other necessities. Upon occasion, I saw Dorrie and other acquaintances. They invariably asked me how I was faring and I assured them that I was happy and doing well. On one brief occasion outside the Red Brick Store, Dorrie, sensed my pretense and began to pry. When I turned my head to hide the sting of tears, she put her arm around me but said no more.

With the weather deteriorating, church meetings in the Grove became less frequent. The Saints met in homes, meeting halls, shops, or anyplace else large enough to hold the neighborhood families. Those of north Nauvoo met in a wainwright's shed, heated by a forge. There was enough room for several dozen of us to meet for Sabbath gatherings. Church leaders, including the Prophet, spread themselves throughout Nauvoo so that at least one was present at each of the several neighborhood meetings. Ned seldom attended, except when the Prophet came to visit. Then he walked regally into the meeting with me on his arm.

When Ned absented himself from these Sabbath services, I usually attended alone but found them increasingly banal. Gone were those high inspirational moments that compelled me to leave everything behind and brave the hardships of a journey to America. Gone were the joys of this new and restored gospel set ablaze by the anointing of God's special Prophet. Gone were the dreams of eternal love and unending increase sealed to the man appointed for me by Almighty God. I had settled into that same ennui that had infused my soul when I attended the Primitive Methodist Church of Preston. I sighed in the bitter realization that I must have had a radical defect of the soul. Willard Richards thought as much in the days before my conversion. That great heart fire I experienced while listening to Wilford Woodruff had dwindled to a tiny flicker.

In mid-October, when the harvesting and gathering had been completed, and we women were furiously canning, drying, pickling, salting, and storing, Arthur Walmsly sent out a notice. The Seminary would open once again for the winter session, beginning in a fortnight's time. I could not have been more thrilled. The children would give me a much-needed respite for at least a few hours each day.

On the opening day of the Seminary, Ned left the house early. I hurried to finish my morning chores and reported to Elder Campbell's home. To our delight, we had over thirty students. Every previous enrollee returned, due, we proudly learned, to the quality of instruction and the progressive approach developed by Arthur. We devoted the first day sorting the students by ability. He may have been exaggerating but at the close of that first day, Arthur remarked that I hadn't stopped smiling since my arrival. I felt happy for the first time since my marriage to Ned Freeman.

I arrived back home in late afternoon. Ned stood just inside the door. His look froze me in place.

"Where have you been?" he said in that low, menacing voice I had come to dread.

"The Seminary," I said.

"And who gave you permission to spend your day at the Seminary with that insipid Walmsley and all of those lice-infested spawn?"

At that moment, a strange combination of panic and anger gripped me.

No, no, no. Ned Freeman will not deprive me of the one thing in my life that gives me pleasure and purpose.

I steeled myself. "You knew when you married me that I was a teacher in the Seminary. If you will recall, you lauded me for my work. I do not need permission to teach. It is my service to the Kingdom."

He walked toward me.

I stood my ground.

When he came to within inches of where I was standing, he thrust his left hand up and encircled my neck in a vice-like grip. With his right hand he took a fallen strand of my hair and curled it behind my ear.

"Let me go," I said through bared teeth.

He lowered his face to mine.

"Dear wife…let me remind you that I am your lord. You will do my bidding and only my bidding. Your days at the Seminary have come to an end. You will stay here and keep up this household, as is your wifely duty."

"Let me go. You are choking me."

"Do we then have an understanding?"

"Let me go!"

To my surprise, he did.

I glared at him for several long seconds before leaning up to his face.

"I will *not* stop my work at the Seminary! I will keep up this house as you wish *and* I will help teach the children."

He looked at me as if to study my face, blinking two or three times.

Instantly, I was on the floor doubled over in pain. Ned had pounded me with his fists, one blow to each of my breasts. Before I could catch my breath, he grasped me by the hair and punched me three more times in the face. I fell to the floor quite unconscious.

I couldn't say how long I was unconscious. When I opened my eyes, I saw that I had been insensible long enough for him to brew tea and take his seat in the rocker to read his paper.

Every breath I drew sent shooting pains through my body and my head felt like Da's anvil after a long day of hammering. I rose to my feet, wondering if I had broken ribs. I could barely see through my swollen eyelids. Blood congealed on my face.

Ned heard me groan and lowered his paper sufficiently to fix his ice blue gaze upon me.

"Tomorrow," he said in a soft, gentle voice, as if talking to a repentant child, "You will walk over to the Seminary and inform Walmsley – that piece of human offal – that you won't be returning. Then you get back here without delay. And, if anyone asks about your condition, you tripped on the hem of your dress and took a nasty spill down the stairs. Do I make myself clear?"

I gave him no answer.

"Good, now get into the kitchen. I am famished."

At that moment, in a plan not yet contrived, I vowed to leave Ned Freeman.

PART THREE

As we said before, so say I now again, If any man preach any other gospel unto you than that ye have received let him be cursed.

Galatians 1:8

And again, verily, verily, I say unto you, if any man have a wife, who holds the keys of this power, and he teaches unto her the law of my priesthood, as pertaining to these things, then shall she believe and administer unto him, or she shall be destroyed, saith the Lord your God; for I will destroy her; for I will magnify my name upon all those who receive and abide in my law.

Doctrine and Covenants 132:64
Church of Jesus Christ of Latter Day Saints

CHAPTER FIFTEEN

Burl

Call

I had a parcel waiting for me, its importance signaled by an ecclesiastical seal impressed in red wax. I wondered what it could be and found myself eager to open it. But first, lamps had to be lit and the fire stoked to take the chill off that fading October day. I had just returned from my labors on the Gasconade Circuit, as it was known, a round of five Methodist churches in central Missouri. The Methodist Church had assigned me to this circuit three years previously. While at age thirty, I was still strong and healthy, I had grown weary of the unremitting travel, often in the worst of weather. I loved my Lord and would continue to do what He asked of me but I dreaded the thought of making my rounds in the winter months ahead. I sighed and pushed these selfish stirrings down the stream of my mind. After all, for the moment I was safely home with two days of rest ahead of me. For this I whispered a brief prayer of thanksgiving.

When all preparations had been made, I settled into my chair by the fire and waited for a pot of water to boil for tea. I slit the red wax seal on the package with a small knife. When the wrapping fell away, a leather-bound book and folded letter greeted my eyes. I picked up the letter and read.

St. Paul's Methodist Church
Cincinnati, Ohio September 18, 1842

My dear Brother Bumbalough:

Greetings in the name of our Lord Jesus Christ. I write to you with all due commendations for your tireless work for the Lord on the frontier of our country. I trust this letter finds you well and that your ministrations continue to bring you the fullness of joy. Word has reached me that our churches thrive under your leadership and that the faithful deem you a veritable gift from the Lord. I could not be in heartier agreement. However, dear Brother, I now write to you about a new field of service to which you are being called.

I lowered the letter and looked up to gaze upon the flames of my fire. "What manner of thing is this?" I said aloud to the empty room. *A new field of service?* I stood and dropped tea leaves into the simmering water along with a small lump of sugar. I returned to the letter, uneasy about what the next lines would tell me.

As you may know, members of the Church of Latter Day Saints, the so-called Mormons, have congregated to form a city on the banks of the upper Mississippi River. They call their city Nauvoo. The city is growing rapidly in population because of a "revelation" to their self-proclaimed prophet, Joseph Smith, that all Mormons from around the world are to gather in Nauvoo to await the end times. The Mormons have been admirably zealous in their missionary work and have converted thousands of misguided people to their strange and heretical beliefs. Some worry that they intend to take over large segments of our country and set up a kingdom with Joseph Smith as the sovereign. I do not know if these rumors are sufficiently founded. I know, however, that there is cause for alarm on the challenges these Mormons pose to those of us who labor to increase the true faith.

Lately, I have returned from a journey to the British Isles. In Ireland I attended a conference of Methodists. It was a most uplifting and heart-warming gathering. From there, I traveled through parts of England, ending my excursion in London. While in London, two leading Methodist Elders and a visiting Anglican clergyman sought me out to voice their concerns over the Mormon movement. Each disclosed to me personal stories about relatives and friends who had succumbed to the Mormon wiles. The Anglican divine, the Reverend James Fielding, serves a working-class parish in Preston, a town in Lancashire that had been the first Mormon foothold in England. He informed me that many of his parishioners converted to Mormonism and many have left for America. The Mormon Church continues to flourish in Preston under the leadership of his very own brother, one Joseph Fielding. Mormon missionaries are active throughout the British Isles and they enjoy astonishing success, to the chagrin of all who profess the true faith.

There is, I am most happy to report, a sprinkling of favorable news in all of this. Some who embraced this Mormon perfidy have become disillusioned with their newfound religion. They seek to return to the confines of orthodox belief. Word has reached me that not far south of Nauvoo, in the tiny village of Sonora, there is a small Methodist mission of some twenty to thirty souls. Among those hardy faithful are a handful of disaffected Mormons. They are of English origin and seek refuge in returning to the security of their religious roots. One would suppose they were once Methodists or Anglicans. While this small congregation in Sonora is without a doubt warm and welcoming, there is no Elder to minister to them. Nor is there someone sufficiently aware of English culture to receive disaffected Mormons with the fullness of understanding. Thus we have a missionary opportunity and obligation in Sonora. We would do well to remind ourselves of Saint Paul's words to the Corinthians: "For a great door and effectual is opened unto me, and there are many adversaries."

What is most urgently needed is a shepherd who will seek after these lost sheep and bring them once again into the fold of right belief. This shepherd must understand the set of the English mind, must be robust both in body and mind to withstand the hardships of frontier life, and must have those gifts of the Spirit that can energize a congregation. In addition, he must have the personal force to retrieve the misguided and lost in what will surely be a place of resistance and possible persecution. My dear Brother Bumbalough, I can think of no one else in all of creation better suited to this role of "shepherd" than yourself. You studied for a time in England and you have worked in the frontier missions of America to build congregations from few to many. You have proved yourself fearless and untiring in the conversion of souls. As a former pugilist and prizefighter, you have the physical strength to engage in this work.

For all the reasons just presented, I am hereby reassigning you to the Sonora Methodist mission. A replacement elder will join you there in Missouri in mid-October. His name is Brother Clive Hensley. He is newly ordained but full of zeal for the Lord. You are to familiarize him with the churches under your care and introduce him to the faithful. When you are satisfied that he is ready to assume responsibility for the Gasconade Circuit, you may remove yourself to Sonora. There you will meet one Gabriel Graham, a teacher who has been leading the congregation in the absence of an ordained elder.

I trust you will accept this call with joy and enthusiasm. I can imagine, though the work ahead is daunting, you will find some measure of relief in shedding the burdens of such wearisome travel as befalls the circuit-riding minister.

In the precious Name of our Lord Jesus Christ, I thank you for your service and bid you every blessing in the weeks to come as you take up your new work.

In His service,
The Rev. Charles Fullam
Bishop

Post Script: Please find enclosed a copy of the Latter Day Saint Scripture entitled, The Book of Mormon. *It would be helpful for you to familiarize yourself with this unusual piece of writing. Certain sections are brilliantly written. Yet, it is pure fiction, except for those portions that are copied directly from the Holy Bible.*
C. F. +

I have no idea how long I sat there blinking at the fire. I found it a strange – or divine – coincidence that on the heels of my silent lament about the hardships of riding the circuit, my relief should come as an invitation to *locate*, a term we circuit riders used for the settling down of a clergyman to serve but one parish church. The bishop's directive could not be refused, and it stirred in me a mixture of emotions. I felt excitement at this new opportunity, fear about my capacity to do the work, and sadness at having to leave the people I had come to love so much. As I grappled with these varied sentiments, I turned to God in prayer.

When finally I said my *Amen and Amen*, the fire had lowered to embers and I had to revive it with fresh kindling and my own hot breath. As the fire roared again upon the grate, I wondered how I might discover more about these Mormons. I had heard of them, of course, and knew of Nauvoo but here my awareness ended. I could not say I had ever met a Mormon nor did I have an inkling about their beliefs. Perhaps in the course of my circuits over the next several weeks I could make inquiries about the Latter Day Saints, though I doubted that anyone else in these rude environs had heard of this new religious movement. Most of my people had only the barest understanding of the true faith, let alone any familiarity with this new sect.

For now, I would have to be content with reading the *Book of Mormon*, which I began with a prayer for the guardianship of my mind. I opened to the first page and beheld the title, *The First Book of Nephi*. For the next hour, before sleep stole my attention, I poured over the contents of this leather-bound volume. On the following two days, as my time permitted, I continued to read this strange tale of ancient peoples with such curious names as Jaredites, Mulekites, Nephites, and Lamanites. I recognized those sections of the *Book of Mormon* that were identical to passages in the Bible. Because the language in which the book was written appeared to be biblical in character, I could see how people, even learned people, could fall under its spell.

Unfortunately, the *Book of Mormon* told me little about the theology of the Church of Latter Day Saints nor did it disclose in any great detail their religious practices. I later discovered that none of the faithful on my circuit had any information to offer me on the subject of Mormon belief. So, it appeared I would open a mission to Nauvoo with little understanding of the world from which I was to reconvert people to the true faith. Then, to my surprise and relief, Clive Hensley, my replacement, came to me filled with useful information.

Clive arrived on October 10th in the midst of a brutal storm that pelted him with buckshot-sized hailstones fired from the heavens. So drenched and chilled was he upon his arrival that I immediately poured him a warm bath and allowed him to soak for a good long while in front of the fire. Once recovered, he ate ravenously the rather middling venison stew I had prepared. (I would never grow portly on my own cooking but Clive offered nary a complaint.) When he had warmed up and his belly was full, he promptly closed his eyes and, if the sonority of his snoring were any indication, enjoyed the restoration that comes from a long and deep sleep.

The next morning we both arose, refreshed and ready to strike out on the circuit. While covering those first miles, Clive informed me that he had once lived in Kirtland, Ohio, an early Mormon colony.

He described to me a rather splendid temple that the Saints had built prior to their virtual expulsion from Kirtland in 1838. Mormons had gained control of the town and the anti-Mormon backlash had become quite menacing. This, coupled with financial difficulties and apostasy within the Church, led to a mass exodus of Mormons to Missouri. There they encountered some of the same difficulties and Governor Boggs expelled them from Missouri on pain of death. Nauvoo became the new destination.

We had been traveling west toward String Town, a mining community laid out on the ridge of a hill much like pearls on a string. We stopped at the confluence of Water Fork and the Maramec River. There we rested our horses and satisfied our hunger with strips of jerky.

"Tell me more about this Kirtland Temple," I said. "I'm curious to know how they worship."

"They held Sunday services in the Temple," Clive said over a mouthful of jerky. "Similar to what you might find in any church. I was never inside but my sister Lois and her husband converted to Mormonism, much to the dismay of our family. In a loud argument with our mother about the waywardness of the Saints, Lois claimed that the Mormons were just like us in many ways. Their worship services consisted of prayers, singing, a sermon, and the Lord's Supper."

"It does sound rather typical."

"I suppose, but over the course of its existence, it appears the Church of Latter Day Saints has drifted further and further from its Protestant roots. Most of the founders and early leaders were Protestants, some were ordained clergymen."

"How have they drifted?"

"They have always held that the Lord bestows upon them, particularly Joseph Smith, certain revelations. Smith has had these revelations in abundance and they have pushed the Saints further and further from orthodoxy."

"Might you give me an example?"

"Perhaps one of their greatest heresies concerns the Trinity. They do not believe the three persons of the Trinity are one in the Godhead. Rather, they think the Father is like a president with two counselors who are separate gods – the Son and the Holy Ghost. These three are separate beings with human attributes. They view

Jesus more as a brother, a created being."

"So I take it they do not follow the historic creeds of the Church."

"They most assuredly do not. They believe the church went astray upon the death of the last apostle and has been wallowing in spiritual deviation for hundreds of years. That is, until the proper priesthood and church order were restored when Joseph Smith received certain revelations in upstate New York."

"Quite strange, to my mind."

"Quite, but I can offer an even stranger notion."

"Please."

"They believe that God lives near a specific star called Kolob."

"You can't be serious."

"I could not be more serious."

"Then God lives near a part of the cosmos he made?"

"It would seem so."

I could not help myself. I began to chuckle. "I guess we'll have to change the Lord's Prayer to *Our Father, who art near Kolob, hallowed be thy name.*"

A good laugh overtook us both.

Upon sobering, we rode on. By the end of our second day on the circuit I had squeezed out of Clive Hensley's mind everything he knew about the Mormon religion. I still felt as if I were an infant in understanding but at least I had learned the rudiments. I could enter my new work with some appreciation of the scriptures and belief system of this strange sect. To my great delight, Clive fathomed the Gasconade Circuit with great speed. I felt certain, after one complete circuit, that I could leave my good people in capable hands. Thus on the morning of October twenty-fourth, exactly two weeks to the day after Clive's arrival, I saddled Buckwheat, my gray-brown horse and bid farewell to a small group of the faithful who had gathered to send me off. I struck out along the road that led west to near String Town where I would catch a connecting road – a new one – that led north through Gasconade County to the German community of Hermann. There I would ferry across the Missouri River and set my course north and east to Sonora and the new mission to which my Lord had called me.

+ + +

Seven days later, in mid-afternoon, I arrived in that small collection of buildings known as Sonora. I quickly located the school and church but no one was in the area. After a few more wanderings I happened upon a farm woman cutting down garden stalks and vines in preparation for winter.

"Good afternoon, Madame," I said, pulling off my hat.

She looked up and squinted at me in the soft light of that early November day.

"Sir?" she said.

"Permit me to introduce myself. I am Brother Burl Bumbalough, the new Methodist minister."

"Oh, dear," she said, dropping her scythe. She attempted to straighten her bonnet and swept her hands down the front of her dress as if to smooth out the wrinkles. "Oh dear me, Reverend Bumbalough. Oh dear."

I dismounted and slowly walked toward her. "Do not trouble yourself," I said. "I am most delighted to be here. May the peace of God rest upon thee."

Upon hearing these words, she smiled and returned the blessing.

"I seek one Gabriel Graham," I said.

"Well, yes. Yes, of course," she said. "I am Abigail, Mister Graham's wife. We didn't think you would arrive so soon."

"Nor did I," I said chuckling, "but the good Lord sent me a replacement that took to my circuit like a duck takes to water."

"That's quite wonderful. We have all been looking forward to your arrival ever since we heard from Bishop Fullam that you would be coming. Mister Graham is not here at the moment. He should be along shortly. He's gone to visit one of his students who has been ill."

"I'm sorry to hear it," I said.

"The boy will be fine. He had a fever for several days. Quite ill, I'm told, but he is soon to be back in the pink. Please, Brother Bumbalough, won't you come in?"

I followed Abigail Graham into their rather large house, one of the few stone structures I'd seen in the area. She bade me sit before the fireplace while she stoked the embers and warmed a kettle of leftover coffee.

"You must be tired from your long journey," she said as she handed me a crockery mug of coffee laced with sugar.

It was the first cup of coffee I had sipped since leaving my home in Steelville and I enjoyed it so much that Abigail graciously poured two refills. We spent a delightful hour drinking coffee and chatting about Sonora, its inhabitants, and the little Methodist Church. I was about to broach the subject of Nauvoo and the Mormons when we heard a stomping on the porch.

"Ah, Mister Graham is home," Abigail said and rose to meet him at the door.

"Gabe," she said, "we have a visitor. Brother Bumbalough has arrived."

I stood to greet my host.

He strode across the floor and extended his hand to welcome me.

"Good heavens," he said, smiling across the width of his face. "We were told we were getting the finest missionary in the Church. They didn't tell us he was the biggest."

I threw my head back and laughed. "I was a wee shaver when a boy," I said, "but along about age twelve I started to grow and didn't stop until I hit the ceiling. My sweet Scottish mama, who barely reached five foot – God rest her soul – used to put her hands on her hips, look up at me, shake her head, and say in her Scottish brogue, 'Burl, whence cometh thou? Ye must be Fin McCool, the giant, reincarnated!'"

We all had a good laugh. Gabe reached up and put a gentle hand on my shoulder, "Come and sit a spell longer. Abby will rustle up some victuals."

Gabe tossed his hat onto one of the pegs and pointed to the chairs by the fire.

"You'll be most welcome to stay with us this evening but we have a house for you," Gabe said. "Old Cordy Taylor, a confirmed bachelor with no heirs, up and died a month or so ago. He bequeathed his house and land, some forty acres, to the Church. I suppose we might have sold it but, knowing you were coming, we decided to turn it over to you. It was a mite run down but some of the men and I put it back in good repair. Shored up the porch, chinked some cracks, scoured out the chimney, white washed the outside, that sort of thing. A few of the ladies cleaned the place, changed out the ticking on the bed, and washed the dishes. Cordy was none too tidy but the place is all spick and span now. I'll take you on over there in the morning."

"Well, this is all right kindly of you folks."

"I suppose you'll be preaching come Sunday?"

"That's correct."

"That will be a relief for me. With my school in full sail, it's difficult to conduct the Methodist classes and get a sermon ready to preach. I'm happy to turn all of that over to you."

"And I'm quite happy to take it off your hands."

+ + +

The following Sunday, I arrived at the Church an hour before the scheduled morning service, put a fire in the stove, and scouted around to see what was what. To my relief, I discovered that there were twenty-five tattered but usable copies of *Wesley's Hymnal*, as it was popularly called. I sang two verses of *O For A Thousand Tongues to Sing* and satisfied myself that I was in good voice after three weeks of rest.

The people began arriving early and I stood on the porch to welcome one and all. A carriage rolled in from the north and as soon as the seven passengers introduced themselves, I knew from their accents they were the estranged Mormons about whom the Bishop had written. I asked if they could linger for a brief time at the conclusion of the service so I might talk with them about Nauvoo and the potential for recovering some of the lost souls. All agreed with considerable enthusiasm.

When all twenty-seven of my faithful new parishioners had seated themselves, I processed in from the back of the church singing in my full baritone *Come Holy Spirit, Heavenly Dove* and inviting all to join me. To my unending delight, the congregation quickly picked up the tune and found the words in their tattered hymnals. So glorious were their collective voices that I bade them sing two more hymns before drawing the music to a close and launching into the service. I followed closely the service prescribed by John Wesley, which would seem formal to most frontier Methodists but comfortable to the English members of the congregation, particularly those who were once members of the Established Church. I preached what was later described as a *rousing sermon* on new beginnings. I took as my text the 29th chapter of Jeremiah, *For I know the thoughts that I think toward you, saith the Lord, thoughts of peace, and not of evil, to give you an expected end.*

At the conclusion of the sermon, I set my large Bible down on the Lord's Table and walked out between the pews and among my people.

"Friends," I said. "I've greeted all of you as you entered this place of worship. Over the next several weeks, I shall get to know each of you better because I will visit you in your homes. But, that you might know me better, let me tell you my story. Before I do this however," I said, chuckling, "I can't help but remark upon my name. Brother Burl Bumbalough. Can you imagine such a name? Well, all I can say is that my parents couldn't help the name *Bumbalough*. I can't help the name *Burl*. And you can't help the name, Brother, for I am truly your Brother in Christ. Now, on with my story. I was a fortunate young man indeed, growing up in a good Philadelphia family with dedicated parents. They saw to my education and brought me up in a household that, while Christian by name, lacked a certain commitment. We attended church, but not always and not with as much devotion as our Lord expects.

"When I was seventeen, both of my parents were killed in a fire that burned our house to the ground. Nothing could be saved. I was the only child and left penniless. Depressed and devastated, I went to work as a stevedore and, absent a strong faith, I fell into evil company and became nothing more than a dissolute tosspot spending my leisure hours drinking, wenching, and fighting. As you can see, the good Lord fashioned me in voluminous form. My size, coupled with hours each day loading and lifting, put me in prime condition for fighting. Before long, several agents saw my success in these brawls and urged me to fight for money. So, I entered prizefights up and down the Atlantic seaboard. Dubbed the *Fighter from Philly*, I won for myself, and for my agents, a sizeable sum of money.

"Then one night, half potted in a tavern in Wilmington, I got into an altercation with another man over a young woman sitting on my lap. Seems she was the man's wife, though I didn't know that. I quickly released her, stood, and offered my apologies. He took the occasion to crack me across the jaw with his fist. Without thinking, I punched once in self-defense and the man dropped to the floor like a stone. He never recovered and some hours later died. I was arrested for murder but at my trial, many witnesses came forward to testify that I did not know the marital status of the young woman and that my blow came in self-defense. I was declared innocent.

"Even though declared innocent, I became quite devastated and despondent over the young man's death and entered a period of deep despair. I realized that, had I been living a moral life, I would not have been in that tavern in the first place and a human being in the prime of life would still walk this earth. A young woman would not have been widowed. I cannot describe for you the melancholy that descended upon me."

The congregation was hanging on my every word but I still raised my finger and paused to alert them to the next point I was about to make.

"But…God was with me. You see, throughout my trial there was an old man who sat in the back, eyes alert, hands clasped atop his walking stick, his back straight as an oak tree. He watched every minute of the proceedings. When the trial ended, he introduced himself as Brother Jonathan Halstead, a Methodist minister. He asked me how it was with my soul. Of course, I had no interest in discussing the state of my soul with him or anyone else for that matter. I suppose because my soul was in a very sorry condition. But he persisted and I finally agreed to talk with him. Over many a cup of tea and glass of lemonade, he managed to turn this bullheaded ne'er-do-well into a man of faith. The Lord was in the midst of all of this. Oh, yes, be assured, the Lord was at work! One thing led to another and before I knew it, I had been sent to England to study theology for a time. Upon my return, I began my work in the Lord's vineyard and now He has sent me here."

When I had finished my testimonial, the people – to a person – came by to welcome me again, to thank me for my moving testimony, and to invite me for a meal at my earliest convenience. It was a heart-warming beginning to my ministry in Illinois. As requested, the Nauvoo contingent lingered behind ready to hear what I had to say about the mission to their city. When I had bid farewell to the last local resident, I joined them.

I asked all gathered what had brought them to the Sonora Methodist Church and what caused them to become disillusioned with their Mormon life. There were slight variations in theme but all seven stated, in one way or another, that what they initially perceived to be the true faith, divine in its foundation, had become for them an arid and unfulfilling cult. It centered on the advancement of one man, the Prophet Joseph Smith.

"'E lives a 'igh and mighty life 'e does," said one of the gentlemen.

"Makes 'imself out to be a king, I should say," said another.

"'He thinks he's holier than our Lord," said yet another.

For thirty minutes they regaled me with their complaints and their deep joy in returning to the true faith. When their litany of grievances drew to a close, I explained to them that I had been sent to Sonora to set up a base from which to draw unhappy Mormons away from false teaching, as well as to be a lifeboat for those who were seeking to return to their true Christian faith. All of the Nauvooians promised to help in whatever way they could. While I had no firm plan in my mind at that moment, I assured them I would come up with some course of action and would draw upon their support for its success.

As they were leaving, one young woman stayed behind and drew me aside. She focused her gaze on the little pink flowers arrayed on the hem of her white dress, not wanting to look me in the eye.

"What is it, sister?" I asked.

"There is one other thing you should know," she said.

"Yes?"

"I did not want to bring this up in front of the others because it is a cause of great mortification for me."

I said nothing.

"But I feel I can…I should tell you."

"Yes, sister, go on."

"Joseph Smith asked me to marry him."

"What? Marry him? I thought the man was already married."

"He is but he has several secret wives and he wanted me to be another. Said I could be sealed to him for time and all eternity. That I would become his special new wife, his favorite. I rejected his proposal, of course."

I stood there in front of the young woman quite speechless, unable to fathom a polygamous prophet.

"You mustn't tell anyone," she went on, 'because I don't want it known I was one of the women he sought."

"Surely you bear no sin, my dear. You turned down the man's improper advance. But I do understand that you do not want to be a source of gossip and rumor. So, you have my word. I shall speak of this to no one. I must tell you that I am shocked to the core. I cannot imagine a man having the temerity to propose marriage to another woman right under the nose of his wife. Does his wife – his first wife – know of this, this philandering?"

"I don't know."

I shook my head and put my hand on her shoulder. "Thank you for disclosing this most embarrassing matter. Stand strong, sister. I shall pray for you."

"Thank you, Brother Bumbalough."

With that she joined the others. I stood in the doorway of the church and waved to the carriage as it rounded a curve and slipped out of sight behind the naked trees lining the road to the north.

"Tomorrow," I said to myself. "Tomorrow I shall visit Nauvoo."

CHAPTER SIXTEEN

Kevil

Summons

Monday, October 31ˢᵗ dawned with low overhanging clouds and bitter cold. With gloved hand, I gathered my watchcoat about my neck and lowered my head so the hat brim could shield me from the gusty wind that swirled around me. I had no idea what had prompted Joseph Smith to summon me to his office on this bleak morning. Yet, I knew he rarely sought my company unless something of import loomed in the offing. His request had come the previous day at the close of the Sunday meeting, which had been held for the first time on the ground floor of the Temple, now sufficiently completed to permit a gathering of the faithful. The place was packed to the walls, but the Prophet was not in attendance on that occasion having sent word that he was ill. In his place, Elder John Taylor had delivered a long and deadly discourse on subjects that have since seeped from my mind. However, it was from Taylor I received word that Joseph wished to see me. Thus as I guided my horse down Granger Street toward the Red Brick Store, I tried to imagine why the Prophet had sought audience with me.

Things continued to brew on the Boggs matter. Joseph had found it necessary to slip out of sight now and again as a precaution against surprise raids from the Illinois authorities. On one occasion, while the Prophet sat eating lunch with his family, three officers sneaked up on the river side of Joseph's house and moved to arrest him. Somehow, he discovered their approach and, while Emma stalled the officers, he made a quick escape through the high corn stalks in his garden. Throughout the month of October, he moved in secrecy from safe house to safe house in and around Nauvoo. He continued in hiding until just a few days before his summons to me. Apparently, he felt matters had simmered down sufficiently to permit him to return to his home and office.

When I arrived at the Red Brick Store, I blew in the front door along with the wind. Piet Van Rijn looked up from his perch behind the counter.

"Mister Freeman," he said, "a bloostery day is it not?"

"Blustery indeed."

"Can I help vit someting?"

"No, I am to meet with the Prophet. I take it he is in his office?"

"Yup, he is."

I nodded and slipped up the stairs. Joseph lolled in his office chair with his feet on the desk. All three hundred pounds of Willard Richards stood by the window reading a letter. Upon seeing me, Joseph jerked his feet off the desk and sat upright in his chair.

"Brother Ned, good of you to come."

"At your service," I said.

"I have received a most interesting letter I would like you to read. Willard, give Ned that letter."

Willard looked up, deflating his second chin, and handed me the letter, irritation etched upon his face. I removed my hat and sat down to read. The letter was dated October 20th and addressed to Elder Sidney Rigdon. The letter had come from one Justin Butterfield, Esquire. I knew of Butterfield. He was a prominent Chicago attorney and sympathetic to the Saints. From the first lines of the letter, I learned that Rigdon had written to him regarding the Prophet's travails over the Boggs affair and the repeated attempts to extradite Joseph to Missouri. As I read on, I quickly grasped that in the letter Butterfield was offering an informal opinion regarding the legality of the arrest warrant. He rightly noted that there was no legal sanction for the governor of one state to deliver a fugitive to the governor of another state unless said fugitive had fled from justice. It could be proved that Joseph was in Illinois at the time of the attempted assassination of Boggs. Therefore, the Prophet could hardly have fled justice – a sound legal analysis, to my way of thinking.

When I finished the letter I looked up to see a smug smile spread across the face of the Prophet.

"Well, what say you about the contents of that letter, Brother

Ned?"

"Butterfield's opinion is correct and buttressed by case law."

"Excellent," Joseph said. "I am glad of your corroborating opinion."

I handed the letter back to Willard who continued to pout.

"What do you intend to do with the letter?" I asked.

"I'm not certain. What do you advise?"

"Well, to begin, the letter does no good sitting in your desk drawer. It must reach the light of day and the opinion expressed therein must be lodged with Illinois Governor Carlin. Unfortunately, the current governor is not likely to receive it with an open mind. Therefore, I urge you to bide your time until the newly elected Governor, Thomas Ford, assumes office. It is only a month until the change in leadership."

"How then do I approach Governor Ford?"

"It will be necessary to present a formal petition seeking Ford's revocation of Carlin's arrest warrant. I'll wager, based upon the contents of the letter, that Butterfield will prepare the petition."

Joseph slapped his hands down on his desk and said in a most gleeful voice, "Excellent and yet again excellent!"

I raised my hand to still his enthusiasm. "Hold on. There is yet another consideration."

"Name it."

"There must be something to bolster the request for a petition. For Butterfield to issue an informal opinion in a letter is one thing; to prepare a petition calling for the revocation of a gubernatorial order is quite another. You cannot approach Butterfield and suggest that I, Ned Freeman, urged you to seek his legal services. He doesn't know me from Adam nor do I want him to. Even if he did know me, I doubt my request would compel him to take action. Therefore, I would suggest that, when the time is right, you send some of the brothers to Springfield with this letter to secure a second letter from Judge Stephen Douglas. I'm told he is favorable to the Mormons and he is a man of considerable stature in the state. If *he* were to write a letter to Butterfield asking him to prepare the petition, you will have a good chance of accomplishing your purpose."

The Prophet's mouth was so tautly stretched in a grin that I wondered how he could speak but he managed to say, "Ned Freeman, you are a genius. I could not ask for better closet counsel than you provide to me and to the Church." At this, he looked up at Willard. "Would you excuse us for a moment?" he said.

Willard Richard's pout turned into a perceptible snarl. "Of course," he hissed and waddled indignantly out of the room.

"Willard is a bit distempered today," Joseph said. "No doubt a result of travel weariness. As you may know, he just returned from visiting a number of churches in the Eastern states where he sought to drum up support for the completion of the Temple."

I said nothing in response.

Joseph leaned over and opened the bottom drawer of his desk.

"I have something for you," he said. "A gift to express my thanks for the laudable service you have rendered. I pray you will continue to offer your wise counsel to the Saints."

He placed upon his desk a hand-forged Bowie knife sheathed in a brass scabbard.

"Take it," he said. "It's yours."

"Brother Joseph," I said. "My services to you are minimal. I surely don't deserve such a fine specimen." (But, of course, I did.)

"Don't be modest, Brother Ned. Take it."

I picked up the knife, checked its heft, and turned it around in my hands to inspect the craftsmanship. It had a beautifully polished stag horn handle with a brass end cap. The hand guard was also wrought in brass. The top of the blade extended to about two inches from the tip where it swept downward to a needle-sharp point. I rubbed my thumb across the blade and knew at once that it had been honed to a razor's edge.

"Why I believe I could shave with this," I said.

"It is yours to do with what you wish."

"I cannot thank you enough."

The Prophet stood from his chair and extended his hand. "It is my pleasure," he said.

A rather awkward silence followed and, assuming our meeting had come to a close, I stood to leave.

"Please," Joseph said, easing back into his chair. "Stay for a moment longer."

I nodded and lowered myself back into the chair.

Joseph returned his boots to his desk, leaned back, and looked at me over his nose.

"So how are things with your new wife?" he asked.

Suddenly, I felt caterpillars crawling on the back of my neck. *Whence cometh this question?*

"Things are well," I said, a certain wariness in my voice. "Why do you ask?"

"Merely curious. I have not forgotten about our conversation in the stand of trees. I take it you still desire the lovely Dorrie Van Rijn as your spiritual wife."

"Assuredly."

"Then your relationship with Elena must be favorable in order for you to secure her permission to take a second wife. You will recall that I mentioned the first wife must grant her approval for a second and, who knows, perhaps subsequent wives."

My stomach dropped. I had forgotten that particular requirement. Elena's permission might be a stumbling block. She had not taken well to my disciplinary measures and, of late, had been displaying a certain resistance to my demands. Had it not been for my quest of Dorrie Van Rijn, I would never have married Elena Arkwright. Her obsequiousness and servility during my sickness had become so insufferably annoying that I could barely countenance her. Then, in our wedded state she had continued to madden me with her infuriating mixture of impudence and hangdog despondency. I found her ugly and repulsive with her long thin body, bland face, and straight hair. To make matters worse, her ugliness became ever more obvious to me the first night I bedded her. I had to force my eyes shut. I had needs, after all. It is no wonder that I found it occasionally necessary to issue a sharp corporal reminder of her proper bearing in my presence. But, now, in the new light of Joseph's reminder, I realized I would have to soften my approach to her. I needed her consent for my *spiritual* marriage to the luscious Dorrie Van Rijn.

Snapping out of my thoughts, I reassured Joseph that all continued well with Elena.

Joseph nodded.

"Good to hear," he said. "Now, there is one more thing and I present it to you under the cloak of secrecy."

"Of course."

"By revelation, I have begun to prepare for the renewed and expanded endowment ceremonies that will take place in the Temple upon its completion. To date, twelve men – you know them – have received the endowment: James Adams, Heber Kimball, William

Law, William Marks, George Miller, Willard Richards, Newell Whitney, Brigham Young, Vincent Knight (God rest his soul), Reynolds Cahoon, Hyrum, and myself."

I listened.

Joseph continued.

"It has come to me that it is time for us to add one more person to this Holy Order, this Quorum of the Anointed."

"I see," I said. "Am I to assume that this person is I?"

"You are."

"And of what benefit is this to me?"

Joseph looked at me with a fleeting expression of incredulity as if he could not quite fathom why I would ask such a question. However, he quickly recovered.

"The benefit is two-fold," he said.

"First…" and at this point he reached over and picked up his leather covered Bible and thumbed through it, flicking pages back and forth until he found his spot. "Here," he said. "Read verses eleven and twelve."

I picked up the Bible and saw the heading – *II Peter 1*. I read the appointed verses: *Wherefore…brethren, give diligence to make your calling and election sure: for if ye do these things, ye shall never fall: For so an entrance shall be ministered unto you abundantly into the everlasting kingdom of our Lord and Savior Jesus Christ.*

I put the Bible down quite mystified as to the message I was to receive.

"I must confess," I said, "as it relates to our discussion, I find the message of this passage inscrutable."

"Do you not see, Brother Ned, that you can have the privilege of being sealed unto exaltation in heaven by ordinances administered while you are still living. The first benefit is your eternal salvation and glory in the life to come. This is not only the first but the most important benefit."

Here Joseph paused and studied my reaction.

I blinked. Nothing more.

He sighed and continued. "The second benefit is like unto it and derives from the first. This is the doctrine of celestial marriage. A woman's sealing unto exaltation is accomplished by her celestial marriage to a man in righteousness before the Lord, a man who has received the endowment to power bestowed upon him while yet in this life. Do you follow, Brother Ned?"

I could see where he was headed. "So you are telling me that receiving the endowment is a pre-requisite to celestial marriage."

"Precisely."

"And not to put too fine a point on it, if I wish to have Dorrie Van Rijn as my own, I must go through this endowment ceremony."

"Yes. Such has been revealed unto me."

"And have the other ten men taken upon themselves spiritual wives?"

"A few. Others are not so privileged as you to have seen the full purpose of the endowment and the joy of celestial marriage. I cannot reveal the doctrine to those who are not yet spiritually ready to receive it."

"In other words, you haven't told them about multiple wives because you are afraid they will oppose the practice and expose you."

"Brother Ned, I much prefer to think they are not yet sufficiently formed in their spiritual lives to understand the purpose and import of this revelation. However, it is within the Quorum of the Anointed that I intend, over time, to reveal what has been given to me by the Lord on the matter of celestial marriage."

"And if I may be so bold as to assume that my inclusion in the Quorum of the Anointed will provide for you certain protections. It is safer to have me in the fortress shooting out than outside the fortress shooting in."

"I do not think of it that way, Brother Ned. I am trying to help you secure for yourself an unending life of joy."

I suppressed an eye roll.

"I shall not betray your secrets, Brother Joseph," I said. "However, I urge upon you all due caution in revealing this radical and, I might add, *illegal* practice to even your closest confidantes. It will be too much for some and, if it becomes widely known, it could break your church apart."

Joseph nodded.

"Does your brother Hyrum know of your revelation?" I asked.

"Not as yet."

"Then who?"

"There are four besides myself who have been taught the principle of celestial marriage – Brigham, Heber, Reynolds, and Vincent. I believe Willard and perhaps Will Huntington are ripe for the telling.

The others will follow."

"Have the four you mentioned taken additional wives?"

Joseph looked at me for several long seconds.

"They have," he said.

I exhaled through pursed lips.

"As your *closet counsel*, to use your words, I must tell you that this is very dangerous. As the practice grows and as more and more wives are taken in marriage, the secret will become impossible to keep."

"What do you advise?"

"Keep the secret for as long as possible and deny it publically at every opportunity both by pen and voice. Meanwhile, have the revelation ready to publish when the civic awareness becomes too powerful to deny."

Joseph nodded. "That was my sense as well."

We sat in silence for a time. Finally, I asked, "When had you intended for me to undergo this endowment ceremony?"

"Tomorrow."

"Tomorrow? That seems rather soon."

"I see no reason to wait."

"And what am I to expect?"

"Am I to understand that you are unfamiliar with Masonic rituals?"

"Heretofore, I have been quite disinterested in fraternal societies, especially those with a religious overtone. Why do you ask?"

"The Masonic rituals are a degenerate and corrupt form of the ancient ritual of bestowing the priesthood. Yet, it is accurate in many aspects. Our endowment ceremony is a restoration of the true practice. In it we perform the proper washings and anointings. We also confer the keys pertaining to the Aaronic Priesthood and the higher Melchizedek Priesthood."

"Washings and anointings?"

"I do not wish to say more at this time, Brother Ned. All will be revealed to you in the morning if you accept this calling."

I cannot describe the incredulity with which I received this nonsense. Again, I found myself amazed that people of at least moderate intelligence could swallow this hogwash. Until that moment in Joseph's office, I could not have imagined myself undergoing ritual washing and anointing, whatever that involved. Nor could I imagine receiving these so-called imaginary and fanciful *keys* to such silly offices as the Aaronic and Melchizedek Priesthoods. Yet, words of acceptance were on the tip of my tongue. A fleeting image of Dorrie Van Rijn released them.

"I will receive the endowment," I said. "Where am I to be and when?"

"We shall meet in this office tomorrow at half past nine."

"I have one condition."

"And that is?"

"I want no record kept of my undergoing this ritual nor do I want any record kept of my membership in the Quorum of the Anointed."

"And why is that?"

"I intend to keep a low profile. I am a fugitive from justice."

"Agreed."

"Very well," I said. "Very well."

I retrieved my knife and excused myself.

+ + +

Upon my way out of the Red Brick Store, I paused to converse for a time with Piet Van Rijn. As I walked out the door, I turned to extend an invitation for he and Dorrie to join us for supper on the following Sunday. He accepted without hesitation. I spent the afternoon doing errands and securing farm labor for the following spring, as I intended to see if my eighty acres of land were, as promised, capable of producing a crop.

When I returned home, Elena was stooped over the oven inspecting a delectably aromatic dish.

"What is that delicious smell, my dear?" I asked.

Slowly, she turned to face me with a look of wary puzzlement. I saw the massive bruise on her cheek and winced.

Her gaze turned to the knife in my hand. Panic spread across her face.

I put up my hand. "Have no fear," I said. "This was an unexpected gift from the Prophet. I shall put it away in a safe place. So, what's in the oven?"

"Sister Mercer came by with several prairie chickens," she said in a voice barely audible. "Doctor Mercer had a good hunt. I've made a pot pie."

I rubbed my hands together.

"I can't wait to sup," I said. "I'm famished. Call me when ready. I shall be in the relaxin' room with my paper."

I turned to leave the kitchen. I could feel Elena's bewildered stare in the center of my back.

Thirty minutes later, she called me to the dining table where the potpie sat steaming amid hunks of hot buttered bread and boiled potatoes. Elena had poured me a flagon of ale. She did not drink any alcoholic beverages but tolerated my own consumption. (What else was she to do?)

Knowing I had no truck with grace before meals, Elena closed her eyes and muttered her own private prayer. I dived into the meal and found its taste as delightsome as its smell. After several mouthfuls, I lowered my spoon.

"My dear," I said.

Elena looked at me with the same expression of chary curiosity I had seen earlier. I pressed on as if I hadn't noticed.

"I have been reflecting upon our time together and it has dawned upon me that I have treated you too harshly. I wish to apologize and to tell you that I have resolved to change my ways. Surely you deserve better conduct on my part. Can you find it in your heart to forgive me?"

She stared at her potpie. "I must say I appreciate what you have just said to me, Ned. Forgiveness and reconciliation are at the heart of the Gospel. They must be part of our walk with the Lord. It will not be easy for me to forgive you. I have been hurt in body and soul."

I held my breath.

"I shall try my best, but do not expect forgiveness to come in an instant. It will take me some time."

"I understand."

"Do you? Do you truly understand?"

I did not know how to respond.

"When I married you, Ned, it was against my better judgment. I felt pressured into it but I resolved to be the best wife I could be — dutiful, responsive, loving. In return I received the back of your hand. Even now as I say these words, I fear you will reach across the table and strike me again."

"I assure you I will not."

"Thank you. That relieves my mind."

I decided to press. "It has been some time since you joined me in my bed. Tonight?"

Again she stared at her potpie, stirring it with her spoon.

"No," she said. "Not tonight."

Her effrontery stopped me cold and in a split second rage exploded in me.

I gritted my teeth and curled my fist.

Then, in a moment of unimaginable effort, I regained control of my emotions and let out a long breath.

"Of course," I said. "As you wish."

We finished our meal in silence.

CHAPTER SEVENTEEN

Elena

Encounter

Ned left the house that Monday morning mumbling something about having to visit the Prophet. I waited until his horse was out of sight down Granger Street before donning my bonnet and wrap. I reckoned that Ned would follow his normal pattern and stay away most of the day. Piet would be at the Red Brick Store leaving Dorrie at home alone. During the night I had resolved to talk to someone about my intolerable circumstances. Dorrie was the natural choice, the only choice. This visit was a risky venture. If Ned were to discover my disclosure to anyone, my life could be in danger.

It took three-quarters of an hour to walk across town to where Dorrie lived. To my relief, the cold weather had kept most people indoors and *en route* I encountered no one of my acquaintance. When Dorrie opened to my knock she immediately focused on the massive bruise that had formed on my left cheekbone.

"Lanie, good heavens! What has happened to you? Please come in. Let me fix some hot tea to warm you."

She pulled me into the house and rushed me to a chair before the fire. When she handed me the cup of tea, she sat down opposite me and looked into my eyes, worry etched on her face.

"Tell me," she said.

I couldn't contain myself. With a torrent of words and a flood of tears I told her the horrific things I had gone through since the wedding. I avoided euphemisms. Ned had *beaten, slugged, flung,* and *raped* me. I described the capricious tyranny with which he ruled me, the limitations in my freedom, and his demand that I quit my work at the seminary.

Dorrie sat there speechless, adding her own tears to mine.

"Lanie, what are you going to do?"

"Leave him."

"But where will you go? What will you do?"

"I don't know, but I will devise something. I'm afraid he might kill me."

"Oh, Lanie, surely not!"

"The thought has lodged in my mind."

For the better part of an hour, Dorrie and I sat, commiserated, and tried to formulate a plan for my leaving Ned. Unfortunately, everything we conceived ended in Ned's murdering me. Since he was so intelligent and cunning, we had little doubt he could stage my death in such a way that would point away from him.

I stayed at Dorrie's until late morning, not wanting to leave the web of support and love she had spun for me. Now at least one other person knew of my plight. At last, I pulled my bonnet around my face to screen the bruise and began the long trudge home. My route took me along Wells Street in front of the Temple. So absorbed had I become in my own problems and so downcast was my gaze that I nearly collided with a giant of a man standing on the side of the street. I halted just inches from him and quickly backed away.

A quick glance revealed him to be several inches over six feet in height and at least eighteen stones in weight. He sported a full, unruly beard of ginger-colored whiskers that surrounded his ruddy cheeks and nose, red and chapped from the cold. He wore a black frock coat and broad-brimmed wide awake hat that suggested he was a minister of some sort. Yet, I could not imagine why a minister would stand on Wells Street with his hands on his hips staring up at the rising Mormon Temple.

"I beg your pardon, sir," I said and gathered my skirts to slip by him.

"Ho ho!" he said. "So there are citizens out on this blowy day."

I nodded and gave him a brief smile but did not break my stride.

"Sister," he said. "May I detain you for a moment?"

"I'm afraid I have to move along," I said, quickening my pace.

"I won't hold you long, I promise."

I slowed to a stop and turned. In doing so, my bonnet slipped off the hidden bruise in a gust of wind.

"Dear me," he said. "You appear to have… Perhaps you've taken a nasty spill."

I gave a quick smile. "Yes, that's it. The stairs, the newell post, a long skirt. It is a dangerous combination."

"Ah," he said. "Permit me to introduce myself. I'm Brother Burl Bumbalough, a Methodist minister just recently arrived to serve the small church in Sonora."

"And I'm Sister Elena Freeman. *Mrs.* Elena Freeman."

He held out his hand, a monstrous ham hock of a hand, "Pleased to meet you Sister Elena."

He closed his hand around mine and I shut my eyes to savor his warmth on such a cold morning.

"And I you, Reverend Bumbalough."

He chuckled. "Naw, nothing worthy of reverence in this old boy. Burl will do or Brother Burl if you insist."

He put his hands on his hips again and returned his gaze to the Temple.

"So this is the great holy building of the Mormons."

"It is."

"What a magnificent structure it will be when it is done. Something far grander than my little church in Sonora."

"I've seen your little church, even peeked inside once."

"You did?"

"Yes, and while it may not be grand, it has a sweetness, an appeal, a sacredness that I must say I miss." I don't know why I said this. I was a devout Mormon woman, after all, a devoted Saint. Why did I, at that odd moment, cherish a tiny Methodist chapel, simple and rustic in its construction, one I had only seen for a brief few minutes?

He looked down at me.

"I note you are English, Mrs. Freeman?"

"Yes, but please call me Elena. My friends call me Lanie." I stifled a sudden gasp. *What is wrong with me? Why do I babble in front of this man? Why am I being so forward?*

"All right, Lanie it is," he said with a smile. "Lanie has a nice ring to it. So where are you from in England?"

"Preston. It's in Lancashire."

"Preston. Of course. I have heard of it. I myself studied for a time in England."

"You don't say."

"Yes. London. I studied at a theological college there."

"And how did you come to be on the frontier of Illinois?"

"The Good Lord directed me. I should add He used as His mouthpiece one of our bishops, Bishop Fullam."

"And you came to Nauvoo just to see the Temple?"

"Among other things."

I waited.

"May I ask you a question, Lanie?"

"I should think so."

"Before you became a Mormon, what faith did you proclaim?"

"You will be sorry to hear I was a Methodist, a Primitive Methodist."

"O dear me. A Primitive Methodist. A dour bunch, I would say." At this he scrunched up his face in a look of ill-tempered peevishness. He hunched over, raised a finger in the air next to his face, and in a reedy voice started to mimic a cantankerous old cleric, "I tell you brethren and sistren," he said. "Thou shalt not escape the all-consuming fire of God. It shall start at the hem of your cuffs and petticoats. From thence it shall crawl up your legs and consume your bodies until it reaches your hair. Then you shall run around with your hair on fire until you collapse in a sizzling heap…"

I could not help myself. I threw my head back and laughed aloud. Burl unscrewed his face and laughed along with me. It was the first time I had laughed, with a full belly laugh, in months. "How did I do?" he asked. "Did I come close?"

I wiped the tears from my eyes. "You did. You most assuredly did."

We huddled in silence for a moment. I knew I should be getting on but, despite the cold, I enjoyed the company of Burl Bumbalough.

"You still haven't told me why you are here," I said.

He sobered for a moment. "To minister to the people of Sonora. That is my first obligation, but I have yet another mission. You may remember the passage from the Epistle of Jude where he says, *Keep yourselves in the love of God, looking for the mercy of your Lord Jesus Christ unto eternal life. And of some have compassion, making a difference: And others save with fear, pulling them out of the fire.* That is what I am here to do, to have compassion on those who have followed false teachers, to pull them out of the fire and turn them to the true faith once delivered to the

Apostles."

"Oh," I managed to say. To suggest that I was taken aback by his blunt disclosure would certainly have been an understatement.

Burl swept his hand over the city. "This place is filled with good people gone astray by false teaching. I make no bones about that. As a minister of the Gospel I am called to contend for the faith and to help my Lord save the lost, to snatch them away from this heresy. It's that simple."

"I daresay you will not find a receptive audience here," I said, finally finding my voice.

"We shall see. God can do marvelous things."

"I should be going."

"I've offended you."

"I'm not offended Brother Burl. You must surely follow your own beliefs but yours are misguided beliefs, beliefs generated in the Great Apostasy."

"Ah, the Great Apostasy…" he said, and I thought I saw a twinkle in his eye. "Tell me more."

"I should go," I said and turned once again to leave.

"Lanie," he called after me, "I should like to discuss this further with you. Would that be possible?"

"I'm afraid not."

"But I must learn more of your faith. Who knows, you may even convert me."

"That I would doubt."

"And yet *you* were converted and something tells me that yours was not an easy acceptance. After all, as a Primitive Methodist you surely read and re-read many times over the New Testament."

"Why do you say that?"

He smiled, and it was perhaps the warmest smile I could ever remember seeing, warmer even than my owd Da's. God rest his soul.

"Join me for discussion and I shall tell you why I say that."

"It wouldn't be proper, Brother Burl. I am a married woman."

"Yes, so I've noticed."

"Good day, Brother Burl."

"Good day, Lanie, I hope to see you again. And…don't forget the New Testament."

Don't forget the New Testament? What prompted that parting comment? My mind was in such turmoil for the rest of my walk home that I had to sit in the rocking chair of our keeping room to gather my wits. Somehow, in the course of a few short exchanges, this colossus of a man had pulled a knot in the lashings of my faith. Looking back on it, these lashings had loosened weeks ago with the Prophet's overbearing efforts to control my life, his insistence that I marry Ned, and his insensitivity during my owd Da's death. Of course I understood Joseph to be subject to human failings. He had said as much about himself on several occasions. However, I expected greater things from a man presumably chosen by God to restore the authentic gospel. Candidly, Arthur's opinions about the man influenced me as well. Without question, my estimation of the Prophet had shifted greatly from the moment I first laid eyes upon him on the ferry landing in Nauvoo.

But this wasn't all. I would have made peace with my reservations about the Prophet if it hadn't been for what he and the leaders of the Church had been saying in recent weeks. During their sermons and discourses, I heard things that seemed new and unsettling. Contradictions were cropping up every which way. When I had my heart fire experience in Preston, I had come to believe that God entered my heart. I took great solace in the Bible verse from Ephesians where Paul says, *One God and Father of all, who is above all, and through all, and in you all.* Yet, just last Sunday, John Taylor quoted the Prophet as saying, *The idea that the Father and the Son dwell in a man's heart is an old sectarian notion and is false.* This baffled me even more when I remembered a passage from *Alma* in the *Book of Mormon.* (I had been reading Alma just two nights previously in search of some solace from the beating I had suffered. Alma has, as a central theme, dwelling in God's protection.) In the passage I had recalled, an ancient missionary named Amulek declared, *...the Lord hath said he dwelleth not in unholy temples but in the hearts of the righteous doth he dwell.* Clearly, Alma and Ephesians agree but the Prophet disagrees? How can such a thing be? After all, the Prophet himself translated the Book of Mormon from the Golden Plates. Did he simply forget this point? Or had he received a new revelation that contradicted both the *Holy Bible* and the *Book of Mormon?* It made no sense.

Also from my recent reading of Alma I recalled Amulek's dialog with Zeezrom. Zeezrom asked Amulek if there exists a true and living god. Amulek said there is and Zeezrom followed up asking if there is more than one god to which Amulek replied, "No." Of course, this is certainly no divergence from the teaching of the Bible. Yet, after one seminary session several weeks ago, Arthur told me that Orson Hyde had written to him from Jerusalem. (Elder Hyde and Arthur had remained close since the latter's conversion.) In one of his letters, Elder Hyde repeated Joseph's new teaching that when a good and devout Saint dies, he will become the god of his own world. How could all of these devout Saints become gods when Amulek, in the sacred *Book of Mormon*, had assured Zeezrom that there is but one God? Was Amulek wrong? Was the Book of Mormon wrong? Was Elder Hyde wrong? Was the Prophet wrong? It would seem that somebody or something was wrong, but I couldn't sort it out.

As I thus reflected upon these contradictions and uncertainties, my mind drifted to the disturbing encounter with Burl Bumbalough. What had prompted me to engage this stranger – this dangerous stranger – in such an unreserved and over-familiar way? *You can call me Lanie?* What was I thinking? And the handshake…(but oh it felt so good, my hand in his…his goodly and ample hand). Why had he asked to meet me again? Was I one he had determined to *snatch* away from false teaching? Was he ready to pounce on me, sensing somehow that I was vulnerable in my thinking with all these uncertainties that had popped into my head? But how did he know? I certainly gave him no indication that I harbored these reservations about Mormonism. Did I? Somehow, though, I detected in him an uncanny, almost supernatural ability to discern the countenance of another person. *Yes, so I have noticed.* What a thing to say… "I am a married woman…" *Yes, so I have noticed.* I shook my head at the thought. Was this a comment on my marital state? Despite his having supplied the excuse for my disfigurement – *a nasty spill* – I was sure he suspected – no, knew – there was something far more ill-boding. But what an act of gentility and grace, to have offered me the means whereby I might steer clear of a painful divulgence.

All of these misgivings were stirred into the stew of apprehension and fear that sprang from my domestic nightmare, the Gehenna of my married life. Sitting there in the rocker, suddenly, my heart seized and I could catch nary a breath. I put my hand on my chest. Panic gripped me. The words *I too, Da?* burst into my mind. Like my father, did I harbor a weak and unsustaining heart? Was it momentarily to fail? Was I on the threshold of the next life? I stood and took two staggering steps, looking upward as if to catch my first glimpse of Paradise. And then, just as suddenly, a strange peace came over me. What a relief, to be *snatched* out of this life and ushered into one of exaltation and joy. Escape, freedom, consolation. Bathed in this radiant thought, I came to realize that I was once again breathing normally. The clutching of my heart had abated. I stood solidly upon the pinewood floor of our keeping room.

I sat back down.

I took a deep breath.

"What am I to do?" I cried to the unadorned walls and then, whispering, "What am I to do?"

I so much wanted and needed someone to whom I could unburden all of this, not just the pieces I unloaded on Dorrie, but the whole boodle. Dorrie had been a wonderful confidante but her love and support could only be limited to my circumstances with Ned. Dorrie was not a person given to reflection or deep thought. Thus revealing my growing consternation over Mormonism and my deteriorating spiritual state would be for her an unfamiliar, strange, and inexplicable condition. On so many occasions she had lauded the Mormon faith and what it had meant to her and to Piet. I understood. She and Piet had been given much by the Church – the solemnizing of their love for each other, meaningful labor, and a deep sense of community. One couldn't ask for more, could one? And what would Dorrie think about my conversation with Brother Burl? I suspect she would react with alarm and adjure me not to have further interactions with him. Not that I anticipated further interactions.

I thought about sharing all of this with Arthur, but that wouldn't work either. Arthur may have held deep reservations about the political scene in Nauvoo but he had never wavered in his conviction that the religious dimension of Mormonism was right and true. I felt certain he would become defensive and argumentative if I were to raise certain questions about the veracity of the *Book of Mormon*. Moreover, as sensitive and caring as he was, I did not see him as an intimate companion in matters pertaining to my marriage. Nor could I see him mustering much sympathy for the unease I felt over meeting Burl Bumbalough.

Aside from Dorrie and Arthur, I had no further candidates for private counsel. My intimate network was, unfortunately, quite limited. I realized that I would have to bear these burdens alone. As I sat pondering this sad conclusion, in the very back of my mind a niggling notion surfaced. Could Burl himself be trusted to bear my burdens with me? Immediately, I shook such an unthinkable idea from my mind. He was, after all, a dangerous man, a spiritual enemy, an avowed *snatcher of souls*. But there was that laugh, an honest-to-God belly laugh, a deep, rumbustious, delightsome moment when I lost myself in uncontrolled and complete bliss. The image of his scrunched up face, his raised forefinger, and his comical voice brought a smile to my face, warmed by the memory of a soft and gentle touch, a protective hand.

My warm enjoyment of this memory was shattered by a sharp knock on the door. I hurried to open it and beheld Portia Mercer, Doctor Mercer's wife, with three plucked prairie chickens dangling from her hands.

"Portia, do come in," I said.

"I can't stay, Lanie. Tobias has been hunting and came home with twenty-some prairie chickens. It is more than we can eat before they spoil so I am sharing them. Could I give you these three?"

"Of course, that's very kind of you."

She handed me the birds but did not remove her eyes from the bruise on my cheek.

"Is everything all right, Lanie?"

"Of course. Oh," (I forced a chuckle and rolled my eyes toward the bruise.) "You must be wondering about this. I fell on the steps. Clumsy me."

"It is a nasty bruise."

"Yes it is."

"Do be careful, Lanie dear."

With that she returned to her carriage.

+ + +

My stomach clutched as I heard the front door open. Ned was home. The peace I had enjoyed vanished with the snick of the door latch as it closed. I looked up from checking the potpie to see Ned standing in the doorway to the kitchen with a large knife in his hand. I held my breath.

"What is that delicious smell, my dear?"

My dear. Panic flooded within me. He fingered a large hunting knife in a brass scabbard. Sensing my alarm, he promptly assured me it was merely a gift from the Prophet, a small recompense for the services he had rendered to the Church. He then slipped away leaving me in the consternation of a superficial but strangely normal and non-threatening exchange. Was this not what one might expect from a husband and wife after a long day apart? My suspicions and misgivings did not dissipate. Something strange and ominous was afoot.

The evening got even stranger. During dinner, he offered an apology for his weeks of cruel and oppressive treatment of me. He vowed to turn over a new leaf. I did not believe him and told him that, while I hoped to forgive, I had been sorely wounded. Then, this beast of a man had the effrontery to seek my company in his bed. I could not imagine anything more repugnant and refused him. I could see the rage building in him but he managed to hold it in check. Silence descended upon our meal and we moved into a stony truce.

+ + +

It is scorching hot. I walk through a thick forest. Branches slap at my face. Locust thorns threaten on all sides and I am forced to tread slowly for fear of punctures and gashes. My feet are constantly entangled in the coiling underbrush. I have to kick periodically to free my shoes. I don't know where I am going. Suddenly, I break into a natural clearing and trickling before me is a small creek, watered by the runoff from recent rains. I stop and watch the waters swirl before me, coursing over variegated pebbles lining the creek bed. The creek offers some measure of peace, a respite from the toils of an uncleared path.

I look up. A few yards away, partially shrouded by the overgrowth, I see the opening to a cave. It beckons me. I course up and down the creek searching for a narrow point to cross. Finding a suitable spot, I gather my skirts and leap across. I don't quite make it. My lead foot splashes down in the water and I feel the cool liquid seep through the eyelets of my boot. To my relief it feels good, refreshing on such a hot and humid day. I edge toward the cave wondering if it is a lair of some wild beast or the roost of a million bats. I hate bats. I am terrified of bats. They are demonic and if a colony were to suddenly fly out of the cave, I scarcely would survive. Closer now, I sense that the cave is empty. Just inside the rounded entrance I see a narrow cleft leading to an inner chamber. Should I go through it? What is beyond? Somewhere in the deep recesses of the cave I can hear drops of water falling into a pool below. There is a glow in the room beyond the cleft.

I walk closer and peer through the cleft. I first check the ceiling of the interior room. I let out a long breath stream. No bats. Something compels me to squeeze through to the interior room but the cleft walls are jagged and almost too narrow to admit me. I let out all of my breath and step through. My dress snags on the jagged rocks – my bodice and backside. I step back and look down. To my horror, my indigo dress has been completely shredded. I undo the front hooks and allow the tattered remnants to fall to the rocky floor below. Then I remove my petticoats leaving me only in my cotton chemise. With arms and lower legs exposed, I try again and find it easy to slip through the cleft and into the interior room.

Despite the dim glow, I must stand there for a moment to let my eyes adjust. When finally, I can see my surrounds more clearly, I notice a figure standing in the far shadows of the cave. It is a man, an enormous man, in a long, flowing white robe. He wears no hat and no shoes. I cannot see his face. I gasp in fear. I am nearly naked – a married woman – in the presence of another man, a monstrously large man. I step back to the cleft.

He holds out his hand to calm me.

"Lanie, I should like to discuss this further with you…"

His voice…his words.

It is Burl.

"No," I say and put out my hand to hold him back (as if I could).

"I mean you no harm."

"I am a married woman."

"So I have noticed."

"Stay away!"

"But I am warm."

"No."

"Warm and gentle."

"You mean to snatch me."

"Yes, I do."

"I can't."

"Come to the warmth."

"No…no…no!"

I shot upright in bed, drenched in sweat, my chest heaving. I stared at the pitcher on the bureau trying to still my pounding heart. My breathing eased and reflexively I found myself saying *I want to come* on each intake of my breath and *to the warmth* on the subsequent exhalations. *I want to come to the warmth.*

I shook my head several times but could not rid myself of the words. Finally, fully awake, I stood up and walked over to the pitcher on the nightstand. I poured a basin of cold water and splashed my face. When I dried off, to my relief, the words had evaporated in my mind. I struck a locofoco and lit the lamp on my nightstand. Two books rested there, *The Holy Bible* and the *Book of Mormon*. I reached for the Bible but stayed my hand momentarily before redirecting it to the *Book of Mormon*. I crawled back in bed and began to read, hoping this diversion would shield me from the frightening images and implications of the dream I had just experienced.

+ + +

Sleep escaped me for the balance of the night and I was fully awake when I heard Ned stir in the next room. Hurriedly, I dressed and went downstairs where I lit the stove and prepared to warm some ham and stewed peaches for Ned's breakfast. I set a pan of water on the burner to heat water for tea and waited.

When finally he came down to his breakfast, I served him and sat opposite him at the table with only my cup of tea.

"Are you not eating my dear?"

He was still at it. *My dear.*

"I'm not hungry."

He looked at me with his ice-blue eyes, eyes without feeling. "It's very good and I thank you."

What had gotten into this man? Something was ajar but I could not imagine what it could be. However, his sudden change in temperament seemed to me opportune and I decided, at understandable risk, to press for some changes.

"Ned, you sought my forgiveness. Do you still desire it?"

"With all my heart."

"I must know that you truly mean to change."

"How may I convince you?"

"I would request certain reliefs."

"Such as?"

"More freedom to come and go as I wish. I will guarantee that the household chores will always be completed in satisfactory fashion and at the appropriate time. But I do not wish to be cooped up like a breeding rabbit."

"Granted," he said.

My eyes widened. Did I dare take it a step further? The opportunity might not again present itself.

"I would like to continue at the seminary."

"No ma'am."

"I will reduce my time there."

"To what?"

"Three days instead of five."

He chewed pensively on his ham.

I awaited his decision.

"Very well. Three days."

Reflexively, my hand shot to my breast. "Thank you, Ned."

Without response, he carved off another bite of ham and put it in his mouth. When he swallowed, he dropped his utensils in the pewter dish.

"I've invited the Van Rijns to dinner on Sunday. They have accepted."

"Oh. That will be nice. I shall prepare a fine meal."

We both stood from the table. He walked around, put his hands on my shoulders, and gave me a small, chaste kiss on the forehead – the first kiss he had given me since our wedding day.

"I shall be in a long meeting with the Prophet and others today," he said.

He stifled a belch, turned on his heel, and strode out of the house.

CHAPTER EIGHTEEN

Burl

Challenges

For several long minutes, until she turned out of sight a few blocks away, I watched the sway of her skirts. A lovely woman to my mind, intelligent, perceptive, proper, attractive, vulnerable, and completely deluded. She was suffering as well, and something told me that whatever wind once filled the sails of her Mormon faith had stilled. Questions and confusions teemed under the surface of her mind. I wanted to see her again, not only to pry her from this Latter Day Saint claptrap, but because I wanted to see her again.

She glanced back at me when rounding the corner. I waved, but she turned her head away. Even at that distance, I could see the discoloration on her face. Unlikely, I thought, that Lanie's bruise and black eye resulted from an accidental encounter with a newell post. As a prizefighter, I'd seen enough faces bruised by a human fist. To my shame, I was responsible for a good many bruises myself. Moreover, I knew most people, falling on a stairway, will turn their heads or put out a protective arm to prevent a blow to the face. It would take a very hard fall indeed to equal the power of a human fist – a man's fist – striking directly upon an unguarded facial bone. She had been violently punched and I placed my wager on her husband.

I looked at the Temple again and shook my head. Impressive but an *abomination that maketh desolate* as it says in the Book of Daniel. After several more minutes watching the workers labor at their misguided efforts, I left the Temple precincts and made my way down the slope to the Red Brick Store. One of the disaffected

Mormons who worshipped with us had mentioned that to find Joseph Smith, my best bet would be to seek him in the Red Brick Store. One of the few occasional passers-by had given me directions and so, on that blustery morning, I re-set my sights on meeting the infamous Mormon Prophet.

To my surprise, the Red Brick Store was a delightful little establishment, chock-full of merchandise – spices, bolts of cloth, staples in gunnysacks, pickles in the barrel, canned preserves and fruits, cured meats hanging from the rafters, candies, and an impressive array of tools and utensils including a waffle iron and two china tea sets. Spices, brine, and wood burning in the pot-bellied stove gave the place a homey and pleasant air. Behind the counter sat a handsome, sandy-haired lad with a vigorous smile. When I walked in, he greeted me in that accent I had heard so often among the Dutch sailors who frequented the docks of Philadelphia.

"Goot day, sir. Velcome to de Red Brick Store."

"And good day to you. A fine establishment you have here," I said, removing my hat.

"I tank you sir. Vat can I do for you?"

"I'm not here to purchase anything, though those sweetmeats in the jar…"

The Dutchman did not rise from his chair but pointed to the jar. "Help yourself to one of dem, no charge."

"Oh but I couldn't do that. Surely there is a charge."

"Not for yust one. Help yourself. Go ahead."

Delighted by my good fortune I unstoppered the jar and tried to get my hand inside to pluck out one of the sweetmeats. As was often the case, I couldn't get my hand in the jar.

"Hand it to me," the Dutchman said, "I vill get one for you. Dems big hands you got dere."

The sweetmeat was delicious. I nipped off tiny bits with my front teeth, swirling each morsel around in my mouth, savoring the flavors. The Dutchman seemed amused at this simple delight and watched my every bite and chew.

"Dat vas good, huh?"

"A foretaste of heaven," I said.

"Vell, den, so much de better for you dat it vas free."

I threw my head back, laughing at the irony of getting a free foretaste of heaven in the Prophet's Red Brick Store, a tiny moment of grace.

When my chuckles abated, I informed the Dutchman that I was there to visit with the Prophet.

"He is purty bissy at de moment. I don't know vat, but dere is some solemn tings going on up de stairs. He might be avile. Can you come back later?"

"Certainly. How long?"

"Dat's hard to say but I vould think an hour or more."

"Very well. I'll wander around for a time and return in an hour."

"Goot. I'm Piet Van Rijn, by de vay."

"Bumbalough, Brother Burl Bumbalough," I said, extending my hand.

He took it and shook with a firm grip but he did not stand. Then I realized he could not. He had been crippled, and I reckoned he could neither stand on his own two feet nor walk.

I leaned over the counter.

"Piet, my apologies. I had not noticed that standing and walking are a challenge for you."

"Ja. Dat vould be de truth. I vas a sailor but I fell from de rigging and hit my back on de taffrail of de ship. Den I fell in the vater and come near to drowning."

I winced and reflexively arched my own back.

"Ayi! You are fortunate to be alive. The Good Lord was surely there to rescue you."

"Ja, vell maybe it vas the Lord but He sent one of de other sailors – Patty O'Neil, de Irishman. He come in de vater after me."

"Praises to God. So how did you come to be in Nauvoo?"

"Vell, I guess you could say it vas love."

"Love?"

"Ja, I vas betrothed to a Mormon girl, my sweet Torrie. She vas gathering to Zion and I yust come along. De Prophet married us and give me dis job in de store. I'm very tankful."

"And well you should be, Piet. That was most generous of the Prophet."

"Ja, he is a vonderful man, dat's for sure."

"Good. I'm glad it has been working out." I donned my hat and turned toward the door. "I shall take my leave and return in a short while."

"Dat's fine. I'll tell de Prophet you vas here."

For the next hour I wandered around Nauvoo trying to engage the few citizens I encountered in conversation but most of them, while polite, avoided me. I finally wound up in the Webb Brothers' Blacksmith Shop. Several other men were gathered there, I presume because it was a warm haven from the blustery cold.

"Good morning, gents," I said as I strode through the open doors.

The men nodded in unison but said nothing, eyeing me with wary stares.

I smiled as warmly as I could. "There's a chill in the air, wouldn't you say? Winter is upon us. Mind if I warm my hands?"

No one objected, so I came near to the forge and spread my hands before the fire. One of the proprietors, Chauncey Webb, was fashioning a steel blade. I watched him work, marveling at his ability to hammer into shape a long, curved blade.

"Would you call that a scimitar?" I asked.

He nodded. "Aye, you could call it that."

"Speaking of scimitars, I have a question for you gentlemen."

No one said a word. They stared at me with hooded eyes.

"I was glancing through the *Book of Mormon* the other day and noted that it mentions scimitars."

Chauncey continued to pound on his blade, the cadence uninterrupted by my observation.

"Don't remember the exact chapter and verse," I said, "but I think it was in your *Book of Enos*. The Lah-mun-ites. Do I pronounce it correctly? The Lah-mun-ites were said to be skilled in the use of scimitars.

The pounding continued. "*Lay*-mun-ites," he said.

"Ah, thank you for correcting me. Now, I've been wondering about this reference since the scimitar is a Persian weapon, if I recall. Never saw the word *scimitar* in the Old Testament, among the Hebrew people, that is. But was it not from the ancient Hebrew people that the Nephites came?"

No response.

"Oh, I suppose the Lay-mun-ites could have fashioned curved swords and the Prophet used the term *scimitar* to describe them. He translated *curved sword* as *scimitar*. Would you think that the case? I don't know. Found the whole matter curious is all I can say."

Chauncey looked up at me. "Yes, that would be the case. The

Prophet used the word *scimitar* in translation."

"Ah, well that makes sense. I appreciate your clarification. And I've been wondering further about the blade mentioned in *Enos*. Do you suppose that was made of steel? Like that nice blade you're fashioning?"

"I would suppose so."

"Yes, yes it is interesting. I note the *Book of Mormon* mentions steel. It was Shule, wasn't it, who fashioned steel out of molten ore from the Hill Ephraim? Again, can't remember the passage but it was in one of the later books, maybe *Ether*. You can correct me if I'm wrong. Funny thing, though... I didn't know they had steel in those ancient days, especially on this side of the Atlantic. If memory serves, steel production came considerably later in the history of civilization. Twenty centuries later. Didn't think the ancients could fire iron ore to a high enough temperature to fashion steel. No mention of steel in the histories of antiquity. I find that curious, don't you?"

Chauncey wielded his last blow on the curved blade and tossed the hammer on to a workbench as if it were a feather duster. He plunged the blade in water and through the steam that rose from the bucket, he said, "Time for you to move on, sir. Your hands are warm now, so I'd advise you to shuffle off."

Two of the bystanders stepped forward as if to enforce Chauncey's order.

I put both of my hands in the air, gesturing surrender, and stepped back.

"Certainly. Certainly. No offense intended. Just curious, that's all. I bid you good day gentlemen." Here I raised my hand in the air. "May God's blessing be upon you."

I lowered my hand certain that none of the men there present appreciated the sentiment behind my benediction.

+ + +

As I approached the Red Brick Store a second time, a tall, red-haired, dandified man stormed out of the door his scarred lip twisted in a snarl of rage.

"Good morning, sir," I said as he stormed past me.

He gave no return greeting.

My goodness, I thought to myself. *I wonder what has drawn his ire?*

Piet nodded as I entered the store and said the Prophet could see me. I thanked him and bounded up the stairs to the small office. I knocked.

"Enter," came a voice from within.

I slipped through the door and strode toward the Prophet as he rose from his desk. Extending my hand, I said, "Brother Burl, Brother Burl Bumbalough."

"Welcome Brother Burl," he said receiving my hand.

A handsome man, I thought, with a winning smile and an easy manner. I noted that he was not in his fighting trim but clearly a man with great physical strength. (As a former prizefighter I had learned to take the measure of a man, a necessity if one wishes to win.)

"So you are the new Methodist minister in Sonora?"

"I am. How did you know?"

"Well, I am a prophet, after all."

"Touché," I said, and we both had a good laugh.

"And, may I ask Brother Burl, what brings you to Nauvoo?" The smile remained on his lips.

"I am here to proselytize."

"You don't say." The smile faded, though not completely.

"Yes. I've been asked by my Bishop to assist the Lord in the spiritual repatriation of those who have left the true faith for Mormonism."

"I admire your forthrightness, Brother Burl, but doubt you will have much success."

"And why is that?"

"Because the people who have converted, most of whom have gathered here to Zion at great personal expense and risk, believe they have found the true religion, the restored Gospel."

"And have they?"

"But of course."

"Tell me how you know this."

"Oh, my good man," he said with a huffing chuckle. "It is a matter of considerable record. But, in brief, I was visited by the angel Moroni some fifteen years ago as I slept. The angel revealed to me the story of Hebrew people who had journeyed to the Americas. That same angel directed me to a set of golden plates containing a record of these ancient people. Surely you know all of this."

"Yes, I've read about it. I have a copy of the Book of Mormon." I laid a finger on my nose. "If I may, I'd like to ask you a question about the three gentlemen – I've forgotten their names – who were the first witnesses to have seen the golden plates. I read their testimony in my *Book of Mormon*. As I recall, these three men said an angel had shown them these plates. Is that correct?"

"It is."

"Where are these three men now?"

"I couldn't say for sure. They are no longer affiliated with the Church. I believe Cowdery and Harris are still in Ohio. David Whitmer is in Missouri."

"Why did they leave the Church?"

"You ask too many questions, Brother Burl."

"Just trying to understand."

"But, if you are honest with me, the motive behind your questions is less than honorable, nefarious even. You wish to lure my people out of the Church."

"As you did in England, Canada, throughout these United States, and elsewhere – *luring* people out of the Church, to use your words."

Joseph made a sucking sound through the chip in his front tooth.

"I'm curious," I said, cocking my head. "I understand you translated the *Book of Mormon* by using a special seer's stone? Is that correct?"

"Yes it is."

"And you placed that stone in a hat, looked into the hat, and some symbols emerged along with the translation into English. Am I still on point?"

"Yes, the symbols were Reformed Egyptian."

"But you didn't translate from the plates themselves?"

"No."

"Then why in thunder did the Lord preserve those plates for over fourteen hundred years if they would not be used someday to present this new testament?"

"The words on the plates appeared to me by the power of God."

"In your hat."

"Yes."

"So if the words are now translated and available for all to read, why don't you put the plates on display? They do exist don't they?"

"Of course they do but they are sacred."

"Too sacred to be seen."

"They must be protected and to put them on display would put them at risk of theft or defacement."

"But couldn't a few trusted folks have a little peek?"

"It isn't necessary."

"Don't you realize you could do much to enhance the veracity of your faith by letting a few trustworthy people have a brief glimpse of the plates?"

"Again, I say it is unnecessary."

"I see. One other question."

"Which I may or may not answer."

"Were there any witnesses to your visitation by this angel Moroni?"

"No there were not."

"So your whole Church, its entire foundation, rests on second-hand information, am I correct?"

"No you are not. We have, besides the three witnesses, the eight others."

"Ah yes, I seem to remember reading about them as well. Tell me again who they were."

"Four of them were members of the Whitmer family."

"And where are these Whitmer men now?"

"Excommunicated."

"Excommunicated. Dear me. And the others?"

"Hiram Page is also no longer with us. This leaves my father, may God rest his soul, and my two brothers Hyrum and Samuel. Unfortunately, my little brother Samuel has also gone to be with the Lord."

"So, Brother Joseph, let me see if I have this straight. Of the eleven witnesses who viewed the original documents of the Church of Latter Day Saints, only one is left among the faithful – your brother Hyrum. And does he not hold a position of high honor in the Church?"

"He does."

"Don't you find that strange, that no one is left within the Church to testify to its veracity except your devoted brother?"

He shrugged his shoulders. "Time passes on. People change. The Lord calls some home. But…" and here he leaned over his desk and pointed a finger at me. "Not one of the living witnesses, nor any of those who have died, has ever denied the authenticity of the golden plates or the *Book of Mormon*." Joseph stood, put his hands on his desk, and looked me in the eye. "Our meeting is over, Brother Bumbalough. I have other matters to attend to. It would be prudent for you to watch your step here in Nauvoo."

I smiled and rose.

"Thank you for your time, Brother Joseph. I bid you good day and the Lord's blessing."

"And likewise to you sir."

We did not shake hands upon my dismissal.

+ + +

I had a brief parting conversation with Piet Van Rijn and thanked him for his kindnesses. I found myself famished and, upon Piet's recommendation, made my way to the Foster Hotel. As I sat to enjoy a bowl of venison stew, which warmed my innards on that cold day, I reflected over my meeting with the Prophet Joseph Smith. I had come to appreciate the force of his personality. This was a man of uncommon intelligence and, if he authored the fanciful *Book of Mormon*, he would have to be counted as a religious genius. Through the ages, powerful personalities had deluded large populations, convincing them of certain heresies and infidelities – Montanus, Arius, Pelagius, Mahamet, and now Joseph Smith, among others. And, from what I had seen, Smith was second to none. The Lord had placed me in a leathery field of service – difficult, foreboding, and perhaps dangerous. With a few sharp words and stern looks, Smith had put me on notice that he intended to brook no opposition.

I spent the rest of my day wandering around Nauvoo, hoping to corner a few more citizens to examine their faith and looking for chinks in their spiritual armor. I daresay some would label my motivations and tactics despicable and unbecoming in a land that had popularized freedom of religion. But, as a called and ordained minister of the Gospel, I considered it my bounden duty to contend for the faith. In the words of Paul to Titus, I must *hold fast the faithful words as...hath been taught, that* I *may be able by sound doctrine both to exhort and convince the gainsayers.* And surely on that day I was in the midst of the gainsayers. Sad to say, my best efforts came to naught. I found no one willing to converse with me beyond the pleasantries a polite encounter required.

Toward late afternoon, as I walked Buckwheat east up Sidney Street, six men rounded the corner and spread out to block my way.

"Good afternoon gentlemen," I said.

Without so much as a word, they surrounded me.

"Can I be of service to you gentlemen?" I asked. In the silence that followed, I became uneasy, not so much because I was frightened by any of them singularly or in combination. I daresay I could have dispatched any or all of them in a good old-fashioned fight. But if they did mob me, I would turn the other cheek and I could suffer a severe beating at their hands. I surmised that no one would come to my aid in this hostile environment and therein lay my unease. So, I did the only thing I could do. I whispered a quick prayer for protection.

"You been declared a public nuisance," said their spokesman.

"A public nuisance?"

"That's right, and we are on orders to send you packing out of town."

"In what way was I a nuisance?"

"You been stirring up our folk."

"Which is my right under the Constitution."

"Laws of Nauvoo override the Constitution."

"I wouldn't want to test that assumption in a court of law."

"Ain't going to be no court of law. You are going to head on out of town."

"I will leave when I am good and ready, sir."

"That would be right now. Now is when you are good and ready."

"Not quite."

He stared at me for several seconds and suddenly threw a right haymaker, a weak and imperfect punch, easily spotted by the practiced eye. I whipped up my hand and caught his fist in midair, interrupting his blow. His eyes widened in disbelief. I held his fist until I could feel the tension ease. Five jaws dropped and no one moved to back up his friend.

"Gentlemen," I said. "I have no wish to fight you in the middle of this peaceful street. Nor is there any need. I am on my way out of town. So why don't you be off to whomever sent you and report that your mission is accomplished. Before you go, I would like to offer you the blessing God gave to Moses for the blessing of the children of Israel." Before they could protest, I raised my hand. The lead enforcer flinched, which made me smile. "The Lord bless thee and keep thee. The Lord make his face to shine upon thee, and be gracious unto thee. The Lord lift up his countenance upon thee and give thee peace."

With that I gathered Buckwheat's reins and started back up Sidney Street thanking the Lord for my deliverance.

I had only gone about a mile out of town when I heard hoofbeats coming fast behind me. I reined Buckwheat to a stop and turned in my saddle to see a young man in a flapping greatcoat. The speed of his approach had flattened his brim against the crown of his hat. His scarf had been so tightly drawn around his face by the force of the wind that I could see the outline of his mouth. When he came alongside, he stopped and pulled down his scarf.

"A moment, please," he said.

"Yes, my good man. How can I be of service?"

"I was in the blacksmith shop earlier today when you came in."

"Ah yes, I recognize you now."

"You raised some hard questions."

"I suppose they would seem difficult for some."

"Are you a minister of some sort?"

"I am." I put out my hand. "Brother Burl Bumbalough. I am a Methodist clergyman serving the congregation yonder in Sonora. And you are?"

He reached across to take my hand. "Barnabas Potter, but folks call me Barney."

"Very well, Barney. What has sent you rushing after me?"

"My family are all devout Saints, you must understand. We recently gathered from Canada, from around Toronto. But, I don't quite cotton to it, to Mormonism, that is. I would like to meet and talk further if you would be fain to do so."

"Certainly. But I hasten to ask, would this meeting put you in danger with your family or others? I ask this because some of the Mormon brethren just threatened me and one tried to assault me."

"My family will be disturbed, to say the least, but they would not attempt to harm me."

"Can you excuse yourself on Sunday morning and come to our church in Sonora?"

"Yes."

"There is a group that comes by wagon. Six or seven others who are abandoning the Mormon faith. You could join them."

A smile crossed his face at learning that there were other Nauvoo dissidents who had sought relief from Mormonism. I gave him the names of several of those who would join us on Sunday next. He thanked me and spurred his horse in a joyful gallop back to Nauvoo.

I relished the rest of my journey home, thrilled to know that my mission had not been a complete failure. One more – Barnabas Potter – had seen the glimmer of light

CHAPTER NINETEEN

Kevil

Endowment

It began in Joseph's office. Standing before me were the Prophet, Brigham Young, Heber Kimball, and Reynolds Calhoun, the same men who had been initiated into plural marriage. A tin tub about three feet in diameter stood in the center of the office. Several white towels and a large pitcher of water rested on the Prophet's desk. In those tight quarters, the collective smell of unwashed Saints suffused the room.

"It is necessary for you to remove all of your clothing," Joseph said in a soft voice.

"I beg your pardon?" I said.

"You are to remove all of your clothing."

I looked at the other men.

They nodded.

"I did not understand this to be part of this ceremony," I said.

"We have all gone through it," Brigham said. "No harm will come to you."

"It is in accord with the revelation to Joseph regarding eternal salvation," Reynolds said in an effort to provide additional assurances. "It will be a short time you are naked before the Lord."

"I think not," I said turning to leave.

"Recall the prize that awaits you," Joseph said. "Both in heaven and here upon the earth."

The image of Dorrie Van Rijn flitted through my mind.

I paused in mid-step.

"Very well," I said, sighing. I doffed my clothes, including my drawers. My emotions at that moment were difficult to describe. I had never been embarrassed about any aspect of my physique, nor was I fearful and apprehensive. I knew I could leave that room in a moment's notice. No, I suppose you could describe my feelings as a swirling mixture of disdain, and indignation. However, I suppressed these emotions as best I could and allowed this mad ritual to unfold.

Without comment, Heber and Brigham put their hands on my upper arms, one on each side and led me to the tub motioning for me to step into it. Reynolds picked up the large pitcher of water and poured its contents over my head. As he did so, Joseph intoned the words, "I wash you that you may be made clean to receive your sacred endowment and to perform the work to which you shall be assigned." Then, with a light touch, he scrubbed me from head to toe. "I wash your eyes that you may clearly see the glory of your Father in heaven. I wash your ears that you may hear the Father's voice. I wash your mouth that you may proclaim the restored Gospel and sing the praises of God. I wash your arms and your breast that you may have strength to perform the services of the Church. I wash your loins that you may be pure and issue increase, bringing spirits into this world that they may be tested and walk by faith." (Here he discreetly and briefly washed the lower region of my belly.) "I wash your feet that you may stand strong and be fleet of foot to win the race set before you."

At this point, Joseph pronounced me clean and prepared for the continuation of the ceremony. Using the towels I had previously spied, the men dried me. Joseph then retrieved a flask of scented oil, lavender I believe, and poured it over my head. Heber Kimball read, in stentorian voice, fragments from the Bible. *"Then Samuel took a vial of oil, and poured it upon his head, and kissed him, and said, Is it not because the Lord hath anointed thee to be captain over his inheritance?...And the Spirit of the Lord will come unto thee, and thou...shalt be turned into another man. And let it be, when these signs come unto thee, that thou do as occasion serve thee; for God is with thee."*

When Kimball had finished his reading, Joseph seated me in a chair and laid his hands upon my head. "As in the ancient of days, men of virtue and nobility were anointed to be kings and priests. In the name of God, I anoint you Brother Edwin Freeman to be a king and I ordain you as a priest for time and all eternity."

Just as I thought the ceremony could scarcely become more

bizarre, Joseph raised me from the chair and presented me with a muslin undergarment bound with red thread. Sleeves extended to the wrists and leggings to the ankle. A reversed L-shaped emblem had been cut into the right breast and a V-shaped emblem in the left.

"What manner of thing is this?" I asked.

Joseph motioned for me to be silent. "Brother Ned," he said, "You are to wear this sacred garment as a reminder of your ordination to the hallowed office of priest, of the covenants which you have made, and of the secrets you must keep. Please put it on."

Resigned to the inanity of it all, I put on the new undergarment. It was tight fitting and uncomfortable. (I would not be wearing it for long.) Joseph then explained that the V-shaped symbol on the left breast represented a compass by which we were always to bow in the direction of the Lord. He traced the L-shaped emblem. "Just as Scripture assures us that he who overcometh will be given a white stone upon which shall be written a new name, so this square symbolizes that white stone of Scripture. As he said this, it dawned on me. These two symbols – a mason's square and draftsman's compass – were those of the Masonic Order. I had been exposed to these markings years earlier during my defense of a Mason who had been charged with murder.

I stared at him with undisguised incredulity. He saw my expression but paid it no heed. Then he placed his hands on my shoulders. "I will now pronounce in secret your new name. This name you are to reveal to no one save he who greets you at the great door of the Celestial Kingdom." At this, he bent over me. I could feel his lips brush my ear. "Thy name is *Pachumeni*."

"Pach…"

Joseph put his hand over my lips to hush me. "This name is to be revealed to no one."

He turned and retrieved a sharp knife from his desk and deftly cut short slashes in the garment across the right knee and the abdomen. "The slash across your knee," he said, "is a reminder that every knee shall bow and every tongue shall confess Jesus as Lord. If you violate the secrecy of the vows you have taken and the ceremony to follow, you shall be disemboweled." He poked his finger through the slash on the abdomen and said, "As this cut reminds us."

I managed to keep from rolling my eyes.

With my hair still dripping oil, the four men then led me into the large upper assembly room of the Red Brick Store. It had been transformed from the last time I had been in the room for the meeting of the Municipal Court.

The three windows on the front of the room had been draped in a black curtain. A large canvas curtain hung down the center of the room splitting it into two chambers. In the dim recesses of the first chamber I could see potted shrubs and small trees arranged against the far wall. On the canvas was painted a scene but I could not make out the features of this mural in the low light. Within a few feet of the entry into the first chamber, I was halted. There, Joseph instructed me to lie upon the floor on my side, curl my knees up to my chest, and close my eyes. The entire upper room then descended into silence. All I could do was wonder with swelling impatience how long this farce would continue.

Just then a thrumming vibrated through the floor. I recognized it to be the synchronized stomping of the four men who had just attended me. I suppose it represented a drum roll or perhaps thunder. From beyond the canvas a voice sounded above the stomping feet, which summarily begun to slow and soften. The voice was to be that of the Lord, but I had to laugh. It was none other than that same stentorian voice of the pompous Heber Kimball. *"Let the light be divided from the darkness. Let the light be called day and the darkness night. Let there be a firmament in the midst of the waters. The firmament shall be called heaven and the waters below the firmament shall be gathered and the dry land that appears shall be called earth. Let the earth bring forth grass, the herb yielding seed, and the fruit tree yielding fruit after its kind..."*

This went on for a few more minutes as Kimball gave a rough recounting of the creation story from Genesis. Then, I heard soft footsteps coming around the canvas. A man I presumed to be Joseph knelt down next to me as Kimball droned, *"Now let us go down and make man in our image, after our likeness.* Joseph then put his hand on my shoulder. *And the Lord God formed man of the dust of the ground, and breathed into his nostrils the breath of life, and man became a living soul."* Joseph blew a long stream of malodorous breath over my face. At this I was instructed to leap up as if springing to life. Joseph walked me down to the end of the room where the potted plants had been placed.

"This is a beautiful place," the voice said. "Everything here is delightful for the eye and taste. Of all these things you may freely eat

but of the tree of the knowledge of good and evil you shall not eat."
Joseph placed his hand under the distal leaves of a small walnut tree,
careful not to touch them. *"Thou shalt not eat, neither shalt thou touch it,
for in the day thou eatest thereof thou shalt surely die."*

"Am I to understand that I am now Adam?" I asked.

Joseph nodded and, by placing a finger on his lips, admonished
me to remain silent. He motioned for me to remain in place. Then he
slipped away. As Joseph left, Brigham and Reynolds came around the
canvas. Brigham was dressed all in black. Reynolds had donned a
long white robe and he carried an apple in his hand. I discovered that
Brigham was to play the Devil and Reynolds, Adam's wife Eve.
While I stood there, they enacted the fall of man in a hilarious parody
that forced me to bite off chunks of my inner cheek to keep from
laughing.

From there, the ceremony festered into complete nonsense. I was
taken to the other side of the canvas, a dark and foreboding chamber
in which nearly all light had been blocked. Here the Devil Brigham
Young assumed the voices of various churches (Catholic and
Protestant) and engaged in a long contrived diatribe against the Saints
until Reynolds leapt into the room. There, disguised as the Almighty,
Reynolds drove the Devil out of the room. Thus I had been rescued
from the perfidies of the denominations.

Joseph walked in and knelt with his back to me. Reynolds, still in
the guise of the Almighty, rehearsed the words Joseph heard during
his vision in Upstate New York. Before my eyes Joseph was once
again commissioned by God to propagate this new gospel to a sinful
and apostate world.

While Joseph continued to kneel in prayer, Reynolds the Almighty
took me back around the canvas to the original chamber. The
curtains on the windows had been removed and the room was bathed
in a light representing the Celestial Kingdom. I could now see more
clearly the large pastoral scene painted on the canvas. All I remember
about the painting were lots of cottony clouds tufted against a blue
sky. Here Heber Kimball forced me to take a vow of secrecy never to
reveal what had happened in this upper room. But I must confess I
was at a loss as to why this taradiddle should remain confidential.

My vows of secrecy were confirmed by a required sign. As
directed, I drew my right hand from my left shoulder across the body
to my lower right side as a symbol of disembowelment. Presumably, I

would suffer disembowelment were I ever to disclose what I had heard and seen. There were other signs during which I raised my arms and repeated certain oaths, all of which passed through me like water through a sieve. If one were to put a gun to my head today, I could not recall them. As a concluding ritual, the four men welcomed me using a secret handshake in which the little fingers were interlocked and the right forefinger placed upon the wrist of the other man.

When the ceremony came to an end, Heber, Reynolds, and Brigham busied themselves restoring the upper room. Joseph called me into his office and slumped into his chair.

"That ceremony is not as it should have been, Brother Ned, but we do the best we can under the circumstances. The whole Endowment rite will be much more dramatic and meaningful when the Temple has been finished."

"I'm certain that will be the case," I said. Nothing could have been more cack-handed than what I had just experienced.

"I hope you felt touched by the Almighty and warmed by your entry into the Quorum of the Anointed, Brother Ned. Is that so?"

"But of course."

"Good. Now, please sit, Brother Ned. We are not yet finished."

"What else could there be?"

"Please, this is important."

With grudging obedience I took a chair opposite the desk.

"Now that you have received your endowments and been ordained as a member of the Quorum of the Anointed, the Lord is calling you to a special task."

I raised uneasy eyebrows.

Joseph remained silent for several seconds as if he were contemplating how to introduce this *special task*.

"As you know," he said, "flocks of faithful Saints have been gathering to Zion over these past several years. Large contingents from Canada, particularly Upper Canada, have been among those who have undertaken the hardships of the journey to Nauvoo. I must confess I fear for those branches of the Church left behind. While it is the Lord's desire that all Mormons gather here, it is still necessary to retain viable congregations for the faithful throughout the world until they have time to gather. I have no knowledge of the condition of the branches we have established in Upper Canada. Do you understand my concern?"

"Of course."

My uneasiness intensified.

"The Canadian immigrants worry, as do I, that not many are left to sustain the mission work in their native land. Therefore, the Lord has urged me to send a good and faithful man to Upper Canada to appraise the churches there."

My stomach dropped. *Not Canada!*

"As you might have concluded," he continued. "the Lord is calling you to what I shall call a *mission of discovery*. You are to make your way to Upper Canada, beginning in Toronto, and visit as many of the branches as possible. You are to take stock of the number of conversions and baptisms, the number in faithful attendance, and the overall spiritual condition of the churches in these several places. Then I would ask that you report back to me on what you have found."

"Brother Joseph," I said, trying to contain my outrage over this request. "It is nearly December. Winter is upon us. It is an act of sheer madness to journey to Canada at this time of year."

"It can be done. Brigham has done it. I myself did it along with Sidney Rigdon and Freeman Nickerson. We suffered bitter cold, blizzards, and deep snows. However, when in the service of the Lord all necessary protections will be provided. I am particularly interested in the condition of the branch in Mount Pleasant, which I helped to organize. It is a branch that holds a special place in my heart. Your contact person in the area is Asa Hoard."

"What if I were to refuse?"

"Come, now, Brother Ned. Refusal of a commission from the Lord coming on the heels of your ordination and admission to the Holy Order is unthinkable."

"And how do I know this commission is from the Lord? How do I know you didn't put me through all this ceremony just to soften me up so I might spy for you in the frozen wilds of Canada?"

Joseph leaned forward and put his elbows on his desk to form a triangle with his arms and hands. He rested his chin on his clasped hands and stared at me. I must admit I grew uncomfortable under his unblinking gaze.

"None may refuse when called," he said. With a wave of his hand, he added, "Besides, there is the matter of your entry into celestial marriage. Conditions are not yet suitable for this to happen. More of the brothers must be initiated into the practice and come to peace about it. This is particularly true in the case of my brother Hyrum. He is not with us and his compliance and acceptance are crucial. Then, too, there is the problem of Dorrie Van Rijn. From all appearances, she is devoted to her husband and it will take time to, how shall I say it, *prepare* her to become your spiritual wife."

"And how is that preparation to be accomplished?"

"Don't trouble yourself. It shall be my duty to you and to her to undertake this delicate work."

"And my being absent is, I presume, of salutary benefit to your efforts."

"I should think so."

I nodded. The man had a point.

"And what of your wife?" Joseph asked. "Will she give her consent?"

I thought about this for a moment before answering. "You are, I'm sure, aware of the old saying that absence makes the heart grow fonder."

Joseph nodded.

"I can," I said, "make a case for the value of my absence. It should make Elena better appreciate my presence in her life. The many things I do for her that she will miss while I am gone. It might soften her to accept the idea of my taking a spiritual wife. It will not be an easy quest but this might move things in the right direction."

"So I take it you will go."

I closed my eyes and sighed. "I shall go."

"Splendid!" Joseph said.

"When did you plan to dispatch me? For how long?"

"I see no point in tarrying. If you can put your affairs in proper order, I should think you could depart next Monday."

"Next Monday!"

"I see no reason why not. I would envision a two-month mission. You should be able to accomplish your task in that span of time."

I shook my head. This was coming upon me with unexpected speed. However, I could muster no argument to oppose either the early departure or the protracted time I would be gone.

"One more thing," Joseph said. "When you arrive back at your house today, you will find a young gelding, black, strong, spirited, and ready to ride. We call him Lampblack. Brother Brigham has taken him there for you to use on your mission. Your current steed – also a gift of the Mormons – is aging and may not be up to the journey. Besides, your wife will need a horse in your absence."

"Thank you," was all I could say. "I shall put my affairs in order. We will sup with the Van Rijns on Sunday evening. I will be off the following morning."

"Very good. Very good indeed."

We stood and shook hands. I had momentarily forgotten the secret grip and fumbled around before grasping Joseph's hand in the prescribed manner. We both laughed at my clumsiness.

As I walked down the stairs, I said to myself with a snarl, "You had better deliver on your promise Brother Joseph. I will do my part." I knew if Elena refused my request for a second wife, I would be compelled to force her acquiescence. That could present certain inconveniences I would wish to avoid. But I would do what is necessary. I managed to nod to Piet as I stormed out of the Red Brick Store.

+ + +

"Canada?" Elena said. "You are going to Canada?"

Her attempt to suppress a smile at the thought of my impending absence was futile. Quickly, she turned so I might not witness her delight. *Yes,* I thought to myself, *this trip will have its advantages.*

For the next several days I put my affairs in order. On the Friday before my departure I retrieved sufficient specie from my secret stash under the floorboards of the privy to keep Elena supported in modest fashion. I also arranged for credit at the Red Brick Store should she run short of funds before my return.

Throughout the day on Sunday, Elena prepared for our dinner guests. She slow-roasted a small pig over the coals in our fireplace. Flames shot up with each sizzling drip of fat. Mindful of the belief that un-skinned potatoes caused the disease called Black Tongue, Elena peeled hers and boiled them in water on the stove. She also cooked turnip greens in fat and vinegar. Resting in the pie safe were several cakes and a plate of molasses cookies, which I permitted her to purchase at Lucius Scovil's Bakery. This was to be a feast indeed. Elena dusted and polished the furniture, swept the floors, and set the table with our fine china. She cleared a light dusting of snow along the pathway from the house to the privy. As I sat in my chair reading the paper and observing these domestic labors, I had to admit there were notable advantages to the married state. No doubt, Elena's industry arose in part from her glee at my imminent departure. My own well-being derived from the excitement I felt at Dorrie's soon-to-be presence in my home.

I had just finished donning my gray trousers and matching waistcoat when a knock sounded at the door. I tugged my ruby-colored cravat into place, smoothed my hair, and strode in stately fashion to the door, prepared to usher Dorrie and Piet into my house with all the gallantry I could muster. When I opened the door, to my surprise, the Van Rijns were nowhere in sight. Instead, there stood the Prophet and his wife Emma.

"Joseph? Emma?" I said.

"Yes, hearing your plans to host the Van Rijn's tonight, we took the liberty of coming along. It will be some time before we see you again and I wanted to give you my blessing for a safe and productive mission. I trust it is no inconvenience."

"None at all," said Elena from behind me. "We have more than enough food."

Furious at this unintended visit, I gritted my teeth and welcomed the Prophet and his wife into our home. As I took their coats, Joseph whispered, "Relax Brother Ned. This is all a part of my plan for you and Dorrie." He glanced over his shoulder. "Speaking of Dorrie, here she comes now."

Through the doorway I saw the Van Rijn carriage pull up in front of the house.

"Let's go help with Piet," Joseph said.

When we had Piet seated at the dining table, Joseph and I took our chairs and watched as the women brought steaming dishes of food from the kitchen. I could not take my eyes off of Dorrie who wore a beige dress spread with tiny pink flowers and wispy green stems. Her corset had been tightly drawn allowing a teasing glimpse of her features beneath a broad neckline that exposed her lovely shoulders. She wore pink chandelier earrings and a matching necklace. She had removed her bonnet to serve and once again I marveled at the cascade of black ringlets that curtained her face and neck. So black was her hair, it shone blue. My mouth watered.

Before the meal could begin, Joseph rose and stood behind my chair. He placed his hands on my shoulders and announced the important mission to which I was being called. He then offered a prayer for my safety and success. Closing with a blessing over the food, he reseated himself and we all dived into the delicious meal that Elena had prepared.

I had arranged for Dorrie to sit to my immediate right. As the meal wore on, now and then, I grazed her leg with my own, lightly so as not to arouse undue suspicions on her part. Each time, she recoiled. I kept my eyes from her and continued my part in the conversation, thus averting any clear sign that my movements below the table were purposeful. From time-to-time, as the conversation permitted, I would lean over and make a side comment, a little joke perhaps, to establish a special intimacy between us. She never acknowledged these asides save for a brief nod, her eyes affixed to her plate. At one point, just after I had made one of these incidental comments to Dorrie, Elena stared at me from across the table with cold disapproval.

When the main course had ended, Elena excused herself and brought in the cake and molasses cookies for our dessert. I poured more chokecherry wine except, of course, in Elena's glass. She never consumed strong drink but preferred a glass of warm milk, pronouncing it a much better accompaniment to the desserts she served.

As he munched on a cookie, Brother Joseph leaned back and focused his gaze on Dorrie.

"Sister Dorrie," he said and, as an intended afterthought, "Sister Elena, Sister Emma, Brother Piet, I hope you are all proud of our good Brother Ned. Today I had the great pleasure of ordaining him as a priest."

Elena's head snapped up, and a frown creased her face. She seemed both puzzled and somewhat offended that I had not shared this circumstance with her. Joseph continued between bites.

"And he has, as I mentioned, accepted this important call from the Lord to sojourn in Canada on a special mission. He will, no doubt, suffer hardships along the way so, Dorrie, and the rest of you, I bid you say your prayers for his safety and well-being."

Dorrie's cheeks flushed, and she nodded, embarrassed at having been called out by the Prophet in such an obvious way. Piet stared at the Prophet, also flummoxed by his directness. Emma stared at her lap. Elena trained sympathetic eyes on her friend Dorrie. I found myself rather amused by the discomfort of everyone in the room.

The Prophet continued his accolades of me for several more minutes, championing my services to the Church, my dedication to him, and my assurances of eternal salvation.

"Any woman sealed to Brother Ned will enjoy a glorious life as goddess in the celestial kingdom."

His eyes drilled into Dorrie.

A long and uncomfortable silence followed save for a gust of wind against the windowpane.

"Ha!" Joseph shouted at last. "Enough of this. We don't want Brother Ned's head to get too large. A toast to him and to his lovely wife, Sister Elena, for this splendid collation. With that, the women excused themselves and began to clear the table. The Prophet, Piet, and I remained at table discussing current events. Piet remained quiet, speaking only when spoken to. When he notified us he needed to visit the privy, Joseph and I drew his arms around our shoulders and bore him out into the cold. When we closed the door to the privy, we huddled in close contact to wait for Piet to finish.

"You were too obvious" I whispered.

I could see his smile in the moonlight. "The seed is planted," he said. "Now we let it germinate."

The evening ended shortly thereafter. The Prophet and Emma left first. Dorrie and Piet did not take their leave until the dishes and cookware had been cleaned and shelved. Dorrie, Elena, and I managed to get Piet into their carriage. To my delight, the opportunity presented itself for me to assist Dorrie up on to the carriage seat. I placed my hand on her hip to assist her ascent. She scooted away from my touch and snapped the reins.

When Elena and I returned to the house, I said, "Tomorrow I leave my love. Will you join me this night in my room to bid me farewell?"

She looked into my eyes.

"I think not."

CHAPTER TWENTY

Elena

Questions

A typhoon of freedom blew through the house as soon as Lampblack bore Ned out of sight on that Monday morning as he began his journey to Upper Canada. Since reducing my time in the Seminary, Monday became a free day for me. I wasted no time in hitching the horse to our carriage and making a quick run to the Van Rijn cabin.

Moments before her departure on the previous night, Dorrie had whispered with unbridled urgency, "I must talk to you, Lanie."

I assured her I would come as soon as possible.

When I walked through the door of the Van Rijn home, Dorrie threw her arms around me. We hugged in silence for several long seconds.

"Lanie, Lanie, what is happening?" she asked. "Last night was a most shocking evening. Oh, it was not the supper – that was wonderful! It was the behavior of the Prophet. Why did he single me out? Why did he direct all of his comments to me? Why did he not take his eyes off of me when talking so fondly of Mister Freeman?"

"Dorrie, I'm not certain," I said. "I cannot explain Joseph's behavior. It was a most uncomfortable time. The Prophet was unexpected. He and Emma had not been invited. I presume he feels he can join any of us at any time because he is, after all, the Prophet."

"And Lanie, there is more you don't know."

"More?"

"Yes, and I don't know how to put this delicately."

"Do you mean my husband's disposition toward you?"

262

"Yes, how did you know?"

"I have eyes, dear Dorrie. Mister Freeman has an unhealthy affection toward you."

"So you have sensed it?"

"More than sensed it. In comments over the past weeks he has spoken of you in lofty and almost covetous terms."

"Covetous?"

"Yes, he would say such things as, 'That young Dutchman is a lucky man. Such a pretty wife.' Just this morning as he prepared to leave, he said, 'Tell Dorrie I shall miss her and look forward to seeing her upon my return.' He didn't say as much to me."

"Oh dear."

"It is good he is gone."

"Yes... and, oh dear, oh dear, how shall I..." Dorrie started to wring her hands. "I caught him trying to rub my leg with his... his leg under the table. Oh Lanie... I am sorry to have to tell you this."

"Don't be. It doesn't surprise me."

"At first I thought it was my imagination, but it happened too frequently to be accidental."

A frosty anger spread through me. Oddly, the anger did not arise from any offense to me. To be honest, Ned's lack of affection toward me had become something of a relief, an excuse even for my own parched affections for him. No, my anger arose from his placing my good friend in such an uncomfortable frame of mind. Dorrie's disclosure did nothing more than stiffen my resolve to leave the man. I needed a place to go, a safe place, a haven far from his wrath. I would seek to divorce him but that would be problematic. Nowhere in Nauvoo could I secure a favorable judgment. Ned was too well placed in the system controlled by Joseph Smith and his male sycophants.

I stayed with Dorrie for the better part of two hours. We continued to visit about less ominous things and tried to enjoy a cup of freshly ground coffee, a rare treat in Nauvoo. Piet was able to procure coffee beans at the Red Brick Store as a perquisite of his work. When I took my leave, I bundled myself against the cold and settled onto the seat of the carriage.

On a whim, instead of proceeding west along Parley Street, as if to return to my home, I steered the wagon in an eastward direction. After several blocks, I caught the road toward Quincy, which would lead me to Sonora. If I were completely honest, this journey could not be described as a whim. I had been thinking about it ever since Ned made his blessed announcement that he would be gone for two months. I thought it divine intervention. With Ned gone for a season, I was free to do as I pleased.

For reasons that were still rather nebulous in my mind, I wanted to visit with Brother Burl again. I had religious questions I wished to pose but, to be truthful, I also just wanted to see him again. Something in that brief encounter near the Temple stirred me deeply. I didn't know if it was my unraveling faith, my disastrous marriage, the need for a man – a real man – to replace my owd Da, or just simply Burl himself. Whatever the circumstance, I knew it would be outrageously forward to visit him in Sonora. Yet, somehow, I knew he would understand my coming, and I had a hunch he would be pleased to see me again. I also suspected (or at least hoped) that his delight in seeing me would not derive exclusively from his missionary ambitions. I wanted him to be interested in me, just for me.

These feelings were not only forward but also risky. I knew it was completely inappropriate for a married woman to have an interest in seeing another man even if no romantic future were possible. When I say *romantic future*, I must insist that there were no such aspirations. I simply wanted to be with a man who seemed to understand me, who exuded a rare warmth and compassion, and who made me laugh like a carefree child. Nor could Burl Bumbalough develop unseemly feelings for me (not that I had detected any such feelings). He was, after all, an ordained clergyman, a man of God, and interest in a married woman would be a sinful misappropriation of his emotions.

I shook my head to rid me of all of these thoughts. Who was I to savor such ideas! Why would I even assume that Long Lanie, Upright Arkwright, the wych-strong willowy one, could spur romantic interest in a man anyway? Such things were the stuff of schoolgirl chitchat, the clucking of silly geese in their teen years, not the stuff of a teacher, a matron, the mistress of a household.

A skiff of snow on the Quincy Road had blown off and since the ground was frozen, I made good time, reaching the Sonora Landing by noon. I stopped at the little school and peered through the window. I saw Gabe Graham pacing back and forth in front of several students seated at rustic tables. In one of his turns, he looked up and saw me through the window. He said something to the class and motioned for me to meet him on the porch.

"Good day," he said. "If I remember, it's Miss Arkwright or, should I say, Sister Arkwright?"

I did not try to correct him. I so wished I were still Sister Elena Arkwright instead of Mrs. Edwin Freeman.

"Mister Graham, thank you. It is nice to know you remember me. I am flattered. Please excuse my interruption. I assure you, I shan't take but a moment of your time."

He chuckled. "Don't worry, the class will survive my absence for a few minutes."

"I'm looking for Brother Burl Bumbalough. Do you know where he is?"

"I can give you directions to his house but I suspect he is gone. He has been keen about visiting his parishioners and is out and about most days. I'm sure he would not mind if you waited for him. May I ask why you seek him?"

"I met him in Nauvoo some days back. He raised in my mind questions of a religious nature. He offered to visit further with me about them should I be of such a mind."

"I see. I'm certain your interest in further conversation on such matters will be gratifying for him. As he may have told you, he would love to help the Lord conquer, or perhaps I should say *re-conquer*, a wayward Mormon soul."

"Well, Mister Graham, I'm flattered by his aspirations, but I assure you I am not a prize to be won in a contest between the Saints and the Methodists."

Gabe Graham smiled and his eyes twinkled. "I would rather imagine he sees it the other way around."

I shook my head and offered a brief smile in response. With that I thanked him and took my leave, following the route he outlined until I came to the house that had been lent to Brother Burl. As anticipated, he was not home but the front door was unlocked. I took a deep breath and, with flickers of trepidation, entered the house. I took off my wrap and blew the glowing coals into a blazing fire, which took the chill off the room. Against my better judgment and out of sheer curiosity about this fascinating man, I began to snoop. I confined my browsing to the lower level of the house. To go upstairs into his personal space would be an unthinkable violation, but I must admit I was tempted. The house was sparsely furnished, which I found as no surprise for a single man who devoted his time, energies, and scarce resources to furtherance of the Kingdom. There were few personal items by which to get a better measure of the man. I found his large leather Bible, tattered and dog-eared from constant use. I thumbed through it, marveling at the copious notes and comments that filled the margins on nearly every page.

On one side of the keeping room, there stood an old scarred kneehole desk accompanied by a cockeyed swivel chair that groaned and squeaked when I sat in it. Papers, inkbottles, and assorted quills were scattered about the desktop. Tentatively, I moved a few of these items around to see what occupied Brother Burl during his hours alone. As expected, I found cryptic sermon notes, the names of his parishioners with directions to their homes and farms, and scribblings that appeared to be lines and stanzas of poetry. *Interesting,* I thought, *a poet.* Somehow, this bear of a man did not fit my image of the fragile poet brooding over his pages searching for the right word to end a line of iambic pentameter. I was about to rise from that cock-a-hoop chair when my eye spotted something on the desk. I swept aside several pages to reveal a partially formed letter. My breath caught as I read it.

Old Webb Farm Road
Sonora Landing
December 4, 1842

My Dear Mrs. Freeman,

On this Day of our Lord, I take pen in hand to

That was all he had written. My heart beat like a hummingbird's at the discovery of this letter and its cryptic opening line. Take pen in hand *to what?* So he *was* thinking of me. Our chance encounter had not slipped from his mind. I warmed at the thought. What was I to make of all of this? I could only imagine and imagine I did.

The afternoon wore on and the cumulative effect of Ned's physical abuse, the stresses of a failed marriage, and preparing a grand supper had taken its toll. I made myself comfortable on the horsehair settee in front of the fire to wait for Brother Burl. I hoped he would not be too late since I didn't want to be on the road to Nauvoo after dark. Before I knew it, I had slipped into a deep and dreamless sleep.

I attempted to open my eyes several times but could not sustain the effort. When finally I awoke, I saw that the fire had been stoked, and the flames were leaping high. A quick glance out the window revealed that dusk had settled upon the land and I sat upright. I had slept too long. Night was at hand.

"Good evening, Mrs. Freeman."

I gasped, startled by the realization I was not alone. I looked over the back of the settee and saw Brother Burl sitting quietly with his Bible.

"Oh, dear!" I said. "You surprised me. I had not heard you arrive."

"I wondered who had parked a carriage in front of my house and liveried a horse in my barn. It might have been an intruder. Imagine my shock to see Mrs. Freeman sound asleep on my couch."

"I'm very sorry, Brother Burl. I hope I have not inconvenienced you."

"Not in the least. Though I am rather curious why you made the journey from Nauvoo, discovered where I lived, and settled in for a long nap."

"I can…"

He held up his big hand.

"We've got plenty of time. You must be hungry."

"Well, I am, now that you mention it. But I mustn't stay. I don't like to travel at night alone. If I leave now I can cover several miles while there is still light."

"Don't be daft. The temperature is dropping like a rock. More clouds have rolled in from the west. It would seem we are in for a snowstorm. It is a bad night to be on the road. You will stay here tonight."

"But that would be inappropriate."

"Mrs. Freeman, you are safe here. No one would think ill of me for putting you up on such an inclement night nor would anyone hold you in contempt. The major issue is your husband. Does he know where you are? Surely, he will be worried for your safety."

"My husband is on his way to Canada to serve the Prophet for a few months. Neither he nor anyone else knows I am here except Mister Graham who gave me directions to your home."

"Ah, well, I doubt he will be a problem. In the short time I have been here Gabe and I have become good friends. We trust one another. He will, if he ever finds out, concur in my decision not to let you travel alone on this perilous night. Now…" He slapped his hands on his knees. "I must rustle up some chuck, as we say here on the frontier."

"Oh no, I don't mean to inconvenience you."

"Well, my dear Mrs. Freeman…"

"Lanie, remember."

"Well, my dear Lanie, we both have to eat. I'm sorry all I have are cornmeal johnnycakes but they are edible as long as they are smothered in molasses. I can heat up tea water."

Johnnycakes and hot tea did not compare to my feast of the previous day. Yet, I was much happier to be eating this modest meal with Brother Burl than struggling through the sumptuous feast I had prepared.

When supper had ended, we took tin cups of tea and returned to the warmth of the keeping room. After a few sips in silence, Brother Burl turned to me. "Now, I think all has been readied for you to explain why you have sought me."

"I'm not sure where to begin."

"May I surmise you have questions of faith?"

"I do."

"I thought as much. Please, toss me a question."

"Before I do, I believe it might be a useful beginning for me to explain to you how I became a Latter Day Saint."

"I would be most interested in that story," he said.

For the next half hour, I recounted the Mormon mission in Preston, the conversion of my owd Da, and my experience of heart fire in the presence of Elder Wilford Woodruff. I told him of my visit to Ann Dawson, who confirmed my heart fire episode had been a visitation of the Holy Ghost, a summons to be baptized in the LDS Church. I coursed over the decision to gather in Zion and shared with Brother Burl the hardships of our Atlantic voyage. When I finished, he stared at me while rubbing the lobe of his right ear.

"So wherein lies the question?" he asked, breaking the silence.

"As I said, I'm not sure."

"May I venture a guess?"

"Please."

"Is it possible your Mormon convictions are crumbling but you cannot imagine how you could have been so wrong, given the power of those emotions and events surrounding your conversion?"

I shook my head in wonderment. How could he read me so well? How could he frame my questions, even when I could not do so myself?

"Yes…I believe that sums it up," I said.

"I don't know if I can answer your question," he said. "However, perhaps between the two of us we can arrive at a suitable explanation. May I ask you some questions?"

"Of course."

"What was your spiritual state before you had this experience in the presence of Elder Woodruff?"

I thought for a moment. "I suppose you could say I felt barren spiritually, not moved by my religion, finding it all rather tedious and sterile."

"Ah," he said, nodding. "So you were *ripe*, so to speak, or perhaps even yearning for a deep and meaningful religious event, something that would pluck you out of the desert. After all, you had just witnessed the powerful transformation in your father, a transformation you desired for yourself. Am I correct?"

"Yes, I think so."

"And may I suggest further that you were so moved by this experience, it has become etched in your memory. For a time, it produced in you a sense of being caught up in great, portentous, and inexplicable events. You were in the swirl of wondrous things. Was this not the case?"

"It was."

"So, I would venture to say, your spirit bore a restlessness to which the Mormon faith seemed to provide a solution. Mormonism offered a lovely rain to the arid soil of your soul."

I nodded.

"Lanie, do you think that powerful experience – the heart fire, as you call it – was from God?"

"I can imagine no other source."

"Nor can I."

"What are you saying?"

"You interpreted your experience as evidence of a present and caring God."

"But it was the source of my conversion to Mormonism, which you take to be a false religion."

"Ah, but you did not instantly convert. In the first hours following your experience, you were still searching, still wondering what had happened to you."

"Yes, that is true until I visited Sister Ann."

"Tell me, what was the hymn Brother Woodruff sang."

"*Come let us anew our journey pursue.*"

"A hymn written by Charles Wesley, an Anglican priest – of the Methodist persuasion, I should hasten to add."

"And you think it was the words of the hymn rather than the singer of the hymn that sent me into a swoon."

"Perhaps it was both song and singer. True words sung beautifully by an untrue believer are still true words. Lanie, I believe God came to you in that moment. Things went awry in your search for an explanation and you searched in the wrong place. I daresay had you gone to your Methodist minister, he would have come up with a far different explanation than your friend Ann Dawson. Both would have agreed that the Holy Ghost came upon you. But they would have claimed different destinies for you under the guidance of the Spirit."

"Then, how is one to know? How is one to know which destiny is right?"

"It is difficult at times. When a person has an experience such as yours, that person is in a weak and vulnerable state, like a newborn infant. A spiritual infant cannot survive on its own any more than a newborn infant. There must be care and nurture from a loving family. Should a newborn come into a bad family, the baby will grow up in a distorted and deformed way. So it is with a spiritual infant. You were born into – or perhaps it is more accurate to say – kidnapped into a bad family and raised in a deformed way."

"Then that means my owd Da was too. But he died in this *bad family* as you call it. I cannot bear the thought."

"Oh, dear Lanie, you mustn't think like that. I gather your father was a simple man, pure in heart."

"Save for Christ Himself, the world has not known a man of purer heart."

"And you have heard it said, *Blessed are the pure in heart...*"

"*For they shall see God.*"

"There you have it. Your father is safe now. He is in Paradise, perhaps even hammering out horseshoes for the heavenly chariots. Remember that passage from Second Kings, and, behold, the mountain was full of horses and chariots of fire round about Elisha? Where do you suppose these heavenly horses get their horseshoes?"

He laughed and his laughter was so infectious that for the second time in less than a week, Brother Burl had made me laugh so hard my cheeks hurt. When finally, my laughter trickled off into titters, I looked up at Brother Burl.

"What am I to do?" I asked.

"Leave it. Leave the whole Mormon apostasy and come back home."

"I don't know if I can. My husband is a priest in the Church. All of my friends are devout Mormons. I have put my whole faith and stock, to say nothing of the family resources, in the LDS Church."

"Lanie, it is a false religion. It is a religion that preys upon your emotions. In your heart you know this...you know heart fire. But there is so much more to Christianity, to true religion, than emotion. You have to be transformed in your mind as well. God made us thinking beings. That's why you are here. The Book of Mormon is a false document. It holds doctrines contrary to the New Testament, the books of which were written in apostolic times and have held fast for centuries. Joseph Smith is a false prophet, a brilliant man, but a false teacher. He is the very sort the New Testament condemns. Lanie, to continue in this false teaching when you know the truth puts your soul in danger. As I said on that blustery day, don't forget the New Testament. Read it again. See how it contradicts the Book of Mormon and the teachings of your erstwhile Prophet."

I didn't know what to say.

Burl stood and poured us more tea. He returned to his seat and beheld me with compassionate eyes. "How is it with your marriage?" he asked, his voice barely above a whisper.

Oddly, this personal question caused me no offense. If the truth were known, I had wanted to disclose to him the awful circumstances of my marriage. When he broached the subject, I wasted no time in painting the grim picture of my domestic life. When I finished, I heard him issue a long, downhearted sigh.

"I was afraid of that," he said.

"How so?"

"Your eye."

"My eye?"

"Yes, I'm a former prizefighter. I know an eye blackened by a human fist. You didn't fall on a newell post. We both know that."

"Yes, but thank you for not saying so when we first met. I was grateful you gave me the excuse I needed. Who knows? If you had pressed your hunches, I might not have come today."

"I am glad you came."

We sipped our tea in silence for several minutes. I could feel Burl's gaze on me.

"So what will you do?" he asked.

"Leave him."

"But you have taken a vow before God."

"A Mormon vow. I shouldn't think it binding if what you say is true – it is a false religion."

"No matter. A vow is a vow. You promised to cleave to Ned Freeman for better or for worse. You did this in the presence of God and, in so doing, made God a partner in your marriage. Divorce is not a Christian option."

"What am I to do?"

"Weather the storm. You said yourself that he has shown more respect for you in recent days. Perhaps he is mending his ways."

"I doubt it. On top of his ill-treatment of me, he has unhealthy affections toward my dearest of friends. He is unashamed of his misbehavior."

"Yet, I fear you owe more time to him, to yourself, and to God."

"I fear for my life."

"Then I shall pray for you."

My anger sparked. "That's easy for you to say."

He set his cup down, placed his elbows on his knees, and spread his giant hands in a gesture of openness. "A thoughtless thing to say," he said. "I beg your forgiveness. You are quite right. I do not understand what you have gone through nor do I appreciate the depth of your fear. However, I will still pray for you. It's all I can do. Do you forgive me?"

I melted. "Of course."

"Come," he said. "We have ranged over too many high mountains for one night. Let me light a lantern and show you to your room. The bedclothes are washed. Just two days ago I tightened the bed ropes.

You should sleep well."

"Oh, no. I can't take your bed. I shall be fine here on the settee."

"Nonsense, you are my guest. You will have the best I can offer, such as it is."

"Burl…"

I caught myself. It is the first time I used his first name alone, without Brother. It slipped from my mouth.

He smiled.

"I'm sorry, Brother Burl…"

"Please, Burl."

"Brother Burl, I can't take your bed. You are so… so, well, big. You would be uncomfortable on the settee."

"My dear Lanie, I have slept in gutters, on docks, on hard ground and rocks. This settee, as you call it, is a blessing of comfort. Come now. I'll fetch a pitcher of warm water so you may freshen yourself on this cold night."

I followed him up the stairs, amazed not only at his sensitivity and hospitality, but the size of his feet and how delicately he placed them on the narrow steps.

"I must be off early in the morning," I said. "I'm due at the seminary tomorrow."

"I shall drive you."

"That won't be necessary. I know the way."

"Yes, but the road could be treacherous. I wouldn't forgive myself if your carriage slipped into the ditch and no one was there to help. I'll tie Buckwheat to the carriage and drive you to the seminary. Then I can ride back."

"That's kind of you."

When we reached the top of the stairs, he led me into a large room with a four-poster bed. He poured warm water into a bowl and turned to take his leave.

"Thank you," I said.

"And thank you for coming," he said.

I can't explain it. In looking back, I suppose it was a combination of his protectiveness and confident wisdom. Perhaps my own hunger entered into it. The moment he set the pitcher on the bureau, I swooned directly into his arms. He caught and held me. Seconds later, I came to and found my footing, but I did not move from his embrace. I felt his warm breath and soft whiskers on the top of my head. I shuddered when he pressed a light kiss on my hair. All of my well-formed precautions had flown out the window.

Seconds ticked.

Finally, we parted.

"I'm sorry," I said. "I don't know what came over me."

"Nor I me," he said with a sigh. "Nor I me. But here it ends. We are on a precipice and we must back away."

I looked into his eyes and nodded. "A pity."

"A pity indeed."

Burl turned and without looking back walked out of the room, shutting the door behind him.

+ + +

Burl and I were up early the next morning. We arrived at the seminary a few minutes before nine o'clock. As Burl mounted his horse to return to Sonora Landing, I stepped close and grasped one of his reins.

"Thank you," I said. "For everything, but I have one parting question."

"And that is?"

"I noticed a letter on your desk addressed to me."

A sheepish smile crossed his face.

"What did you intend to write?" I asked.

"I planned to invite you to join us for worship on Sunday morning."

"Is that all?"

"I would have urged you to linger after the service so we might talk."

I smiled. "That would have been nice."

"Now I can invite you in person. There are Nauvoo residents coming each Sunday by carriage. I know they would carry you along."

"Perhaps."

"I hope to see you Sunday."

He tipped his hat and turned his horse down the streets of trampled snow and out of the Mormon city.

"Who was that gentleman?" Arthur asked as I stomped the snow from my boots.

"He is a friend of mine, someone I just met. His name is Burl

Bumbalough."

Arthur chuckled. "That name is a mouthful."

"He would agree."

"And how did you meet him?"

I put my hand on Arthur's cheek. "Dear Arthur, you ask too many questions."

"I see," Arthur said, his little round mouth spreading to a pink slit. His brow remained furrowed.

For the next five days, I debated with myself. Should I accept the invitation to attend the Methodist Church? On the one hand, I could see Burl again. On the other, if seen and reported, I would be in hot water. Such exposure would alarm my friends and acquaintances, especially Dorrie. They would wonder what had possessed me to attend a Methodist Church. If I embarrassed Ned, my circumstances could be dire. He would punish me for compromising his position with Joseph.

It wasn't until Sunday morning that I decided to attend the worship service in Sonora. I had awakened in the early hours, tossing and turning, wrestling with the decision. Finally, I arose at six o'clock, dressed, and rode to the pre-arranged house where dissident Mormons were to gather. Ten of us crowded into Jim Siegenthaler's carriage and huddled under blankets for the frigid trek to Sonora.

Along the way, several of the passengers recounted their stories, sharing reasons they had fallen away from the LDS Church. Their estrangement revolved around one of three primary objections: the inconsistencies and irrationalities of the faith, control over the lives of adherents, and disaffection with Joseph Smith. They saw the Prophet as a man consumed with lust, desire for power, and the unseemly pursuit of wealth. I also listened attentively as these fellow travelers discussed their first impressions of Brother Burl.

"What a marvelous preacher," one said. "I was enraptured by his first sermon to us."

"And what a powerful singing voice," said another.

"He has a good voice?" I asked, wanting to hear more.

"Oh, my dear," said one older matron, "Wait until you hear him. He can bring down walls."

I smiled inwardly. There were new surprises every day with this man.

"And a marvelous sense of humor," Jim Siegenthaler said, turning his head toward me with a smile. "Have you met Brother Burl, Sister Elena?"

"I have," I said but offered no further information.

When we arrived at the small wooden church in Sonora, Burl strode our way, removing his hat in a gesture of welcome. His ginger hair spiked in all directions and it made me smile. He gave me a brief nod.

"Brethren and sisteren from the North," he said in his booming voice. "All hail to thee. Welcome, welcome. Come. A fire burns in the stove to warm one and all."

As he ushered us into the church, lightly, briefly, he put his hand in the small of my back to guide me through the door. I nearly swooned again.

Another fifteen minutes passed as other congregants arrived and took their seats on rough-hewn pews. Throughout the church, now full, there were soft whispers of greeting and private prayers murmured in silence. Then a hush fell over the people. Suddenly, a thunderous baritone shattered the calm. Burl marched into the room bearing his great Bible and singing *Come Thou Long Expected Jesus*. What an appropriate hymn, I thought. I remembered we must be in the Gentile season of Advent. A wave of nostalgia washed over me. I missed this time of expectation and preparation for the incarnation of Christ. I no longer observed Advent because it had never been a practice of the LDS Church.

When Burl reached the front of the church, he put his Bible on the Lord's Table and turned to face us with a smile of radiant joy. He spread his arms, looked heavenward, then closed his eyes and finished the four verses of the hymn, *a capella* and from memory. I sat awestruck by the power of his voice that filled every nook and cranny of the church. I marveled at the joy and warmth that radiated from his smile. A man with a heart for the Lord. No question about it.

"My dear brothers and sisters," he said, "we shall follow the order of worship Brother John Wesley recommended to us." Then he raised a finger. "But with a few variations here and there, which I trust the good Lord won't mind. Let us then begin." He closed his eyes. "As the psalmist says, *The sacrifices of God are a broken spirit; a broken and contrite heart, O God, thou wilt not despise.* Bow your heads with me and let us confess our sins."

We proceeded through the service of Morning Prayer, which was familiar to me. Though I had worshiped with the same words for many years in Preston's Primitive Methodist Church, there was something different in this little frontier chapel. I felt a fervency, a unity of spirit, and an affection I had rarely experienced in worship, even in those first heady days of my conversion to Mormonism. This was especially true as they sang from the little tattered hymnals. Everyone lent a voice, even the men, and while they may not have equaled in numbers the great choir of Nauvoo, these Methodists took no back seat in the power of praise. I so wanted to plunge into the worship of God with the fullness of my being, to join them with my whole heart. But I held back, leery of my feelings because I had been betrayed by these feelings, betrayed by heart fire.

As we concluded another lovely hymn, *Lo He Comes with Clouds Descending*, Burl picked up his heavy Bible, handling it as if it were a flimsy pamphlet. He looked to the heavens again for the umpteenth time.

"Guard my lips, O Lord, that I may speak nothing that is not of thee. Guard our ears, O Lord, that we may hear nothing that is not of thee. Guard our hearts, O Lord, that we may harbor nothing that is not of thee. Guard our lives, O Lord, that we may do nothing that is not of thee."

He studied the congregation with arms spread, Bible resting in one hand.

"Friends, I have come among you to be your minister, to walk with you on the journey of life. For this I am grateful to God. And while I am to be among you I am also to lead you in an important mission. We have been placed here by God to be a witness to the true faith. North of us dwells an apostate faith that perverts the children of God and He has given us the awesome charge to reclaim his children. To rescue them. To guide them back into the fold. With this in mind, please listen as I read from Peter's Second Letter. *But there were false prophets also among the people, even as there shall be false teachers among you, who privily shall bring in damnable heresies, even denying the Lord that bought them, and bring upon themselves swift destruction. And many shall follow their pernicious ways; by reason of whom the way of truth shall be evil spoken of. And through covetousness shall they with feigned words make merchandise of you; whose judgment now of a long time lingereth not, their damnation slumbereth not.*"

He put the Bible on the Lord's Table once again.

"Does this not sound familiar to you?" he said, pacing the center aisle of the church. "My dear ones, we are in the near presence of a false prophet, a false teacher. Burl moved gracefully around the pulpit to retrieve a small leather bound book. He waved it back and forth causing the covers to sway under the force of his gesture.

"And here is a composition of feigned words, the *Book of Mormon.*"

From there, Burl launched into a diatribe against the Mormon scriptures. I remember little of what he said that morning but I do remember how I felt. As discontented as I was with the Mormon faith, hearing Brother Burl's condemnation of all I had come to believe unnerved me. My heart so pounded in my chest that I feared others would hear it. It had become too much.

As the sermon drew to a close, Burl raised a forefinger. "We Christians put our faith first in a person, the person of Jesus Christ. We do not put our first belief in a prophet. We do not put our first belief in a church structure or its human authority. We do not put our first belief in a set of rules by which we are to live. We attain eternal life, not by our own works but by the grace of God alone, by faith in God alone, and by Christ our God alone. Christ only, for as it says in the Acts of the Apostles, *Neither is there salvation in any other; for there is none other name under heaven whereby we must be saved!*"

Burl walked back to the second pew and sat among us. Next to me. I could feel his presence. I could smell his exertion. Silence descended upon the whole church. After what seemed an eternity, he rose again. The intensity with which he concluded his sermon had melted away.

"One last thing," he said. "We must at all times bear the compassion and mercy of that One to whom we pledge our fidelity. So while we condemn the teachings of the LDS Church, we also keep a light burning in our homes for those who have lost their way. When they see that light we must open our doors in friendship and our arms in love."

Our service concluded with another familiar hymn, *O Come, O Come Emmanuel,* but my emotions were in such turmoil I could not find voice to sing it. When the service ended, I rushed passed Burl, refusing to acknowledge the man who had kissed me on the forehead. Tears stung my eyes.

I heard Brother Burl ask Mary Siegenthaler, "Is she all right?"

"I pray she will be," Mary said. "You can't know how hard it is for some of us.

I walked out of earshot.

CHAPTER TWENTY-ONE

Burl

Fall

I could see it happening. She arrived, reserved and guarded to be sure, but pleased to be a part of our little congregation. At first, she seemed comfortable in our presence. Then, as I began to preach, her countenance clouded. She dropped her eyes and stared at the folds of her dress. Something I had said unnerved her, but I knew not what. I fought with my pillow for two nights before deciding I must make my way to Nauvoo and discover what had caused things to become so unhinged.

I planned to make my trip to Nauvoo early on Tuesday afternoon. I would first stop at the Siegenthalers and then try to intercept Lanie at the close of the school day. The bitter weather had not abated. As I mounted Buckwheat, I drew a heavy scarf around my face. I had not gone a mile before the wind began to rage over the waters of the Mississippi, blowing snow, leaves, and other debris across the road. Cakes of icy snow formed on my scarf, the brim of my hat, the reins, and bit straps of my horse. At the half-way point, I stopped and considered turning back but concluded it would have been just as foolhardy to return home as to continue my trek to Nauvoo.

When I reached the Siegenthalers, visibility had been reduced to a few feet. The streets and roads were deserted. The Siegenthalers, huddled in their house, were shocked to hear a knock on the door. When they saw me standing on their porch dripping in icicles, they jerked me into their house. Jim donned his great coat and led Buckwheat to the barn. Mary snatched my coat, hat, and boots from me. She shoved me into a chair, removed my stockings and vigorously rubbed my frozen feet and toes. When my feet turned pink, Mary wasted no time in serving me a glass of warm milk.

"Well, now Reverend, to what do we owe this unexpected pleasure?" Jim asked, stomping the snow from his boots.

"Not *Reverend*, remember," I said. "Just Burl. It seems I picked a bad day to come north. The storm gathered as I was en route. By the time, I realized I was in a dangerous situation, it was too late to return home. So I thank you for your kindness. I'm warming up."

"Am I to assume that you didn't come here to see us, that you had another purpose?" Mary asked.

"Yes and no. I came here to see Sister Freeman."

The Siegenthalers exchanged glances but said nothing. I continued.

"She was distressed by our worship service or, more directly, my sermon. I don't want to frighten her away so I thought I would pay her a visit. I had intended to stop here first to hear your assessment."

Mary shrugged. "She is fraught. She said little on the ride back to Nauvoo. When we arrived, I invited her to come in for a few minutes. She resisted, not wanting to talk, but I insisted. Jim excused himself to the barn. She disclosed little save for her anxieties over leaving the Mormon Church. Her husband is a close confidante of the Prophet. She does not wish to cause Ned any embarrassment. As I'm sure you understand, the decision to leave the Mormons, after throwing in all you are and all you have, is difficult. I would venture to say she is in the throes of such a quandary."

"That is all she said?"

"I'm afraid so."

"She mentioned nothing about what I might have said or done to cause her pain?"

"No she did not."

"I thank you for this information. May I linger for a time until my clothes have dried and my body has been roasted by this welcome fire?"

"Of course."

An hour later, after pleasant conversation and prayers with the Siegenthalers, I trudged back into the unremitting storm. The Seminary house was shuttered, and I concluded that school had been called off due to the weather. Still, I knocked on the door in hopes I might rouse someone. After several attempts, the door opened a crack, and I beheld a tiny little man with mouse-gray hair and beard.

"May I help you?" he asked.

"Yes, I am in search of Mrs. Freeman. Is she here?"

"Alas, no. We have canceled our session for today. May I ask why you seek her?"

I detected an air of protectiveness.

I smiled. "Gracious me! I apologize for my ill manners. Permit me to introduce myself. I am Brother Burl Bumbalough, the Methodist minister from Sonora."

"I know who you are but I don't know why you seek Sister Elena."

"Good sir, she is an acquaintance of mine. Let's simply say, we have mutual interests, and I came to engage her in further conversation."

"And this could not have waited until the storm passed?"

"The storm had not intensified when I departed my home."

"I'm afraid I can't give you her whereabouts."

"I mean her no harm."

"Sir, I should warn you that I have recently learned that you seek to recover souls – Mormon souls – you deem to be lost. I surmise that Mrs. Freeman is among those you wish to pluck from our Mormon tree. She is an intelligent woman and capable of making her own decisions. She may harbor reservations about our faith. If so, she has not told me. I, too, bear reservations but my concerns have little to do with the truth of the *Book of Mormon*. I have no doubt the *Book of Mormon* is inspired of God. I say all of this for two reasons. First, I warn you that you are a marked man. Your presence in Nauvoo is, may I say, unappreciated. These people will seek to keep you at bay with whatever force they need. I assure you, they are not timorous when it comes to the use of force in defense of their faith. You could be in considerable danger. Second, despite my reservations concerning Mormonism, I do not wish to become one of those fruits you seek to pluck. Have I made myself clear on these points?"

"Abundantly."

"Then I bid you good day."

He started to shut the door, but I put out my hand to stay its closure.

"My dear fellow, the weather is frightful. Won't you please tell me how I might find Mrs. Freeman's home? If you don't tell me, I fear no one will. As you say, she is an intelligent, capable woman and can come to her own conclusions. Do you believe she *needs* your protection?"

He looked at me for several seconds, weighing the decision to help me. Finally, he shrugged and gave me the directions I sought.

For the third time that day, I stood on a porch and knocked. This time my heart was in my throat. Given Lanie's abrupt departure from the church, I had no idea how she would receive me. I feared she would not admit me into her home. When she opened the door and peered through the crack, saying nothing by way of welcome, my fears were confirmed. I took off my hat and began to spin the brim.

"Good day, Mrs. Freeman, Lanie," I said.

"Reverend Bumbalough."

"I'm out visiting people."

"So I see."

"May I come in for a moment? To talk."

"There is nothing to say."

"Please, Lanie. Whatever might be your future intentions, it is not good to end things on this note. May we visit for a moment? Then I shall take my leave, never to bother you again."

She stared through the crack. At last, she opened the door and, without saying a word, led me into the keeping room, warmed by a hot fire on the grate. I could smell bread baking in the kitchen. Her long gray housedress, cinched around her waist by an apron, swayed as she walked before me. Lanie pointed to a rocking chair but did not offer to take my coat and hat, which I took as a sign that my visit would be brief. She sat opposite me on a ladder-back chair, hands clasped in her lap.

"Lanie," I said. "I have come to offer an apology for whatever I said or did that so distressed you this Sunday past."

"You owe me no apology, sir."

"I fear I do. You entered the church full of anticipation and excitement. You left quite nonplussed, even distressed, if I may say so. I can only conclude that something I said caused you to become alarmed."

She heaved a big sigh and shook her head a few times, little shakes. Her eyes remained fixed on the folds of her dress, much the same countenance I saw during the waning moments of my sermon.

"What was it?" I asked, my voice soft and pleading. "I must know."

She shook her head again, the same little shakes.

We sat in silence. I did not know what to say. She remained inscrutable, so I started talking, not knowing where my thoughts might lead.

"I spoke with Mary Siegenthaler before I came here. She explained to me how difficult it is for Mormons to abandon the Church. Mary also informed me that your husband is a close advisor to Joseph Smith and that your disengagement from the Church could cause him considerable embarrassment. Is that what disturbed you?"

She made no response.

"I fear it is more," I said. "I have presented my missionary intentions with fervency. Perhaps I was too intense. On the one hand, I do not repent of this. To my mind, Mormonism is a bane to religion. It is growing at an alarming rate. While it may suffer certain setbacks in the years to come, I have little doubt it will continue to grow and prosper. From what I have seen, it offers security and relief to spiritual seekers, most of whom will not question the origins and propositions of their new faith."

Here I paused to spin my hat again.

"On the other hand," I continued. "The last thing I wish to do is cause you consternation. You have no idea just how much I value your presence in my life and in my church. I flowered within when I saw you sitting in that wagon from Nauvoo last Sunday. It caused me great joy to hear your voice singing the hymns and I could tell the old service, properly rendered, gave you great satisfaction. Then, your countenance flagged. I can pinpoint with some accuracy when, in the course of my address, your ardor waned."

She said nothing.

I studied her for several minutes until I realized I could not reach her. Elena Freeman was a complex woman. Intelligent, sensitive, in some ways innocent and pure, defiant at times, unsatisfied and yearning, tender and unhardened by the vicissitudes of her life. She aroused in me a shielding instinct but she rebuffed my assurances. I had little doubt that her resistance stemmed in part from fear of the dangerous and volatile Edwin Freeman.

Resigned to her silence, I took a deep breath and stood. I put my hand on the latch and turned back to see her, perhaps for the last time. She had not moved.

"Thank you for letting me in," I said. "I shan't bother you further."

The instant I stepped out on the porch, a gust of icy wind sucked the breath from me. I gazed out at the churning snow and the rapidly forming drifts, giant white pillows on the streets of Nauvoo. The return trip to Sonora Landing would be hazardous and I pondered getting a room in Nauvoo for the night. However, if what the little headmaster said was true, I was a marked man. I feared no innkeeper would receive me on this dreadful night. Besides, I had no money with which to pay for a room or livery. I would have to rely on God's protection and, to that end, I paused before mounting Buckwheat and said a prayer for safekeeping.

I didn't hear it through the howling wind but at the end of the block, something caused me to turn back. Lanie was running toward me.

"Wait!" I could tell she was shouting, but it sounded like the faint wail of a kitten burrowed in hayloft straw. "Wait!"

I turned Buckwheat to face her as she drew near. She gathered her shawl around her shoulders, reached up and took hold of one of my reins.

"Come back," she said. "You can't travel in this weather."

"I'll make it," I said. "You are not to worry."

"Please, come back."

Our eyes locked for a long moment.

"Please," she said again. "Put your horse in the barn. There are blankets and a bucket of oats for him. Then come back to the house. Please."

I nodded, relieved at not having to make my way home in the storm. Perhaps, I thought, I might yet make peace with her.

Something must have snapped within her because when I had seen to Buckwheat's care and returned to the house, she was different. She bustled about with what I knew to be her natural hospitableness. She placed my hat, coat, boots, and stockings on a bench before the fire to dry and warm them. When she took my socks she held them away from her, grasping them with her thumb and forefinger, wincing at the smell. Despite my discomfiture at her smelly face, the recovery of her emotions made me smile.

For several minutes we stared at the fire, listening to the pops of exploding pitch.

"Turnabout is fair play," she said at last.

I raised my eyebrows.

"You would not let me travel in the storm and gave me shelter for the night. I should do no less for you. I fear you would lose your way in this blizzard. You may stay here tonight."

"Thank you," I said. "Do you suppose God has whipped up this storm to keep us together?"

"I shouldn't think God wants us together." She stood abruptly. "I must tend to my bread."

When Lanie returned, she served me a cup of hot tea and warm bread with butter. We spoke in snippets and only on subjects safe for superficial conversation. She busied herself with knitting and I browsed Mister Freeman's old newspapers. At nine o'clock sharp, she stood, picked up a lantern and bade me to follow her. We went upstairs, and she showed me to the back bedroom.

"This is Mister Freeman's room. You may sleep here tonight. Everything is clean and there is water in the pitcher. I bid you good night."

She backed out of the room shutting the door behind her. I can't say how long I stood where she had left me. Though I felt certain I understood the source of her detachment, I sensed irritation budding within me. She was overreacting. After all, I had never intended to hurt her by what I said in my sermon and I had every right to say it. I harbored no doubts about my call to Sonora nor did I intend to quail in my duty to help God reclaim His deluded children. With these thoughts teeming in my mind, I stripped to my underclothes, knelt by the bed, and lifted my cares to the Lord in prayer.

+ + +

I did not sense it at first. As I awakened to a pitch-black room, I felt a presence. I saw nothing so I reached out, startled when another hand grasped mine. Lanie sat on the edge of my bed.

"Lanie?"

"Yes. Don't be alarmed."

I propped myself on my elbow. The bed ropes groaned under my movement.

"How long have you been here?" I asked. "Is something wrong?"

"I have been here for a spell wondering if I should waken you."

"What is amiss?"

"My soul."

"I don't understand."

"I have tossed and turned all night."

I waited.

"I don't know what has come over me but I want you to know that I bear no ill will toward you. You have done nothing for which you must apologize."

"But I…"

"Shhh." She put a finger on my lips. "I've been thinking about what you said yesterday. I believe you were accurate on all accounts."

"All accounts?"

"Yes, you spoke of my consternation at the thought of leaving the new Zion. I have given my time, my resources, my abilities, and my father to the Mormon Church. I suppose you could say I have surrendered my whole being. Then, in the middle of your sermon it struck me like splitting maul."

"What hit you?"

"This… " She swept her hand in an arc. "All of this may be a colossal heresy, a monstrous error. Then, from the pulpit, you brought forth such powerful words so fervently delivered that I felt you were crushing me. Now I am sorely disillusioned. Mormonism appears a sham, yet I don't know if I can make a break. I don't know if I can come back to your church. It frightens me."

I found her hand and took it in mine. She offered no resistance.

"Time, Lanie. Time. This has all happened so quickly. Give it time. I want you to be with us on Sunday, but I will understand if you and the Lord need freedom to sort out the tangle of your emotions."

"Thank you for that," she said. "But I must assure you that you owe me no apology. You were simply doing what you believe God has called you to do, and you did it with the zeal I would expect of you. You are a soldier of Christ."

"The true Christ."

She shook her head, uncertain.

We lapsed into an awkward silence. Unable to endure it, I sat up and put my arm around her shoulder. After the briefest of hesitations, Lanie's resistance dissolved, and she melted into my chest. I held her, knowing full well that I was failing the test set before me by the Prince of this World, and no longer caring. Her warmth, the silkiness of her skin, and the fresh scent of cloves that wafted from her lips produced in me a bliss I had never before experienced.

It happened quite naturally. She raised her face. Our lips brushed together. Then, in an instant, everything exploded in passionate ecstasy. We gave our mouths to each other until at last we broke apart, catching our breath and savoring the moment.

"I must go," she said.

"Please stay."

"No. I can't. I am a married woman."

She stood, brushed the front of her nightgown to iron out the wrinkles and raced from the room. I had little doubt. I had fallen in love with Elena Freeman but my joy in this awareness was sullied by the knowledge that, together, we had just torn down the walls of the Eighth Commandment, *Thou shalt not commit adultery.*

PART FOUR

I opened to my beloved; but my beloved had withdrawn himself, and was gone: my soul failed when he spake: I sought him, but I could not find him, but he gave me no answer.

Solomon's Song 5:6

Verily, verily, I say unto you, that whosoever shall put away his wife, saving for the cause of fornication, causeth her to commit adultery; and whoso shall marry her who is divorced committeth adultery.

3 Nephi 12:32
also
Matthew 5:32

CHAPTER TWENTY-TWO

Elena

Visitations

The spring of 1843 wandered in, timid in the face of a tenacious winter. I had not seen Burl Bumbalough in eight weeks. We had withdrawn from one another by mutual consent. Shamefaced, on the morning after our indiscretion, a moral lapse in which two vows had been vacated, we stood in the kitchen facing one another. The smell of fried eggs and fatback wafted about us. He took my hands in his.

"I am mortified," he said.

"As am I."

"Now I must repent and I must suppress the feelings you have stirred in me."

Tears stung my eyes. All I could do was nod.

"We cannot let this develop further," he said.

I nodded again, in wretched agreement.

Gathering myself, I looked at Burl through filmy eyes. I offered a tight smile and clasped his hands. "At least the weather has cleared. It is still cold but sunny. The way home should be clear."

"Yes."

"But, let me serve you some breakfast, food for the journey."

"I think it best I go."

"Oh, please don't go. All is prepared."

"I am most grateful you prepared this meal for me but I mustn't linger, much as I would like to."

My heart sank. This was our farewell.

"I hope what happened between us will not stay you from coming to church," he said.

"I don't know. My mind and heart are in knots. It will take time."

"I understand," he said.

He released my hands and, without a word, left the house.

I watched him walk to the barn and whispered under my breath words I had never spoken to any man before, save to my owd Da, "I love you." With that I dissolved into uncontrollable weeping.

+ + +

The Mormon leadership discovered I had attended worship at the Sonora Methodist Church and had missed several Sunday meetings in Nauvoo. A week after Burl and I parted, I heard a sharp knock on the front door of our house. When I opened it, I beheld Emma Smith, Elizabeth Durfee, and another woman whom I did not know.

"Good day," I said. "To what do I owe this visit?"

"May we come in?" Emma asked.

I stood aside as the three women entered in silence, not waiting for my invitation. Elizabeth and the unknown woman sat down, Emma and I remained standing.

"Please, won't you have a seat?" Emma said, more by way of command than question.

I took a seat, my heart crawling into my throat.

Emma remained standing.

She took a deep breath. "Sister Elena, word has reached us, on good authority, that you have forsaken your obligations to the Church. You have not attended scheduled meetings on the Sabbath. More disquieting, you have attended the Methodist Church in Sonora. You have been seen in the company of the Reverend Burl Bumbalough, a vile man who seeks to persecute the Saints."

I nodded but said nothing. While I had been careful not to expose my movements, neither had I been overly cautious. I realized there could be any number of possible informants, some of whom may have exposed my actions. People talk after all.

"It is true," I admitted. "I attended one service of the Methodist Church but I did so more out of curiosity than commitment."

"There is no need for curiosity. They do not possess the restored Gospel."

I remained silent.

"We are here not to judge but to urge upon you repentance," Emma said after a long silence.

If they have not judged me why would they seek my repentance? I steeled myself. "I have nothing to repent."

"For your waywardness, you do," Mrs. Durfee said.

"I think not. One visit to Sonora does not constitute waywardness."

"It does if you have not been otherwise faithful in your attendance here in Zion," the unnamed woman said.

I could feel the steam rising.

"I must say that your mission this morning does not set well with me," I said. "My spiritual health is something between my Lord and me. I need not answer to you."

"Oh but you do," said Emma.

"So you are now the self-proclaimed spiritual police for the sisters of Zion?"

"We are."

"And on whose authority?"

"My husband Joseph's. When he established the Relief Society by revelation and prayer, he established me, his *Elect Lady*, as its president."

I threw all caution to the wind.

"What would you say, Madame President, if I announced I do not believe that by revelation you have been anointed to serve as an enforcing officer? And what would you say if I refused to accept your authority?"

The unnamed woman gasped. All six eyes of my visitors widened to the size of halfcrowns.

"Sister Elena," Emma said, trying to control her voice. "May I remind you that your husband is a priest of the Church, on an important mission to Upper Canada, and a valued advisor to the Prophet. Your actions and your impenitence are a public affront to him. If not for your own sake, for his you need to reform your ways."

I stood and faced Emma with a level gaze. "The three of you should leave. This conversation has come to an end."

"And if we refuse?"

"Then I shall leave and the three of you may sit here and stew in your own juices an entire fortnight, for all I care."

Emma was speechless. Elizabeth Durfee mumbled something to

the effect of *Well, I declare!* The unnamed woman made gargling noises. But to my relief they all left as requested.

The next day, Jim and Mary Siegenthaler came to my house expressing their sorrow that I had missed Sunday services at Sonora Methodist. I thanked them for their concern but remained evasive in response to their questions.

Several days later, the Prophet himself stood on my porch. Upon admission, he waltzed into my house sporting a *hale-fellow-well-met* attitude. His voice carried no tone of judgment. Joseph issued no condemnations nor did he call me to repentance. He rocked back and forth in Ned's chair, chewing on a burnt locofoco, musing about the inevitability of spiritual lapses and religious doubts. With a casual wave of his hand, he confessed that he had such episodes himself, if I could possibly imagine that. He reiterated the importance of respecting my husband's position, given his extreme value to the Church.

Then, for the first time in my hearing, he unfolded his doctrine of celestial marriage including the necessity for me to be sealed to my husband. In so doing, I would enjoy eternal life in the highest realm of heaven. "Now that the Temple is nearly completed," he said with a proud smile, "you can be among the first to be sealed in that sacred space." His jaunty tone gave way to a light scolding tone. "By the way, I note that you and Ned have not been forthcoming in contributing to the construction fund for the Temple."

I listened respectfully but pledged nothing with respect to celestial marriage or earthly tithes. He cajoled me for another ten minutes. When he saw his entreaties would come to nothing, he shook his head in vexation, removed himself to the door, and stepped through with a slow turn. I watched him until he rode out of sight.

Let him simmer. I was highly incensed by these intrusive attempts of the Prophet, Emma, and her toadies to stifle my free will. Despite what they said, their visits had nothing to do with my spiritual health. Their motivations were grounded in power and public appearance. I suppose because I was the first woman crew chief in the mills, had served as a respected teacher, and had become widely read, I enjoyed an independence unseen in most women. I tried not to be arrogant or self-righteous. I was grateful for my blessings. On many occasions, I had striven to be more compliant and less independent, the most glaring instance of which was my ill-fated consent to marry Ned

Freeman. I had no doubt that Ned's absence and Da's untimely death had released me to a level of freedom I had never before enjoyed. With that freedom came an intensified will to be more my own person, albeit under the yoke of Christ. Whose Christ? The Christ of the Bible or the Christ of Joseph Smith's youthful vision in upstate New York? I felt like the center knot on a tug-of-war rope with two Christs trying to pull me across their respective victory lines. The harder they pulled, the tighter the knot.

And then there were the letters. They began coming about ten days following Ned's departure. He wrote every day if the dates on the letters were to be believed. Because of the sporadic delivery of mail on the frontier, his letters came in bunches. I was forced to arrange them by date to establish a proper chronicle of his mission. In each letter, Ned devoted several paragraphs to the details of his journey, which I found interesting, despite my loathing of him. Always, as the letter came to a close, he would seek my forgiveness for past abuses. He would profess his undying love for me, and assure me he longed for the day when we would be reunited.

A part of me – the proper moral part – wanted to believe what he said but the other part – the corrupt and self-interested part – did not. I still held Burl in the center of my heart and no matter how hard I tried, I could not evict him to make room for my treacherous husband. I thought about Burl day and night. As I went about my chores and duties, I wondered what he would be doing at that precise moment. When my head hit the pillow at night, my thoughts turned to him and to unmentionable fantasies. On many an occasion, down on my knees, I asked God to relieve me of my obsession with this Methodist minister. Either God chose not to answer this prayer or I was too hard-hearted to accept His grace.

My constant thoughts of Burl caused me to reprise our conversations and play them again in my mind. *Don't forget the New Testament.* That strange admonition surfaced in my mind many times during what I have come to call the *long winter of confusion.* One early afternoon, as a blizzard swirled about our house, I accepted Burl's challenge and opened the Bible to the New Testament. I had no particular destination in mind. As it happened, the Bible parted to Ephesians, the second chapter. I began to read until I came to the eighth and ninth verses, *For by grace are ye saved through faith; and that not of yourselves: it is the gift of God: Not of works lest any man should boast.* I stared at the flames of the fire before me and remembered Burl's words as he preached, *We attain eternal life, not by our own works but by the grace of God alone, by faith in God alone, and by Christ our God alone. Christ only...* The *Book of Mormon* says something quite different. I recall Nephi, in his second book saying, *for we know that by grace we are saved, after all we can do. After all we can do?* That would be works. Paul says *not of works*. Was Paul wrong? Was the Prophet wrong?

As the days wore on, I continued to struggle with the contradictions between the New Testament and the doctrines of the LDS Church. The Bible teaches that God is Spirit but Joseph contends that God the Father has flesh and bones. The Bible teaches there is but one God. The Mormon *Book of Abraham* refers to the *gods* who *organized and formed the heavens and earth.* The Bible teaches that no sin is beyond redemption save for cursing the Holy Spirit. Yet, Mormonism teaches that adultery committed a second time is unforgivable. These and many other contradictions clogged the workings of my mind, leaving me in a state of unresolved perplexity.

To add to my burdens, Dorrie flew into my front room one afternoon in a state of complete disarray. Her hair hung not in delightful curls about her face but in a stringy bun poorly bound on the back of her head. She still wore her apron and her face bore an expression of utter despair. She fell into a dining room chair and with one elbow on the table, held her drooping head.

"Dorrie, whatever is the matter?"

"It's happened again, though much worse this time."

"What has happened?"

"Joseph. He came to my house this morning. Piet was at work. The Prophet made himself at home. He requested a flagon of ale, which he drank down in one gulp. Then, he talked of the most distressing things. He once again brought up the subject of celestial marriage."

"I know what you mean. He's done the same with me."

"What is this about, Lanie? Does he do this with all the women or are we being singled out?"

"I don't know. I don't understand. He seems possessed by the subject of sealing and marriage for eternity. It is a wonderful thing to believe in eternal marriage, but what if one marries the wrong man?"

"Yes. What if..."

Dorrie pulled a handkerchief from her sleeve and wiped her nose.

"Lanie, there is yet more I feel I must say."

"Yes?"

"He kept probing me on the subject of my relationship with Piet. I mean my intimate relationship."

"Intimate relationship? I should think that none of his business."

"I would agree and when I said as much, he brushed it aside. He said, 'I am the Prophet of God in these latter days. You should reveal all to me.' I truly believe – oh how can I say it – that he wants to know if Piet has been able to consummate our marriage. He brought up the word *virgin* more than once."

"Oh, Dorrie…"

"Lanie, I am not a virgin. I was when I married Piet but there are no problems with intimacy."

"You needn't have told me this, Dorrie. It is none of my affair."

"Someone needs to know. But not Joseph. What can it mean, Lanie?"

"Dorrie, you have heard the rumors…the rumors of spiritual wifery."

"Yes, but I can't believe them."

"What if they are true and Joseph is cultivating you to become his spiritual wife?"

Dorrie's hands flew to her mouth. Her eyes widened. She let out a long low wail, stifled by her hands. "Nooo," she said. "You can't be right."

"I pray I am not."

"It shall never happen. I love Piet and only Piet. For me, there is no one else in all the world."

"Bless you," was all I could say.

Dorrie stayed with me for the rest of the day.

+ + +

Just when I thought matters could get no worse, I suffered a terrible blow. I reported to the Seminary in what I thought would be a routine day. And so it was until the session ended and the last pupil walked down the lane toward home. As I gathered slates from the student tables, Arthur asked me to sit with him for a moment.

"Lanie, I must inform you of something."

"Yes," I said, instantly unnerved by the tone of his voice.

"This will be my last term at the Seminary."

"Last term?"

"Yes."

"I don't understand."

"I am leaving Nauvoo to return to England."

My heart crashed to the floor.

"England?"

"Yes. I am returning to pursue studies for the doctorate at Oxford, Saint Edmunds Hall."

"Doctorate?"

"Yes, in theology of all things. I have corresponded with one of the dons who has agreed to take me on. He thinks it will be amusing and challenging to have a Mormon among his charges."

I closed my eyes to a collapsing world. The Seminary had been my lifeline. It gave me purpose and meaning. It had been the only sustained joy in my life.

"I am happy for you, Arthur," I said. I *was* happy for him too. A man of his astonishing intellect and scholarship should take it as far as he could. This was a splendid opportunity. "But for me it is an announcement of great sadness."

"Lanie, you could continue in my absence. As Headmistress, I should say. Now that Doctor Bennett has left Nauvoo, I could speak to Mister Kelly, the President, in your behalf."

I shook my head. "I am flattered by your recommendation but couldn't do it, Arthur. Mister Freeman would forbid me the time and energy it would take to manage the school. Besides, I am certain there is someone else better qualified than I."

"I would think not. You are masterful with the pupils. Degrees and credentials do not guarantee that rare ability to reach students and help them master complex material. You have a special gift."

"Still, I could not do it. I will be pleased to stay on as a teacher a few days a week but to head the Seminary, no. That I could not undertake."

Arthur sighed. "Very well. I shall begin to consider other candidates. The Seminary is important and it must continue."

I walked home mired in despondency. I could not imagine how I would cope with these trials. That night – the 28th of February – just as I prepared to recite my nighttime prayers, I heard the front door open and close. I hurried to the top of the staircase.

My heart seized.

In the parlor below, Ned Freeman removed his hat and lowered his saddlebags to the floor.

CHAPTER TWENTY-THREE

Kevil

Accident

I placed my hat on an empty peg by the front door and took a deep breath. So now the charade begins. My proclamations of love in each of my letters must now be made real. I would show Elena I had mended my ways and that she, my first wife, would hold a special place in my heart. On this night, I would take her to my bed and try to remove any doubts or misgivings she might yet harbor. To this end, I wasted no time in ascending the staircase. To my surprise, she greeted me at the top of the stairs.

"Elena," I said.

"Yes, husband. You're home."

I sensed a measure of warmth in her voice. Perhaps absence does make the heart grow fonder. Carefully, I took her hands and drew her into my arms. She stiffened, then yielded. I placed a small kiss on her forehead but did not push my affections further.

"I have missed you," I said. "It is good to be home."

"You must be tired," she said.

"Not too tired to profess love to my wife."

"Are you hungry? Need I fix you something to eat?"

"Hungry only for my wife."

She stiffened at my words.

"Come," I whispered.

I grasped her hand and led her down the hallway to my room. I could feel her resistance but she complied. An auspicious reunion, I thought to myself.

+ + +

I slept late into the morning and descended the stairs to delightful smells of frying eggs and, could it be, a slab of beefsteak? I chattered away in bits and fragments about my trip. Elena listened without comment. When breakfast ended, I saddled Lampblack and hurried to the Red Brick Store to find the Prophet. I gave a hearty greeting to Piet.

"It's good to haff you back to Naufoo," he said. "De Prophet, he is in his office. Vy don't you go on up. Vee can talk later."

I thanked him and sprinted up the stairs two at a time. When Joseph saw me he leapt to his feet and skip-hopped to embrace me.

"Come sit down," he said. "I am ready to hear your report. Tell me. I am eager to hear of what you learned in Upper Canada."

For the next hour, I briefed Joseph on the condition of the branches in Upper Canada. Suffice it to say, the churches I visited, twelve of them, were in dismal shape. The most devout had, as Joseph well knew, gathered to Zion leaving the remnant churches weak in leadership and bereft of zeal for the conversion of souls. I opined that at least two were on the verge of closure.

When I had finished my report, the Prophet sighed but said little. Sensing that my business with him had drawn to a close, I secured the flap of my leather portfolio and stood to leave.

"A moment more of your time," Joseph said, raising an index finger.

I reseated myself.

"We have a problem in Springfield," he said.

"What sort of problem?"

"The legislature is considering a bill to rescind the Nauvoo city charter."

"Rescind it. Whatever for?"

"We are growing and gaining in power, Brother Ned. Some are fearful. Some are jealous. Some are bigoted. It's the *habeas corpus* clause that sticks in the craws of our opponents. They feel it has obstructed justice, particularly in my case."

"But the Nauvoo charter is similar to the charters of several other cities in the state. Are those charters also in jeopardy?"

"Of course not and therein lies part of our defense. We are being singled out for unfair treatment."

"What do you wish of me?"

"I fear this bill will pass in the House. If this happens, we must defeat it in the Senate. I would beg you to go to Springfield immediately and provide the senators, behind the scenes, arguments necessary to defeat the bill. I need someone with a sound legal mind and the power of persuasion. You are that man. I should add that defeat of this bill is in your best personal interests. The *habeas corpus* provision could protect you in the event you are implicated in the Boggs affair and tracked to Nauvoo."

I was loath to go on the road again but the Prophet's point was well taken. I was the man to do this work and I might need Nauvoo's robust *habeas corpus* provision in the future. "Who are my contacts in the Senate?" I asked.

Joseph gave me several names of sympathetic senators. Then, unexpectedly, he asked, "Why don't you take Piet Van Rijn with you? He's been complaining of late that he hasn't been out of Nauvoo in over a year. I know he would enjoy the trip and would keep you good company. Piet thinks highly of you."

"Forgive me, Brother Joseph, but I do not wish to play nursemaid to a cripple on this important trip."

"I shouldn't think he would be a great burden. In your absence, he has become quite capable of getting around. He has metal contraptions he straps to his legs that give him stability when he stands. He swings them while on his crutches."

"Yes, I know. I've seen him wearing them."

"He now rides on his own and is a capable horseman. You take him along. It may give you opportunities to advance your *other agenda*."

"Speaking of which," I asked, "how have you fared with Mrs. Van Rijn? On my behalf, that is."

"It's been a struggle. She is very devoted to Piet. Here is the rub. Though she has not said as much, despite my probing, I have the impression that her marriage is not, shall we say, as *incomplete* as I once thought."

"And what difference does that make?"

"None. The revelation on celestial marriage specifies that spiritual wives must be virgins, but this has not always been the practice." He smiled awkwardly and shrugged his shoulders.

I nodded. "So, is the time ripe for me to move forward on this matter?"

"When you get back, I should think we can press our intentions, you with your wife and I with Sister Dorrie. See if you can soften Piet up for this eventuality. Poor man can't be a fully suitable husband to such a lovely woman."

"Indeed," I said and, with a nod of approval, rose to take my leave.

"So I take it you will permit Piet to accompany you?" Joseph called out as I walked out of his office.

"I shall," I said. There were possibilities in his companionship.

Piet was delighted by the invitation to accompany me and all arrangements for our departure were completed by noon that day. When I arrived at the Van Rijn cabin, Piet was already mounted on his horse with his steel braces strapped to his saddle. Before mounting to begin our journey, I drew near to Dorrie. "I shall take good care of him, Mrs. Van Rijn," I said with a gallant bow.

She stepped away from me. "Please do, for he is very precious to me."

+ + +

We rode hard for three days, up before dawn, not resting until after dark. As Joseph predicted, when we arrived in Springfield, the House of Representatives had already voted to rescind the Nauvoo charter. The Senate was scheduled to take up the bill two days hence, which left little time to accomplish my purpose. I went to work at once, meeting with friendly legislators and drawing up a list of solons who might be persuaded to vote against the bill. To my surprise, Piet provided useful assistance in my lobbying effort. He testified to the Prophet's good character and generosity.

"Look at me," he would say, "I'm just a poor cripple but de Prophet, vy he done good by me. He give me a job and take care of me and de vife. If you have heard othervise, you is misinformed. De Prophet, he's a great man."

Sitting on edge in the statehouse gallery, Piet and I watched the debate unfold on the floor of the Senate. Finally, a roll call vote was taken, and it seesawed back and forth until the last vote, which tipped it in our favor – sixteen nays and seventeen ayes. The bill failed. Piet gave out a whoop of delight and I felt rather pleased by my own excellence.

Our return trip to Nauvoo was much more relaxed, and it permitted me to turn to my *other agenda*, to use the Prophet's phrase. We rode west to Jacksonville and then north to Beardstown where we would cross the Illinois River. It was a cold, blustery evening when we arrived in the Beardstown area. The ferry got hung up in mid-river and it took the better part of an hour to free the vessel. When we reached the western bank, dusk had settled upon us.

"Had I known we would be this late in getting across, I would have found lodging for us in Beardstown. No point in going back now."

"Ve can find a place on de river and camp for de night," Piet said.

The thought of sleeping on the ground put me in a peevish frame of mind but we had no choice. We could not make Rushville before nightfall, so we set up camp on the bluffs of the Illinois River and built a small fire. As we gnawed on leathery venison jerky, we promised one another that we would get a real dinner upon arrival in Rushville.

I had just settled under my blanket and nestled my head into the soft leather of my saddle when Piet informed me, apologetically, that he had to relieve himself. The man needed help coursing across the open ground with his braces. In high irritation, I obliged him. I walked with him as he swung himself to the bluff of the river and relieved himself over the embankment. As he leaned over to button his breeches, one of his crutches slipped out from under his arm and toppled to the ground.

"I'll get it," I said.

As I reached down to pick it up, opportunity struck. Swiftly, I picked up the crutch, rammed the underarm strut into the small of Piet's back and launched him over the rim of the embankment. He struck the cliff side once and catapulted into the river. In the pale moonlight, I saw him surface twice, flailing and gasping, before his braces dragged him under. His hat floated away on the currents of the swollen Illinois River.

I smiled to myself.

+ + +

Two days later, when my news of Piet's *accident* reached Nauvoo, the entire town went into mourning. Because of his visibility in the Red Brick Store and his affable nature, Piet was a well-known and popular man. Dorrie was inconsolable. Elena stayed with her day and night to offer comfort and support. The Prophet wasted no time in setting up a memorial service for the Grove, which drew over two thousand people. Throughout the service, Elena held Dorrie in her arms.

At the end of his eulogy, Joseph motioned for me to join him at Dorrie's side.

"Sister Dorrie," he said. "You have my condolences once again. Piet was a fine man who suffered greatly in this life but I assure you he is in the heavenly realms at this moment. And now you must move forward in your life. It is important to you to find the right man and enter into a second marriage. Since you and Piet were not sealed for time and eternity, your own salvation depends upon a new marriage, one in which you can be so sealed."

Dorrie stopped crying and simply stared dumbfounded at the Prophet.

Then, like a protective mother bear, Elena stepped between Joseph and Dorrie and drew herself up until she met the Prophet eye-to-eye. "I cannot believe my ears!" she hissed through clenched teeth. "What manner of man are you that you approach a grieving widow at the very moment of her husband's funeral and talk of remarriage! You sodding cur!"

She punched him in the chest. He winced.

I had never seen Elena so undone nor had I ever heard such intemperate language from her lips. As I stood there, bemused by the whole event, Elena turned, put her hand on my chest, and shoved me backwards with surprising force.

"And you back off too!" she said seizing Dorrie and hurrying her from the Grove.

The bystanders watched with wide eyes and mouths agape.

It has begun, I thought, *it has begun. The ball rolls. A rocky start, perhaps, but the ball rolls.*

CHAPTER TWENTY-FOUR

Elena

Bounty

After that horrifying scene in the Grove, I rushed Dorrie home and sequestered her behind closed doors. I ran interferences with the well-wishers who came by with food and condolences. Several who had heard Joseph's unseemly suggestion commiserated with Dorrie. They urged her to forgive their beloved Prophet who, at times they said behaved not as a man of God but simply as a man. I became increasingly appalled by these entreaties. To my mind, Joseph acted very much as the leader of the Church, in his guise as a man of God, when he commended a second marriage to Dorrie. This was part of his celestial marriage doctrine. His motivations had little to do with Dorrie's eternal salvation in the highest heaven. He had begun to spread the principle of plural marriage and Dorrie was merely a pawn in his greater scheme. I also believed that he meant to have her as a spiritual wife for himself. Joseph repulsed me, as did my husband, the Prophet's devoted lickspittle.

I stayed with Dorrie through the night, knowing full well that I might incur Ned's wrath in so doing. I no longer cared. Dorrie needed me and if I had to suffer a beating for my ministrations, so be it. On the morning following Piet's funeral, Dorrie and I awakened at the same time. We rummaged among the many plates of donated food for something to eat. As we nibbled our food, Dorrie whispered into her plate, "I don't know what I am to do."

"I should think it too soon to worry about what the morrow will bring," I said. "We will take care of you. You must take your time."

"That is not what I mean. You are such a dear one, Lanie, and I know you will not let me suffer want. No, that is not what concerns me. Rather, I am flummoxed by the Prophet's proposition that I soon remarry and, I daresay, not a little frightened."

"The man is a fiend," I said. "All of this flannel among the Saints about his lapses from being a true Prophet of God and acting merely a man is just that – flannel. I don't trust him and neither should you."

"I don't know, Lanie. He has always been so good to us. I'm sure he has my best interests at heart. His suggestion was just so… so unexpected yesterday. I cannot make out his purpose."

"He means to have you for himself. Of this I am quite certain."

"I can't accept that, Lanie. I know you believe the rumors that have swirled about, the rumors of plural marriage, but it doesn't make sense to me. He is a great man and a true Prophet. He has a wonderful marriage to Emma and a family of fine children. Why would he want me? Or any other woman, for that matter? He has so much. Despite all of the tribulations and persecutions he has had to suffer, he is still a blessed man and, it would seem, a man protected by God."

"He is a philanderer and an adulterer."

Dorrie's hands flew to her mouth. "Oh, Lanie, please don't say such things! Please, please don't say them."

Her words pierced me. What was I doing? This poor woman had just lost her husband, suffered through a dismal memorial service, beset by the uncouth overtures of her great hero, and awakened to a foreboding future. And here I was, her best friend, engaging her in an argument over the man who had been her beloved husband's benefactor. I softened.

"I am sorry, Dorrie. You are quite right. It is not proper of me to behave so rudely in the time of your mourning." I put my hand on hers. "But I must say one more thing and then I shall be quiet. I want you to know that I have no choice but to leave the Church. I can no longer abide what I see and hear. Yesterday's outrage in the Grove became the proverbial straw that broke the camel's back. I am leaving. That is certain. Still and all, I will always be here for you. Of this you must be assured."

"Lanie, you mustn't condemn the whole Church on the basis of one comment by the Prophet."

"If that were the sum of it, I would not. Alas, there have been many incidents and my decision is well-informed."

"Oh, Lanie, no! You can't go from the Church. Where will you go?"

"I don't know. I visited a small Methodist church in Sonora some weeks ago but there are, shall we say, *problems* there. But we mustn't dwell on such things right now. Let's finish our breakfast and rest for a time."

Dorrie gaped at me. Tears formed in her eyes and spilled onto her cheeks. My own heart puddled and I dropped immediately to my knees before her chair and drew her into my arms.

+ + +

I parted company with Dorrie in the early afternoon, promising to return as soon as possible. She assured me she would be fine. She had to attend to certain matters consequent to Piet's death, which would occupy her for the rest of the day. I walked toward home, my mind a maelstrom of thoughts and emotions. I truly had come to the breaking point with the Latter Day Saints and saying so to Dorrie seemed to solidify the decision. I could not follow a prophet of such contemptible character. Nor had I any use for Emma and her attempts to intrude into my life. Joseph's circle of leadership, including my own husband, was a boorish and self-serving lot. To top it off, I had growing reservations about the veracity of the *Book of Mormon*. The history, at times, seemed so contrived as to be silly. Yet, on the whole, its contents were of such a cosmic sweep and contained such powerful truths that I could not grasp how one man, of his own accord, could pen such a document. It beggared the imagination. At that moment, I could contrive no better explanation for the authorship of the *Book of Mormon* than divine inspiration. Was it possible that Joseph Smith had been stirred by the Holy Ghost to write this additional testament of Jesus Christ? If so, why would God choose a man of such base affections?

I had also come to the breaking point with Ned Freeman. The incident in the Grove and Ned's fawning attentiveness (I even thought I detected a hint of amusement in his attitude) provided the final impetus to divorce him. I would waste no time in telling him so. No doubt this would bring on a good old-fashioned whipping but, I thought, I might as well give him something to whip me for.

I paused in front of the Temple, exactly in the spot where I had first met Burl Bumbalough. The chiffon yellow of that day's pale sun spread a pastel sheen on the white limestone, now rising well into the second story. Burl had been correct. It would be a magnificent structure. One could only imagine its towering influence over the city when once finished, to say nothing of the shadow it would cast over the lives of Mormon people. I thought of my owd Da and his unflagging dedication to the construction of this building. Standing there, I could not help but wonder, was it all such a colossally misdirected effort; an architectural sacrilege?

When I arrived home, I sighed in relief. Ned was gone. I busied myself in tidying up the place, waiting on tenterhooks for my husband to appear. The time for confrontation was at hand.

I didn't wait long.

Thirty minutes later, he strode through the front door.

I met him in the keeping room.

"Elena," he said. "You are home."

"For a time," I said.

"What does that mean?"

"I'm leaving you Ned."

"Leaving me?"

"Yes, as soon as I can possibly get my affairs in order and make arrangements, I will vacate this marriage."

His affable mood clouded before my eyes. His mouth twisted into the snarling smile I had so often seen before, usually moments before he beat me. I steeled myself for what was to come.

"I won't grant you a divorce," he said. "Besides, the Church doesn't believe in divorce. You know that."

"I could care less what the Church believes. I will leave you."

To my surprise, he did not strike me. In fact, his cloudy countenance lightened again. His voice softened.

"Elena, hear me out. I have a proposition for you, one that I believe will not only satisfy you but preserve our marriage and forestall any public embarrassment."

I frowned.

"As you know," he said, his voice steeped in pedantry, "the Prophet Joseph Smith has received a revelation concerning the eternal nature of marriage when the man and woman are sealed one to another."

"Yes. I have heard this."

"There is an aspect of this doctrine that has not yet been revealed to you."

I waited.

"It is proper, according to the revelation, that in certain circumstances, a man may take a second wife."

"So it is true. What I have been hearing."

"It is."

I grunted in disgust and put my hands to my ears not wanting to hear any more of this nasty bilge. Ned reached up and grasped my wrist, tenderly, and drew my palm away from my ear.

"Please hear me. In some cases, when a woman is abandoned or widowed, provision must be made for her care and protection. It is biblical, after all. One might suppose, for example, that Boaz, a prosperous middle-aged man was already married when he took the widow Ruth as his wife."

I was surprised that Ned used a biblical reference. I had never known him to be a student of the Bible but, given his great intellect and substantial education, perhaps it shouldn't have surprised me. But when it came to Scripture, I was on solid ground. "There is no mention in the Book of Ruth that Boaz was married," I said. "But all of this is quite beside the point. That was an ancient polygamous culture. We live in Nineteenth Century America, and multiple marriages are prevented by law. So, what is your point?"

"I should like to be Boaz to Dorrie. I should like her to be my Ruth."

I stood there staring at Ned. I had missed the boat. I had not seen it coming. The Prophet's recent attempts to soften Dorrie in the matter of celestial marriage had nothing to do with his own lusts. He was acting on behalf of Ned Freeman, my own husband, for whom my loathing had just deepened beyond description. I had no words.

"The requirement," he continued, "is that the first wife must give her permission for the second marriage. I want your permission and I aim to get it. Think of it this way. In granting permission, you will become the revered matriarch in our family. Both you and Dorrie will be sealed to me when the Temple is completed and the sealing ordinance is available. You will both enjoy a life of eternal bliss as sister wives and sister goddesses."

I stood there blinking in dumbfounded silence.

Ned nattered on. "In this proposed arrangement, you will be given complete freedom to live as you wish. You may resume full-time responsibilities at the Seminary, if that would be your desire. You will no longer have any marital responsibilities to me save for oversight of the home and tending to its upkeep. I shall leave you be, in other words. All of your needs and securities will be met. I simply need your permission."

"Go to hell!"

He leaned back in disbelief. The cloud returned. The scar on his lip twisted into a fishhook. "Do you dare to curse me?"

I grasped my skirts, leaned forward, and jutted my face to within inches of Ned's prominent nose. "Go...to...hell," I said, my voice hissing with venom.

He struck.

With lightning speed, he hammered me in the face. Stars swirled around my eyes and, in less than a second, I could feel myself losing balance. Before I hit the floor, he battered me again with his fist, straight across the jaw. I collapsed in a heap and counted six pendulum kicks of his right boot at full force on my chest and abdomen before I lost consciousness altogether.

He left me there, a heap on the floor. I awakened moments later with my right cheek on the hardwood floor. One of my molars lay several inches away. When I probed my mouth with my tongue, I discovered a throbbing gap in my lower left jaw. I drew myself up to a sitting position. Shooting pains accompanied every move. I turned my head. Ned rocked back and forth in his chair, reading a newspaper.

"You knocked my tooth out," I said, my voice raspy and barely audible.

He pursed his mouth in a *so-what* expression. "I need your permission," was all he said.

I offered no response.

I clawed the wall to an upright position, and dragged myself up the stairs to my room. There I cleaned up as best I could, removed my housedress sprinkled with blood and laid myself on the bed. In an odd sense, I was thankful. I had survived the beating even though, if my painful breathing were any indication, I had suffered several cracked or broken ribs. As soon as I felt a measure of recovery and could stand without the room spinning like a greased wagon wheel, I would leave.

I must have dozed off for a few minutes. I was jarred into wakefulness by a knock on the front door and the shuffle of feet entering the keeping room. I heard the muted voices of men. Rising from my bed, I wobbled to the top of the staircase. There I could shield myself behind a wall and with occasional glances survey the scene below me. I could hear all that was being said.

After admitting his visitors – the Prophet and Brigham Young – Ned reseated himself in the rocker. Brigham eased himself into a chair. Joseph remained standing.

"We have a problem," Joseph said. "Or, more directly, *you* have a problem, Brother Ned."

"And what is that?" Ned asked.

"Earlier today, a man named Jeremiah Trumbull visited us. He is a bounty hunter. He peppered us with questions. About you."

Neither Ned nor Brigham said anything.

Joseph continued. "As you know, there is a bounty on your head from the prison break and, by the way, where is Sister Elena?"

"She is not feeling well," Ned said, "and has taken to her bed."

"There is no chance she can overhear this conversation?"

"She is dead to the world."

"Very well. As I was saying, there is a bounty on your head for the Missouri prison escape and the murder of a guard."

I stifled a gasp. *Murder? Escape? What was I hearing?*

"I'm not surprised," Ned said. "How much is the bounty?"

"Three thousand dollars."

"A goodly sum. What about Doctor Mercer? A bounty on him as well?"

Doctor Mercer? Was he part of this? Whatever this is. I could not believe my ears.

"He didn't mention Brother Tobias," Brigham said. "There is no bounty on his head. The surviving guard, one Mister Nathan Philpott, fingered you and you alone."

"Did this bounty hunter say why he came to Nauvoo?"

Brigham answered. "He is one of the last ones hunting for you. Most have given up. Somehow, Trumbull found out you were from the Carolinas and over the past year or more he has been snooping around your old haunts hoping to find you. When he did not find you in the Carolinas, he traveled to New York, Boston, and

Philadelphia because some of your neighbors said you often frequented those cities. He found no traces of you there and so began his trip back to Missouri, journeying by way of Chicago where he has a sister. He has been staying with her the past couple of months."

"But, how did he come to inquire here in Nauvoo?"

"He knew Mercer was a Mormon and thought by chance the two of you might have come here. He had these papers."

I sneaked a peak around the corner of the wall. Joseph had just handed two sheets of tattered paper to Ned who spent several minutes reviewing them. One page bore the drawing of a face.

"What did you tell him when he showed you these?" Ned asked.

"I simply told him that I didn't recognize the man in the drawing but I did disclose that Doctor Mercer has opened a practice here in the city."

"Why in heaven would you do that?"

"To give myself credibility in throwing him off your track. Mercer is not the subject of a manhunt. I reckoned honesty regarding the good doctor might purchase Trumbull's acceptance when I told him that you weren't here. He would waste his time searching for you."

"What did he say?"

"He agreed, but he asked permission to interview Brother Tobias."

"What did you say?"

Joseph shrugged. "I told him that he was free to visit with Doctor Mercer. Simple as that. I also told him if he left me these pages, I would provide them to the sheriff and we would keep our eyes peeled for the likes of you."

"I must say I find it unsettling that you told this Trumbull that Mercer is here. How am I to know that Mercer won't give me up?"

I could tell from Ned's voice that he was alarmed.

"Mercer won't betray you."

"I pray you are right about that. I will confront Doctor Mercer immediately. May I have those papers?"

"They are yours to do with what you wish. I would recommend you burn them."

"I shall but first I must speak with Mercer."

"Very well," Joseph said.

The Prophet and Brigham took their leave. Ned stood in the

keeping room staring at the papers. Did I detect a slight tremor in his hands? He looked around, took a deep breath and strode over to the stack of newspapers. I slipped down three stairs to keep him in view. He picked up several papers and inserted the two tattered sheets in the middle of the stack. He then hurried to the barn and saddled Lampblack for what I presumed would be a beeline for Doctor Mercer's office.

When he had left, I stole downstairs, rifled through the stack of papers and withdrew the two sheets of paper he had hidden. A charcoal drawing of Ned's face stared from one of the pages. The other was a yellowed newspaper clipping bearing the headline, *Two Escape Missouri State Prison: Guard Murdered.* In the upper corner of the clipping, someone had written *Jefferson Enquirer, December 9, 1839.* I eased into the rocking chair, favoring the bruises on my right side, and began to read.

In the late afternoon of Monday last, two men, trustees of the Missouri State Prison, overpowered two guards, murdering one, and making their escape. The escapees, Doctor Tobias Mercer and Mister Kevil Pape, Esq., had been trustees in a lumbering detail and were on their return to the prison when the aforementioned incident occurred. Mercer had been imprisoned during the recent Mormon difficulties in Caldwell and Ray Counties. He had been convicted of manslaughter in the killing of a man who trespassed upon his property. Pape was incarcerated for attempted murder of a Cherokee woman in Greene County. The guard who lost his life in the skirmish with prisoners was Howard Boling, recently of Kansas City. One other guard, Nathan Philpott survived but not without injury.

Prison guards pursued the felons but with the onset of heavy snowfall and under the cloak of darkness, the chase had to be suspended for the night. Cornelius Rayford, the Warden, vowed to scour the earth for these dangerous escapees and return them to justice. "This is the first escape from the Missouri State Prison," the warden said to the guards who assembled last evening to prepare for today's search. "And I assure you it will be the last!" Mister Rayford was considered in high dudgeon over the escape and uttered his remarks with reddened face and pounding fist.

I lowered the article to my lap and stared at the far wall. My stomach twisted in knots. *So his name is not Edwin Freeman. It is Kevil Pape.* I shook my head. My husband. A convict. A felon. As I tried to grasp the enormity of what I had learned in these last minutes, I heard the landing of a boot on the front porch.

I glanced out the window and caught a fleeting glimpse of Ned's coattail as he rushed toward the front door. He shot through the door and fixed his eyes on me as I rose from his chair. The drawing and clipping fell to the floor.

"Did you forget something?" I asked, my voice breathless with panic.

He looked at the scattered pages on the floor.

"What are you doing?" he screamed.

Like a viper coiled to strike, he leapt at me.

I dodged out of his way and, despite the considerable pain I suffered, I ran into the kitchen. Ned – or Kevil – spun after me screaming curses, his emotions bursting into a crazed frenzy.

I grabbed a lantern and, as he rounded the corner into the parlor, I pivoted and swung the lantern at his head with as much force as I could summon. Fortunately, despite my injuries, I was *wych-elm strong*, and the blow sent him reeling backward to the floor, stunned and disoriented.

I ran out the front door still in my underclothing.

I had to escape. He would kill me and dispose of my body. He would declare to all of Nauvoo that I had left him against his will. Dorrie would confirm this. I told her as much.

Ned's boots pounded on the porch floor behind me.

Lampblack stood there, reins loosely wrapped around the porch rail. I grabbed the reins and, grimacing in pain, vaulted myself into the saddle. I had never ridden Lampblack, but I was glad for his youth and speed.

I spurred him toward the yard gate.

Just as I reached the gate, Kevil's hand encircled the cheek piece of Lampblack's bridle.

I slapped Lampblack's withers with the reigns, kneed him, and drew him sharply to the left.

Kevil's hand was caught in the cheek piece and I could hear bones snap as the horse twisted to the side. The man screamed as Lampblack surged forward and pierced the gate dragging Kevil behind. After several yards, the vile man extracted his hand and slumped to the ground writhing in agony.

+ + +

Racing through the cool March air along the Mississippi River in my thin cotton underclothing chilled me to the point of swirling dizziness. I leaned against Lampblack's neck to capture his warmth and to keep from falling from his back. I shivered uncontrollably and moaned through my chattering teeth. Each hoof beat sent shocks of pain through my ribcage. I no longer had complete control of my faculties but I held fast to one thought – get to Burl's house. He would protect me. I stole glances over my shoulder. To my relief, I saw no rider closing upon me.

It took nearly an hour to reach Burl's house. It stood, rising into the afternoon sky atop a slight rise. I had made it. I had escaped. Safe at last. Even if Kevil – I still couldn't get used to saying his real name – determined where I had gone, he would have difficulty capturing me with Burl as my protector. I patted Lampblack's neck. What a magnificent horse, my savior horse. I slid from his back and guided him into the barn where a water tub rested half full. There, with as much sweep as my aching ribs permitted, I raked hay scattered about the floor and piled it near the water tub. Throughout it all, I staggered like a common drunk. My frozen hands were like Stone Age tools, clumsy and imprecise in their movements.

After repeated knocks, I realized Burl was gone. I would have to wait for his return and I prayed it would not be long. Once inside the house, I stoked the fire and brought life back into my hands. I latched both doors and moved from room to room securing the windows. Four of the latches were broken, which flooded me with worry. There was nothing I could do or…was there? If I could find a hammer and some nails…

Unlatching the back door I returned to the barn in search of tools. Just inside the barn door, I heard a horse galloping hard from the direction of Sonora. I flattened myself against the wall of the barn and, without breath, prayed that the rider might pass by. The hooves pounded closer and closer. I squeezed my eyes shut. Then, to my great relief, the rider sped by the house and continued at full tilt down the road.

I scrounged through the tools and located a hammer with a loose wooden handle. The metal wedge was missing. I knelt over and slammed the heel of the handle several times on the hard dirt floor. I had seen my owd Da do this on occasion in his blacksmith shop. It worked. The handle seemed much tighter. I resumed my search, which yielded only four rusty, bent nails. I thought it providential that there were four windows with broken latches.

Once back inside the house and with the door locked, I set about trying to angle a nail through the window sash and into the frame. The nails were dull and the hammer was worth no more than two strikes before I had to reseat the head on its shrunken handle. Eventually, after repeated and painstaking straightening of the nails, I had the windows anchored. Kevil, if he found me, would have to break the glass. At least that would give me a warning.

A weapon.

Yes, I need a weapon.

I searched for a gun but found none. I wandered throughout the house. When I reached the upstairs bedroom, I spotted two clothes irons sitting on the bureau. I gave them a good heft and practiced swinging them with different arcs and thrusts. Once, I overextended my reach and nearly passed out in agony. After several deep breaths and sufficient ebbing of pain, I reasoned that as long as Kevil himself did not have a gun, I had a fighting chance. He was much stronger, but I was still limber and quick after all of those years as a little doffer. I reckoned that the many games of dodge ball helped too. This weak confidence paled further when I acknowledged to myself that any vigorous movement would cause sharp stabs to my ribs. I would simply have to power through the pain.

With these preparations completed, I started back downstairs. After three steps, I realized that I was still in my underclothing. I returned to Burl's room and rummaged around in his wardrobe for something to wear. Everything was impossibly large. With no other options, I extracted a white dress shirt, put it on, and rolled up the sleeves. The tail came to my knees. I was embarrassed to have so much underclothing showing beneath the shirt so I found a pair of rough wool stockings to complete my makeshift attire.

Back in the parlor, I sat on the horsehair settee, balancing an iron on each knee, and waited.

Hurry Burl.

CHAPTER TWENTY-FIVE

Kevil

Chase

That rotting bawd! She broke my hand. I sat holding my right arm close to my side and fingered the small bones below my wrist. *Uuungh!* The pain was excruciating and the movement below the skin unnatural, disordered.

I stood, grasped the gate post to steady myself, and waited for the pain to subside. When I stabilized enough to think, I knew I had no time to nurse myself. I took a deep breath and raced to the barn. I had to catch Elena. She now knew who I was and would expose me at the first opportunity. Of this I had no doubt. And that damnable strumpet took Lampblack, leaving me with the aging brown mare. Furious at my misfortune, I raced to the barn and, struggling with one hand, saddled the mare.

Ten minutes later, at a full gallop, I tore into the small yard in front of Dorrie's cabin. Lampblack was nowhere in sight but, if anyone knew where Elena had gone, Dorrie would. Without knocking, I shoved the door open and strode into the cabin. Dorrie stood by the fire clothed in a long, black mourning dress.

"Where is she?" I snarled.

"Where is who?"

"Elena."

"I have no idea."

Without permission, I looked in both rooms of the cabin, under the bed, and in every potential cranny where she might hide. Then I burst through the back door and ran to the small barn.

Nothing.

Next stop – the Seminary.

Arthur Walmsley, the little scrub, seemed clueless as well. I lifted him by the throat and rammed him up against the wall behind the student desks. To my surprise, he showed no fear in confirming he had not seen Elena in several days. A thorough inspection of both floors of the Campbell homestead revealed nothing.

I made the Smith homestead my third stop. Joseph was at home with Emma when I stormed into the house.

"She's gone!" I shouted.

"Who?" Joseph asked.

"Elena."

"Gone where?"

"I don't know. She found the picture and article and lit out. She's not at Dorrie's and not at the Seminary. Have you seen her?"

"No, not a glimpse."

"What happened to your hand?" Emma asked.

I looked at my swollen hand. It had begun to purple.

"The wench broke it."

Emma lifted my hand gingerly and inspected it. "It appears she broke several bones."

"Can't worry about that now."

Emma looked into my eyes. "You know she has been seen with a man named Burl Bumbalough."

"I do not. Who is Burl Bumbalough?"

"A reverend. Methodist," Emma said. Her lip curled. "He has a small church down in Sonora. Elena attended that church in your absence."

"You think she went there to find him?"

Emma shrugged. "It's a possibility. If she is bent on escaping you, she knows Nauvoo wouldn't be the best place to seek shelter. She has few close friends. There aren't many safe places for her to hide within the city."

"If you are wrong and I travel all the way to Sonora without finding her, I will have lost valuable time."

"Let her go," Joseph said. "If she turns you in, you will need to escape yourself. I would suggest that you leave Nauvoo forthwith and lose yourself somewhere. Perhaps in time, you can rejoin us. Save yourself."

"Not until I wrap things up with Elena."

"What do you intend to do?" Emma asked. I detected alarm in her voice.

I pivoted on my heel and sprinted from the Smith homestead leaving Emma's unanswered question hanging in the air.

The old mare could not sustain a full gallop for more than a mile. I stopped several times to rest her, which only added to my soaring agitation. When I arrived in the Sonora region, I spotted a small church, which I assumed to be Bumbalough's cure. I tried the door and found it locked. It took three full-body slams to batter down the door.

No Elena.

I saw activity in the nearby school.

I threw open the door to the school.

Fifteen pupils spun on their benches.

"Sir, I beg your pardon, but we have a school session," the teacher said in full stride to intercept me and bar my entrance into the classroom.

In an instant, I could see he would not respond to bullying nor did I have time for a prolonged altercation. I softened my approach.

"No, I beg *your* pardon, sir," I said. "Permit me to apologize for my abrupt behavior. My dear wife is at death's doorstep and requires the ministrations of the Gospel. I am in a great hurry to find Reverend Bumbalough."

"I don't believe I know you, sir," the teacher said. "I know all the Methodists in this region. Why don't I know you?"

"I'm not Methodist. We are – uh – Catholics but there is no priest in the area. The prayers of a Methodist minister will surely suffice. Can you point me to him?"

The man looked at me with undisguised suspicion. At last, he relented. "You can find his house down Old Mill Road. Turn left a half mile to the south of here." Without further ado, he dismissed me from the school while the children looked on, alive with curiosity.

Thirty minutes later, I spotted the house on a slight rise in the land. I pulled the mare into a small stand of trees where she could not be seen from the road. To my relief, there was a considerable patch of field grass beneath her feet. Knowing this mare, she would occupy herself with feeding on the grass and would not even raise her head if someone came down the road. I had few worries about being discovered. If Elena were in the house, it would not take long to complete my business. I had no fear of the Bumbalough fellow. No doubt an anemic little prig. If necessary, I would dispatch him too.

For several minutes, I surveyed the terrain, determining my best approach. The house rested on a prairie elevation, solitary save for a small barn in the rear. Not a tree, not a shrub, stood within one hundred yards of the house. Generous windows adorned the front and sides. Sneaking to the house unseen in either direction would be impossible.

I widened my scope. To one side of the house and to its rear, in the far distance – perhaps a quarter of a mile away – several clumps of trees studded the horizon. Though it would take time, my best opportunity lay in leapfrogging that L-shaped string of tree stands until I reached a point directly behind the barn. From there, I could crawl through the low grasses to the rear of the barn. Though I could not see from where I stood, I hoped there were fewer windows on the rear of the house.

I took thirty minutes to dash from tree stand to tree stand. Just as I was about to reach the final group of trees, I stumbled in an animal hole. Reflexively, I put out my broken right hand to break the fall and jolted the jumbled bones. I rolled onto my back writhing in pain but somehow I stifled the scream. It took ten minutes to recover. I wiped cold sweat from my forehead and neck. Still lying on the ground, I shifted the Bowie knife from right to left side. I could not wield a knife with my injured hand.

I smiled.

Ambidexterity is a wonderful thing.

I began my crawl. Dusk had descended upon the prairie. Darkness, my welcome companion, would soon be upon us. Crawling from the tree line to the barn took far more effort than I had imagined. Fifteen minutes later, breathless and flagged, I sat resting against the barn, calmed my breathing, and recovered my strength. I glanced at the sky. I hadn't noticed before but black clouds had rolled in and the air temperature was plummeting. I turned my head in both directions and pricked my ears. Save for small gusts of wind now and then, silence surrounded me.

Then I heard it.

The soft nicker of a horse.

I turned and peered through a crack in the barn siding. In the dim light I could barely make out the silhouette of a grand horse.

Lampblack!

CHAPTER TWENTY-SIX

Elena

Terror

An iron crashed to the floor.

My eyes shot open and I gasped. My skin tightened. I scanned the darkened room, stilling my breath.

Nothing.

Slowly, I calmed and, without taking my eyes off the room, I leaned over and retrieved the iron.

I must have fallen asleep. How, in the name of everything holy, could I have fallen asleep? I was angry and recommitted myself to unwavering vigilance. Stiff with pain, I sat up and resumed my guard, unmoving.

Where was Burl?

Evening was at hand.

Where was Burl?

Two light clicks and a clunk.

The back door.

Someone at the back door. *Burl? Please be Burl.*

Silence.

Then…the voice.

"Elena? Oh Elena?" Sing-song voice. "It's Ned. I know you are in there."

I sucked three quick breaths. He found me! O Dear God, he found me!

"Let me in, Elena."

I sat, paralyzed. My knuckles whitened on the iron handles.

"I won't hurt you. I want to talk. To explain. You don't

understand."

Hurry Burl.

"Talk to me, Elena. Just let me explain and then I'll leave you alone."

Finding a scrap of courage I stood and walked toward the front door. I could run from the house but where would I go? No, best stay inside. I pressed my back against the door.

Silence surrounded me again.

Minutes passed.

Nothing.

Wham!

Kevil heaved himself at the front door.

Then again, wham!

And yet again, wham!

"Let me in, dear Lanie." His voice was soft, buttery with confidence. "You can't stop me. If you let me in it will go easier for you."

I squeezed my eyes shut and stood several inches away from the door to avoid another blow.

I waited, my breaths coming in shallow gasps.

Suddenly, a crash of breaking glass!

I spun to my left. A large stone lay in the middle of the floor amidst a scattering of glass shards from the front window.

Several long seconds later, a hand rather delicately grasped a piece of glass lodged in the sash and, in one quick movement, broke it. Thrice more and the window was clear. Large enough to admit a man.

The blade of a knife slid through the window. *The Bowie knife!* I watched it with horrified fascination.

Then a hand.

And an arm.

And the head.

That awful red head!

In one great winding move, I crashed an iron down squarely on the back of Kevil's head.

He howled in pain.

As did I.

I hammered him again with the other iron.

And again.

He slumped over the sill of the window. The knife clattered to the floor. I waited for several painful minutes to see if he would move. Nothing. I walked over to him and stood there with the irons on my hips, ready to strike again. He lay draped over the windowsill, unconscious. I set one of the irons down and grasped a shock of his hair. I raised his head. To my undying horror, he looked at me with those ice-blue eyes and spread a wicked grin. In one quick motion, he snatched my legs from under me, toppling me to the floor and stormed through the window.

I found my feet and ran up the stairs to the bedroom, slamming the door, and latching it. I looked at the latch with chagrin. A tiny decorative thing. It would offer little security.

Hurry Burl!

I could hear the stair treads creaking. In slow perfectly timed cadence – *queek...queek...queek.*

I readied myself to deliver one more blow with the iron.

Queek...

Silence,

The latch rattled.

Wham!

The latch popped its screws.

The door slashed inward, crashing against the bureau.

I swung the iron through the doorway, screaming in fear and pain.

I missed.

My iron landed a glancing blow on his right hand.

He shrieked in agony, a cry far beyond the pain of such a weak blow. He dropped the Bowie knife and fell to his knees clutching his hand to his chest. I pounded him twice on the top of his head, rendering him senseless.

Rage exploded in me and, against all resistances of my conscience, I rolled him over on his back, grabbed his knife, and straddled him.

Savoring my fury, I dropped to my knees and raised the knife high above my head.

I took a painful breath, gritted my teeth, took aim at Kevil Pape's gaping maw, and plunged the knife.

Or...I tried to plunge the knife.

Oddly, my arms did not move. They were immobilized above my head as if caught in a giant vise.

I thrust downward again.

To no avail.

I raised my eyes to the knife and saw two massive hands grasping my wrists.

Burl.

"Perhaps it would be best if I took this," he said, peeling my fingers apart.

He threw the knife on the bed and pulled me to my feet. I turned to bury myself in his chest. I came unhinged and poured a torrent of tears and babbles. When finally I sniffled into coherence, we separated, keeping our arms linked.

"I take it this is Ned Freeman," he said.

"Yes and no."

"I may need help with that answer."

"This is Ned Freeman. But it is also Kevil Pape."

"That certainly clears it up."

I glanced up at him. He sported a wide grin.

"I should explain," I said.

"Please do."

For the next several minutes, I explained the events of the past several days with special emphasis on the bounty hunter's visit. Burl simply stood there with his eyebrows lifted in complete amazement.

"I believe we should turn this Mister Pape over to the authorities," he said.

"Tonight?"

"No. It's best to wait until daylight. Let's get him downstairs."

Burl hoisted Kevil over his shoulder and hauled him downstairs where he dropped him into a parlor chair.

"Would you feel comfortable going out to the barn?" he asked. "There is a coil of rope there. We'll secure Mister Pape until morning."

I was overjoyed at the assignment.

When I returned, Burl lashed Kevil to the chair, and motioned with me to sit with him on the settee. Opposite Kevil.

Kevil stirred. His eyes opened and he raised his head. "My hand…"

"Yes, I noticed your hand," Burl said. "It appears as if you have a considerable injury."

"I need help with my hand. That wench broke it."

"Sorry, Mister Pape," Burl said, "but I'm short on sympathy

tonight and I would imagine Lanie shares my sentiments."

Kevil let out a low groan.

Burl stood and placed himself squarely in front of Kevil.

"Look at me," Burl said, his voice firm, controlled.

Kevil raised his eyes.

"Here is what will happen, Mister Pape. Tomorrow morning we will load you into the wagon and lug you to Carthage. There you will be turned over to the sheriff for transport back to Missouri to stand trial for murder. Then I aim to pay a call on your good friend, the Prophet, and arrange for an immediate end to your marriage. Follow?"

Kevil nodded.

"Now, as a minister of the Gospel, I am obligated to pray for your sorry, depraved soul and I will do so. Of that you may be certain. I am also obligated to inform you it is highly unlikely, given what I have heard, that you will escape justice in Missouri. It is also highly unlikely you will escape godly justice unless you repent of your sins – all of them – asking Jesus to come into your mucky soul and scour it. Here you sit, defeated and restrained. It is a propitious moment for such a confession. So what say you?"

Kevil spat on Burl's pant leg.

"Well, I can't say I'm surprised by that response," Burl said. "So be it."

Burl returned to the settee.

I leaned against Burl, my arm encircling his.

"You're tired," he said. "Why don't you go upstairs and crawl under the bed covers."

"I will. Just let me stay here for a time."

+ + +

The sun was high above the horizon when I awoke the next morning. I donned Burl's massive shirt once again before taking my battered and bruised body downstairs. Burl perched on the settee much as I had left him the previous night.

Kevil was nowhere to be seen.

"What...?"

He laughed. "Don't fret. He's down in the cellar with the spiders."

"I don't understand."

"Oh, he got a little rowdy during the night. Tried to hop around on the chair. Even managed to free his good hand. So I dragged him downstairs and tied him to a support beam. Then I bolted the cellar door. Hope he likes spiders."

We ate stale bread smeared with honey, which Burl graciously shared with Kevil, and readied the wagon for the trip to Carthage. Before turning east, Burl drove by the Grahams and asked Mary to lend me a dress. An hour later, we arrived in Carthage. Burl drove directly to the sheriff's office, heaved Kevil over his shoulder, marched into the jail, and threw his prisoner into the tiny cell.

"Better lock that door," Burl said. The sheriff sat slack jawed. "Name is Kevil Pape. He's wanted in Missouri for murder."

"That's Kevil Pape?" the sheriff asked.

"Yes, indeed."

"I don't know what to say. I thought he was long gone. Thank you, good sir, for your assistance in capturing him. I will make certain he is sent back to Missouri."

Back atop the wagon seat, Burl and I made a beeline for Nauvoo and the Red Brick Store. Two hours later, with me in tow, he strode past the shelves of merchandise. Customers watched us with quizzical expressions. Up the stairs we went and Burl burst through Joseph's office door without knocking. The Prophet, Brigham Young, Willard Richards, and William Law stood behind the desk. Burl grabbed Joseph by his vest and pulled him over the desk as if he weighed no more than a half sack of oats.

"What do you think you are doing?" Joseph shouted.

Brigham and William rushed to protect the Prophet. Willard held back. *And to think I once harbored feelings for that lily-livered man.*

"Back off," Burl snarled. "You don't want to get into it with me."

They complied.

Burl returned his attention to the Prophet.

"Now, let me give you some clear directives," Burl said. "First, your man Pape is in jail. I put him there myself. I suggest you not interfere with Pape's transport back to Missouri lest you be charged with aiding and abetting. Am I clear so far?"

"Put me down," Joseph said.

"I will when I'm finished. But I want your undivided attention. Am I clear so far?"

Joseph nodded.

"Very well. Second, you will arrange for an annulment of this woman's marriage to Pape. Not a divorce. An annulment. I want it clear there never was a marriage in the eyes of the law. I want no stigma attached to her whatsoever."

"We don't have a provision for annulment."

"Then figure one out. You are the King of Zion are you not? Fraud and deception ought to be reasonable causes for an annulment, I should think. And you'd better get to cracking because I'm taking Elena to her house to pack her belongings. She is leaving this Sodom. When I return, I expect the decree of annulment to be properly executed and recorded. Am I still clear on my expectations?"

Brigham Young found his voice. "Why are you so exercised over all of this? Why do you insist on an annulment? What is this woman to you?"

Burl turned to Brigham, "I want her never to have been married to Mister Pape. I want her to suffer no future legal or ecclesiastical entanglement, because, you see, if she will have me, I intend to marry her myself."

EPILOGUE ONE

Kevil

1868

I finished the last drop of my brandy and listened to the winds wafting through the treetops before returning to my reverie.

I had languished all day in that Carthage jail, the same brig where Joseph and his brother Hyrum were killed six months later. A physician examined my hand and informed me I had fractured and dislocated three carpal bones. He bound my hand, but it never healed properly. I don't have full motion of my wrist and fingers. My hand is clawed with arthritis.

Sometime during that first night of confinement, a shadowy stranger, cloaked in a cowl slipped into the jail. He stole by the sleeping guard, unlocked my cell, and led me to a saddled horse behind the jail. The man disappeared as quickly as he had appeared. I wasted no time setting an eastward course toward Macomb. Once again, I was on the run.

I made my way to New York and then Boston. If anyone tried to follow me, they were unsuccessful. Through additional deceits and forgeries, I opened a law office. Of course, I was extremely successful at the bar and soon had accumulated sufficient means to live a life of luxury and ease.

One day, fifteen years later, as I lounged about my capacious waterfront home, I received a post and repaired to my veranda to read the letter.

May 14, 1858

My dear Ned (I cannot think to address you as any other than Ned):

Grace and peace to you. It has taken considerable effort on the part of our investigators to locate you. Please be assured we have no intention of disclosing to anyone where you are. This letter comes as an invitation to you. I fear you will reject the invitation but I feel the Lord is directing me to make the effort. As you know, a decade ago, the Saints vacated Nauvoo and made the trek to the Salt Lake Valley. We have created a paradise here in the desert. Our city is bigger and more prosperous than Nauvoo. Utah, as it is known, is now a territory and may one day be a state. It is a haven of peace and security. We have had occasional skirmishes with federal troops and there are continuing efforts to persecute us but we practice our religion according to the revelations bestowed upon our beloved Joseph. May he rest in peace. You will be pleased to know that celestial marriage is now publically accepted and practiced. For this we all give thanks to God.

This said, permit me to offer the invitation. I have always been enamored of your legal acumen and I admired the great service you rendered to the Saints during the troublesome years of Nauvoo. I greatly desire to have that service at hand once again. Several of the Church authorities and I have given this offer prayerful consideration. We would like to invite you to come to Zion and re-establish your credentials as a Mormon leader – always working behind the scenes, of course. You will be provided a suitable home and a generous compensation. You can once again be part of a grand and holy movement.

Please, I beg of you, give this invitation prayerful consideration.

Awaiting your earliest reply, I remain…

Brigham Young
President
Church of Jesus Christ of Latter Day Saints

I laughed aloud when I finished the letter. Not a chance. Why would I abandon all I had achieved? Why would I forsake all I had accumulated here in the fashionable northeast? What could cause me to cast my lot once again with those religious rubes? Certainly not this pathetic invitation from Brigham. Utah? I laughed again.

I gave the matter no further thought for several days. Then, one bright Sunday morning, I awakened with the invitation perched on the front steps of my mind. I could not shake it. It ate its way through me like a termite through dry wood. I could not rid myself of the notion. *What was it? What was it about the Mormons? What was it about me?*

I wrestled with the matter for two months until I realized my frame of mind corresponded exactly to what I experienced in Mrs. Perry's Saint Louis boarding house. Languor, boredom, and ennui had me in their collective grip. I had everything a man could want. But, my life revolved around courtroom appearances in cases of no particular interest, and trips abroad to spark a measure of excitement. And I knew. Oh, I knew. I had never felt more alive than with the Mormons in Nauvoo.

Six months later, I put my affairs in order, closed my law office, sold my house, and made the arduous trek to Salt Lake City. That was 10 years ago. To be honest, it was among the more fortuitous moves of my life. I have enjoyed a splendid mixture of prestige; prosperity; and, at times, exhilaration among my old friends – Brigham Young, Willard Richards, Tobias Mercer, Porter Rockwell, and Orson Pratt, among others. I have seven wives, all comely and accommodating. My one regret is that I can find no trace of Dorrie Van Rijn. People tell me she did not make the trek to Salt Lake City. Her whereabouts are unknown. Ah well, not all plans come to the desired end.

So there it is – quite a tale, if I may say so myself.

"Minnie! Minnie! Another glass of brandy!" I shouted to my fourteen-year-old wife. Such a sweet young thing.

Ha! I laughed to myself. A splendid life.

EPILOGUE TWO

Elena

1858 (II)

What a proposal! Not the proposal of my dreams. I had imagined a dashing man down on one knee staring pleadingly into my love-struck eyes. So when I heard Burl utter that wonderful subjunctive, *if she will have me*, I had to rehearse it several times in my mind. Of course, I accepted his proposal, which he later repeated on one knee, staring pleadingly into my love-struck eyes.

Things unfolded that morning in Nauvoo as Burl had ordered. We rode to the house in Old Commerce. I took what I had brought to the marriage. When we returned to the Red Brick Store, Willard Richards presented me with a hand-written decree of annulment. It bore the signature of the Prophet himself. Willard assured us the annulment would be properly recorded in Carthage, the county seat.

"See to it immediately," Burl said. "You wouldn't want me to visit you on this matter again."

I suppose such threats are not fitting for a clergyman but I was relieved to hear them. Burl could be intimidating and I knew few would oppose him if he chose to brandish his power.

"I suppose this means you are spiriting me off to Sonora," I said as Burl snapped the reins.

"It does. I spoke with Gabe Graham while you were donning Mary's dress. I asked if they might put you up for a time. They agreed."

"May we then stop at my friend Dorrie's house? I would like to tell her what has happened and I would like you to meet her."

Burl agreed. We stopped at Dorrie's and, despite her grieving, she played the gracious hostess serving tea and almond cookies, recently given by a well-wisher. As we sat at Dorrie's table describing the events of the previous day, the door burst open to reveal Piet Van Rijn hanging on the shoulders of two strangers.

Dorrie gasped.

"Sorry I'm late," Piet said. "I had a little mishap, I tink you could say."

Dorrie ran to Piet and threw her arms around him nearly toppling the three men.

"Dat husband of yours..." he began, staring at me.

"He is not my husband any longer," I said. "It's all over."

"Vell, dat's good. Turns out, he's a bad man all de vay around. He pushed me into de river. I near drowned. Dem braces drug me under de vater but I got dem off, sure enough. Venn I vas a sailor, I learnt to hold my bret unter de vater. So I got dem braces off an' swum to de shore vit my arms. Oh vas I colt! Dat vater vas icey colt. I crawled up de bank an' den I passed out. Dese men, dey bachelor farmers. Dey found me an' took me to deir place. Dey varmed me up by de fire."

"He was makin' no sense 't'all," one man said. "Colder'n a dead fish an' talkin' jibberish. We laid him out by the fire for a whole day to get him warmed up. Then he come down with a fever so we poured likker down his throat an' kept him by the fire. Fever broke a few days ago but he was too weak to travel. He started talkin' sensible-like and told us who he was. We lit out for Nauvoo as soon as he was fit to ride. He's still weak as a kitten, but we reckon he'll find his strength afore long."

"It's a good thing Kevil Pape is in jail," Burl said. "Now to murder, we add a charge of attempted murder. May God have mercy on his soul."

The two rescuers left bearing our heartfelt thanks and two dozen almond cookies. Burl and I stayed a few minutes longer before leaving Nauvoo.

+ + +

The time has come to bring this narrative to a close. One month later, Burl and I were married in the field next to the white prairie house on Old Mill Road. A Methodist minister, a friend of Burl's, came up from Quincy to perform the ceremony. For the next five years, we lived in Sonora and watched with joy as the little congregation grew under the Lord's good favor.

Joseph and Hyrum were murdered (the Saints would say martyred) in the Carthage jail after their incarceration on charges of violating the constitutional right to freedom of the press. They had been complicit in destroying a printing press that had been used to publish the one and only edition of the *Nauvoo Expositor*. The *Expositor*, published by Wilson and William Law, who had defected from Mormonism, contained scathing articles exposing the deceits and treacheries of the faith. Not long thereafter, the magnificent Temple was completed, but growing local opposition to the Mormons finally forced them to abandon Nauvoo. They made the long trek to the great Salt Lake valley, to a territory completely outside the United States.

Nauvoo itself became something of a ghost town with only a handful of Mormons remaining along with scattered Gentiles. To my great delight, Dorrie and Piet remained in Nauvoo. Piet continued to manage the Red Brick Store for a time, but business faltered and the store closed. One Lewis Bidamon, who would soon marry the widow Emma, set up a store in Nauvoo and hired Piet to be his clerk. We often saw the Van Rijns. They suffered no repercussions for fraternizing with Gentiles because the Mormon leadership had all relocated to the West. To Burl's great disappointment, he had no success in his efforts to re-convert the Van Rijns.

Emma Smith attended the Methodist Church for a time, though not ours. Around eighteen sixty, her son Joseph was ordained as the Prophet for a new church comprised of Midwestern Mormons who disavowed polygamy. Emma was accepted into that new church and not long thereafter, the Van Rijns also became members of the Reorganized Church of Jesus Christ of Latter Day Saints. They moved to California, and I have long since lost track of their whereabouts. It is a source of great sadness.

In 1850, seven years after our marriage, Burl was reassigned to Ebenezer Methodist Church on the north side of Springfield, Illinois. We moved there with our three children, Matthew, David, and Annie. During our time in Springfield, we became close friends of the late Abraham Lincoln, God rest his great soul. We knew him before he was President. He and Burl would get into the greatest discussions about theology and Mister Lincoln often turned to my husband for advice and counsel. I enjoyed Mary. Few enjoyed Mary, but I found her intellect and her great education compelling. For hours on end we would discuss the great books. At last, I had someone with whom I could talk about my passion for literature. To our great delight, our Matthew was a good friend of the Lincoln's oldest son Robert, Bob as he was known to us.

It all sounds idyllic but I will tell you that the early years of our marriage were difficult ones and that must be laid entirely at my feet. My struggles with the truth of Mormonism did not completely disappear the instant we drove out of Nauvoo that day. I had a long fight with myself over it all. I had such a deep and radical history with the Mormons that it was something I could not easily dismiss. Burl was patient. He provided me the space to work through my emotional and intellectual thrashings. He did not club me with the New Testament nor did he decimate the *Book of Mormon* with his education and intellect. He never repeated his admonition, *Don't forget the New Testament.* He did not need to. I spent hours reading the Bible, seeing it again for the first time. I will admit I loved the little church in Sonora but much of that had to do with Burl's magnificent preaching and the genuine friendliness of the people. I can't name a date when I no longer considered myself a Mormon. The whole thing just winked out at some point between 1843 and 1850.

Then too there were the horrible feelings I harbored over my near murder of Kevil Pape. I had to confront the murderous rage that brought me to the point of killing another human being. Despite all the affirmations poured upon me by my husband, I sank into a deep pit of self-loathing, unable to forgive myself. On many occasions Burl and others assured me that by accepting Jesus as Lord and Savior, my sins had been forgiven, including my attempted murder of Kevil Pape. I knew this on an intellectual level, but I could not accept it in my heart. It took a long time.

Unlike the slow, imperceptible decay of my belief in the Mormon religion, there was a precise moment when I finally felt God's grace and loving forgiveness. When he was six years old, little Matt had gotten hold of a tin of locofocos and was out in the barn playing. Burl was gone on one of his many visits and the other children were napping in the house. Something prompted me to look out the window. Flames had engulfed the barn. I ran out of the house and met little Matt running toward me. I told him to stay right where he was and ran into the barn where I led the frantic Lampblack to safety. When I returned to Matt, he looked up at me with tears streaming down his cheeks.

"I'm so sorry, Mama. I'm so sorry," he said. "Please don't kill me."

What else could I do? I swept him up in my arms and assured him that I wasn't going to kill him and neither was Papa. "I know you didn't mean to do it. It's just an old barn anyway."

He pulled away from me and looked through his tears into my eyes. "You love me Mama. You love me just like God loves you."

That afternoon I held little Matt for much longer than he wanted to be held.

The End

AUTHOR'S NOTE

In his book, *The Art and Craft of Writing Historical Fiction,* James Alexander Thom writes: *To be really good historical novelists…we have to take our obligation to historical truth just as seriously as the historians do theirs. But we don't have to bear the burden of being the authority on every factual detail. Our disclaimer is right there on the cover:* a novel.

Mindful of this obligation, throughout *Heart Fire,* I have tried to provide a historical context that is truthful. Thus, the broad sweep of events surrounding the attempted assassination of Governor Lilburn Boggs; the Mormon mission to England; the gathering of Saints to Nauvoo; the early unfolding of the doctrine of celestial marriage; the general activities of Joseph Smith; the knavery of John Cook Bennett; the social character, culture, and institutions of Nauvoo; and many other details in the story are accurate and based upon established historical records.

Two intentional anachronisms must be pointed out. First, the fiery Welshman, Dan Jones, captain of the Mormon steamer, *Maid of Iowa,* did not actually take command of the vessel until 1843, several years after the time in which he appears in this story. Second, wanted posters, such as presented in the novel, were probably not commonly used in the United States until Civil War times.

It is widely held that the attempted assassination of former Missouri Governor Lilburn Boggs in 1842 was perpetrated by Orrin Porter Rockwell, an associate of Joseph Smith. However, John Cook Bennett, in *The History of the Saints,* demurs, suggesting that, while Rockwell may have been involved, he did not actually pull the trigger. Bennett writes: *I feel certain…that Rockwell…acted as the* conductor *or* guide; *and that one of the twelve composing the Destroying Angel, assisted by Rockwell, did the deed.* Bennett's demurral provided the first seed of ideation. If not Rockwell, then who? My musing on this question provided the fictional flowers that bloomed from that first seed of ideation.

The assassination attempt on Governor Boggs' emerged in the wake of Joseph Smith's prophecy that the Governor should die as punishment for his expulsion of the Saints from Missouri. The expulsion occurred approximately one year after several Mormon leaders established a missionary beachhead in Preston, England. They first preached in the Reverend James Fielding's working-class parish and therein lies the second seed of ideation. What must it have been like to sit in that small congregation in Preston's Vauxhall Chapel and hear these frontier missionaries from America present a whole new gospel of Jesus Christ? The story of two such congregants provided the fictional flowers blooming from this second seed of ideation.

My task then became the unification of these two literary bouquets – the shooting of Lilburn Boggs and the consequences of Mormon missionary preaching. This I did with an accelerating dance where one partner begins in Preston and the other in Missouri's capital, Jefferson City. Throughout this dance I have tried to be sympathetic to my Mormon characters in their quest to find meaning and purpose in life. However, I have pulled no punches in my critical rendering of Joseph Smith and his leadership cabinet, nor have I been well-disposed to the early doctrines and practices of the Church of Latter Day Saints. *Heart Fire* is unabashedly, unashamedly an apologetic for orthodox Christianity.

Along with all conscientious novelists, I am deeply indebted to others for their assistance in creating this work. A special thanks is extended to my "reading team" who gave of their time, good counsel, and encouragement when I sluiced around in the whirlpool of self doubt – Lorrie Scott, Christina Blackmore, Jan Schumacher, Lindsey Robison, Ruth Benedett, and Mary Ann Campbell. I am also deeply indebted for the incredible insights offered by prominent Mormons who have converted to evangelical Christianity. Bishop Lee Baker and his wife Kathy (Witnesses for Jesus, Inc.) offered valuable historical insights regarding the early days of the LDS Church. Dennis Higley of H.I.S. Ministries International gave me important information on the early LDS Temple ceremonies and the construction of temple garments. Finally, a particular debt of gratitude is owed Dr. Lynn Wilder, former B.Y.U. professor, author of *Unveiling Grace*, and a founder of Ex-Mormons Christians United for Jesus. In her delightful professorial fashion, she provided three pages of detailed edits on an early manuscript and suggested the term *long winter of confusion* to describe Elena's uncertainties as the threads of her Mormon faith began to unravel. Finally, a deep thanks to my wife Jean Ann, as always, my first editor.

www.ingramcontent.com/pod-product-compliance
Lightning Source LLC
Chambersburg PA
CBHW070641180626
46817CB00006B/2192